Blue Devil

B. R. Lynch

The Book:

Blue Devil, the sequel to Liberty Bodleigh, is historic romantic fiction, Regency Period in England, with adventures in the Peninsula War in Spain and Portugal.

The Author:

Blue Devil

by

B. R. Lynch

1. Edition, 2021

Chapter 1

Portsmouth, England

December 1811

    Captain Ronan Trevelyan, his soggy greatcoat dripping with rain, dismounted his sweat-soaked charger in the inn yard. While the ostler led Gunpowder away, the captain strode into the inn to find his servant. Jacob had followed instructions, packing campaign chest, saddle valise and his own few belongings, traveling by coach to Portsmouth the previous day and taking a room at the inn. Upon reaching his room, the captain ordered Jacob, in Spanish, to procure dinner and a hot bath. Jacob, in the beginning throes of learning that language, guessed what his master had said.

    After dinner Captain Trevelyan tramped out in the rain to check his stallion. Gunpowder consumed quantities of hay in the stables. Satisfied with the animal's care, Ronan marched to the docks in search of transport to Lisbon. He soon found what he sought and discovered a cousin, Aaron Brandolyn, was the ship's first lieutenant. Aaron was twenty-five. Ronan would be twenty-five the coming January. Lieutenant Brandolyn introduced his cousin to Captain Asper, who explained he was taking several officers and horses to Lisbon and had room for Ronan and his horse. They would depart on the first favorable wind.

    That evening, Ronan, appareled in his silver-laced, indigo, Hussar dress uniform, wearing sabre and sabretache, supped with his Cousin Aaron, Captain Asper and several Peninsula officers. One of the officers had heard of Captain Trevelyan and his nom de guerre, Blue Devil. Over beef and home brew, that officer recited some of the Devil's daring exploits. Captain Trevelyan claimed they were much exaggerated. True, he'd fought in the charge at Sahagun, but had not sabred twenty 'monsieurs.' After he had been captured on an intelligence patrol, he and his fellow prisoner had only killed six French soldiers in their escape, not sixteen. Captain Trevelyan only led a few dozen men to safety at Talavera, not several companies. And he and the guerilleros had merely attacked supplies and messengers, not brigades. However, he had been shot returning from behind the French lines, and he had been further injured when his horse had been killed. The captain had spent recent months recovering in England.

Aaron informed the diners that his parents, the Reverend Eugene and Mrs. Brandolyn had raised Captain Trevelyan, an orphan, with Aaron's seven brothers and two sisters. "You've probably heard of my brother, Captain Samuel Brandolyn, who fought at Trafalgar. As did Captain Trevelyan, as a ship's passenger!"

"I commend your parents for raising such fine men," Captain Asper declared.

The next morning, Ronan rode Gunpowder to the ship. He held the stallion as the sailors pulled slings under its body. Ronan let go as they raised a mystified Gunpowder up and lowered him into the transport's hold with the other horses. The ship got underway that afternoon. Ronan walked the deck with Aaron, who like most people in Ronan's company, did most of the talking. "I suppose if you hadn't been such a hand with horses you'd have gone to sea like me and Samuel."

"Possibly," Ronan replied, leaning against the gunwales, picking his teeth. "I like the sea."

Aaron waxed poetically on how he loved the sea and all its moods.

Below deck, horses plunged back and forth in their narrow stalls, making the ship rock. Jacob, who shared a cramped cabin with Captain Trevelyan, became bilious from the ship's rocking. An officer's servant told him ships transporting horses were the worse.

While Jacob suffered agonies of seasickness, Captain Trevelyan dined and played music with officers in the captain's cabin. Now his shoulder was healed, Ronan thought he could live without Jacob, an unwanted gift from his godfather. He could easily find a Spanish-speaking servant in the Peninsula. After three rough days at sea, Jacob showed no signs of improvement and was too incapacitated to perform his duties.

"Comer," Ronan ordered, setting a basket of bread, cheese, apples and nuts in front of Jacob.

"I can't eat. I'd as lief you shot me. In fact, I wish you would," Jacob replied, reverting to English. He felt too ill to practise the Spanish his master demanded of him.

"Bah! The food is fresh now, later it will be maggoty biscuit and five year old beef," the captain warned him in English.

The thought of that drove Jacob to his basin. His master ate an apple and cracked nuts. Then he put on his reading glasses and read out loud from a Spanish version of Don Quixote he'd bought for Jacob. Jacob realized this irritating behavior would continue until he ate something. He tried the bread. The captain continued reading. Jacob soon learned he felt better with a full stomach. Once Jacob overcame seasickness, his master resumed teaching him Spanish.

Christmas passed at sea. The sailors received extra rum and the officers celebrated with drink and music. Ronan, as usual, listened more than he spoke. He habitually collected information and stored it away for future use. Ronan studied other officers as much as he studied the French in his reconnoiters, learning their strengths and weaknesses.

An officer of foot mentioned a man in his regiment, Sergeant Collins. Ronan had inquired about Sergeant Collins before he left Spain. He listened. The officer said the man deserved promotion, and that two commanding officers had intended to request it, but both had been killed before they did so and the sergeant's memorandum had not reached the proper people.

"Just damned bad luck. Happens all the time. The man's thirty-six years old and been a sergeant for nine years. Good man, reliable, conscientious, unquestionable courage and not empty in the brainbox."

The officer went on to tell of the sergeant's losing his wife and two children. But two sons and a daughter survived. One son was a private in the regiment and the other a drummer boy. He described the daughter as a real beauty, but "wild as they come, typical camp follower."

~~~~

A calm day, Captain Trevelyan took out his Brandolyn and Trevelyan breech-loading pistols. Jacob tied a worn neck cloth to a rope near the bow, while the captain stood on the poop deck. Officers gathered to examine the pistols and bet on Ronan's marksmanship.

"I see no advantage to a breech-loading pistol," one officer grumbled.

"I also have a breech-loading Brandolyn rifle," Ronan informed him, raising a pistol, aiming and firing at the target.

Jacob held out the rag, showing a hole. The captain needed a new target. He offered to shoot the rope, itself, betting a guinea.

"An impossible target!" the others agreed and bet against him.

Captain Asper considered his rigging safe and also bet against the captain. Only Lieutenant Brandolyn refused to gamble. He was too familiar with his cousin's marksmanship.

Balancing himself on the wavering deck, Ronan leveled his pistol and fired. The rope blew apart. Captain Asper cursed. Five officers resolved to buy Brandolyn and Trevelyan guns.

~~~

Boscawden, Hampshire

Liberty Bodleigh finished painting the portrait of Captain Trevelyan in his Hussar uniform. She derived satisfaction that she'd captured the dreamy, far away look he sometimes revealed, and lifelike color. Her Aunt Sarah and Uncle Augustus claimed it was her best portrait and certain to be a success in the Academy exhibit.

With Christmas approaching, she spent much time with Edith Westerly and other friends, but their company failed to alleviate her longing for Ronan's company. She rode her little gray mare to the Westerly's one day.

"How dull you are, Berty!" Edith complained. "You were in Captain Trevelyan's pocket and now you ain't fit company for anybody. Not like you to have a fit of the dismals."

"I wasn't in his pocket! We spent time together because he would be leaving and I painted his portrait," Berty replied.

"I must see it now it's finished. I'd ride Slug over, but Papa says I must ride with Claude or a groom. How inconvenient! Claude makes excuses and we only have one groom."

"Claude didn't mind riding with us when Captain Trevelyan was here. What's changed his mind? Have you two been dagger drawing again?" Berty asked.

"Of course, who could refrain from arguing with anyone as corkbrained as Claude. He rode with us when the captain was here because he says the captain is an out and outter and he was proud to be seen with him!"

"And ashamed to be seen with us? Claude is empty in the cockloft. It's not as if he has anything better to do. I don't see why you can't ride with just me. Nobody could fall off Slug," Berty said, but this was not the subject most on her mind.

"How much does it cost to travel to Lisbon?"she asked.

"Really, Berty! How should I know? Do you intend to make a complete fool of yourself and elope to Lisbon?" Edith snapped.

"I wouldn't elope. I'd go there to sketch and paint. I could paint battles and become famous."

Edith laughed. "I daresay you'd paint battles and your dear captain would be the hero of every one!"

"Newspapers would carry engravings of my sketches of battles," Berty expanded, "Think of it, Edith!"

Edith laughed. "Who ever heard of a woman's sketches appearing anywhere! And Captain Trevelyan wouldn't let you near a battle field. You'd be terrified, anyway, and all that gore would make you ill. A fine lot of paintings you'd accomplish!"

"Captain Trevelyan doesn't have any say in what I do. We shall never be leg shackled. He says he won't marry until he's two score, if he lives that long. And I shall not marry under current marriage laws. And what's more, I've not the sensibilities you accuse me of. I've seen animals butchered without cringing. When I sketch, you know, I don't see things as you do, I see lines and shadows and I get so involved that I don't even think about what is going on."

"Hmm. Now I see you on a battlefield, sketching, while bullets and cannon balls fly around you. You beat everything, Berty!" Edith replied, then resumed with, "I wouldn't commit myself to spinsterhood on account of marriage laws. I've never known a lady to read marriage laws. 'Honor and obey,' indeed. Mama only obeys papa when she agrees with him. You Americans make too much of your rights. And no, I'm not reading your Tom Paine again!"

"Besides, didn't you tell me you would never travel by sea again? That you were so seasick when you were sent here after your papa died, you thought it was the period to your existence?"

"I was only twelve then and Lisbon is not as far to travel," Liberty countered.

Edith had more to say about Berty's friend, "I collect Captain Trevelyan intends to continue as an unrepentant rake. You know people will talk about his behavior at the Pendleton's ball for years. He made you look fast, Berty."

"I'm not and I don't care what people think. I'm not saying Captain Trevelyan isn't wayward at times, or maybe just too forward, but he's better than anyone else I've met."

"Now you insult my brothers!"

"No, no, I didn't mean to!" Berty replied, alarmed at her unintended solecism.

Edith laughed, "I daresay, I'd prefer your dashing captain to my dear brothers, too! Walter, bless him, is a bracket-faced giant and Claude, well, we've already discussed him."

~~~

Liberty visited Cedric Trevelyan at Boscawden Hall. His eldest brother, Sedgewick, was spending Christmas with Sedgewick relatives, including his fiancée, in Kent. Captain Alexander Trevelyan had returned to his regiment. Lord James Trevelyan retired to live as a recluse in the new wing. The visiting cousins had gone to their families for the holiday and Captain Ronan Trevelyan had returned to the Peninsula War. Peace and tranquility had returned to Boscawden Hall.

Since Ricky no longer needed a tutor, Lord James had appointed his former tutor, Welspent, librarian and antiquarian for the Hall. Welspent cataloged the Hall's books, paintings, furniture, armor, plate and other collections. He also worked on the family genealogy. Berty sat with him and Ricky in the library.

"The Trevelyans hold one of the oldest baronies in England," Welspent said.

"If we weren't so disagreeable, we'd have a dukedom by now," Ricky joked.

"There is a good chance that Mr. Sedgewick will inherit the Marquesate of Leith. Neither of the aged Marquis' heirs have wed and both are sickly denizens of Bath."

"God help us!" Cedric lisped softly, "Sedge is already top lofty and over-bearing. If Alexander was home, I daresay, they would come to blows. I'm glad father has designated our stipends in his will for Sedge would make us beg for the clothes on our backs. Alexander says he'd have poor Cousin Ronan put up in the stables and I very well believe it!"

"Pray don't speak of your brother so, Cedric," Welspent adjured him.

Liberty admired this show of spirit from her childhood friend. At nineteen, Cedric had overcome his stammer and grown into a well-made, handsome youth. Although he disdained horses, he was a skilled swordsman, a graceful dancer and a loyal friend. His current passion was the Classical Greeks. He read Greek and when in London, spent hours studying the Elgin marbles in the British Museum. He still had no interest in females, other than his platonic friendship with Liberty. She gazed at the Van Dyke portrait over the mantel, the one Ronan resembled.

"I've finished Ronan's portrait," she told them, "Uncle Augustus thinks t'is good enough to enter in the academy as my associate's probationary picture, even though I'm only nineteen and a female. He is ordering a frame and planning our trip to London in the spring."

"I say that's dashed exciting, is it not, Welspent? We must drive to the Bodleigh's to see it," Ricky said, "Father should have Alexander's portrait done in his splendid regimentals."

"That should be achieved before his regiment sails for the Peninsula," Welspent said, adding, "Someday I may be cataloging your paintings with the Hall's other masterpieces, Miss Bodleigh!"

Berty flushed.

Cedric continued to inform Berty, "Sedgewick is betrothed to a distant cousin, on mother's side, Hester Sedgewick. She is mother's brother's ward and heiress to her father's estate when she is of age next year. I apprehend it is a very fine property with a modern house. Sedgewick told me the estate produces an income of over 5,000 pounds a year. He, of course, would know these things!"

"I think it unseemly and mercenary to consider such things before marriage," Welspent opined, "I can conceive such consideration in a gentleman like Captain Ronan Trevelyan, who was not provided with an income suited to his station. In fact, no income at all, due to his father's disobeying Lord Victor. A disgrace for a child to suffer for his father's disobediance, esspecially when that disobediance is over an arranged marriage. But Mr. Sedgewick Trevelyan will inherit the barony and an a excellent income."

Ricky replied, "In our family, you can't have too plump a pocket. My own allowance doesn't permit me to stay in London unless I reside with Priscilla and her husband or stay at a hotel with father. He prefers a hotel to our own town house since he has allowed Priscilla to live there. I daresay, Ronan will end up with more blunt than Alexander and maybe all of us. He is very clever."

"Cedric, you know it is improper to discuss family money matters," Welspent proscribed further talk on the subject.

They visited Berty's atelier, as she called it, the next day.

"He looks as if he is breathing!" Cedric exclaimed, admiring his cousin's classical features.

"Very lifelike, Miss Bodleigh," Welspent expressed a more restrained opinion.

"You have quite captured him," Cedric continued.

"I daresay the only way any female will capture him," Francis Bodleigh said, stepping into the studio with Augustus. He turned to his niece, saying, "I would you had chosen a more fitting subject for a female painter to show. Perhaps one of mothers and children."

"Why must female painters only depict women and children?" Berty asked, "I'd prefer to paint horses and soldiers."

Francis snorted derisively. Augustus pointed out Berty had signed her name, L. R. Bodleigh. "Most viewers won't know it was painted by a female. They will judge it without bias."

"Father should buy it for the Hall to hang with the other family heroes," Cedric declared, staring at the painting.

When Cedric later presented this idea to his father, his Lordship dismissed him. "I might have a wedding portrait done of Sedgewick by one of the London painters. Sedgewick mentioned a Lawrence."

"But, father, you should see this one."

Lord James would not leave the Hall except to attend church services. He expressed disappointment that Sedgewick intended to marry in Kent. "In that case, I shan't attend. I can not travel that far."

"No, not if you can't travel as far as the Bodleigh's," Cedric whispered. This was the closest he had ever come to criticizing his father.

His lordship, used to his stronger minded sons, didn't perceive this. "I suppose you must travel for the wedding," he said.

The idea of escaping his dull home even for a dull wedding made Cedric smile.

~~~

Edith praised the portrait. "I'll insist father have our entire family painted. Do you think Alexander will sit for you?"

Berty shrugged and replied, "Cedric said Alexander will sit and pay me from his allowance if his lordship isn't forthcoming with the payment."

"Everyone knows the captain, Ronan, that is, has a tendre for you," Edith claimed, "Is he going to write to you?"

"It was mentioned, but you know how fickle gentlemen are."

"I'd love to have an officer writing to me," Edith said.

"You have your brother," Berty teased, suspecting Edith would like to throw her cap at Alexander.

~~~

Miss Penthwaite descended upon the Bodleighs just before Christmas. Enough snow had fallen to beautify the countryside without making roads impassible.

"I do love Christmas in the country," she declared, "London's rather dull for those of us without family."

Augustus insisted Miss Penthwaite see Berty's studio and new work.

"Most of her commissions have been collected by their owners before the holiday, but there is one you must see."

Hilda stepped into the tiny cottage and stood thunderstruck.

"A golden Adonis! Is that a real person or did you imagine him?" she finally asked.

Berty laughed. "That is Captain Ronan Trevelyan, Aunt Sarah's cousin."

"The captain looks as if there is blood in him, as if he could step out of the painting. How do you accomplish this? Is he as dashing as he looks?" Hilda asked.

"More so!"

"Then you must be in love! I may be an old blue stocking, but I still admire a beautiful man!"

Berty blushed at such a confession.

"He is Lord Victor's grandson, is he not? There is a strong resemblance. I knew Lord Victor when I was young. A handsome, detestable creature! A rake of the first order. Of course women adored him. Is your Adonis of a rakish desposition?"

"I can't say. He conducts himself as a gentleman to me, although he provokes Aunt Sarah," Berty replied, cautiously.

"I venture to say, if he provokes Sarah, he is an imperfect gentleman. You may be blind to his true character," Hilda replied, and they returned to the house.

The Bodleighs celebrated Christmas with a feast shared with their servants, Betty, John, Peggy and Joe. Augustus' brother, Francis Bodleigh, Boscawden's steward, had traveled to Birmingham to be with his sons, their wives and children.

Sarah steamed a plum pudding and Augustus made his yearly comment about it lacking plums. The women gave gifts of stitchery, including an embroidered waistcoat for Augustus. Augustus and John gave wooden boxes. Berty gave miniatures she'd painted of each of them. Joe gave the Bodleighs a bird he had whittled. They gave him new clothes and shoes. Miss Penthwaite gave everyone books. Berty gave her a small, misty landscape.

"Oh, I love this. I shall hang it prominently in my drawing room. But if you could do me a miniature of your captain, I would not object!"

"Hilda!" Sarah cried, "He is not Berty's captain and surely you are not taken with him?"

Hilda laughed.

"I assure you he is vexing and, often, grim," Sarah said.

"I'm sure," Hilda agreed, "And probably has dozens of mistresses and all the vices that plague our young gentlemen."

Immediately, Sarah came to his defense. "No, no, he's not a spendthrift or sot, nor does he gamble away his money."

"He doesn't have any," Augustus added.

Miss Penthwaite noticed Sarah mentioned nothing about mistresses.

They finished the evening in song. The next day, Boxing Day, the Bodleighs and Miss Penthwaite took Hilda's carriage to the Hall to watch his lordship distribute boxes to servants and tenants. Sarah, Alexander and Cedric helped with the distribution in the great Hall.

After the gift giving, Berty showed Miss Penthwaite the collections of armor, weapons, sculpture, objects of art and portraits.

"Antiquaries from all over come to see these old family pieces," Berty said. She iterated the painters, some renown. From the great hall, Berty led Miss Penthwaite to the upstairs gallery with its portraits of Elizabethans, 17th century cavaliers and their ladies, as well as paintings and sculpture brought home from grand tours. Such pieces were scattered throughout the house. The early 18th century wing, considered modern, where his lordship reposed most of the time, was closed to visitors, but Berty took Miss Penthwaite to the library.

"This is my favorite room and probably the coziest," Berty said.

Miss Penthwaite examined the pictures and the books, most of which were in Latin.

"Many of these books are quite old and valuable, but I see very few modern works," Helen remarked. "This house seems to have stopped a hundred years ago. Indeed the the original building itself shows no alterations. Quite remarkable."

~~~

Alexander came to see Ronan's portrait and left impressed. He broached the subject of his own portrait with his lordship and worked on his father's filial feelings by telling him his regiment would be going to Spain and who knew when or if he would return. "I may fall in battle!"

His lordship, having no judgement of his own, preferred known painters. When Alexander compared the charges of known painters versus Miss Bodleigh's tiny stipends, Lord James immediately agreed to pay for the work. Sedgewick would have dampened the project or any other that would take money from his future estate, but Sedgewick remained in Kent planning his wedding.

Alexander desired a life-sized portrait of himself on horseback. Berty pointed out that her studio wasn't large enough to accommodate such a painting and, although she could find some place else to paint it, the cost would be considerably more than the price she'd given him for the three-quarter length portrait that they had originally discussed. There were time constraints, too, due to the limits of Alexander's leave. Cedric also informed Alexander that the horse would distract from him. "Do you want a portrait of you or a horse?"

Alexander's vanity convinced him the horse would have to go. He would stand in his red uniform, holding his elaborate, horse-maned helmet.

When Edith heard that Alexander was sitting for Berty, she invited herself to stay with the Bodleigh's that she could be present for the sittings. Sarah laughed when Berty explained Edith's request. Miss Penthwaite continued ruralizing after Christmas and sat in as chaperon.

Once she had decided on a pose, Berty began with a preliminary color sketch as with the portrait of Ronan. Unlike Ronan, Alexander squirmed like a child and talked constantly.

"Your mouth is going to be a blur," Berty admonished him.

She arranged for Edith to sit where Alexander could see her.

"There, that's better, now keep your eyes on Edith."

"Easily, Miss Westerly is very handsome!" he said.

Edith didn't mind his staring at all. She pretended to embroider and talked as much as Alexander. By the time Berty had completed the sketch and started on the portrait, Alexander had asked permission to write to Edith. Miss Penthwaite enjoyed the young people's nonsense immensely. She thought Alexander a bit of a coxcomb, but he was well favored and well-made. To her, it was a shame he hadn't joined a Hussar regiment since his red uniform clashed with his red hair.

After a few days, Alexander returned to his regiment. Berty finished the painting from her sketches. Cold January set in with little occupation. Liberty changed her mind about consulting Miss Penthwaite regarding traveling to Lisbon. What had been a great love affair to her, could have been a mere flirtation to Captain Trevelyan. He was correct; she knew little of men or the world. Hilda left to visit other friends.

Berty waited for Captain Trevelyan's first letter and Edith waited for Alexander's. Sunday church services marked their weeks. Both day dreamed during Reverend Wingfield's usually bland sermons. Sometimes Berty got the gist of his more edifying efforts. She admitted to herself, most sermons were wasted on her. One had to attend services, however, or be considered an eccentric, or worse, like her dear free-thinking father. Liberty did not want to be a lonely outcast.

Chapter 2

Late December 1811, through April 1812

Lisbon and Spain

Jacob viewed Lisbon's filthy streets in disgust. Apparently the residents threw the contents of chamber pots and everything else out of windows, adding it to the horse dung on the streets. He thought it worse than anything he'd smelled in London. And priests, why did they need so many priests? Priests and soldiers everywhere. On the other hand, all the houses looked new. In fact, an earthquake had destroyed Lisbon in the last century and all had been rebuilt.

The boy rode in a baggage cart while his master rode ahead on his prancing charger. Another officer greeted the captain, and they stopped for a brief talk, then rode on. Ronan led them out of town to a clean neighborhood of walled homes.

They entered a courtyard over run with noisy, playing children. A multitude of servants, then more children and, finally, the lovely, buxom mistress of the house burst out of the house to greet the captain. They all spoke rapid Portuguese, of which, Jacob didn't understand a word, but he understood the embrace he saw his master give the lady.

The captain instructed Senora de Sousa's groom how to tend his horse before joining the lady and her children. Two footmen carried baggage into an austere bed chamber. Here, Jacob found his master's old campaign chest, guitar and other belongings left behind when he'd campaigned in Spain. The Portuguese footman told Jacob something, he wasn't sure what, but they brought in a copper tub and the accouterments for bathing. Jacob assumed his master wanted to bathe after the voyage, but first they dined.

While the captain dined with Senora de Sousa, Jacob joined the other servants. None had much English, but they were friendly to any servant of the captain and offered Jacob foods he had never eaten, such as olives. He found them tolerable, but not good. He liked the pretty, friendly maids and gathered the mistress of the house was a generous employer. There were so many young children about, Jacob wanted to ask if the lady operated an orphanage, but no one understood what he said. He resolved to ask his master later. He also wondered about her husband and debated asking his master.

After dining, the Senora led Ronan to her private sitting room. The nursery maid brought the captain's daughter, two-year old Serafina, and presented Ronan with his infant son, Arthur Vivian Trevelyan, a name Ronan had instructed Antonia to give the baby months before. Ronan held the baby a while before kissing him and handing him to Antonia to suckle. There was little he could do with an infant, but Serafina commanded his adoration. He sent for his guitar and played for her until her bedtime.

After that enjoyable interlude, Ronan joined Jacob in the austere chamber for his bath. Glad to have someone who understood him, Jacob began rattling in English. "Why are there so many children here?"

"Hablar Espanol," Ronan replied. He explained, in Spanish, that the war had left many orphans. The Senora loved children above all and had taken them in. She also aided adults.

While his master dried, Jacob struggled to say, in Spanish, he would need to purchase such things as boot blacking, tooth powder and soap. He also inquired, mostly via gestures, if he should purchase wax for the mustaches the captain had been growing since leaving Boscawden.

"No, I don't use wax. One of the footmen will take you," the captain replied in Spanish and gave Jacob unfamiliar coins. Ronan explained the approximate value of each coin in British coinage and said that some things were expensive in Lisbon. Ronan took a dark blue silk dressing gown from a hook and put it on.

"You'll sleep here," he told Jacob, "Have my uniform ready at dawn."

Ronan swung out of the room to join Antonia in her chamber. He felt comfortable and unconstrained with his mistress, unlike the restraints he'd endured when courting English maidens. Not that he didn't approve of such restraints. A gentleman didn't satisfy his lust with virgins. A voluptuous thirty-eight-year old widow, who didn't wish to remarry, particularly not to a soldier of twenty-five, was another matter. And they both loved children, particularly the act of creating them.

~~~

After an early breakfast, the captain graced Wellington's headquarters with his stunning presence. When the other officers had last seen the Blue Devil, he'd been shabby, haggard and wounded. He'd returned a gleaming, healthy officer of the first stare. His many friends and acquaintances greeted him warmly, particularly Captain Vivian Ramsey, who he invited to dinner at the señora's that evening.

When Wellington looked up to see his exploring officer swagger into his office, he paused to study him. "I see you've visited your tailor, Trevelyan," the Beau commented dryly.

The general immediately set down his needs. The captain must find the guerrilleros he'd worked with and engage their assistance in the coming siege of Cuidad Rodrigo, and he was to make contact with Sir Colquhoun Grant, somewhere in Spain. Ronan left to choose his men and prepare for the expedition.

In the course of a busy day, he also received his back pay. Thanks to Nathan Rothschild, Wellington no longer had to borrow from shady Maltese bankers. Rothschild had gotten the gold to pay the British army passed through France and into Spain. Captain Trevelyan visited his agent in Lisbon and purchased Consoles. He now had a little daughter to endow and a son to educate.

Ronan returned to Senora de Sousa's after dark and informed Jacob he would be leaving in the morning. A soldier would come with transportation for Jacob and the baggage. He was to leave one chest behind. Jacob would be following the army. The boy packed the saddle valise with shirts and necessities for the captain's expedition.

Captain Ramsey arrived and Ronan sent the señora for their son.

"I've never had the honor of having a baby named after me," Ramsey pronounced, adding, "But I'm glad you put the Beau's name first."

~~~

The captain rode into the cold mountains seeking his old associates. They soon found him. After much discussion, their leader and a few choice men rode to a hill overlooking Cuidad Rodrigo. The captain studied the fortress with his spyglass. He noticed cattle grazing on the glacis. They could supply the defenders with beef during the coming siege.

Captain Trevelyan's first action presented itself. He led his men and the guerrilleros against the defenseless cattle of Cuidad Rodrigo. They herded 200 cattle off the glacis before the fortress's governor rode out to retrieve them. Ronan and the guerrilleros captured the governor. After this success, they dined on roast beef.

The captain dispatched a man with a prisoner, led by the nose. The soldier delivered the prisoner to Wellington, with a message from the Blue Devil. "After interrogating this prisoner, I thought you would like to further interrogate him with fork and knife."

Wellington whooped when he saw the bullock. Devil's message also contained information on Cuidad Rodrigo.

Blue Devil next paid a call on Sir Colquhoun Grant, who was, as the captain chose to put it, touring Spain and keeping an eye on Marmont. While the captain rode, Wellington ordered Cuidad Rodrigo invested. On January eighth, his men captured the Great Teson, an outwork on a hill overlooking the fortress. In the days following, the army dug trenches to the walls.

The captain returned to report that Marmont was at Salamanca. With little time before Marmont reached Cuidad Rodrigo, Wellington ordered the breaches stormed on January nineteenth. From his post on the Great Teson, amid cannon fire, he used Captain Trevelyan as an Aid de Camp and messenger.

When the fort had been captured, soldiers drank themselves into a wild mob. The captain joined officers trying to bring order to the trigger-happy rabble, but in the end the soldiers sacked the place. The next morning, Ronan stood with Wellington at his headquarters, watching soldiers march out wearing ladies' gowns, festoons of shoes and carrying hams and other victuals on their bayonets. The sick and wounded followed and then traitors were marched out and shot.

In a moment of repose, following the siege, Ronan began his first letter to Miss Bodleigh. He was as laconic in his writing as in his speech.

"Dear Miss Liberty Bodleigh,

I have led an action against cattle grazing the glacis of Cuidad Rodrigo. They offered little resistance, giving my men no opportunity to distinguish themselves. We captured 200 cattle and the Governor, M. Reynaud. He wishes to join his brother in England and shall be obliged.

We captured Cuidad Rodrigo and our soldiers sacked it. They marched out the following day draped with ladies' gowns and carrying hams on their bayonets.

We will next lay siege on Badajoz.

Your devoted servant, Captain Ronan Trevelyan"

He filled the rest of the page with one of his music compositions for his Cousin Sarah to play on her pianoforte.

The missive arrived in Boscawden in late February. In its passage from the mail coach, to the Tavern keeper, to the boy who ran to the Bodleigh house with it, everyone noticed the blue wax seal stamped with a devil's head. Sarah Bodleigh observed the Blue Devil's seal with mixed emotions. She paid the boy a half pence and left the letter on the passage table for Berty, who was working in her studio.

Berty saw it as soon as she stepped in and, trying to restrain her raptures, ran upstairs to her room to carefully break the seal and read it. It's brevity neither surprised, nor dismayed her. She felt her heart beat when she read, "Your devoted servant."

She later shared it with her aunt and uncle. Sarah copied the music so that Berty could keep the letter in her room, when not showing it to Cedric and Edith.

Berty wrote back, with a touch of drollery.

"Dear Captain Trevelyan,

Must we be so formal, Ronan? I read your brief passage on Cuidad Rodrigo to my Aunt and Uncle. You make war sound like a lark, which I'm sure it isn't. Aunt Sarah has played your beautiful piece many times and gets better each time.

I've finished your portrait and Alexander's and they are now drying. I have some requests for miniatures.

Edith's father refuses to replace her abominably lazy gelding. She remains an even worse rider than I and rather lazy herself. So we ride out together like brigands, me with my little pistol and Edith with her father's horse pistols. Since I carry a pistol, she decided she must, also. Sometimes her brother, Claude, accompanies us, but usually not, since we are slow and boring. We ride, armed to the teeth, to visit our friends within a five mile radius!

The most pressing matter I've faced of late has been whether to trim my hair. Edith has had her hair cut in the latest mode, and our friends have copied it. Even Mrs. Wingfield has had her hair cut and Aunt Sarah is considering it. They say it is much easier to pin up in back, but the front and sides must be curled if not naturally curly or it hangs down like spaniels' ears. At least, Edith's does. It is very flattering to her when curled, though. I would not bore you with this trivial matter, but you know something of pinning hair and I thought to consult you. I have already asked Uncle Augustus, Ricky and Mr. Wellspent. None has ventured an opinion, claiming ladies' hair styles are beyond their comprehension. I hope you feel flattered that I consider nothing beyond your comprehension. Although if you recommend I cut it, I will probably not do so. Not so much because I am perverse, but because I'm really asking someone to stand by me against the mode.

Your devoted Friend,

Liberty"

The captain received this letter in March, during the third siege of Badajoz, but before the storming. He enjoyed it immensely and kept it with his other letters, including one from his business partner, Cousin Benjamin, and one from Master Tristan Burlington. Senora de Sousa did not write. She was only a little over one hundred miles away and the captain visited her as often as he could on one of the three blood horses he used. As Wellington said, the Peninsula was the graveyard of horses. Exploring officers were provided with the fastest, but hard riding in the mountains required rest. The captain alternated between Gunpowder and two good army horses.

Blue Devil spent most of his time with the partisans, watching the French and reporting to Wellington. One evening, after his master had dined with the general and enjoyed enough port to loosen his tongue, Jacob spoke to him, in much improved, Spanish.

"Do you have a birthday, sir?"

"Of course, everyone does."

"I don't," Jacob replied.

"You do, but you don't know when it is."

"Yes, that's it. I don't even know how old I am. Josiah thought I was about fourteen last year. I was wondering, when is your birthday and how old are you?" Jacob asked many questions at once for his master seldom volunteered information.

"January seventh, I am five and twenty."

"Would you mind if I used that date for my birthday and made myself fifteen?" Jacob continued.

"Why should I mind; I don't own it? January, derived from the two faced God, Janus. He looked to the past and faced the future. Now we are in March, derived from Mars. The month armies march to resume battle," the captain elaborated.

"But we began fighting in January," Jacob said.

Devil shrugged.

At the end of March, Blue Devil reported to Wellington that Marmont was marching on Cuidad Rodrigo. Badajoz's breaches were barely sufficient, but as good as they were likely to be. On April sixth, Devil and other ADCs delivered the general's orders launching the assault. Bloody disaster followed.

A Forlorn Hope advanced on the steep ramparts to be blown to pieces by powder barrels. Storming parties found the ditch at the bottom full of water holes and mines. They climbed over planks with foot long spikes and reached a wall of sword blades. After forty attempts, no one had reached the top.

Wellington ordered Captain Trevelyan to ride to General Picton and order him to assault the castle on the other side of the breaches. This attack seemed impossible. Ladder after ladder was thrown down or broke, but finally, one man made it and the others followed. The British army marched into town to exact revenge on the recalcitrant inhabitants. Murder, rape, plunder and drunken debauchery followed into the morning of April seventh when Wellington issued orders to end the plunder. The following day, the Bloody Provost set up gallows to end the sacking.

Five thousand British soldiers lay dead. Captain Trevelyan and many officers thought the pillaging excusable. Murder and rape, inexcusable, but the officers could not stop an army bent on revenge. The captain and two other officers guarded a house occupied by several ladies, who generously offered their jewels for saving them. The officers refused all but token mementos. Ronan later bought gold chains, rings and jewels from soldiers for a fraction of their worth.

He wrote Berty a sober account of Badajoz, the multiple bloody assaults, the lost of over fifty officers and 5,000 men, the explosions and swords. Leaving out descriptions of rape and child murder, he stated those things happened in the sack of the city. He saw no point in sparing Berty the truth, for she would read it in her uncle's radical papers. He gave her permission to share the letter with her family and Cedric, begging Cedric's forgiveness that he did not have time to write to him. In the end, the captain wrote, "Don't cut your beautiful hair."

~~~

While billeted in a town, Sergeant Collins encountered a drunken captain he'd seen with Captain Trevelyan in their first encounter. When Collins helped the man up from a fall, Captain Winot addressed the sergeant, "Dammit, ain't you the mad sergeant who thinks Devil ought to marry your wanton daughter?"

Rather than express his offense at being so addressed, Collins thought to use the opportunity to obtain information. Besides, he couldn't punch an officer. The sergeant reserved his fists for his men when they got out of line.

"My daughter is married, sir. What Devil would this be?"

"Captain Trevelyan. You pressed him with your absurd claim."

When questioned further, Captain Winot described the captain as the descendant of earls and viscounts, fifth in line to a barony and seventh or eight to a marchessate. "A bit too blue blooded for a sergeant's daughter, don't you think? Anyhow, Trevelyan has to marry an heiress for he was born with pockets to let. Dash it, he wasn't born with pockets at all!"

Coincidentally, the Sergeant came up on Blue Devil on Gunpowder the next day. Captain Trevelyan, who'd just met with Wellington and his staff, glittered in full hussar uniform and ornate shako. His mustaches glinted gold when he halted his mettlesome steed, the most beautiful horse Collins had ever beheld. The Devil greeted Sergeant Collins.

"Captain Trevelyan! Just the man I wish to see," replied the sergeant, as amiably as he could manage.

Devil waited for more.

"My daughter has married an ensign."

"My felicitations," the captain replied, coldly.

"Accepted, but it puts me to trouble for he don't want your brat around. So with a broken heart, my Mary has left the child with me and my woman. Now if Mary's mother had lived, t'wouldn't be so bad, but she died as soon as we reached the Peninsula after considering herself lucky to come with me. And Mrs. Jones, my woman, a soldier's widow, has two brats of her own and another on the way."

Sergeant Collins displayed his usual loquacity. The Devil stared at the sergeant's weathered face and shifted his left foot out of the stirrup.

"Mount," he ordered.

Collins hesitated a moment, then climbed behind the Devil and directed him to the house where he was quartered.

"So much better in a house than to bivouac with women and children to look after," the sergeant said.

He clung to Devil as the horse leaped into action. Collins thought they fairly flew to his quarters, but what Devil intended he could not imagine.

The sergeant dismounted while the captain waited. Collins looked in the house, but his family was gone. Soldiers and camp followers gathered to stare at the Blue Devil.

"You'd think they had never seen a Hussar before," Collins grumbled, "Ah, there's Mrs. Shotwell."

A handsome woman of about twenty-five waddled towards them with her bonnet askance, a basket of provisions on her arm and three barefoot little boys running around her, two still in skirts. Sergeant Collins, grabbed one of the smaller boys, a very blond and very dirty two-year old and held him for the Devil to examine.

From his tall horse, the Captain looked down on the urchin.

"What did his mother look like," Devil inquired.

"You don't know?" Collins ejaculated.

"It was dark."

Mrs. Shotwell, collecting this was the Hussar the Sergeant had told her about, looked up with mild surprise. She first noticed he was exceedingly handsome. Then she said, "Mary looks like her father, gray eyes, sandy hair, a well-favored girl. Christopher is six and thirty, not in the bloom of youth, or the resemblance would be more apparent,"

Mrs. Shotwell spoke with remarkable clarity. She had been a governess before eloping with her soldier.

Devil assumed Christopher was the Sergeant. He looked down at the urchin's very blue eyes, like his own and remarked, "He looks like the rest of mine. Hand him to me."

"Well, I'll be a monkey if we will do things as shabby as that. You could intend to throw him in the river for all I know!" the sergeant protested, "Let's go inside and discuss this like gentlemen instead of out here diverting every soldier and whore."

The Devil collected Gunpowder as if to depart. Realizing, he'd possibly insulted and then given an order to a captain, Sergeant Collins quickly made amends. "I beg pardon, sir. I didn't expect you'd want him.

Would you not like to know his birth date and name? Perhaps inform me of your intentions? He is my only grandchild."

Devil alighted from his charger and handed the halter strap to a nearby soldier, warning him not to touch the reins. The captain removed his shako to walk under the low door to the house. Collins sized him up, the way he did all men. The captain stood four or five inches taller than Collins, about six feet, two inches, Collins figured and probably weighed the same as the sergeant. Tall for a light cavalryman, but slender.

They sat at a bare table, while Mrs. Shotwell tried to clean the boy. The house served as quarters for numerous soldiers and their families, but they were left alone to talk.

"His name's Christopher Collins, same as mine," the sergeant began.

"Trevelyan," the captain corrected him.

The sergeant thought it a good sign that the captain was giving the brat his surname, but grew cautious in his speech in case the Devil was touchy. Things were going too well to offend the officer. Mrs. Shotwell put on a pot for tea. The sergeant, who was proud to have a relationship with a woman of such quality, explained she had been a governess, of respectable family, but poor. "She speaks French!"

Upon inquiry, Collins learned that the captain intended to send the child to his godfather, Sir Richard Burlington, in Dorset, as companion to Sir Richard's son. Christopher would be educated according to his capacity.

"You mean if he has a good mind, you will send him to university?" Collins asked, incredulously.

"Yes," Devil replied firmly. He intended to have the means for sending both Arthur and Christopher to Oxford by the time they were old enough, if he lived.

Collins asked if he and his daughter would be allowed to visit the child. Ronan said Sir Richard would likely allow this and if not, the captain would arrange for them to meet elsewhere.

"You will find Sir Richard the kindest of men beneath his gruffness," Captain Trevelyan assured him.

He asked Collins how long he'd been a sergeant, to see if the information he had, matched what Collins would say. It did. He judged the sergeant to be a man of integrity.

"Write a memorandum and I will see that the right person endorses it," Ronan told him. Men who wanted promotion wrote memorandums listing their qualifications for endorsement by their commanders, but again and again, Collins' commanders had been killed.

While the sergeant wrote, Mrs. Shotwell told the captain that the sergeant's current commanders had bought their promotions and Christopher knew more about soldiering than the two of them. The captain didn't doubt her. He told her he would send the boy back to England with the wounded. If she or Christopher knew of a reliable man to accompany the boy, he would pay him well. The Devil was to leave on patrol again that week, but would keep the boy until then.

Christopher gave him the memorandum and Ronan stepped out of the house. He found a commotion. Gunpowder had escaped his holder and stood rearing in the middle of the street, attacking anyone who tried to catch him. Devil casually put on his shako and whistled. Gunpowder hit the ground and galloped to him. His master stroked his neck as if he'd been a good horse, then leaped on him and gathered the reins. Sergeant Collins handed up the quiet child. The captain grasped the boy with his right arm and galloped away. Little Christopher enjoyed the ride.

Soldiers stared when the captain rode to his quarters carrying a child. Jacob frowned in dismay when told to scrub "Master Christopher Trevelyan" and find him clean clothes. Wisely, Jacob decided to find the clothes first. Taking the child with him, he trod to his laundry woman. She knew most of the women in camp who had children or sewed and promised to have a clean infant's dress for him that evening.

Jacob returned with Christopher, an apparently contented child, used to a ramshackle life among strangers. If he missed mother or grandfather, he didn't show it as long as he had something to eat. Jacob soon learned that. He procured goats milk, bread and cheese and those victuals kept Christopher in high gig. Jacob scrubbed the lad in a basin and combed his verminous head with a fine toothed comb.

Captain Trevelyan returned from meeting with Quartermaster General Murray regarding the next patrol, to find a clean, well-fed little child.

"He don't talk much, sir, unless he's hungry. Women fuss over him; coo over his big, blue eyes and say he looks like you. He ain't as much trouble as I thought he'd be," Jacob said.

Vivian Ramsey shook his close-cropped head. "You're a rum one, Devil! If you won't avoid getting bastards, at least get them on women who won't know who the sire is. You're plowing the wrong fields."

After supper, Vivian smoked a pipe while Ronan played guitar. Christopher sat in front of him, fascinated, until Jacob put the boy in a little bed he'd made of blankets. Ronan woke during the night to find Christopher next to him, a trait he must have acquired from Mary. They slept together until two wounded veterans were found to escort the boy to Dorset.

Sergeant Lightfoot had lost part of his right foot at Badajoz. Private Handy had lost the use of his left arm, which hung limp at his side, and he was blind in one eye from the same battle. Both were from a village near Burlington. Sergeant Collins knew them to be sober and trustworthy.

"I have a wife and two children in Dorset," Sergeant Lightfoot said, "I'll be glad to take the child to Sir Richard. Between Handly and me, we can care for him. He's got the feet and I have the arms." Despite the pain in his foot and his loss of career, Sergeant Lightfoot laughed.

Ronan gave them several pounds for their trouble and letters to deliver to Sir Richard. Some were for forwarding. He assured them Sir Richard would compensate them and help them find employment. If Sir Richard was in London, they were instructed to forward one of the letters to him there and wait his return.

Sergeant Collins and his bride, the former Mrs. Shotwell, watched the Devil hand the child up to Sergeant Lightfoot on the wagon taking them to port.

~~~

Weeks later, the two ragged, scruffy soldiers stepped off a stage coach with Christopher at Burlington's tavern. While they refreshed themselves with food and ale, the tavern keeper inquired their destination. They didn't look like the sort the villagers wanted about.

"We are going to Sir Richard Burlington to deliver this child," Lightfoot said.

"What does he want with that urchin?" the tavern keeper asked.

"I don't know. We're following orders from Captain Trevelyan."

"Captain Trevelyan! Is that blade fobbing off his bastards on his lordship now?" the keeper asked.

"Dammit, how should we know? The captain could have lost his wife. We ain't nosy like some!" Lightfoot retorted.

The keeper snickered, "Well known, the captain never had a wife of his own."

Having fortified themselves, the travelers walked and hobbled down the long drive to Burlington House, stopping occasionally to rest. They were resting on a grassy bank when Sir Richard drove by in a curricle drawn by two mettlesome young horses.

Sir Richard halted the horses he was training and turned around. "Who are you and what are you doing here?" he asked.

Lightfoot told their story.

"The effrontery of it! Is that libertine going to send me his byblows now? My God, he must have a quiver full!" Sir Richard pronounced, then broke into a laugh, "A pretty little lad there. My godson marks his get."

Sir Richard ordered Lightfoot to get in the curricle and hold the child. There wasn't room for Handy. Back they dashed to the house. Ann and Tristan fussed over Christopher like a new toy. Gervace shook his head, claiming, "They'll ruin him."

When Handy reached the house, Gervace took the veterans to the kitchen where they talked about the war, and he learned their needs.

~~~

April, Spain, Wellington sent Captain Trevelyan to find Sir Colquhoun Grant. Blue Devil met the guerilleros and discovered the French had captured Grant. The captain would have led them to his rescue, until they told him Grant had accepted parole.

Chapter 3

1812-13

Spain, England and Portugal

Captain Alexander Trevelyan's regiment arrived in May and joined Wellington's army in Spain. Brimming with news from home, Alexander searched for his cousin, Ronan, but learned the Blue Devil was on an exploring mission. The army marched.

One morning while on the road, Alexander saw a rider on a distant hill. The rider pounded down the hill, bounded over a rocky stream and leaped his horse over a caisson traveling on the road. He rode up another hill where Wellington and his staff stood. Alexander heard the general's loud guffaw from a great distance.

"By Jove! That officer is my cousin!" Alexander informed his companions, "I have so much to tell him tonight!"

After Ronan delivered his report, he sat on his horse eating a meal brought to him, then dismounted and mounted a fresh horse with replenished supplies. The captain galloped off the way he had come, taking the shortest route between two points.

In the following days, Alexander heard multiple tales of his cousin's daring deeds and rumors of his mistress. Finally, Ronan rejoined the army. Alexander discovered him in his billet having the dust of Spain scrubbed from his weary body.

"Found you, at last! Dash it if you don't take more baths than anyone I know," Alexander began.

"Yes, once a week, needed or not, but usually in an icy stream," Ronan replied.

Alexander laughed and began his news. "Have you heard that Perceval was assassinated in the Commons?"

"Yes, and Liverpool has replaced him. Jacob told me."

"Then I'll get on with family news. Sedgewick still ain't married. I think he's as reluctant to get leg shackled as we are and maybe he's as big a pansy as Cedric. Such brothers! It's enough to cause me to suspect Mama of misalliances. A shocking thing to say, but such brothers!"

Alexander held up letters from Miss Bodleigh and Cedric and set them aside while Ronan dried off and pulled a clean shirt over his head. He pulled on stockings and cavalry overalls and slipped the braces over his shoulders. Jacob tied a black neck cloth and helped him into his jacket.

Ronan offered his cousin the warm bath water. Alexander, still a greenhorn, declined. Vivian took a turn in it, instead, followed by three other officers. At that point, Alexander realized what a rarity a warm bath was on campaign. In the following days, he found himself waiting a turn to use warm shaving water and missing his English valet, who'd not traveled with him.

Devil offered Alexander port, which he accepted. While Alexander lubricated his tongue, Ronan put on his spectacles to read Berty's brief missive.

"You wear spectacles? I had no idea!" Alexander spoke.

"For reading," Ronan replied and read the letter to himself.

"Dear Ronan,

I have nothing as exciting as battles to write of, but you know that. I'm distressed that the Untited States of America has declared war on Britain. As poor and weak as my country is, its leaders would not have taken such a desperate measure without provocation. The pressing of sailors and hindrance of trade has been intolerable. I saw three sailors pressed from the ship that brought me to England. It was most unjust. Aunt Sarah and Uncle Augustus agree, but advise me to keep my opinions to myself except among close friends.

Aunt Sarah, Edith and I will be traveling to London soon. My painting is in the Royal Academy! I try not to be TOO proud of that. I shall have more to write from London.

Your friend, Liberty"

The cousins shared a good meal. Alexander, as usual, proved himself an Atlas at holding up the conversation.

"Where do you think the Peer intends to strike next?"

"I hazard a guess that he will attack Salamanca," Ronan replied.

"Oh no one thinks that! Why do you?"

"That's what I would do." He kept his intelligence knowledge to himself.

"Do you care to wager?" Alexander asked.

"No. Particularly not with someone with empty pockets."

Alexander chose to change the subject, "You know, I've never been in battle. Cedric says I'll wet my breeches. What should I do?"

"Take them to a laundress."

Alexander sputtered a laugh. "I meant what should I do in battle?"

"Do as you were trained."

"I hope I may, to be sure. I suppose your faith sustains you, as it should me, although I sometimes think I'm going to the devil," Alexander retorted.

"I no more believe in the devil than I believe in centaurs, nor do I believe there's a heaven and hell, except on earth. Take heart, my dear, one doesn't need faith to prove oneself in battle," Ronan replied.

"You shock me! I always suspected as much, but not being one for metaphysics, well, lets not discuss that. I suppose you mean what one needs is these," Alexander replied, putting his hand in his crotch.

His cousin smiled slightly.

"You do believe in God?" Alexander asked.

"Yes, I believe in a Creator of the universe and all in it. I know not why we were created, but we are not discussing metaphysics."

"No, by Jove, we were discussing battle. Pray tell me all you can, cousin."

Ronan shrugged. "It thrills me," he said, paused, and added, "Like nothing else. One waits and watchs for action. Most of us get used to the howls of the wounded and dying, the stench."

Alexander grew somber. June thirteenth, they marched for Salamanca.

~~~

Salamanca's forts surrendered on the twenty-seventh and the army marched into the beautiful city. Alexander could truthfully write to Cedric that he had not wet his pants. He had performed with valor and his cousin promised to write home with that information.

"I did pray, though," Alexander said.

"As did I," Ronan replied.

Blue Devil, Alexander and some Oxford alumni among Ronan's friends strolled about admiring the university city. Don Julian Sanchez, the famous guerrillero chief, with whom Devil had frequently worked, strode towards Blue Devil. They embraced and kissed, much to Alexander's disgust. Don Julian, too, wore Hussar uniform, of a sort. He called Ronan, "Le Diable Bleu," the name the French had given him, and told the officers of horrible tortures that awaited Diable Bleu if Monsieur caught him.

"But the rules of war forbid harming a uniformed intelligence officer," a green officer said.

Don Julian laughed at such naivety.

Their joy proved brief. For three dusty weeks, the British and French armies marched back and forth, often within cannon shot, accomplishing nothing. Alexander contended with hot days, cold nights, exhaustion, bad water and dust.

The army's baggage had been sent to headquarters at Cuidad Rodrigo, but Devil and his valet always traveled light. Since Jacob had grown too big for a donkey, Ronan provided him with a good mule. Besides Jacob, the mule carried necessities and supplies, including dried peas, oat meal and beans in waterproof containers. A donkey carried baggage, as well. Ronan suggested that Alexander obtain such emergency rations, but Alexander trusted the army and thought he could buy provisions from peasants if need be. Ronan explained that often peasants had been robbed of everything eatable.

On July twentieth, when crossing the River Tormes, an ominous thunderstorm struck. Two days later, the armies positioned themselves on two hills. The French, who arrived first, on the Greater Arapiles and the allies on the Lessor Arapiles. During the battle, Devil, attached to the fifth dragoons, charged with them. In the end there were 14,000 French casualties to 5,000 allied.

The victorious army marched to Madrid, crossing an excruciatingly dusty plain in August. Soldiers drained their canteens and lips became parched. As they neared the city, people brought them wine to quench their thirst. They entered the city to massive, ecstatic celebrations, but in the backstreets, people died of starvation. Alexander and the other soldiers suffered the kisses of grateful Spanish men.

In a billet they shared, Ronan wrote a cheerful missive, detailing events, to Miss Bodleigh. He also told her Britain's politicians had mishandled America .

"If they hadn't been such dunderheads, America would still be a colony."

Alexander grumbled, "I promised Edith, Miss Westerly, I'd write. I don't mind writing a few lines to Cedric, but what do I say to a miss? I've never written to a girl in my life? What a botheration I've gotten into. Never did like to write."

Ronan suggested he pay someone to write his dictated letters.

"Capital! Why, I should have thought of that."

While in Madrid, Alexander hired a Spanish valet to replace the one he'd left in England, found a private with excellent hand writing, flirted with senoritas and thoroughly enjoyed himself until he saw bodies of starved people thrown on the streets.

~~~

The letters eventually reached Liberty and Edith in London at Miss Penthwaite's. Sarah had returned to Boscawden, leaving the girls under Hilda's supervision.

"I dare say, I've never seen such beautiful writing as Alexander's," Edith boasted.

Berty glanced at the letter. "He had someone write it for him. Cedric has shown me Alexander's letters. His writing is worse than mine. If mine looks like hen scratching, his looks like bull pawings."

"I don't believe it," Edith replied.

"Suit yourself," Berty said.

Edith read Alexander's letter out loud, "It thundered before the battle. Thundering cannon initiated the battle," began a lengthy account of battle.

Berty suggested Alexander paid his scribe by the word. "Go on, Edith, what else was thundering?"

Edith cut Berty a pouting look, and continued, "Thundering hooves..."

Berty laughed to unladylike excess. She strode to the writing desk to begin her reply to Ronan's letter.

After thanking him for his brief descriptions of the battles, she took issue with the idea of America remaining a colony, but at least he agreed British dunderheads had made a dog's breakfast of things. She told him about the art exhibit.

"My painting is hung higher than I would like, but just to have it in the exhibit suffices. When Aunt Sarah, Edith, Miss Penthwaite and I visited the exhibit, two gentlemen stood before my painting. One of them said the portrait was idealized, 'No one ever looked that perfect.' and the other man agreed and suggested I had copied a classical bust! Aunt Sarah turned to Edith and Miss Penthwaite and said, loudly, "It's the very likeness of Captain Trevelyan, don't you agree?"

"Edith agreed avidly. Miss Penthwaite has never seen you, but she put in that all my portraits are exact resemblances. The gentlemen then turned around and asked if we knew the sitter and Aunt Sarah told them she not only knew the sitter, but was his cousin and very close!"

"Fearing my friends would introduce me as the artist, I left the room. The gentlemen's remarks affronted me. They shouldn't have and I left to compose myself."

"Miss Penthwaite has taken us to concerts, exhibits, the theater and private art collections. Most of those works make me feel quite inadequate, but I think I do good portraits. She entertains the most interesting people. You would describe them as radicals. They argue constantly."

"I hope you meet Miss Penthwaite someday. She works on projects to save climbing boys and child white slaves and educate orphans and numerous other good things."

"Miss Penthwaite rented horses for Edith and me to ride in the park. They were described as gentle ladies' hacks. Mine had a mouth as hard as an anvil and Edith's was as lazy as Slug, which we thought impossible. She could barely get him to move until a piece of paper in the wind startled him. The nag bolted and two gentlemen stopped it. Both men were old and married; no cause for jealousy there. We failed to impress the ton."

"We have been subjected to the most abysmal flattery, especially in the form of poetry. God spare us from anymore, would-be John Donnes. At least half the young men of Miss Penthwaite's acquaintance believe themselves poets. She also knows a fair number of dandies. It pains me to see their shirt collar points poking their faces and their taste in raiment torments to behold. I've come to appreciate our country bumpkins with their buckskins and top boots. No poets or toad eaters among THEM!"

"I prefer Boscawden to the city, but Miss Penthwaite says if I am to be a successful artist, I must show my work here and she said when I am older, I should have a London studio. I don't see how I could pay the rent or live here."

"Edith was in raptures over Alexander's beautiful handwriting. It has improved since I last saw it. I dared to say he'd hired a letter writer. Most considerate of him."

Berty wrote her letter, uncrossed, on two sheets of paper. One of Miss Penthwaite's noble friends franked it for her. He also franked Edith's letter to Alexander. "I'll gladly frank any letters from young ladies to our Peninsula soldiers," he said.

Liberty's letter cheered Ronan during the melancholy siege of Burgos. As usual, the army was ill-equipped and lacking enough engineers, tools and siege guns. With no tents, the soldiers bivouacked in the open.

During the siege, the French shot and killed Ronan's friend and fellow intelligence officer, Major Cocks. A beloved young officer, his exploits were as legendary as Devil's. Wellington shed tears over him.

In the end, Burgos had to be abandoned. Wellington waited a week to do battle. Instead, the French army of over 100,000 tried to cut off Wellington and Hill's army of 70,000 from Cuidad Rodrigo.

With the lost of Grant and Cocks, the Blue Devil acted as Wellington's favored intelligence officer. For a while, Devil received messages from Grant via Spanish spies. Grant's captors finally disallowed his visitors and Grant escaped into France.

Wellington thought about his Devil. The indefatigable Captain Trevelyan followed orders, yet took initiatives and showed evident genius. If he hadn't fought a duel, the Peer would have promoted him. Trevelyan wasn't likely to do that again, yet he was notoriously unpredictable. The French thought so. Ronan would have preferred to be less well known to them. Wellington recommended the captain's promotion to brevet major. Quartermaster General Murray, who supervised intelligence, agreed. If captured, he might be treated better as a major than he was as a captain.

During the siege of Burgos, Captain Trevelyan led a daring patrol to assess the French advance. Devil, himself, stalked close enough to count the enemy before returning to his men. They encountered a brief skirmish when returning to their lines. Soon after, Devil fell forward in the saddle, dropping the reins. Gunpowder halted and stood waiting for his master to cue him.

The captain's men rode round him. One dismounted and held the captain on the horse while another man led. They saw blood flowing from under his shako and removed it to discover a head wound. At the hospital a surgeon stated a spent bullet had hit the captain over his left forehead causing a concussion. He had an assistant clean and bandage the wound and departed. Devil did not awake.

Devil had shared his findings with a reliable lieutenant, who presented them to Wellington from memory. He was unable to answer the general's questions as his captain would have.

"Grant, Cocks and now Trevelyan," Wellington repeated, despondently.

~~~

Vivian Ramsey soon removed his unconscious friend from the hospital and placed him in his own tent, where Jacob and Ramsey's Spanish batman tended him. The general sent frequent inquiries as to his condition.

~~~

A cannonade exploded in Ronan's head. Gradually, he regained consciousness. He remembered who he was, but not where or what had befallen him. Ronan felt tremendous thirst, sat up on the cot and gripped his head in his hands to stop it from blowing apart.

"Captain?" a voice asked.

Ronan tried to see the speaker, but it was dark. He asked for water and the speaker held a cup for him to grasp, but the captain didn't see it. Why was there no candle?

"Here is is, sir," Jacob said.

Ronan's hands waved towards him and caught the cup. He gulped the water, felt suddenly sick and threw up.

"They said you might be sick. Here, just sip a little," Jacob advised.

Ronan did so and then asked Jacob to light a candle.

"A candle, sir? It's daylight."

Jacob passed his hand before Ronan's eyes. Nothing.

"You don't see me, sir?"

"No, it is dark."

"I'm sorry, sir, it isn't dark. You can't see. Maybe it will pass. You were hit in the head, you know."

"No, I don't know. Who are you?"

"Jacob, sir, your valet. Do you remember being hit?"

He did not. Jacob told him a day had passed and the army was preparing to retreat. The boy helped his master outside to relieve himself and vomit again. Jacob worked to get a little food and water into Ronan. He sent for the surgeon who said the captain might regain his sight or not. No one knew with head injuries.

An ADC and Captain Alexander came to check on Ronan's condition and spoke to the surgeon before he left.

"First we lose Grant, then Cocks and now Devil's blinded. I've not seen the Peer so discouraged," the aide said, before turning to Ronan and saying, "We are retreating. You can ride in the Peer's carriage with Doctor McGrigor, whose horse kicked him."

"Bring me my horse," Ronan ordered.

"You're in no condition to ride, Ro," Alexander objected, but Ronan insisted.

Vivian, who had been seconded to the Corps of Guides, where he had been deciphering messages, returned to the tent. "What the deuce is this? Ah you've come around, Devil."

"But he can't see," Jacob told him, adding the surgeon's statement.

He listened to the aide's sensible proposal, but knew Ronan would not agree. "We will leave in the morning, Devil. You rest for now."

Ronan obliged, laying back upon his cot, overwhelmed with headache, in too much pain to think about his blindness.

Dawn, Jacob cleaned his master, changed the bandage, fed and groomed him. Ronan evinced no improvement. Alexander obtained permission to accompany his cousin. Jacob packed his mule and the donkey. Vivian's batman packed the tent and other accouterments on a mule and mounted his own. A groom brought up Gunpowder, now worn and thin. Alexander helped his cousin into his greatcoat and a low-crowned, broad-brimmed hat. Ronan could not wear anything else over his wound and it was raining. Jacob then led him to Gunpowder and the captain mounted. The boy gave Ronan directions to guide his horse. Once on the muddy road, Gunpowder followed the rest.

The November rain fell all day. Evening, Jacob and the batman set up the tent and Jacob ground together the remaining rations in water to make a cold gruel. The rain made it impossible to build a fire. During the following incessantly rainy days, Alexander learned why his cousin and Captain Ramsey carried their own rations. The commissariat misdirected the army's supplies and men starved. They roasted acorns when they could build fires, but found little else to eat.

Alexander apologized for bringing only a goat cheese. The others agreed to share with him. Jacob and the batman estimated the amount to use each day based on an estimated five days march to Cuidad Rodrigo. This came to less than a pint a day for each man of dried beans, peas and grain, plus a bite of Alexander's cheese. Jacob expertly ground the porridge each day and, when weather permitted, cooked it. When the batman found wood, it tended to be too wet to burn.

Ronan vomited half of anything he ate.

"Damn your eyes, Ro! That was my cheese!" Alexander grumbled and immediately added, "Dashed sorry. Shouldn't have put it that way."

"A damnable waste of food," Vivian claimed, "You want me to feed it back to you, Devil?"

"No, thank you, you may have it," he replied seriously.

They marched on until the famished army discovered a herd of wild pigs and went wild shooting them. Disorder followed. The French caught some of the men. Punishments, including hanging, brought the men back to order.

They reached Cuidad Rodrigo two days later. Dr. McGrigor and two other surgeons examined Ronan's wound. One surgeon said the captain's head required trepaning, drilling a hole in the skull, to reduce pressure. Another said bleeding was the answer. Dr. McGrigor thought it best to let nature heal and the surgeons left the patient alone. The wound stopped bleeding and the captain recovered his strong stomach, but not his sight. His headache eased somewhat. When his friends inquired about his sight, Ronan replied, with sangfroid, "I'll see, or not."

Ronan resigned himself to probable permanent blindness and seemed contented. He played his guitar and drew crowds doing so, partly for the beauty of his music and partly for his fame. Lieutenant Phillip de Sousa paid him a visit.

Phillip resembled his mother in beauty, amiability and rare tolerance. He was almost of age, knew his father was dead and contemplated taking a wife. His mother's liaison with the captain and their children presented a dilemma. No decent bride would approve. Senora de Sousa promised to move to her rural estate when Phillip came into his inheritance. She considered marriage between herself and the captain out of the question. Age, religious differences and her love of independence were too great. Phillip loved his mother and respected the captain as a man of great courage, but the captain dominated the household when he was there, which, fortunately, was rare. Any objections to his rule met with stony silence. Even so, Phillip considered the captain a friend he could count on.

Phillip wondered if the captain would be moving in with his mother permanently now he was blind, yet dared not ask directly. "What will you do?" he asked Ronan.

"I can only wait and..." he started to say see.

"Will you be coming to Lisbon?" Phillip inquired.

"I'd like to see... be with my children for a while. I shall not be a burden, if that concerns you. I have ways to earn my keep in England. I will go there."

After a silence, Ronan added, "Will you act as guardian of my children?"

Surprised, Philip replied, "Certainly, they are my siblings. I have leave to visit my family. What shall I tell mother?"

"I shall ride with you," Ronan said.

Phillip knew Ronan was on medical leave and free to go to Lisbon, if able, which he doubted.

"This may be my last opportunity to visit the senora and my children. If I recover, I will be with the army in Spain. Wherever I am, I will find means to provide for the children."

Most people would have disbelieved an improvident soldier, but Phillip trusted that, even blind, Ronan would succeed.

~~~

"Ride 200 mountainous miles in your condition!" Vivian boomed, when apprised of Devil's plans, "Madness! Sheer madness. I will go with you."

Alexander joined Ronan, Phillip and Vivian. Jacob and the officers' batmen packed mules with provisions and fodder. Several other friends volunteered to accompany them, but were refused permission.

The rain continued in the treacherous mountains. When it let up, Ronan played his guitar. Music soothed concerns about his sight. During the trek, he suddenly saw light so strong, it brought on a searing headache. He pulled off his black neck cloth, tied it over his eyes and rode on. Come nightfall, he removed it and discovered he could see forms in the darkness. His companions tentatively rejoiced, but come morning, the strong light blinded him again and his headaches resumed.

Exhausted riders and horses stumbled into Senora de Sousa's courtyard of an evening. Phillip led them into the house where his mother embraced him and Ronan before Phillip told her of the captain's blindness. The usual mob of children surrounded them.

Alexander, not speaking any Portuguese, followed Ronan and Jacob to Ronan's chamber.

"Filthy town, but I came to see the sights and I will. Oh, dash it, sorry, I shouldn't have said see the sights. Upon my soul this is awkward, but I have such a brief leave," Alexander blundered.

"I believe you requested leave for selfish motives," Ronan responded.

"Upon my word, I did not! I mean to see you get the best care. Dash it, there I go with see again. And by the by, I collect that handsome lady is your mistress. You do like them matronly, don't you? I dare say she's old enough to be your mother."

His cousin didn't reply. After a hot bath, Ronan took Jacob's arm to Senora de Sousa's chamber.

Ronan spent the following days in rooms with shutters closed, playing his guitar for the señora and all the children. He dumbfounded Alexander when he introduced Serafina and Arthur Trevelyan. Almost three years old, Serafina curtsied, one-year-old Arthur stared from round blue eyes. Alexander struggled to digest the situation. He could hardly object when Phillip de Sousa didn't, but he spoke to Ronan alone in the captain's private chamber.

"Everybody knows soldiers have mistresses or strumpets, well maybe not everybody, but, dash it, why didn't you use the officer's brothel? Instead you take on a respectable, or used to be respectable, lady and have children that you acknowledge. It ain't the thing, Ro! What will they say in Boscawden? What will Miss Bodleigh think?"

Receiving no response, except the all too familiar stony silence, Alexander continued, "I guess in your present condition, it don't matter what she thinks, does it? You've written to her?"

"Four times," Ronan astonished Alexander with an answer.

"By Jupiter, it's been a year, hasn't it. I daresay I haven't written Edith more than that. I rather thought you might marry Miss Bodleigh someday, when your career had advanced. Damn it! Damn that bullet! And now these children! Such a botheration!"

"My children are not a botheration. I cherish them."

"What about Miss Bodleigh? She might not cherish them."

"She doesn't need to. She is not my wife and they have a mother. Miss Bodleigh is a blue stocking and an American republican. We could not possibly be suited," Ronan replied, icily.

"What the deuce! I thought you had been taken with her for seven years and her with you.Why did you write to her, then?"

"We are friends."

Alexander stared at his cousin. "Humdudgeon, Ro! You know she don't approve of your rakehell ways and if she knew of these by blows of yours, you'd never get near her. You ain't humming me with that friends nonsense. 'Not possibly suited," bah! Well, none of my bread and butter, thank God!"

~~~

After paying his own mistress a visit, Vivian had to return to duty. The army was now in Portugal. Alexander and Phillip also returned to duty. Slowly, Ronan's sight returned, although he remained sensitive to light.

Senora de Sousa was supervising her household downstairs, when her footman announced visitors. With much pomp and celebration, Wellington had arrived in Lisbon that week. Now, he and three ADCs paid a private call on Senora de Sousa to learn how Captain Trevelyan went on.

Antonia welcomed the great general. She spoke no English, but enthusiastically described the captain's progress and told them he was playing his guitar for the children. The visitors heard the guitar from the entrance. When the Peer announced he would like to see the captain, Antonia said of course, then recalled, "But he is dishabille. I shall tell him he has guests that he may dress properly."

The soldiers laughed, entertained by the idea of surprising the captain, "dishabille." They would see the captain as he was. Antonia led them upstairs to a large, dark room. Most of the shutters were closed to protect Ronan's eyes. Besides the guitar, children laughed and danced as the company entered. A hush fell. The children stopped their play. The captain sprung to his feet and bowed. As the visitors' eyes adjusted to the darkness, they saw the captain wore a dark blue silk robe over shirt and trousers. Blonde little Serafina stood next to him. A Portuguese nursery maid held Arthur's leading strings nearby. Fourteen children, five women and one British officer. Even Wellington was dumbfounded.

The captain introduced Mrs. Tarkington, his daughter's governess, a British officer's widow. She curtsied. He introduced a Portuguese lady in charge of the eight orphans in the room. He introduced Mrs. Tarkington's two boys, Senora de Sousa's two children by her husband and the eight orphans. All bowed or curtsied. Then he introduced, "My daughter, Serafina and son, Arthur."

Serafina curtsied. Year-old Arthur stared from round eyes.

His lordship looked at the two blond children and smiled. "Arthur, eh?"

"Yes, my lord, after you. In a few years there will be many boys named for you," Ronan volunteered, unusual for him.

"I'm honored," the general said dryly. He would have been more honored had the child been legitimate. His older brother had several illegitimate children. The Beau did not approve.

The Portuguese lady herded the orphans out of the room and the other ladies sat. The gentlemen then sat, also.

"I apologize for the darkness. I can not bear light yet. The French might change my nom de guerre to la chauve-souris bleue."

The blue bat. His lordship exploded in one of his horse laughs. He and the captain had lost their usual laconic grimness in the relaxed atmosphere of the señora's house. The lady and her lover exuded contentment. Ronan's regained sight would have been cause enough for their smiles, but they were also happy in their children and, as one of the officers observed later, got on better than most married couples. In fact, got on better than the Peer and his wife. Wellington had not seen his wife in three years and seemed glad of it.

"Your sight is improving, captain?"

"Yes, my lord. The surgeons believe it shall be completely restored by the spring campaign."

Antonia whispered to the captain. "The senora wishes to know if you could stay for dinner?"

"By Jove, I'd be delighted. Perhaps you will play for us until then."

Antonia excused herself to speak to her cook. The men rose and resumed their seats after she left. Ronan began to play a piece by Sante, explaining he had found the music in Salamanca. Serafina sat on a stool by her father with her own little guitar. He finished that piece and played one by Vivaldi. The señora returned and the men rose until she had seated herself by the captain. When Ronan finished playing, Serafina boldly asked Wellington, in English, "Would you like to hear the piece papa taught me?"

His lordship, who loved children, could not refuse. The captain and Antonia smiled like the adoring parents they were. Serafina played a short simple melody, perfectly. The gentlemen applauded and she curtsied. Arthur squirmed and his nursemaid took him away.

Serafina asked her father to play the fandango he'd composed for her mother. The day went on with one enthralling piece of music after another until it was time for Ronan to dress for dinner. Serafina kissed her parents, curtsied to the gentlemen and left to join the other children.

Senora de Sousa kept a fine table with a great deal of fresh seafood. His lordship presided at the head of the table, while Antonia sat in her place at the foot. Ronan sat to her right in the dimly lit dining room. After dinner, the gentlemen sat over port, not his lordship's favorite wine, but the señora kept only local wine. The captain abstained. His doctor advised against it as having a deleterious effect with head injuries, but Ronan felt no desire for it. While the others smoked cigars and drank, he ate an orange.

"I apprehend you interrogated Major Fremont. Was it not a bad policy to deny his parole? The Frogs could repay in kind. Did you do so out of revenge?" an officer asked the captain.

"When he had me in his power, he offered me an insult. When I refused, he had me beaten and shackled," Ronan replied, glacially.

"I had not heard that. In that case, he deserved to hang."

The others agreed, although Ronan remained more tolerant than most. His beauty had drawn such offers all his life. Even the third small facial scar did not detract. That fresh scar disappeared into his hair. It occurred to some that Ronan grew his Hussar side beards and moustaches to hide some of his troublesome beauty.

"I daresay, you've received such offers before?" the inquisitive officer asked, but received no response.

His lordship found the subject repugnant, and chose that moment to draw out a paper for the captain. Ronan accepted, opened it and did not need his glasses to see his promotion to full major, not the brevet majority Wellington had originally intended.

Ronan smiled and thanked the Peer. "Senora de Sousa will be pleased."

He would have more money to provide for his three children. He already did more work than most majors. The new major decided to celebrate with a glass of port after all, but one glass of strong drink overpowered his injured head. He refused another.

Ronan spoke of "annihilating monsters of depravity" and driving any left back to France and their "Corsican ogre."

Much amused, his companions asked if he intended to steal more cattle.

"I'll steal everything they have; their ammunition, their horses, their pay, their breeches, their women! Telle est la guerre, ma passion."

"I thought to make you a staff officer, Trevelyan," Wellington joked.

"S'il vous plait, non, mon seigneur," Ronan had stolen the enemy's language, before realizing his mistake, "Ah, I beg pardon, my lord. My physician is correct, I can not take strong drink now." Followed with a disquieting giggle.

His lordship thanked Senora de Sousa, adjured his new major to take care and departed.

~~~

Major Trevelyan, sat at his desk writing to friends. He wrote of Grant's capture, Cox's death, the failure at Burgos, the misdirection of supplies; a litany of misfortune. Yet, he insisted Wellington's army would drive the French from Spain in the next campaign. He picked up a fresh sheet and wrote, "Dear Miss Bodleigh."

She'd asked him not to be so formal, but he chose to be so. She was only a friend, after all, although no friend stunned him the way she did. Not even Antonia, of whom he was extremely fond. And Liberty thought him a rake hell. Everyone did. Although he'd never seduced a virgin, nor did he frequent brothels. His conquests were too blatant to be considered seductions. He'd taken the señora by storm one night four years ago, but he'd never forced an unwilling woman. Nor had he made any vows to them. He had warned Antonia he would not be faithful. Ronan owed his bad repute to criminal conversations, id est sexual liaisons, with unhappily married ladies and three duels.

Carpe diem. He wrote the same letter to Liberty Bodleigh as he'd written to the others. He didn't mention his concussion in any of them. He did, however, sign them, Major Ronan Trevelyan.

Chapter 4

In Boscawden, Edith received a letter from Alexander before Liberty heard from Ronan. Alexander enumerated the "worse experiences" of his life, horrid marches, the failed siege, rain, inadequate food and chaos. He credited Ronan with saving him, but hoped he never had to eat another uncooked dried bean.

Alexander had carefully mentioned Ronan's injury. He didn't mind upsetting his father on his own behalf, but didn't want to disturb ladies. Edith might share her letter with Berty. Alexander claimed a bullet had bounced off Ronan's hard head, giving him a blinding headache. "He couldn't see for a few days, but he's recovering."

None of this information assured Berty when Edith read it to her. By then Berty hadn't seen Ronan in a year, nor heard from him in three months. She and Edith had returned to Boscawden and suffered the ennui of rural life after a city visit.

"You are blue deviled, Berty," Edith claimed.

"Yes, I am. I had great expectations of the exhibit, but no one cares to visit an artist so far from the city; so I'm back to painting brats and pigs."

Edith laughed, "That would put me in the dismals, too. And no letter from Ronan?"

"None. It's that blinding headache Alexander mentions. I think it's worse than he would have us believe. Maybe Ronan is actually blind and can't write and knows I would suspect something was wrong if he had someone else write. It's quite worrisome."

"I never thought of that. I think you are right and I will write to Alexander presently for more information and none of his bouncers."

~~~

In London, Sir Richard and Lady Burlington and Master Burlington attended the exhibit at Somerset House.

"If you see anything that strikes your eye, Ann, I shall purchase it," Sir Richard told his lady.

They wandered about, examining the paintings. Having seen all the ones at eye level or below, Ann happened to look up.

"Good Heavens!" she exclaimed, "Captain Trevelyan!"

"By Jove, it is! A perfect likeness. I had no idea he was sitting for a portrait, did you?"

"L. R. Bodleigh. Who could that be?" Ann looked in her catalog, "L.R. Bodleigh of Boscawden, Hampshire, Portrait of Captain Ronan Trevelyan, Kings Hussars, not for sale!"

"Balderdash, everything is for sale. I shall purchase it. So this is what he was doing in Boscawden last year. I thought he was dangling after some damsel. The devil probably wanted me to think that!" Sir Richard said.

"Now, Richard, please don't call him a devil in front of Tristan."

Tristan interposed, "Yes, my godbrother should be called a Hussar and we should buy the painting for Christopher so he will know what his father looks like."

"Sweet child," Ann said of Tristan. Christopher, still in skirts, was home in the care of his nurse, Miss Brown.

At that point, acquaintances of the Burlingtons entered and the portrait was forgotten amid greetings and chatter.

~~~

Cedric took leave of Berty and Welspent to travel to Kent for Sedgewick's wedding. He promised to write. His lordship remained cloistered in his rooms, claiming ill health prevented him traveling to Kent. Sarah claimed he had inherited Lady Catherine's hypochondria upon her death. Lord James had been active before her demise. He expressed joy at his son's matrimony.

Welspent cataloged the Hall's collections and longed for the unattainable Tabitha Palmer. He could not support a wife on his meager earnings and studied other ways of earning a living. Berty and Mrs. Goodyer assisted in the inventory. Berty had not seen the new wing, built in the reign of Charles II, excepting a few brief visits to Lady Catherine with her aunt. Since Lord James had become a recluse, only a few servants entered that wing. He stayed in his bed chamber while Welspent inspected the collections. The paintings and sculpture astounded Welspent and Berty. Works by Caravaggio, Canaletto, Barbieri, Titian, Claude, Poussin, Ruysdael, Culp, Van Dyke and Lely hung in the gallery. Classical marbles and bronzes stood there and in the orangery. After an eighteenth century remodeling, the saloon and drawing room were furnished with gilded mahogany furniture built by Thomas Chippendale to designs by Adams.

Throughout the house reposed furniture from all ages, Gobelin tapestries, inlaid marble tables from Italy, blue john, ormolu, silver and so forth. The Great Hall held armor, weapons, ancient oak furniture, antlers, musical instruments and family portraits. Sixteenth and seventeenth century beds filled the chambers. Gibbons carvings decorated over-mantles. Silver dressing sets rested on well-made dressing tables. Grinsby, the butler, supplied a list of silver bowls, plates, trenchers, etc, as well as wine in the cellar. Mrs. Goodyer kept a list of chinaware and linen.

Welspent asked Barnstable for a list of horse furniture and carriages, which he promised to make. There were twelve attics full of old furniture, trunks of clothes and papers. Not to be left out, Mr. Gardner claimed the formal gardens held rare plants, fountains and statuary.

"Before Sedgewick departed, he told me he would like to sell many of the collections when he inherits. He has no interest in art, particularly of nude pagans!" Welspent told them.

"That would be terrible!" Berty exclaimed.

"Indeed!" Mrs. Goodyer and Mr. Grinsby agreed. Mrs. Goodyer went on to explain, "Antiquaries come from all over and on public days, it allows the local people to enjoy a bit of culture. A pity, his lordship has disallowed visitors to the new wing."

"The art has certainly inspired me. We have nothing like this in America that I know of," Berty said.

"Oh yes," Mr. Grinsby added, "This is one of the oldest family collections in the country. The Trevelyans never sold anything and brought back masterpieces from their grand tours. I do hope Sedgewick doesn't sell off anything."

"It would be dishonorable," Berty said.

Welspent and Berty also inventoried the unoccupied chambers in the living quarters. Sedgewick's chamber surprised them with its luxurious, modern furnishings in the neoclassical style.

Priscilla's former chamber bloomed with floral wallpaper, curtains and pale painted furniture. They found Captain Alexander's armoires filled with clothing, paintings of actresses and singers hung on the walls and an expensive silver dressing set resided on his dressing table. Red velvet served for bed curtains.

They entered Cedric's chamber through Alexander's. Surprisingly, it emanated masculinity, with dark Tudor furniture, dark brown velvet hangings and austere plaster walls. Berty's sketches of male nudes from her art lessons hung on the walls.

Returning through Alexander's chamber through the dressing room, they entered Ronan's chamber. An Elizabethan bed, hung in silver embroidered, indigo velvet, dominated the small room. Oak linen-fold panels covered the walls. The meagerly furnished room held a chest of drawers, a chair and an armoire containing Ronan's civilian raiment. Reminded of Ronan, Berty found the empty chamber melancholy. She stroked the high quality, superfine wool coats.

"I wonder why his valet left the coats; they will not be the thing when he returns," Welspent said.

Mrs. Goodyer informed them, "This was formerly Lord Victor's chamber. We thought it fitting to assign it to the son of his disowned son. One would think his lordship would have chosen a finer chamber in the new wing. I shall hang lavender with those coats to keep out moths."

The adjoining chamber had historically belonged to the baroness and could only be accessed through the baron's chamber. It had been unoccupied since Lady Grisella's death over twenty years before. Mrs. Goodyer, batting aside a cobweb, apologized for its dusty state.

"Lady Catherine told me not to bother about it, but the new lady may think otherwise. I shall have these dry rotted hangings taken down and the room scrubbed. Our new lady will probably want new furnishings, wall paper and the like."

"Good heavens, I hope not! That would require covering those lime-washed linen-fold panels," Welspent objected.

Berty agreed, saying, "We have nothing so ancient as those panels in America. And the workmanship! Yet the family takes it for granted and doesn't seem to care."

"I pray Lord Sedgewick and his lady stay in Kent. I understand the house there is quite modern," Welspent said.

"Ah, but it would be good to have children in the Hall again," Mrs. Goodyer said, but on second thought, couldn't imagine the stuffy Sedgewick as a warm and loving father.

The Honorable Sedgewick married in late December and traveled to the Holy Land on his honeymoon. When this news reached Alexander in January, he laughed and told Ronan. The major still suffered from headaches and light sensitivity, but promised Alexander they would celebrate Sedgewick's wedding when he was in good point and high force again. They would dance fandangos with Portuguese belles.

Cedric wrote to Berty that he liked Kent immensely and had met a friend, Sylvan, a boy of sixteen. Ricky described the estate Sedgewick had acquired through his marriage as a rich one with a fine, modern, Palladian house, separated by a haha wall from a landscape garden with streams and a lake. "Such a welcome change from dark and ancient Boscawden! All is bright, white and classical."

Berty wrote back that she liked dark and ancient Boscawden and that Ricky and his family didn't appreciate the treasures they were blessed with.

Appreciate them or not, Ricky soon had to return to comfort his suffering father. Lord James fell into a mysterious decline. He refused to go to Bath for the waters and a change of scene. Bleedings, purgatives, medicines failed to revive him. The Bodleighs thought the Baron's old surgeon did more harm than good, but Lord James refused to see the new surgeon.

Meanwhile, Cedric told Berty about Sylvan. "He's as beautiful as Ronan. Younger and softer and smaller and ever so charming. And he loves me, Berty, he really does. I wish I could have him here, but father would not approve and you know what tattlemongers are like here."

"You sound downright romantical, Ricky," Berty observed.

"Do I? I must be prudent when Sedgewick returns. I suppose he shall be a pattern husband, he plumes himself so on his morality."

"I'd think he'd be rather a cold fish. Probably doesn't know how to kiss. And when that high stickler inherits, he'll be unbearable," Berty offered her opinion.

"Sedgewick's unbearable now," Cedric agreed, "Whoever heard of going to the Holy Land on a honeymoon? I do hope father recovers. But if he don't, I'll have my allowance and shall live in a cottage with Sylvan."

~~~

Benjamin wanted his cousin's advice. Ronan had not replied to his last letter, weeks before. It was now February. The gun company flourished, but Benjamin struggled to develop their other ideas. He left the factory in the capable hands of its manager and traveled to London to look into central heating and plumbing in houses. These advances would occur in London, not the country. Ronan had told him to study hydraulics and he did, meeting several scientists his cousin had mentioned, but most important were the builders. They had practical knowledge of how to get things done.

Benjamin also checked on their gun store, Brandolyn Arms. Ronan would approve the sign above in plain black letters on white. The Peninsula veteran he'd hired to operate the enterprise was also an excellent choice. The man showed Benjamin advertisements he'd taken out.

By the time Benjamin returned to Devon, he felt confidant he could run the business without his cousin, but would prefer his assistance. A letter awaited him. In it, Ronan mentioned recovering from a slight injury and answered his questions. It was the only letter Ronan wrote mentioning the injury.

Miss Bodleigh also received a letter with the blue devil seal. Besides the same military news Ronan had sent to everyone, he enclosed two of his musical compositions transcribed for pianoforte. He'd titled one, *Liberty's Fandango* and the other *Saraband for Mrs. Sarah Bodleigh.* Liberty grinned when she read "Major Ronan Trevelyan." She immediately told her aunt and gave her the sheet with the compositions. They called the saraband, Sarah's Saraband, and Sarah began playing both works.

Edith received two epistles from Alexander, written a week apart, but arriving at the same time. She read the most recent first. He informed her that Ronan had recovered from a frightful concussion and since Ronan had recovered, Alexander felt free to elaborate on its horrors; weeks of blindness and harrowing headaches.

Alexander enlarged on everything. He not only danced fandangos until dawn with the most beautiful ladies in the Peninsula, but drank so much he was incapacitated for three days. "I would heartily like to let Sedgewick know how we celebrated his life tenancy. Ronan wishes him a quiver full of children, which seems to be his intention himself."

"What does that mean?" Berty asked.

"I reckon Ronan wants a quiver full of children," Edith replied, "Or do you mean life tenancy? I think that is their cant for marriage."

"I might as well tell Ronan not to write, for I get more information from Alexander. Ronan never mentioned a concussion. Doesn't Alexander mention Ronan's promotion?"

"No, he doesn't. Envious, I suppose."

"I dare say, but now we won't have two Captain Trevelyans," Berty reasoned.

~~~

Liberty replied to Ronan's letter by addressing him as Major Ronan Trevelyan. She continued with, "Captain Alexander has written that bullets bounce off your head, which I think is one of Alexander's bouncers."

She expanded with news from Boscawden and the progress of her painting career.

In the Peninsula, Ronan and Alexander joined officers in hunting fox and other creatures, but Ronan also spent days suffering from headaches in dark rooms. He spent time analyzing intelligence and in planning sessions with Wellington and his officers.

The major's regiment, the King's Own Dragoons, arrived, splendid in new red shakos. He reunited with old friends, including Captain Denton Langley, the regiment's dark Adonis. The men called Ronan their Adonis. Denton had introduced Ronan to two of his British mistresses before the war. They had fought together at Sahagun and shared blankets on the freezing retreat, but while Denton had returned to England with the rest of the regiment, Ronan had been seconded to General Beresford in Portugal. Captain Langley brought interesting news to Ronan in his private quarters. Denton had heard Ronan was in London the previous fall. When he visited the Burlingtons, they told him Ronan had departed, but he met the most beautiful lady, Mrs. Sophia Winton.

"Your cousin, I collect, and everything I wanted in a lady; beauty, wit, Money. So we wed. And Sophia presented me with a daughter, a very fair daughter, a few months later!" Langley said.

"I felicitate you," Ronan replied.

"Thank you, Adonis. Your wits must have gone begging not to have made Sophia an offer. She told me you both agreed not to marry, but she accepted me. Maybe changed her mind with the wee one on its way. I can understand a lady refusing a rake like you. How many by blows does this make now?" Langley asked.

"Six, that I know of."

"Upon my word, Adonis, you should have your fall front sewed shut if you can't you keep your wedding tackle in you breeches!"

Ronan looked at him quizzically and asked, "Do you still frequent Haymarket ware?"

"Curse you! Not now I'm hedged. One doesn't like to think what happens to those harlot's children, if they are even born."

Langley chose to change the subject. He told of the regiment's activities in England. "Putting down Luddites was not what I expected to do when I joined the cavalry. I suppose someone had to do it. Can't allow ruffians like that to destroy stocking looms. Still it's a bloody shame. They don't have work."

~~~

Langley wasn't the only one objecting to Ronan's libertine behavior. In Boscawden, Augustus and Francis Bodleigh argued over the hanging of the major's portrait.

"It should hang in the Hall. You should sell it to his lordship," Francis declared.

"His lordship won't pay what it's worth. The major is Sarah's cousin and Berty's friend. It shall remain in our parlor," Augustus said.

"Berty's too particular friend, if you ask me. She shouldn't wear the willow for that rake and you shouldn't have it in your parlor. You're doing our niece no favors by encouraging this undesirable friendship," Francis insisted.

Berty walked in from her studio at that point. Sarah, sitting by the fire shook her head and rolled her eyes. Berty thought her uncles were arguing politics and sat down to listen.

Augustus turned to her, "Francis thinks we should sell his lordship the Major's portrait for a pittance."

"I'd rather not. His lordship has all kinds of family portraits to look at. This is my friend," she replied.

"Balderdash! Friend, indeed. I hope you haven't thrown your cap at him. He's not only above your touch, but he's a rakehell. Augustus was a fool to allow him to pay his addresses to you. I should hope you had forgotten him by now."

"Fool, am I," Augustus bridled, "Too good for Berty, is he?"

"You know damned well he is, Augustus, by blood, not behavior," Francis insisted, in his anger, forgetting to watch his language before ladies.

"I know no such thing. I admit he has indulged in some youthful follies that young men are prone to, but he's an officer and a gentleman and no officer or gentleman is too good for my niece," Augustus argued.

"You feather headed ninny hammer! Upon my word, Augustus, your wits have gone begging if you believe this folderol. The reprobate has overset your judgment as much as Berty's. God grant me patience!" Francis fulminated.

Sarah and Berty often enjoyed Augustus and Francis's disagreements, but this one touched on a personal issue. Berty felt stiff and heated.

Sarah interrupted, "God grant ME patience. Major Trevelyan has been gone a year and we don't know when or if he will return. Berty is free to meet other gentlemen. Francis, you intentionally throw Augustus into a taking. I won't abide this fuss."

Francis bowed to Sarah's rebuke. Augustus snapped open a radical paper and fumed. The painting stayed in its prominent place on the end wall.

Chapter 5

1813

Lord James' London attorney sent word of his lordship's death to Lord Sedgewick's agent in the Middle East. Cedric wrote to Captain Alexander and to his sisters. After the usual condoling calls, Berty visited Cedric at the Hall without Sarah.

Mrs. Goodyer had dressed the Hall for mourning; mirrors turned against walls, clocks stopped, black drapery where appropriate. Public days were canceled. Cedric wore black and looked white by contrast. Berty wore her usual garnet riding habit.

"I never thought I would miss father so. It's worse because I'm alone here. Except for Welspent, of course, but I mean as far as family. I think I shall go back to Kent and await Sedgewick," Cedric decided.

Berty thought that a good idea.

Cedric disclosed that the lawyers had discussed Lord James' will with him. "It felt odd, me alone with them, but there was no one else. Father left an allowance for Boscawden's school on the condition it be named after the Honorable James. Ain't that hilarious?"

"What will they name it, Rake's Progress?" Berty asked.

Cedric laughed. He continued informing her about his generous allowance, various gifts to old retainers and other bequests. "Father was more generous in death than in life. He also stipulated that the contents of the house had to stay intact. I was hoping he'd leave some of the non-entailed properties to Alexander and me, but he didn't. Thousands of acres all for Sedgewick, plus the Kent property. And that's not all, you know we are related to the Marquis of Leigh?"

"Aunt Sarah has mentioned that," Berty replied.

"He is ancient. None of his children survived childhood and his brother's two sons are invalids. Sedgewick is next in line to inherit that title after the nephews. Berty, there will be no bearing him!"

Berty commiserated with Cedric. He went on to tell her he had written to Alexander and Ronan with this news. When Cedric finished his litany of complaints, Berty assured him he was far better off than most people. He agreed and said he intended to pay the traditional tithe to the church out of his limited income.

"I am also assisting Sylvan who was born neither hosed nor breeched. The poor child wants for everything!"

Berty felt foreboding in that and warned, "Don't let your soft heart overset your judgement."

Cedric smiled and assured her Sylvan wouldn't take advantage of him. He asked Berty if she would paint a portrait of Sylvan. She said she would and they agreed to correspond.

Berty returned to her studio to work on portraits. She decided to send the best one to the Academy that year, but longed for spring and equine portraits she would paint when horses had shedded their winter coats.

Edith and Berty attended several friend's weddings, including Amy's to a gentleman fifteen years her senior and Tabitha's to Sir Henry Danford. With every wedding, Edith and Berty felt more like old maids, for both would be twenty-one that summer. Berty's resolve never to marry, weakened. She and Edith attended every local ball, country dance and fête. Berty always had partners and it was her family's profound hope that she would forget Major Trevelyan and meet someone of better repute and fortune, a country squire, perhaps.

A handsome gentleman of two and thirty asked Berty to dance twice at Mrs. Pemberton's ball. Gideon Talbert did not tear up Berty's dance card as Ronan had done, nor did he do anything else outrageous. He behaved with perfect decorum People suspected he had taken a fancy to Berty. And she didn't altogether disdain him. She found his proximity stimulating.

Between dances, he fetched Berty lemonade and conversed. "Liberty, an unusual name, even for an American, is it not?" he remarked. He didn't particularly like its radical sound, but held his tongue.

"I was born on the fourth of July and my father, an avid reader of Mr. Thomas Paine, chose to name me Liberty."

"I see. Do you have a middle name?"

"Yes, Rhiona. My mother's parents were Irish." Berty smiled at the discomfort this gave Gideon. She recalled Ronan Trevelyan had liked her name when they first met.

"That's a pretty name. Don't you prefer it to Liberty?" he asked.

"Not esspecially. I respect my father's judgement in the matter. You may call me Berty, if you like. Everyone else does. I do not like Libby, though."

Berty flashed her perfect smile. That brilliant smile was enough to make Gideon forget about her unorthodox name.

Talbert had been a captain in the Twelfth Dragoons, serving two years in the Peninsula, before his elder brother died, leaving him the family estate. Captain Talbert found it necessary to sell his commission and return to attend family matters. He had to see to the marriage of a younger sister, the support of an older, widowed sister, the education of a younger brother and repairs to his long neglected house, an Elizabethan pile not far from Boscawden. He now had time to satisfy his own needs and everyone knew he sought a wife.

Berty thought Gideon handsome enough, tall and well set up, with regular features, curly brown hair and gray eyes. A pleasant and easy smile graced his aspect. When asked about his experiences in the Peninsula, he admitted he was glad to be out of it and preferred to be titled mister rather than captain. Gideon Talbert intended to spend the rest of his days tending his estate, riding to hounds and raising a family.

Mr. Talbert called on Augustus Bodleigh on a business matter. One wing of Talbert Hall was in such a poor state, it needed to be torn down and replaced. Many property owners recommended Augustus as the man to replace this wing. He would build in a style compatible with the existing edifice and to the highest standards. Besides this business matter, Talbert looked forward to seeing Miss Bodleigh. At the ball, he'd been unable to decide if she were very pretty or beautiful. Perhaps in the cold light of day, he could make that decision and get to know her better. He didn't mind that she had been born in America. After all, she'd been raised in England since she was twelve by a reputable family of the lower gentry.

Talbert arrived at the Bodleigh's when Berty was working in her studio. Peggy ran over to tell her Talbert had come to see Augustus.

"You'd better come to the house and change, Miss Berty, for I'm sure Sarah will invite this gentleman to dine and Betty is all in a flutter to prepare a suitable dinner," Peggy informed her.

Berty supposed she should change out of her painting smock, but she saw no need to impress Mr. Talbert. She felt flattered that he might take an interest in her, but she wasn't throwing her cap at him. As neglectful as Ronan was, having not answered her last letter, he still occupied her mind.

While Talbert spoke with Augustus in the office, Berty ascended the stairs to change. Her limited wardrobe gave her few choices. Sarah was still in mourning over Lord James, but Berty wasn't. She thought the white gown would contrast badly with Sarah's black, and settled on her old primrose muslin. Peggy assisted with Berty's difficult hair. When they finished, Berty descended the stairs and found Mr. Talbert in the parlor with her aunt and uncle.

Talbert gazed appreciatively, bowed and smiled at Berty. She returned the smile. He'd been admiring her paintings.

"One can't help but notice that portrait," Talbert commented on the obtrusive painting of Major Trevelyan.

"A cousin of mine and friend of the family," Sarah informed.

"Major Trevelyan, I collect. He was a captain and an exploring officer when I was in the Peninsula. I still hear of his exploits. He makes so much mischief for the French they call him le Diable Bleu," Talbert commented.

"Yes, so we've been told," Berty replied.

"An unconventional and dangerous man. I don't consider it worth the extra three dollars a day to take the risks he takes as an intelligence officer," Talbert added with a frown.

"You alarm me, Mr. Talbert," Sarah remarked, "I've known him since he was a boy."

"I beg pardon, I only meant he was dangerous to the frogs. He fights with the guerrilleros who are quite unconventional. I don't care for any of those papists, frog or dago," Talbert amended his comment, but the Bodleighs detected something troubling about it.

Talbert adroitly changed the subject to horses, appreciating the paintings Berty had done of the Bodleigh steeds. He was pleased to learn Berty rode.

"But I don't hunt. I'm not up to that," Berty said.

"I wouldn't expect it," Gideon said, "I do like to see a lady hack, but hunting is too dangerous."

"I hunted when I was young," Sarah put in, "But I was never a neck or nothing rider!"

"Of course," Gideon agreed with a smile.

"Sarah drives now," Augustus said, "As does Berty."

Gideon frowned. "Not curricles, I hope."

The Bodleighs laughed. "No, we just drive old Mercury in the gig to visit friends," Sarah said.

Gideon showed obvious relief, "I see. Yes, of course, that would be quite convenient in the country. I had thought of the ladies of fashion I've seen driving in London."

The Bodleighs laughed again. "I can't imagine myself driving a mettlesome pair in the park!" Sarah said, "Now Berty, I can picture that!"

Berty giggled. "I've never driven a pair, let alone a mettlesome pair. I'm quite happy with old Mercury."

This modesty pleased Gideon. If there was anything he despised it was ostentatious women of questionable virtue. He had some uncertainty about painting as a female occupation. His sisters had taken watercolor lessons, though; so he supposed it was acceptable. As long as there was no nudity, but Berty only painted portraits, animals and landscapes, not mythological characters. He thought her a sensible, old-fashioned girl. He was gratified to see few poems or silly novels among the books.

They enjoyed a good dinner and later Sarah played the pianoforte. Gideon wasn't particularly disappointed that Berty neither played nor sang since many women who did, did so atrociously. Gideon returned to his hall satisfied on many points.

Berty went to bed with many thoughts. It occurred to her that she had no desire to be alone with Mr. Talbert, whereas she wanted nothing more than to be alone with Major Trevelyan. She wondered why and if that would change.

Augustus and Sarah went to bed hoping Mr. Talbert would replace Major Trevelyan in Berty's affections.

~~~

In Spain, Wellington met with division officers and intelligence staff, including Major Trevelyan. The general declared how much he needed Grant, who had now escaped into France. "I need someone to communicate with Grant's spies."

"I will go," the major offered.

The general shook his head. Major Trevelyan had been riding on one mission after another, but he and his infuriating escapades were too well known to the French. They would delight in giving Diable Bleu a harrowing death against the rules of war. They could claim he tried to escape or wore civilian clothes.

Devil leaned back in his seat. He longed for the challenge. "I can do it," he said quietly, knowing the general knew no one else could pull it off. For that matter, could the Blue Devil?

Wellington asked how he would go about it. The major stood and strolled to the map. He explained where he would meet the guerilleros in the mountains and how he would travel through Spain to reach Grant's spies. Many shook their heads at such risks. They thought the major overconfident, yet he persuaded Wellington to let him go and strode out to prepare.

~~~

Captain Ramsey stood next to his mare, claiming, "Your stallion offered Bess an insult."

Major Trevelyan studied the Roman-nosed, ewe-necked, roach-maned, bob-tailed cob and remarked, "I believe he tried to pay her a compliment. I'm appalled at his taste."

Ramsey laughed. His homely mare stood fire with the best of them. Gunpowder leaned his elegant head on Major Trevelyan's shoulder. Blood dripped from a leg wound where Bess had kicked him. The groom admitted Gunpowder had gotten away from him. The charger would be lame for days.

"Clean the wound with vinegar," the major told him. He wouldn't use Gunpowder on his mission. The French were too familiar with the animal. Instead, Blue Devil selected the best of the long-tailed, captured French horses.

In the major's billet, Jacob trimmed Devil's hair and shaved his moustaches before applying brown dye to his head and facial hair. Jacob inserted a gold earring in one ear, for there was a custom in parts of France for the oldest son to wear an earring. No one would suspect an English officer of wearing an earring. Ramsey brought a dragoon uniform a tailor had remade to fit the major. It resembled an indigo and buff French dragoon uniform.

"Dark hair becomes you. I could never reconcile angelic gold locks with the Devil," Vivian joked.

Jacob covered the major's shako with a rain cover and brushed off his greatcoat, while Devil packed coins to pay guerilleros.

~~~

Captain Augusto Diaz recognized the familiar, tall, straight-backed horseman from a distance. Who else would ride in these mountains alone, but Diable Bleu? Yet when the Devil rode closer, Diaz paused, then laughed. The Devil was up to his tricks. They dismounted and kissed, before getting down to the business of reconnaissance.

Days later, Devil rode alone in the night. He knew he was near French pickets, but he needed to get through them. Inevitably, a French soldier ordered him to halt. Others came forth with a lantern. Devil appeared inebriated. He gave his name as Captain Dominique La Chance and mumbled the name of his regiment. Upon further inquiry, he grinned and replied in slurred French, "I've been to the bordello in the village."

He pointed in the direction of a village with a brothel notorious for serving officers. Guerilleros acquired much information from the strumpets who worked there.

Captain La Chance regaled the soldiers with a tale of a toothless whore who performed excellent fellatio. He described other interesting entertainments he had enjoyed at this bordello with women who specialized in various positions and erotic pleasures. By the time he had finished, his auditors were convinced he was either a phenomenal lover or a phenomenal liar. He rode tipsily on, singing Clare de Lune.

Days passed. Captain La Chance rode back to the British lines and surrendered to English riflemen without a fight. His English was so bad, a French-speaking Major Dennis interviewed him and gave him parole. Dominique asked to be taken to General Wellington. He had important news for him. Major Dennis was skeptical until Captain La Chance said he had information on the Blue Devil.

Major Dennis took the captain to headquarters. Upon hearing the captive had information on his exploring officer, Wellington commanded he be brought in. Captain La Chance stood before the general, shako under his arm, revealing short, brown hair. Wellington and his ADCs stared a moment before the general whooped. His exploring officer had blue Deviled French and English to bring back information Wellington requested and more.

~~~

Weeks passed with no reply from Ronan to Berty's last letter, while Alexander replied at length to Edith's. Berty wondered if her letter had miscarried. It also occurred to her that if she sent another, she would have to pay to send it. Previously, Sarah had taken Berty's letters to Lord James to be franked. A minor irritation, but an irritation all the same. Berty suspected Ronan had cooled to her in his long absence, although she had not cooled to him. She often gazed at his portrait and handled the golden guineas he'd paid her for it. Other times, she looked at the mementos in her bureau drawer; his long blond hair still tied in a ribbon, as he'd worn it when they first met; her first sketch of him and his letters. She also studied the old continental dollars her grandmother had kept. They never had been worth anything, but they symbolized her country with their mysterious engravings. How odd, she thought, that she, a loyal American, should hold in her affections a British officer and aristocrat.

One bright March day, Berty rode to the Hall to see the daffodil meadows, spring garden and foals. She carried her sketch book in a saddlebag and looked forward to a day of sketching the beauties of spring.

She rode to the stables to put Rose up before walking in the gardens. The usual activities of the grooms halted when she rode into the stable yard. Mr. Barnstable walked out and ordered everyone back to their chores. "Stop acting like you've never seen a pretty female. A bunch of addlepated hicks I have here, Miss Bodleigh."

Berty dismounted and a groom took charge of Rose. Barnstable walked alongside her out of the stable yard and onto a path to the gardens, where the gardeners were busy.

"May I have a word, miss?"

Barnstable had never offered to speak with her alone before. Feeling ill at ease, Berty agreed.

"The boys took some of the mares to Burlington Hall to be bred and came back with gossip. The on dit, I believe you would say, only this ain't news except to us. I think you should know what they learned. Your Uncle Francis is telling your Uncle Augustus right now, but you should hear it from me and have time to think on it."

Berty felt her heart beating and begged Barnstable to get on.

"There were two little boys playing with a pony. One was Sir Richard Burlington's son, about seven years old. The other was one

Christopher Trevelyan, still in skirts and quite blond. The major sent him to the Burlingtons last year."

Barnstable paused for Berty to digest this. She exercised admirable self-control and inquired, "Has the major married?"

Barnstable, thunderstruck by her innocent question, replied, "Has hell frozen? No, he has not married and I doubt he ever will. This brat is his natural child by a sergeant's daughter. T'is beyond me why he chose to acknowledge it. Most men would not."

"But that's not the only tale my boys returned to tell. It's long been the opinion of Sir Richard's retainers that his own son is by the major, too. You see both Sir Richard and his wife are brown in eye and hair. Their son is the image of Major Trevelyan."

This was too much. "Brown indeed. Too brown," Berty declared, "Why would Sir Richard tolerate his wife bearing a child by another man?"

"That's the thing. They think he's never gotten a woman with child and he wanted an heir. He had his godson bed his mistress and when she got with child, Sir Richard married her!"

Berty's mouth made an O.

"I like the major well enough, Miss Bodleigh, but we have to face the truth and the way he was dangling after you last year, it's well he's gone, ain't it?"

Berty couldn't answer. She hated to admit her Uncle Francis was right about Ronan, but she was not glad Ronan was gone. She thought about how to respond.

"Thank you, Mr. Barnstable. I'm sure many girls would be angry at hearing their friend denounced, but you have been forthright and wish me well, I think."

"I certainly do wish you well, Miss Bodleigh, and the major, too, but what can we do?"

"I don't know. I don't know how many mistresses Ronan has or how many natural children, but I see why he has always been mysterious. I'm not sure why he has chosen to be friends with me," Berty said.

"You are very lovely, Miss Bodleigh, that's one thing, and you ain't highty-tighty like so many in his class. In fact, you ain't his class, or mine. You're in a class of your own!"

"That's the nicest thing anyone has ever said to me, Barnstable!"

"Thank you, Miss. I've tried to do right here."

Barnstable walked away. He was the same age as the major, yet Barnstable had always thought Berty above his touch. To him, she belonged to the major.

Berty walked pensively in the gardens. She lost all interest in sketching and avoided the area near the house where the gardeners toiled. She walked past inactive fountains in the parterres. Those fountains hadn't operated in years. Berty followed the central path with the distant focal point, the ruined Norman keep. She hardly saw the garden, so distracted were her thoughts.

Berty turned off the main path to climb up alongside the water stairs, designed like one a Trevelyan ancestor had seen in Italy. Spring water tumbled down mossy steps into a channel and on through the garden eventually reaching a stream. Berty wandered into the dim, shell-decorated grotto under the steps. She sat and thought, but her thoughts went in circles, reaching no end. She noticed beautiful shells in man made patterns. Berty glimpsed herself mirrored in a shallow pool. She studied herself, uncritically. Her face had lost its child's appearance. She realized for the first time, she really was good-looking, even beautiful, if one ignored her unkept hair and plain riding habit. That gave her confidence.

Berty rose and continued rambling about the gardens. She entered the orangery, where classical statues stood, protected from the elements. Here, a slender marble Adonis reminded her of Ronan. She would write to him, but first she rode Rose up the steep, narrow path to the keep. From that high point, she looked down upon the surrounding patchwork of hedged fields, streams and woods. Man and his creations appeared tiny in the great scheme of things. She took heart her concerns were insignificant. Strong wind blew around the exposed tower, tossing Berty's skirt and beating her loose pigtail against her face. She remounted Rose and returned home.

~~~

A turmoil awaited Berty. Sarah and Augustus didn't believe the tittle-tattle Francis had told them. "One doesn't pay heed to servant's tales," Sarah said.

They grew quiet when Berty entered. She tried to seem cheerful when she said, "It's quite alright. I've heard the on dit. It doesn't signify, you know. I'm not betrothed to Ronan. He's wed to his sword, recollect."

The arguments continued. "Well, perhaps he is meeting his obligations to this child," Sarah said, "He certainly isn't accused of getting the tavern maid with child like one of his cousins. She doesn't know which cousin is the father, but she has not accused the major, who never visited the place. And he hasn't seduced the Hall's maids like James did. Mrs. Goodyer considers him a gem of propriety where the maids are concerned."

"No, he'd rather dangle after Cook," Francis commented, acerbically.

"Oh don't use that term, dangle. It reminds me of Mercury when he's at pasture with the mares," Sarah rebuked him, to everyone's embarrassment.

"Very well, he's always made love to Cook."

Sarah laughed. "Yes, as a boy, he was always hungry, but I would say trying to charm Cook is not the same as making love or dangling."

"It doesn't signify," Francis said, "He's unquestionably a libertine, has been for years and everyone knows it. You should drop his acquaintance."

"Bachelor fare," Augustus countered, "Some frequent the muslin company, others take mistresses. It's not spoken of and love children are fobbed off on relatives, orphanages or neglected altogether. I dare say there's not a bachelor soldier who has not visited a prime article. I dislike refining upon this indelicate subject before Sarah and Liberty, but you have brought it up, Francis."

"Major Trevelyan has been the subject of disapprobation for years, Augustus. Are you so hen-witted, you don't know that!" Francis flared, again.

"I'm not a gossip monger. He's had his youthful indiscretions, sowed wild oats. Frankly, I'm rather glad he has acknowledged this child."

"Then you're as dicked in the nob as he is," Francis fumed. "This isn't his only child. He's gotten others in through the side door. And these indiscretions, as you put it, aren't his only transgressions. Dueling, gambling and God knows what he's got up to in the Peninsula!"

"I refuse to believe he's the worse monster in nature you paint him," Sarah defended, "His gambling consisted of games of whist, not hazard or dice and he only does it because he has been denied his rightful means. Really, Francis, we haven't seen Ronan in over a year. We hardly need cut the acquaintance."

"Very well. I just hope Berty isn't wearing the willow for him," Francis said.

"I'm not pining, if that's what you think," Berty said, "I attend dances and gatherings like other girls." Berty then had a thought, "Do you suppose Mr. Talbert indulges in these indiscretions?"

"Berty!" Sarah exclaimed, "That was improper!"

"Why is it proper to discuss Major Trevelyans indiscretions and no one else's? Uncle Augustus just said bachelor soldiers indulged in light skirts, did he not?"

For once her relatives were at a loss for words. Berty left the parlor and climbed upstairs to her chamber. She found herself quaking, for she was upset both by the disclosure of Ronan's licentiousness and by her relatives' reactions. She was surprised by Augustus' vigorous defense of the major, but Augustus would always disagree with Francis.

In the ensuing days, she composed a letter, in her head, to Ronan. When she thought she knew what to say, she took pen and ink and put her thoughts on paper, only to discover she wasn't sure what she wanted to say.

"Dear Ronan,

I have not received a reply to my letter of a few weeks ago and wonder if it has miscarried or if the head injury Alexander wrote of is worse than he said and still affecting you.

Mr. Barnstable sent mares to Burlington and the grooms returned with the on dit. My family is in a taking over news of a child you sent to the Burlington's. I feel quite indelicate mentioning this, but it has brought me much disquiet, especially with so many talking about it. It refreshes memories of your past wantonness.

If you wish to stop corresponding, please inform me. Aunt Sarah can no longer take my letters to Lord James to be franked. I can afford postage now, but this will be my last missive until I hear from you.

Your Friend,
Berty"

Berty read it over and thought it cold. There were so many things she wished to ask, but thought them inapt. She wondered what had happened to the child's mother.

This letter and its reply arrived as fast as packet boats could carry them. Berty felt surprise and relief when a boy delivered a letter with the Devil stamped in blue wax. First thing she saw was a draft for ten pounds. Ronan's letter;

"My Dear Liberty,

Please accept my sincere apologies for being remiss in writing. Your previous letter arrived, to my gratification and pleasure. Knowing you are well is, in itself, a pleasure. Since Alexander has informed you, needlessly, of my concussion, I admit I spent most of my winter confined to dark quarters with nothing to write. Now I am active and have little time for it. Alexander will make up for my silence as he always has.

How comforting to know I am remembered in Boscawden. I hope to be remembered for other reasons in future. Children are gifts.

Please continue to write. I have enclosed funds for postage and an Air for Mrs. Bodleigh to play.

Your true friend,

Major Ronan Trevelyan."

Berty smiled at his sardonic comment on being remembered and his typical reserve. Apparently he wanted children regardless of his lack of a wife. Ten pounds! Such an enormous sum for postage. She often didn't receive that much for a painting. Her family would object to her using the ten pounds, but she would defy them if she had to take the draft to the Portsmouth bank herself!

Sarah grumbled about the impropriety of sending it. Augustus humphed and, after some thought, decided he did not object. "If a man wants a girl to write to him, he should pay the postage," Augustus declared.

Berty hugged him, the best uncle in the world. He had not condemned her when she had danced every dance with Ronan over a year ago, or for any of her other foibles.

Augustus told Berty he needed her to ride with him to Talbert Hall to sketch the disintegrating wing. Now that she had heard from Ronan, Berty had no desire to see Talbert, but this was business.

They took Mercury and the gig since Augustus had not found a carriage that suited him for the price he was willing to pay. Sarah said he didn't really want a carriage and the expense. Corky rode with them.

Berty asked Augustus why people condemned Ronan for his behavior when it was understood that most soldiers did that sort of thing.

"The major doesn't hide his wanton behavior. He ignores proprieties. Society doesn't approve of such insolence. Society prefers secrecy and hypocrisy. The melancholy truth, Berty, is you should forget the major. If he returns, I fear he will bring you dishonor and heartache. Mr. Talbert, on the other hand, is an honorable, responsible gentleman. He respects propriety."

Berty sighed. "He is rather stricken in years, Uncle."

Augustus laughed, "Two and thirty is hardly stricken in years! An ideal age for a man to marry. Settled. Not likely to kick the traces. Quite likely to appreciate a young wife and treat her well. Anyhow, no one is in a hurry."

Berty took some reassurance in that.

As Mercury clopped up the drive to Talbert Hall, Berty admired the quaint old-fashioned charm of the gabled house and it's topiary. Talbert strolled out of the house to meet them, handing Berty out of the gig. He led them and Corky inside, where his housekeeper acted as hostess and took Berty away to refresh herself.

Augustus and Berty quickly got down to business; measuring and sketching the old wing, while Corky romped between them. Talbert watched, unaccustomed to seeing a woman performing a man's job. He was reminded of a lady who rode alongside her officer husband in the Peninsula. When Augustus and Berty were finished, Talbert mentioned that lady.

"I've heard of that admirable lady," Augustus said.

"Yes, so exciting. I think I would be terrified in battle," Berty confessed.

"Indeed, I should think any woman would be. I don't know why seeing you sketch made me recollect her. There's certainly a big difference between sketching and riding with an army."

Berty laughed, "I should think so! No bullets whizzing by when I sketch!"

They adjourned to the house for tea, served by the smiling housekeeper. The Bodleighs spoke of their admiration for Talbert Hall. "I like to see a house kept in it's original state," Augustus said.

"Yes, I'm rather sentimental, I suppose, but I prefer the old styles," Talbert said.

"Oh, yes, they are so picturesque," Berty agreed.

Augustus laughed lightly. "The artist in Berty sees beauty, where I see decay. I admire the craftsmanship in our old relics, but I like a sound, modern house with chimneys that draw and no drafts. The last time we were in London, I visited a house with a furnace in the basement that heated the whole house via pipes. That is the future."

The Bodleighs much impressed Talbert, who no longer debated whether Berty was pretty or beautiful. It mattered more that she appreciated his house.

On their return trip, Augustus expanded on his London visit, while Corky and Berty listened. "I thought it best not to mention that I met the major's cousin, Benjamin Brandolyn, while studying that heating arrangement. A pleasant, downright gentleman, nothing of the dandy about him. He was looking at the heating, too. He knows a thing or two about pipes, engines, pumps, furnaces. Owns a firearms company with the major. Unusual for gentlemen like that to be in business. Not accepted by many and Major Treveleyn insisted only the Brandolyn name be used."

"Why didn't you mention this before?"

"You know how I woolgather. It slipped my mind. When we find a willing client, we're going to install a heating and water system."

Berty laughed. "I fear that house will turn into a fountain!"

"We will practice on a conservatory."

They arrived home to find that Francis had visited in their absence. Sarah greeted them with such anxiousness, her tabby cat hid under the sofa. Berty feared there was more bad news regarding Major Trevelyan.

"Lord Sedgewick and his wife have died!"

"Upon my soul, how did this happen?" Augustus asked.

He and Berty sat down to listen to Sarah's story. The family's lawyers had received a letter from Sedgewick's Mediterranean agent informing them that Barbary pirates had attacked the ship their client and his wife were taking back to England. Normally the pirates would have held the couple for ransom, but due to some mishap, the ship sank and the Lord and Lady drowned.

"What a tragic family! Appalling," Sarah said.

~~~

The family's attorneys sent notice to Captain Alexander, now Baron Boscawden. Upon receiving this interesting correspondence, Alexander read it three times, muttering, "I can't believe it."

He then walked out in search of his cousin Ronan. Ronan put on reading glasses and replied to Alexander's persistent disbelief with, "You've lost a brother and sister and gained a title and estate."

"Upon my soul, Ro, I am thunderstruck! What should I do?"

Ronan recommended that Alexander inform his commanding officer and request an extended leave, possibly consider selling out. Then consult his attorneys and stewards and take their advice on managing his estate and income. Ronan also advised avoiding gaming hells and mercenary chere amies.

"Killjoy!" Alexander pronounced with a laugh, "Dash it, is it too awful of me that I don't feel particularly mournful over Sedgewick and his bride? In fact, I rather feel like celebrating. Will you share a bottle of port with me? And a feast, we must have a proper wake."

While they sat over their wine, Alexander claimed he'd lost interest in gaming hells and would visit only the most genteel bachelor's ware. "I shall be a model lord, behaving with the utmost propriety and conduct. And, Ro, don't call me my lord. I don't think I could adjust to that. I'll always be Alexander to you. After all, you still out rank me unless I buy a commission and why should I do that now?"

Alexander begged for more details of his cousin's latest observing mission. The major obliged with as much information as he could divulge without compromising his informants. Alexander guffawed when Ronan told him he had used tales Alexander had told him of brothels to distract the French.

After emptying their first bottle, Alexander decided Ronan should write to Berty. "I'll deliver the letter," he said.

Ronan said he had nothing to write. Alexander laughed at such absurdity, began another bottle and dictated the letter.

"Dearest Liberty,

Lord Boscawden dictates this letter on my behalf, since I have nothing to say. We are mourning the loss of Lord Sedgewick and spouse with a private wake. My lord objects to my using his title. I will call him Bosky. Bosky insists a proper wake requires quantities of food and wine, which we have just enjoyed.

Bosky orders me to say that you are the love of my life. (all others are temporary ports in a storm- his words) I shan't object. He says that I am to write that I am under your thrall. Also under the thrall of some very good port. Bosky dictates a lot of flummery that I shall not repeat.

We prepare to drive the French from Spain. I am enjoying myself immensely. The more dangerous the mission, the more delight I take in it. Bosky is correct in these assumptions. He desires me to report my latest mission in which I impersonated a French officer in order to pass through the lines. He wishes me to brag and to write how I deceived Monsieur, but that would be superfluous.

        Your devoted friend,

        Ronan"

        Alexander objected to the unromantic ending, but took the letter as it was. He also took a bundle of Ronan's musical compositions to be sent to the Reverend Eugene Brandolyn with instructions to publish them anonymously.

        Alexander received his leave and left the Peninsula with a light heart. He would no more miss the hardship of campaigning than he would miss Sedgewick.

Chapter 6

Augustus Bodleigh and Berty worked on the plans and elevations of Mr. Talbert's new wing. They made it larger and better lit per Gideon's desires, yet in proportion and style to the rest of the building. The design meeting Talbert's enthusiastic approbation, he ordered his people to demolish the rotten wing. Augustus and John supervised a crew of masons and carpenters in the new construction.

While this building was underway, Alexander arrived to take up his barony. He listened inattentively to Francis Bodleigh's descriptions of the estate's farms and sources of income and how part of that income was used to maintain and improve the estate. Alexander only wanted to know how much he had to spend. His lawyers explained the likely income from both estates, less expenses, including his brother's allowance. Alexander left them quite pleased.

He visited Miss Westerly and the Bodleighs, telling everyone not to milord him. Alexander gave Berty the letter, saying, "We were half disguised when I made him write, but in vino verity, right? He left out all the beautiful phrases I dictated. A terrible secretary! But I used the same phrases in my last letter to Miss Westerly; so no loss!"

Lord Alexander described Ronan's adventures to everyone. "I hate to admit it, but Blue Devil enjoys this war far more than I do. He's hardened to appalling sights, sounds and odors. I can't describe the things I have seen that made me retch. He sees more action than most. The major is Nosy's own selected observing officer, remembers everything. And all for a measly three extra dollars a day!"

The new baron recounted Devil telling the frogs about visiting a bordello. "Why else would an officer be riding back at that time of night? He used every brothel story he'd heard and enhanced them. I couldn't have done better myself and I consider myself an accomplished raconteur. I tell you, Ro can be quite entertaining when he overcomes his shyness."

"Is that what it is, shyness?" Berty asked.

"Well, dash it, perhaps not, but sometimes, perhaps so," Lord Alexander stumbled.

Later, Berty reread the lines, "You are the love of my life. I don't object." and wondered if he meant that. Like most women she spent much thought on things men said with little thought and quickly forgot. Did he write it because Alexander told him to? What did he mean he didn't object? Was she really the love of his life? Or were they bamming? She came to no conclusion and did not dare ask. Berty soon wrote back, informing Ronan of the building project and mentioning Gideon Talbert.

The Reverend Brandolyn received Ronan's compositions and sighed at the lack of lyrics. "Such beautiful music," he told Marie, "He suggests which ones could be hymns and which ones are love songs or dances. I shall write words for the hymns and maybe attempt some of the love songs."

"You used to write me lovely poetry, my sweet," Marie reminded him.

"Thank, you, dearest. I can do so again. I shall publish these as written by an Officer in the King's Dragoons, with lyrics by myself. I see no need for me to be anonymous."

~~~

While Ronan rode with the army, Alexander visited his Kent estate, where Cedric resided with his friend Sylvan. Alexander didn't care to ruralize during the London season. The presence of Cedric and Sylvan in Kent provided additional motive to leave for the city.

In London, Alexander arrived at the family townhouse where his sister, Priscilla, her husband and two young children resided. Priscilla had redecorated the drawing and dining rooms in the Egyptian style. Alexander disliked the insipid blue drawing room, previously a bold red with Chippendale furniture and the putrid green in the dining room took his appetite. Most of all, he hated the hideous Egyptian furniture with its ghastly crocodile feet.

Accustomed to thinking of the London house as her own, Priscilla immediately asked Alexander how long he intended to stay. "Until hunting season," he replied, adding sarcastically, "But don't worry, dear sister, I daresay I'll be out most of the time."

"Upon my soul, I hope so. I frequently entertain the pink of the ton," Priscilla replied.

"Oh, am I not good enough for the ton, now? I always was before," his lordship replied, "And do address me as my lord when speaking to me, sister, dear."

"Very well, my lord, if you intend to stay here, I will need additional housekeeping money."

"Dash it, Priscilla, you live here rent free as it is! This is my house, you know!"

"Father said I could live here," Priscilla replied, haughtily.

"Father is dead. I am the baron now. You and your husband and brats should live in your own house."

On that, Priscilla flounced out. She relegated Alexander to a cramped third floor chamber instead of the master chamber where he properly belonged, but disliking quarrels and believing he'd spend most of his time out, he let it pass. He eventually learned that both his sister and her husband had lovers and lived beyond their means.

~~~

In Boscawden, Sarah and Berty prepared for their annual London excursion, something they took with mixed feelings for both loved the country in spring. Berty had shipped one small portrait to the Academy and would begin horse paintings on her return.

She'd attended one dance that spring at the Pemberton's, again dancing twice with Mr. Talbert. At that dance Talbert heard that Berty had danced every dance with Major Trevelyan over a year ago. He did not approve, but blamed the major for taking advantage of an innocent girl. He stupidly mentioned it to her. "I apprehend you know better now than to stand up with one person every time."

"I didn't dance every dance with the major. Wagging tongues exaggerate. I did dance more than the accepted two dances and all were waltzes. And knowing my partner was leaving for an indefinite period, I'd do so again," Berty replied.

Dumbfounded, Talbert stammered, "I find that shocking, Miss Bodleigh."

"Oh, fudge, Mr. Talbert, it was all quite innocent. I'm sure you are not so easily shocked. My Uncle and Aunt gave their approbation," she added the last somewhat untruthfully.

"I'm aghast. I really don't know what to say," Talbert replied and then said more than he should have, "Because of the local gossips, one must conduct one self with complete propriety at all times."

"Then they would be suspicious! Besides it would take the joy out of life to live worried what others think," Berty rejoined.

"I think I enjoy life while living with decorum," Talbert answered.

"As do I," Berty said, "Or perhaps I enjoy life while thinking I live with decorum."

They parted amiably, but when Berty repeated the conversation to Edith, she added, "I don't give a straw for his decorum!"

~~~

Augustus rode to Portsmouth to check on his investments. He returned feeling unwell. "I had hoped to explain to you how I've invested our monies, including Berty's but I feel bilious. Perhaps after a cup of tea and a lie down, I'll be in full force again," Augustus said.

He drank his tea and went to bed. An hour later, while sitting in the parlor, Sarah and Berty heard him retching. Sarah checked on him and returned to tell Berty, "Augustus believes he had bad mutton for luncheon. He feels better now he has rid himself of it."

Augustus retched again and again. Sarah emptied the chamber pot and brought out another while Berty lit a fire in the chamber to keep him warm. He was sick all night and by morning suffered pain in his stomach, back and head. Sarah gave him one of her herbal concoctions and covered him with quilts.

"If only Dr. Waddles was still here," she said.

They had liked Waddles, but old doctor Letting had not retired as expected and most people continued to call him instead of young Waddles. Waddles had left to replace a retiring physician in Dorset, near Burlington.

By afternoon, Augustus was delirious with fever and Sarah sent for the dreaded Letting. "All he does is bleed and purge, but I don't know what else to do," Sarah fretted.

Berty told John Garvey he would have to supervise Talbert's construction. Although not a master joiner, he'd worked with Augustus so long, he knew what to do. He hitched Queen to the cart and drove to Talbert's the next morning with Queen's foal trotting beside her.

As expected, Dr. Letting, bled Augustus, claimed he was liverish and not to give him anything to eat and very little to drink, except brandy."

"Well, if that isn't the outside of enough!" Sarah displayed one of her rare vexations. "Liverish! Is Augustus yellow? No! Nothing to drink when he suffers from fever! Letting doesn't know his business. I have half a mind to send to Burlington for Dr. Waddles."

"I think we should do that, Aunt. I shall ride to the Hall and Uncle Francis will send someone," Berty said.

"I daresay you are right and Francis needs to know of Augustus' illness."

Sarah returned to nurse Augustus, giving him plenty to drink, while Berty saddled Rose and rode to the Hall.

Francis Bodleigh immediately arranged for a groom to ride to Burlington to fetch Dr. Waddles and then followed Berty back to see Augustus. He found his brother barely conscious.

The family took turns staying up with Augustus that night. He moaned with pain and delirium and by morning had not improved. Dr. Waddles arrived the next day, examined Augustus and was as baffled as anyone, but had the honestly to admit it.

"I suspect it is a kidney ailment, but there also seems to be a stomach complaint. Bad mutton? I don't know. Sir Richard had some of these symptoms when he suffered from the stone."

"Dr Letting bled him? I don't see any point in doing that again."

Waddles recommended laudanum for the pain and some herbal remedies. He rode to visit some of his old patients, returned to check on Augustus and spent the night. The next morning Augustus remained the same. Waddles admitted he couldn't do anything and rode back to Burlington and his other patients.

Augustus remained in limbo for a week, his family exhausted from nursing him. Even Francis took a turn every day, as well as Peggy and Betty. Reverend Wingfield prayed over Augustus. Friends sent parcels of food. On the eighth day of his illness, Augustus weakly rallied, but everyone remained cautious. Sometimes the sick get better before they get worse. Days passed and he slowly improved, but remained weak.

Sarah and Berty canceled their London trip. Berty pondered a future with no Uncle Augustus. She'd always taken his presence for granted. Now she realized how important he was to her and how much she loved him, his good nature and good advice. Berty also wondered about their financial situation if Augustus became unable to work. Would they be able to live on his investments? He'd never had a chance to tell them. If they could, it would not be on the level they were accustomed to. A fleeting thought that marriage to Gideon Talbert would secure her future and take one burden off her family passed through Berty's mind. She set it aside.

Berty resolved to work harder and pursue her career. With Augustus improving, she set off in the gig to sketch Mr. Willard Sorbitten's blood stock. Berty spent the day, sketching two stallions in pencil and pastels. She also sketched the surrounding countryside for backgrounds. Sorbitten ebulliently stood by and watched.

Berty decided on conventional poses this time, but eventually she intended to paint the animals in action and sketched the animals in motion. She studied her drawings while Mercury paced home on his own.

Sarah filled the marital chamber with spring flowers for Augustus, since he was too weak and fragile to leave it. Francis brought oranges from the Hall's orangery.

Berty put on her bonnet and worked in the garden, pulling radishes, picking lettuces and peas in the mornings before she went to work in her atelier. One day she rode to Talbert Hall at Augustus' request. Her uncle was well enough to wonder how the work was coming and wanted Berty's opinion as well as John's.

Berty walked around the wing, studying it critically. "Mr. Garvey, there is space framed for two casements there when there were supposed to be three."

"Yes, Berty, Mr. Talbert decided to use that room for a book room and wanted the extra space for shelves. He said to put four casements on the upper floor."

Berty sighed in frustration. "That will look hideous. The upstairs casements should be in line with the downstairs casements and the same number."

"That's what I thought, but it's his house," John replied.

"Yes, and when it looks wrong, he will blame us. Where is he, I'd like to explain this?"

Talbert had ridden to a neighbor's to look at a horse. Berty didn't want to hold up the work. She took out a paper and politely wrote about the casements and how they would look, saying flattering things about his good sense and taste and how she and her uncle cared for the place. She then made a sketch of his proposal on another sheet of paper. Berty gave the note and sketch to John and hoped for the best. She returned to Boscawden without seeing Talbert.

Gideon Talbert had never taken advice from a female and considered the building trades male occupations. He studied Berty's note with surprise and discomfort. Gideon wished to remain on good terms with

Berty, a prospective wife, yet he didn't wish to bend to her every whim.

When making his changes, he'd thought only of room for books and light upstairs, not the change in appearance. After a good deal of pondering and consulting with John and the carpenters, he decided to build as originally planned. Subsequently, Berty received a note from Gideon, thanking her for her suggestions. Gideon added that the carpenters thought it best not to change plans and therefore, he went with their guidance. He then wished for Augustus' quick recovery.

Berty felt an inexplicable resentment at Gideon's condescending tone. Augustus quickly pounced on it. "He depreciates your fine taste and good judgment, Berty!"

"He credits the carpenters instead of you," Sarah put in.

Gideon mitigated this irritation by bringing a large basket of strawberries to the Bodleighs. He arrived in his curricul and offered to take Berty for a drive. She didn't want to be alone with him and since she wore her painting smock, made the excuse she couldn't leave her work at that time. "I'm quite behind on these paintings. You sorely tempt me, Mr. Talbert, but I'm afraid I must decline your kind invitation."

He easily accepted her refusal for her hair was in a messy braid and paint stained her hands and smock. A smear of ultramarine blue graced her cheek, and she reeked of turpentine. At that moment, Berty did not fit his vision of an ideal wife. He didn't want to be seen with such a slovenly looking girl. Gideon imagined a wife who would present him with an heir and spend her time sewing and performing other womanly tasks, while looking like a proper lady. On the other hand, Berty, in spite of her tomboy ways, beguiled him.

Berty finished one of Sorbitten's horse portraits and received payment before it was dry. While finishing the second, she heard that Mr. Sorbitten had lost money at the races. When she realized he would be unable to pay for the second portrait, she resolved to keep it for the Academy the following year. Berty picked up a few human portrait commissions and painted small landscapes with animals on speculation. When she sat down to her account book, Berty figured she made barely enough to live on and fell into the dismals again. However, her paltry income helped with the family's expenses.

One bright spot came from Barnstable. He commissioned Berty to paint his fiancée, the daughter of one of the Trevelyan tenants. He'd courted her for two years and now the grooms said he'd put the cart before the horse as she was in a family way before the banns were read.

"Now that Lord Alexander is Baron Boscawden, I'm not worried about the horses being sold," Barnstable told Berty, "So I offered for Susan and she accepted. Your Uncle Francis is putting us in the cottage near the stables. You don't know Susan very well, but I think you will like her."

Berty proffered the portrait as a wedding present.

"I won't hear of it, Miss Berty, I know you aren't plump in the pocket yourself and now with Augustus being sick, well, I've saved my gold boys and I'll pay like the quality."

Berty laughed, "You'll probably pay better than the quality. "

Chapter 7

Spain, 1813 summer and fall

Major Trevelyan led his regiment, in brigade with two other Hussar regiments under Lieutenant Colonel Grant, part of Sir Thomas Graham's force. They traveled a secret route north across the Spanish mountains. No secret to the major, who had scouted the torturous route with Quarter Master General Murray's mapmakers, and now led the way. They climbed up and down mountains, single file, to turn the French.

Melting snow turned rivers into torrents. On May thirty-first, they crossed the Almeida ford with the Fifty-first Light Infantry clinging to their stirrups and horses' tails. The wild waters swept men away.

The Hussars rode ahead, skirmishing with the retreating French and taking prisoners. The major led his men in many such encounters in the fir groves. They closed with the enemy at Morales, where Grant was wounded.

June nineteenth, they had driven the French to Vitoria. The Hussars bivouacked in the hills above the city. From the heights, they enjoyed a glorious view of Vitoria and the French army.

King Joseph, Napoleon's brother, drew up his 57,000 men and eighty guns behind the Zadorra River, expecting a frontal assault. Behind the city, his enormous baggage train gathered with camp followers, all manner of loose women, escaping civilians and treasure, including the French army's pay wagons.

June twenty-first dawned, cold and drizzly. Wellington arranged his 78,000 men and seventy guns in four columns. Graham would take his men in a flanking movement through the mountains. The first shots were fired at 8:30 A.M.

A peasant informed Wellington of an unguarded bridge. The peasant led a light brigade and Major Trevelyan's Hussars to the spot, losing his head to a cannon ball on the way. The brigade and Hussars soon found themselves on the French side of the river, waiting for battle.

By 3:00 P.M., battle engulfed the valley. Grant ordered his Hussars to attack three squares of infantry and cannon, leading to their slaughter before he realized his mistake. Major Trevelyan and his men avoided that madness.

At 5:00 P.M., King Joseph ordered retreat and the French army dissolved into chaos. Civilians, soldiers, artillery and thousands of carriages swarmed towards the only escape route, the Pamplona Road. Adding to the confusion, Grant ordered his Hussars into the town ahead of the army.

King Joseph escaped from his carriage and galloped away at the last minute. French stragglers directed the Hussars to treasure. They broke open chests, scattering coins, plate and jewels. Peasants and soldiers pillaged French baggage. Grant, himself, was said to have picked up fine gowns for his wife.

Major Trevelyan led his Hussars with Colonel Ponsonby's heavy brigade down the Pamplona Road in pursuit of the French army, but rain, a bad road and inadequate men brought the pursuit to an end. The horses were blown when they rode back to the pillage. Major Trevelyan allowed the heavy brigade to take the main road, while he led his men on another route. On the way back to Vitoria, they met a coach, a baggage wagon and a pay wagon that had gotten lost and thereby escaped the rest of the British army.

Hussars surrounded the vehicles, disarming the drivers. At last, the reward of war, plunder, the major thought, studying the two wagons. But first the coach. He dismounted, holding his sword. Captain Langley stood behind him, pistol at ready. Blue Devil swung open the carriage door revealing a lady and her maid. The lady held a small lady's pistol aimed at him.

He addressed her in perfect French, "Major Trevelyan, madam." he bowed and continued, "If you kill me, madam, fifty angry men will offer you no mercy. Hand me your pistol and I promise you my protection."

His words sounded cold, but his handsome countenance persuaded her.

Major Trevelyan took the pistol and politely asked her name.

"Madam Clotilde Soupert."

"We will restore you to your husband, madam."

"Please don't, major! I have long been a widow," she replied with a roguish smile.

The major observed Madam Soupert icily, noticing her beauty. He suspected she was courtesan to a high-ranking French officer. Major Trevelyan closed the door, mounted Gunpowder and ordered his men to escort the vehicles to an inn further down the road. On the way, he ordered a private to secure a fine Arabian horse wandering riderless. Everywhere, horses, mules and other livestock wandered among coaches and wagons, while soldiers looted everything.

In the inn's court yard, Devil ordered the pay wagon guarded, horses tended and men to set up camp, before climbing on the baggage wagon with Captains Langley and Ramsey. He shot the lock on one chest and lifted the lid, revealing silver coins and plate. The major ordered two sergeants to divide this loot among his men.

Madam Soupert stepped from her coach, blasting the major in rapid French. The contents of this wagon were her property. How dare he touch it!

"I claim this baggage for the fifteenth Huzzars," Major Trevelyan informed her, preparing to fire into another lock.

"My gowns!" she screamed.

"If these are your gowns, madam, you may keep them. And you may keep the jewels in your coach. Perhaps you have a key that we may inspect this chest?"

How did he know she had a jewel chest under the seat in her coach? Madam Soupert wondered, taking a key from her reticule. The major took the key and opened the chest. Langley held a gown in front of himself.

"Do you think the color becomes me, Devil?"

"The color may become you, but the lady would become the dress," Devil commented.

Langley rifled through the contents, found only ladies' raiment and replaced everything. Major Trevelyan requested the innkeeper provide a room for madam and sent her chest with her.

Langley moved on to the next. They discovered chests of coins, plate, more ladies' raiment and a large trunk of rolled canvases, stolen works of art. Devil claimed one, unopened chest for himself and the paintings for Wellington, who would, of course, return them to the Spanish. He retained most of the fine plate for Wellington to return to the Spanish, also, but coins he had divided among the men, including a major's share for himself. Except the gold in the pay wagon.

"The regent will get that to build more domes on his house," Langley alleged.

Some of the men grumbled. Later the major surreptitiously had some of the pay taken and the contents divided. The rest he would deliver to the general, who would never know how much there had been.

Having ordered his men to stay sober, he entered the inn with some of his officers. The rest supervised the remaining distributions. Most washed the dust from their faces before sitting down to await a large repast. Major Trevelyan sent the innkeeper to ask Madam Soupert if she would care to join him for supper.

Clotilde's risky attempt to escape with stolen loot having failed, she considered herself lucky to have kept her gowns and jewels. Perhaps the stony major wasn't so bad. She thought him handsome, unlike her previous lovers, and she needed a new protector. Better an Englishman now that the French were losing. After the innkeeper issued the invitation in Spanish, which Clotilde understood, she changed out of her traveling dress, washed and arrayed herself in one of her more revealing gowns. The light cerulean blue silk matched her eyes. Clotilde's maid arranged her brunette hair in a simple pile, while madam chose a sapphire neckless and earrings.

Madam Soupert glided into the dining room and paused. Every officer rose and some gasped at her beauty. "A stunner," someone whispered.

Major Trevelyan escorted her to his table and seated her opposite himself. Clotilde noticed his Devil's watch fob and commented, in French, "A blue devil, major? I've heard officers speak of le Diable Bleu in your army, a rogue and a spy. Do you know of him?"

"Yes, madam, that is my nom de guerre," he stated.

"You are le Diable Bleu? The infamous one?"

"Yes, madam. Wine?"

Devil filled her cup and his own. Clotilde studied him. His excellent manners and solf spoken French pleased her. She had been born in an aristocratic family, but with the revolution, their fortunes had fallen. Clotilde considered herself lucky to marry an army officer and luckier still when he died, for she had disliked him. She'd learned to please men for their money and sometimes pleased herself as well. By twenty-seven, she'd suffered one miscarriage, but otherwise avoided unwanted pregnancies via use of carrot seed and lemon-soaked sponges. Blue Devil paid more attention to his supper than to her. She thought the English cold.

Clotilde joined in the silent repast. After they were satiated Clotilde resolved it time to thaw the glacial major, "You trust me not to be hiding weapons on my person, major?"

"No, I don't trust you, but a gentleman doesn't search a lady. You may have a pair of nine pounders hidden in your bosom."

She chortled. "That doesn't daunt you?"

"No, madam. I shall find a breech and storm it."

She detected a thaw.

"Indeed and how do you propose to do so?"

"Magnifiquement."

Clotilde grew hot at his braggadocio.

Captains Langley and Ramsey laughed at the exchange and translated for some of the others. There was no privacy in the army. The officers placed bets on whether Devil would bed Madam Soupert that night.

"Devil hasn't seen his mistress in weeks. After allowing madam to keep her jewels and gowns, he'll be wanting his due," Vivian stated.

Langley shook his head, "Ro is no more charming as a Devil than he was as a cornet."

Devil heard that remark, looked into Madam Soupert's eyes and smiled. She returned the smile.

"You are so young to be a major," she observed. He appeared young and angelic in the candlelight. Clotilde found she had to pry any information from him.

She learned he was twenty-six and had joined the cavalry as a cornet at age nineteen. Clotilde had heard the English officers bought their promotions, but when she suggested Devil's family had bought his, he gave her a firm, "Non."

"Ah, so you earned them with your remarkable exploits."

"I earned them by carrying out my missions with due diligence."

Ramsey shook his head. "Freezing again. No way to win fair maiden, eh, Viv?"

"Some of them like a challenge and this light o' love needs a protector."

"Can't think she would appreciate him picking his teeth rather than attending her," Langley responded, watching Devil work his silver tooth pick.

Madam preferred Devil's tooth picking to the reek of the cigars her former lovers had smoked. She played with her fan. Devil put away the tooth pick and cocked his head at her. Her move.

"I wish to retire," she stated, rising. The gentlemen rose, also.

Devil offered his arm to escort madam to her chamber. They disappeared up the stairs.

"Won't see him again tonight," Vivian declared. Some disagreed and the betting was on.

"Isn't that consorting with the enemy?" the sixteen-year old cornet asked.

"Not at all. Devil's conducting an interrogation. I daresay, when he's finished, he'll know more about the enemy than anyone!"

Upstairs, Devil opened the door, Clotilde entered and Devil followed. Her maid waited in the candlelight. Devil placed his arms around Madam Soupert, bent down and kissed her unresistant lips. After a thorough exploring mission, he raised his head.

Clotlide laughed, "You lack finesse!"

"Teach me."

She released his pelisse from the button that held it in place and untied it. Clotilde tossed it on a chair. "Make yourself comfortable, Devil, while my maid unpins my hair."

Esmé unpinned and brushed Clotilde's hair, before removing her slippers. Devil removed his sword belt and stood watching.

"You must do better than that! Please sit," Clotilde objected and sent her maid to remove the major's boots and sashes.

Esmé returned and helped Clotilde out of her gown. She then untied the laces in Clotilde's corset, which had held her breasts to reveal cleavage. Clotilde dismissed Esmé and stepped out of her petticoat, revealing that she wore no shift. Standing in her full exquisite nudity, she said, "You see I have no weapons hidden."

"But you do have weapons," Devil intoned, casting an admiring gaze.

~~~

Clotilde awoke in the dark. Devil stood up lighting a candle. She'd lost count of the number of times they had coupled. His scarred, beautiful, body glowed in the light. He pulled his shirt over his head, buttoned it, pulled on his overalls, tied the black neck cloth and pulled on his boots.

"Mon Dieu, what are you doing, mon amie? T'is dark," she asked.

"I must go."

Devil pulled on his dolman, buttoned it, tied his sashes, swung on his baldric and pelisse. A kiss and he was gone. Clotilde heard horses and men in the inn yard. She donned her petticoat and went to the window to watch as the sun rose on the activity below.

Men saddled horses and hitched others to the two wagons. They loaded loot on two captured mules. Every man had a heavy rucksack. She saw Devil mount his impatient steed and cue the animal to dance in place, piaff and then, passage. Some stopped to watch the major show off. Too soon, all were mounted and Devil spun his horse, only to see Clotilde watching. He blew her a kiss and galloped out with his men.

~~~

Wellington's army jollified all night. The next morning, the general rose to find his army going to sleep and in no condition to pursue the French. He showed particular ire with Lieutenant Colonel Grant and his Hussars, who had stopped to plunder instead of pursuing the enemy. Wellington did praise the men who had attempted the pursuit the previous day, including Major Trevelyan, whose unit appeared in fit and able condition that morning. They also delivered a pay wagon and some of the paintings and valuables the French had stolen from Spain.

Wellington had plenty to be pleased about. His army had captured 151 canon, two million cartridges, 100 wagons, the French pay, millions of which went missing and art masterpieces, some of which were used as tarps before they were discovered, one of the largest captures of loot in history. His army had marched 400 miles in forty days. His casualties were 5,000 to the French 8,000.

Wellington tried, unsuccessfully to get Grant recalled. Instead Grant received a medal as did most officers, including Major Trevelyan, who now had two medals. But Wellington remained dissatisfied with his cavalry and reorganized it. He brigaded the Fifteenth Hussars with the Tenth under General Lord Edward Somerset.

Meanwhile, King Joseph escaped across the Pyrenees to France with 55,000 soldiers.

~~~

When Clotilde found accommodations near the army, she sent a messenger to the major. He read it. The messenger returned to Clotilde with no reply. She fretted. If the major didn't want her, she would find another officer. For the time being, she had enough money. If only she understood English.

Major Trevelyan interrogated prisoners. On hearing le Diable Bleu was going to interrogate them, many prisoners begged for their lives, such was Devil's notoriety. The guerrilleros spread tales that le Diable Bleu cut out tongues, fried and ate them. Instead, he offered prisoners sympathy for their travails, fine food, wine and women. His friends, who had persuaded him to join Oxford's drama club, would be astonished at what an accomplished thespian he'd become. Ronan played more dangerous tricks now than hiding snakes up his sleeve as a boy.

Having spent days and nights interrogating prisoners, Ronan sent them on to prison camps. He now found time for his mistress and with that goal, enjoyed a bath in his quarters before setting off for her abode.

When he stepped into her chamber, he immediately ducked a flying cup. Before Clotilde threw another piece of crockery at him, he grabbed her wrist.

"Two days! I have waited for you two days and you do not come! You do not write. What am I to think? That I must find another man?" She screamed and sobbed and beat Devil's chest.

"Patience, Clotilde. I have duties."

"You did not write," she spat at him, her anger unabated.

Ronan pushed her onto the bed and fell on top of her. An hour in bed and Clotilde clung to her devil. Ruled by passion, she teased him over his English coldness.

When he returned to his quarters, the major sorted his loot of gold and jewels. He made up small parcels to send to England and Lisbon, via reliable means. Ronan put on his glasses to write letters. Jacob copied one that described the last month's actions and the Battle of Vitoria. Ronan sent those copies to Sir Richard, the Reverend Brandolyn and Lord Alexander Trevelyan. He sent the original to Berty with an additional page. In that letter, among other things, he wrote, "Please tell Oliver Barnstable that when crossing the torrent, Gunpowder rose to the occasion with a soldier hanging on each stirrup and one clinging to his tail. Besides Gunpowder, I have a captured Arabian horse to ride as well as the best of the troopers."

Ronan sent Berty a gold chain for her twenty-first birthday. He sent Lady Burlington a jeweled bracelet and Senora de Sousa a perfect, unmounted diamond. He didn't mention details of how he had acquired this loot.

In London, Alexander celebrated the victory with over 8,000 other revelers at a fête in Vauxhall Gardens, held by the Prince regent. Alexander, feeling he was missing the excitement and fame of the war, made plans to return to Spain. He packed large cheeses against the journey and sent for his stud's three best chargers.

Chapter 8

Boscawden

Liberty celebrated her twenty-first birthday quietly due to Augustus' fragile state. Berty received Ronan's package soon after her birthday. Reading the missive, Berty wondered that Ronan had shown so little of the effervescence expressed in the letter in person. She reread the letter and realized they were two letters, one describing the battle and the other to her, both bubbling with high spirits. Ronan enjoyed winning. For all its nastiness, he enjoyed war. What would he do when it ended. She hoped he wouldn't be sent to America.

Berty knew her relatives would disapprove of the gift, but she showed it to them anyway. They could hardly expect her to send it back.

Augustus had recovered sufficiently to sat in his arm chair by the parlor fire, with Corky at his feet. Despite Sarah's warnings against exciting himself, he insisted upon reading his radical papers and chastised her if she kept them from him. Berty bounced downstairs with her letter and chain.

"Good Heavens! Where did you get that?" Sarah exclaimed.

Berty told them and Sarah frowned. "This is inappropriate," she said, carefully, "Cousin Ronan knows better, but I've come to expect such conduct from that devil."

"Devil, Sarah, upon my word, that is strong for you," Augustus admonished her, "Have you come to agree with the French, that he is a devil?"

"I shall amend that. Lord of Misrule, shall we say?"

Berty laughed. "I like knowing at least one exciting person," she said, adding, "Whether anyone approves or not. Besides it has been over a year since I've seen Ronan."

"I would not wear that chain in public," Sarah warned.

"Oh. Let people talk. They are just jealous," Berty retorted.

Sarah sighed in surrender. The older Berty got, the stronger her will. Berty read the battle letter to her aunt and uncle; the other she kept to herself.

"I appreciate these letters. None of that humbug one reads in the papers," Augustus opined, "And that chain was among the spoils left by the French?"

Berty read that part over, "King Joseph abandoned his treasure to the Hussars."

"Then it was fairly won, I think. You should treasure it as a memento of the victory. Upon my soul, Sarah, that the major still thinks of our Berty after this time is remarkable, don't you agree?"

"Yes, I can't accuse him of fickleness," Sarah reluctantly admitted

~~~

Cedric arrived at Boscawden with his friend, Sylvan, and called on "Miss Bodleigh, the artist" in her atelier. Sylvan appeared to Berty as shy, soft-hearted and harmless. Instead of resembling a classical Greek god like Ronan, Sylvan reminded her of a pretty blond child. Ricky desired a life-sized portrait. He was willing to pay well for it. He also mentioned that Sylvan looked grand on a horse.

When he wasn't touching, admiring or talking about Sylvan, Cedric told Berty that Lord Alexander had taken ship for Santander, Spain, to join his regiment.

"I warned him he should not. He and I are the last of our parent's children, I told him. I tried everything to dissuade him. Alexander refused to sell out and said he would not let Ronan have all the glory while he daw-dled in London," Cedric informed Berty, adding, "I told him he should breed and supply an heir. He knows I've never cared for girls. I rather believe as the Greeks that the relationship between men is superior."

Berty felt uncomfortable and asked what Alexander said about that.

"He laughed and said if he didn't have children, Ronan would have a quiver full."

Alexander had told Cedric about Ronan's Portuguese children, but Cedric thought it unwise to repeat that.

"Well, Alexander's always been irresponsible, but no one expected him to obtain the barony. He now must take that responsibility. Edith West-erly has a tendre for him," Berty replied.

Cedric laughed. "She ain't good enough for him now. He must have a great lady, an earl's daughter at least."

"I hope he hasn't gotten so high in the instep that he's forgotten his friends! I declare, Edith would make him happier than any spoiled earl's daughter," Berty defended her friend.

"Perhaps so, but I don't have any say in it and now he's off to the Peninsula."

Berty immediately replied to Ronan's letter, thanking him for the chain, the only piece of jewelry anyone had ever given her. Berty didn't know how she could ever repay him. She informed Ronan of her uncle's illness, slow recovery and how much they appreciated the major's account of the battle.

~~~

One warm morning, Berty and Pete worked with that year's foals. Pete led the great shire, Queen, while Berty led Queen's filly around the meadow. The filly easily followed her dam and then Berty led her away. When she cooperated, Berty praised her and turned her loose.

Gideon Talbert rode up while Pete and Berty were doing the same training with Melody's colt. He dismounted and watched the young woman leading the colt away from its dam and back again. Gideon wondered if this was the sort of thing a lady should do. It wasn't in his realm of experience. He would have to ask his sister the next time he visited her. An invalid, she resided in Bath.

Berty, in old bonnet and boots, smiled. "They are coming along well. We will have to sell the filly, but uncle hopes to keep the colt to replace Mercury. Mercury is sixteen years old."

"Is he? He looks well for his age," Gideon replied.

"Indeed he does. Uncle gives him tobacco for worms and Mercury is always fat though Aunt Sarah and I drive him often."

Gideon definitely didn't think it ladylike to speak of horse worms. Yet Berty's pretty face and cheerful spirit made up for much of her indecorum.

After Gideon left that day, Liberty rode Rose down to the stream in the wood to bathe in private. She took a towel, but kept her shift on to wade in the cool stream. Berty didn't swim and avoided the swimming hole further along. Not only was it deep, but the Hall's many young, male servants often bathed there, nude. She splashed and cooled herself while Rose rolled in the water.

~~~

In Devon, Benjamin Brandolyn finished drawings of a design for a boiler and various valves to be used for heating homes. He followed his cousin Ronan's advice and took the plans to his brothers in London, Brandolyn and Brandolyn, Attorneys at Law, to apply for patents. He wrote to Ronan explaining he was using the profits from their gun manufactury to build a prototype boiler. He wanted to install a heating system in his father's rectory, but the Reverend Brandolyn refused such an expensive and risky luxury, saying he liked nothing better than an open fire. Benjamin found a more forward thinking individual open to experimentation.

~~~

July twenty-seventh, Ronan sat on his gray Arabian stallion next to Lieutenant De Sousa, Antonia's second son, and the Caccadores on a hill overlooking Sorauren, when Wellington rode up. They all cheered, "Douro, Douro!"

The major rode after his commander, joining him on a ridge where the general observed Marshal Soult, the Duke of Dalmatia, through his telescope. The British called Soult, the Duke of Damnation. The Duke chose to take an afternoon nap that day, which allowed British reinforcements to arrive. The next day, the allied army won the first battle of Sorauren.

Exhausted by fighting and heat, both armies rested the next day, to resume on the thirtieth. The French army, expected to live off the land, fought half starved. Both armies suffered from the intense heat, but the allied army beat the French. As usual, the allies failed in the pursuit.

~~~

Captain Daniel Rollings lay in his own blood, more of it oozing from his face and arm. He thought his eye pain unbearable, yet he bore it. From his good eye, he saw Major Trevelyan approach with his stiletto in one hand and a shirt and canteen in the other. He kneeled by Rollings and ripped the shirt with the stiletto. Devil gave Rollings water and cleaned the gash in his face. The sabre cut began in the right forehead, passed through the eyebrow and cheek. Blood filled the eye socket, but Devil couldn't tell the degree of damage to the eye. He bandaged it as well as he could with strips of his spare shirt.

Ronan helped Rollings to a surgeon where he supervised a surgeon's assistant stitching the wound, including the eyelid. The major held Rollings down while the stitches went in that delicate membrane.

Captain Rollings was a promising exploring officer, well-educated, but impoverished. He and Major Trevelyan shared many interests: jewels, which they bought from soldiers and auctions of dead men's property; music; philosophy. When Ronan had time to visit him later, Rollings repeated the surgeon's diagnosis. He might not regain the use of his right arm, and probably wouldn't regain the sight in his right eye.

"I'm useless to the army and myself. I'd be happy to be able to work as a menial laborer."

"Bah! You have an education, use it," Ronan retorted.

"Tutoring, teaching, gladly. My visage would scare brats into behaving!"

They chuckled. Time would mitigate the ghastly wound, leaving an impressive scar.

"I know a village school in need of a master. The last man I recommended died after a few months." Ronan told him.

"The students were that bad? If I exercise my arm, I might be able to wield a cane with the best of school masters! Life in a sleepy village appeals after this war. Green meadows, plenty of beef and lamb. Milkmaids!" Rollings continued.

He tried to grin, but the wound pained him.

"I'll be glad to chew without pain," he remarked.

While they talked, Langley walked up with a letter for Major Trevelyan from Lisbon.

Ronan put on his reading glasses and broke the seal. The letter, in Portuguese, stated;

"Mother and Arthur are dead.

An infection started among the orphans. Mother insisted on nursing them and caught the disease. There was fever, cough, difficulty breathing. She succumbed after a week, followed by Arthur three days later.

Mrs. Tarkington, at the first sign of the disease, took her sons and Serafina to the home of a British family. She had attempted to persuade mother to avoid the sick children.

Mother recieved the diamond before her illness. I am keeping it for Serafina."

The letter was signed Phillip de Sousa. The sudden grimness of Ronan's expression told his friends it was bad news. He volunteered that

Senora de Sousa and their son had died. "Serafina is safe and in good hands with Mrs. Tarkington."

He immediately dispatched a letter to Phillip offering condolences and requesting an address for Mrs. Tarkington. In the dispatch, he also mentioned that Antonia The major was unable to ride to Lisbon at that time.

Ronan, Vivian, Denton and Daniel and held a wake for the dear señora. This involved entering various states of inebriation and much foolish talk. Devil sought further consolation with Madam Soupert. She served to remind him the greatness of his loss. Clotilde's explosive temper compared unfavorably with Antonia's tranquil nature.

~~~

Alexander Trevelyan arrived a few weeks later. He marched to his cousin's billet with cheese and wine. Jacob opened the door and led Alexander to an airy room, where Ronan sat in his shirt sleeves with no neck cloth and his mistress sat in her petticoat.

Shocked by their undress, Alexander bowed and apologized for arriving unannounced, as if he were in a London drawing room. Ronan laughed and introduced Alexander to Madam Soupert. Alexander attempted to speak to her in his atrocious French and neither understood the other. Therefore, he introduced his cheddar and wine, which everyone understood.

In the scorching heat, Alexander soon took off his red coat and loosened his neck cloth.

"Devilish hot!" he commented, "Does Madam know you are the Blue Devil?"

"Oui, le Diable Bleu!" Clotilde responded, cheerfully.

Alexander thought she didn't show much loyalty to Bonaparte.

Ronan treated her much better than her previous master, but he didn't love her.

Ronan promised, "Bosky, I shall entertain you in the style I entertain prisoners."

"You alarm me, Ro!"

They dined on veal and lamb, accompanied with fine wine and a courtesan for Alexander.

~~~

On August eighth, San Sebastián fell, followed by a murderous sack and fire that destroyed the city. The sack appalled Alexander. When he shared his shocked sensibilities with his cold-blooded cousin, Ronan shrugged. "That's what soldiers do when they are thwarted too long."

"I thought war would be man to man fighting, you know. But it's drudgery and misery and brutality," Alexander confessed.

"Go home and get heirs, Bosky," Ronan advised.

"Dash it, I will not be so soft. I want to see this war through," Alexander replied and then turned soft again, "This bit of muslin you've provided me. Upon my word I'd hate to get a woman with child, even a trull. She uses preventatives. Are they effective?"

Ronan shrugged.

"Whenever I think of those little girls sold in London, I cringe, especially the red headed ones. You know that tavern wench in Boscawden got with child by one of us. Not you of course, but one of our cousins or me, although I was damned careful. I'm afraid to go there. Stings my conscience, 'pon my soul it does!"

The more he drank, the more maudlin Alexander became and the more acute his sense of his obligations until he became prostrate with remorse for all his sins, mostly in the petticoat line.

Finally, Ronan could bear no more. "Dear cousin, permit me to inform you, if you are going to suffer from such refinement of feeling, you should not be in the army."

"Oh, I know, I know, but I can be as tough as the next man when my blood is up. It's after the event and seeing how others act. I hope never to see such a thing as San Sebastian again."

"Of course not. That was pure evil. That is how men are."

They drank until numb to such feelings, carousing until late and laying with their women.

The army fell into exhaustion from heat and exertion. During the weeks of recovery, the major explored and collected intelligence. Ronan rested his worn horses and used Alexander's instead. Alexander saw little of him and Clotilde complained bitterly of Ronan's absences to Alexander, his mistress, who had become her friend, or anyone who would listen. Alexander wondered that a soldier's courtesan would take exception to his absence in the line of duty. When he suggested as much, she threw a wine bottle at him. He dared not suggest she spend the time learning English.

"You, ma'am, are a shrew and short of a sheet, as well," Alexander told her in English.

"Ah, my poor Milord Alexander," his own mistress consoled him, "Only Devil knows how to pacify Clotilde."

"Why should he bother when there are so many sweeter game pullets who would have him?"

The major's absences continued until October.

When back in quarters, the major took Lord Alexander to dine with General Wellington. Alexander felt nervous as a girl at her first ball, but "Nosy" as Alexander chose to call him, was in high spirits with recent successes.

Alexander learned that Nosy favored Cousin Ronan. Major Trevelyan had never been one of the croakers whose tongues wagged behind the general's back, nor was he an arrogant know-it-all like so many easily offended, inexperienced aristocratic officers. Once they took offense, they refused to do anything. Wellington appreciated Ronan's public taciturnity and devotion to duty. In private, the general found Ronan's well-furnished mind impressive and his wit amusing. The major's morals were the major's own business.

Alexander enjoyed claret while Nosy and Ronan played whist for small change. The general was one of the few people with whom the major played. Wellington whooped when he won, which was rare against Ronan.

In the course of the evening, Alexander heard his cousin tell the general that he had spoken with cockle harvesters. They told him the River Bidassoa, separating Spain from France, could be crossed at low tide.

"I rode across one dark night," the major stated, as if he'd walked across Bond Street.

"By Jove, did you?" the general ejaculated.

"Yes, it wasn't above three feet deep."

On October seventh, the allied army crossed the Bidassoa estuary, at low tide, into France, turning Soult's army. During that battle, Alexander heard the unnerving hissing and whistling when the French marched to their drums.

On October thirty-first, the blockaded city of Pamploma surrendered. Alexander's heart ached to see skeletal men march out.

Chapter 9

Boscawden

Through August and September, Berty painted Sylvan. She and Sylvan persuaded Cedric to sit for his own portrait again.

"You are much more mature now than when I painted the first one," Berty said.

Gideon Talbert rode up one afternoon to see Cedric and Sylvan leaving Berty's atelier. He came in upon Berty as she cleaned brushes. She immediately felt uncomfortable, for Sarah did not sit in on the painting sessions with Cedric and Sylvan and Berty feared Gideon might make her an offer, which she would refuse.

"Who was that chit-faced youth with Mr. Trevelyan?" Gideon inquired.

"That was his friend, Mr. Johnson," Berty replied, while swishing brushes in turpentine. She hoped the smell of turpentine repelled Gideon and kept him at a distance and it did. She wiped the brushes on a rag.

"I see you have done his portrait," Gideon remarked with a frown. He felt it improper to say to Berty what he thought of Mr. Johnson.

Berty felt mischievous. "Yes. Mr. Trevelyan has proposed that I paint the two of them together, nude."

"Of all the outrages! You certainly do not entertain the thought!" Gideon ejaculated.

Berty smiled. "I do entertain the thought. Not to be mercenary, but these portrait commissions have been most welcome under our current straightened circumstances."

Gideon bristled. "But surely, you will not paint nudes?"

"Why not?"

"It's most unseemly! No respectable woman would do such a thing."

"Why not?" Berty persisted, feigning innocence.

Gideon tried again, "I just explained that it is not proper."

"Do you really think so? I was going to ask Aunt Sarah, who would never breech the canons of propriety," Berty replied.

"Please do ask her!"

Berty thought it expedient to invite Mr. Talbert to tea since that hour approached. He offered his arm as they walked to the house, She accepted. He thought her very pretty in spite of her braided hair and paint-stained smock, but was unable to contrive what he considered a fitting way of saying so. Berty didn't mind walking on Gideon's arm. She wondered if in time, she could grow to like him, if he wasn't so infuriatingly concerned with proprieties and acceptable behavior of women. No, it wasn't just his stiffness. Something else repelled her that she couldn't explain and couldn't reason away.

Talbert sat in the parlor opposite Augustus and Corky. Augustus, knowing Talbert was Tory, put away his radical paper and engaged in conversation. Yes, he was much improved, but not in full force.

Sarah, who had been helping in the kitchen, joined them. Talbert thought she would never approve of Berty painting nudes, but dared not mention it, since he began to think Berty was humming him. He didn't know what to think of that.

Liberty bounced downstairs, in an unladylike fashion. At least she didn't slide down the railing, Sarah thought. Talbert had to admit, Berty looked lovely in her demure primrose gown with her hair braided neatly around her head. He'd not noticed that gold chain before.

They went in to tea with John, Betty and Peggy. Gideon didn't approve of the Bodleigh's custom of dining with people he thought of as servants. He wasn't sure if the Bodleighs were old-fashioned or modern, but he conducted himself with exemplary manners. He praised the scones as worth the ride over, which ingratiated him with Betty.

"Thank you, sir. They were always favorites with our boys," Betty said.

Now that Betty had brought it up, Augustus asked how the boys were doing. John had last spoken of them before Augustus' illness and he had forgotten.

"Didn't John tell you? We got a letter from John and Andy in Canada and Ned is faring well in London," Betty replied.

Sarah interposed, "Augustus has forgotten things said to him just before his illness."

They returned to comfortable subjects like food until Gideon mentioned the successful crossing of the Bidassoa and Napoleon's fall at Leipzig. Everyone agreed the war would soon end.

"What will happen to the soldiers?" Liberty asked.

"Some will go to America, some to India and some to Ireland," Gideon replied.

Liberty tried not to wince when he said America. Finding the rrest of the conversation tedious, she daydreamed. Gideon took his leave soon after tea. Berty helped carry dishes into the kitchen.

Betty, reminded of her sons, rattled on about them. The youngest was apprenticed to a London cabinet maker. The two elder boys were making their fortune in Canada. She'd had five, but two had died of small pox.

"You stayed trim after having children," Peggy said, "Why hasn't Mrs. Wingfield?"

"The Reverend needs to preach on gluttony, that's why," Betty said, "Did you see how she ate half my cake and most of the scones the last time she came to tea?"

"She was eating for two," Liberty put in.

"More like a dozen. She's gotten far too plump. Babies have nothing to do with it. Look at Mrs. Witherfield, ten children and she's thin as a stick. I dare say she could do with my scones."

"But enough of that, what do you think of Mr. Talbert, that's what I want to know?"

Berty bridled at the mention. "Why I haven't thought about him, why should I?" she asked disingenuously.

"Don't try me with that flummery! He don't have the major's dash, but he's good and settled, which is better," Betty said.

"Better for what?" Liberty asked.

Betty threw a wet dish rag at her.

Liberty admitted Betty had a point. The major had not responded to her last letter. She wondered what would happen when, or if, he came home. They had said they would not marry anyone ever. Berty began to think that was a foolish thing to have committed herself to. No wonder one wasn't considered adult until the age of one and twenty. Ronan had been older, but he had other reasons to forgo marriage. Berty's reasons dissolved at the specter of a lonely old spinster living on the parish. Perhaps she shouldn't try Gideon with her vexing quirks and hums, which he had tolerated with grace.

Gideon, a creature of habit, visited the Bodleighs regularly, arriving to tea every Thursday. He expressed his satisfaction with the completed wing. Augustus apologized for having been unable to supervise it, but John had performed with knowing expertise and Liberty had also reported back to Augustus.

The Wingfields joined the Bodleighs and Gideon for tea one Thursday. Augustus praised the Reverend for the comfort he had given him during his illness.

"I only performed my duty, Augustus, praying and reading comforting Bible passages," The Reverend said.

"Yes, of course. I confess, though, I did get tired of the Lord's Prayer," Augustus said with his wry grin.

Sarah gave him a warning look, for he liked to tease.

"Most people take comfort from it, but I do agree it is most overused," The Reverend admitted.

Cynthia Wingfield mentioned the American war, a taboo subject in the Bodleigh house. Sarah adroitly changed the subject while Cynthia indulged in three more scones.

Gideon excused himself early and the Wingfields lingered, enjoying the tranquil respite from their four boisterous children. The Reverend and Augustus talked in the dining room, while the ladies retired to the parlor.

Sarah explained to Cynthia, "We don't discuss the American war. We are quite against it and, as you know, Berty is American. Mr. Talbert, though, is in favor of it, but realizing our disapprobation, he doesn't speak of it. A most considerate gentleman."

"Most certainly. I can find nothing exceptionable about him," Cynthia agreed, "I daresay he will make some fortunate female a wonderful husband," she hinted to Berty, "I'm sure many have set their caps at him, but he seems to have a tendre for Liberty."

"Really, I wouldn't know," Berty rejoined, "He isn't the least romantical."

"One shouldn't expect a sensible man to express the romantic nonsense young girls pick up from novels and other un-improving literature," Cynthia replied.

"Then I should say, he isn't warm," Berty amended.

"She means Gideon lacks Major Trevelyan's swash and dash. Ronan would swagger in here, kiss our fingers and seat himself next to

Berty as if he owned the world, although he hadn't a feather to fly with," Sarah said with a languid smile.

Berty grew pensive. For a while, no one spoke. Gideon couldn't compete with the memory of the major.

"If he survives the Peninsula, he could be sent to America," Berty muttered moodily.

This inspired Cynthia to praise Gideon again. Sarah joined in, mentioning how conscientious Gideon was in paying the workmen, unlike too many gentlemen. Berty grew weary with their praise of Gideon's excellence. She thought him a dead bore.

The next day, she received a letter from Ronan that was anything but boring. He wrote with élan of riding Gunpowder over the Bidasoa estuary, the battle, Alexander 's arrival and the beauty and plenty of the country. Elated, Berty read the letter to her Aunt and Uncle. Sarah heard it with mixed feelings. She knew these letters kept Berty from favoring Gideon. Augustus listened with rapt attention.

"Why the major sounds like he's in high gig. The war is going well and he seems to have become comfortable writing us about it," Augustus commented.

Berty agreed. The next day, she told Barnstable of Gunpowder's accomplishments.

"The rough colt makes the best horse. I hope the major brings him home to stand stud here."

Chapter 10

November tenth, the armies fought the battle of the Nivelle. Weeks
of rain and mud followed. Then the investment of Bayonne and five days
of fighting before the allies won. For the next two months of rain and
storms, Wellington settled in his headquarters at St. Jean de Luz.

Major Trevelyan billeted there with a K.G.L. surgeon, Major Manfred Jurgens and other officers. Manfred wished to improve his English and
Ronan wanted to improve his German. Alexander visited often on the rainy
days. On good days, they rode on the beach or fox hunted with the Duke.

Mrs. Collins sought Major Trevelyan and found him on the street.
He offered his arm and they walked along. Honoria explained the purpose
of her visit.

"Mary has died. Typhus. Her baby died, also. Her husband is sick
and Kit, Captain Collins, now, thought you should know, that you could
write the Burlingtons."

"Yes, I will. I'm very sorry. I doubt they will tell Christopher for a
while," the major replied.

"No, of course not. He is so young. Perhaps he has forgotten his
mother. She was Kit's favorite, but we have a little girl now. That is something."

Ronan nodded. They walked a while without speaking. When Mrs
Collins had to go in another direction, the major kissed her fingers and they
parted.

Clotilde and Alexander's mistress, Artemisia, who shared quarters,
happened to be walking on the opposite side of the street. Clotilde hastened
across, causing riders to jab their horses' mouths and carters to curse.

"Devil! Who was that?" Clotilde accosted the major.

He tilted his head back and stared down at her without answering. The major walked on, ignoring her. Infuriated, Clotilde drew out a stiletto and thrust at him. Devil spun round, grabbed her arm and tore the weapon from her hand. He half dragged her back to her quarters. Artemisia followed, while passersby murmured.

In the privacy of her chambers, Clotilde screamed and beat her fists against the major.

"It is none of your concern who I speak to, or whether I have other women," he told her.

She called him cold and cruel and tried to scratch his face. Without a word, he strolled out of the apartment. A piece of crockery crashed against the door as he shut it.

~~~

One wet afternoon, Alexander showed up at his cousin's billet with wine and a basket of food, both of which were good and plentiful. Major Jurgens greeted him.

"And where is my dear cousin?" Alexander inquired.

"Vere do you tink? He's vith his insatiable whore. He's de most concupiscent man I've ever met. Dey disgust me!" Manfred expatiated, practising new words.

Alexander laughed, "Upon my soul they can't be too long about it."

He sat down with Manfred and shared the wine. They asked Jacob to go to Madam Soupert's quarters to fetch Major Trevelyan.

"He ain't there," Jacob retorted.

"Vere is he den?"

"With his Irish wench, I reckon."

"Anoder one!"

The tousled Devil swooped in his wet greatcoat.

"Speak of the Devil!" Alexander cried.

Alexander and the surgeon lit cigars. All drank fine wine and ate. They talked of war and women. Alexander expostulated with Ronan on his disastrous incognita.

"Clotilde's very demon of a woman," Alexander said, "Pay her off and send her away!"

Ronan grinned. "A devil's bride."

"In a left-handed marriage! You're as touched in the upper works as she is!" Alexander said.

"You see vat I mean. Besotted vit lust, a very satyr. A disgrace to de cafalry," Manfred claimed, humorously, practising words..

His auditors laughed.

"I don't doubt it. But my cousin enjoys good health and a healthy man must have a woman."

"I've nefer seen such health! She's a dangerous baggage to play vit," Manfred said.

"Ah, you have hit it. My cousin loves danger and, you know, he is dangerous himself! More so than he seems," Alexander stated.

"Oh, I haf heard," Manfred replied, smoking his cigar, "If half de stories of Le Diable Bleu are true, he is very dangerous indeed. Yet speaks as gentle as a referend! I don't vant to see him injured by dis harlot. She suvers hysteria, tempestuous moods and excessive lust. The last, very unhealthy vor a man."

His friends laughed.

"By Jove, we must take a physician's advice, Ro. I understand the only way to avoid women with excessive lust is to marry. You're four months older than I, you be the first."

"You wish me to marry the French courtesan?"

"Dash you, no. Send her away and take leave for Boscawden."

"I can not take leave now. You are the one who needs to wed."

Alexander sighed. "I rather dread getting hedged, myself. I know I must get an heir, but the idea of being shackled to a woman for life daunts me. They are so changeful."

~~~

Ronan continued to rack up with women and return to his quarters during the day. He and Manfred alternated between speaking German and English. Manfred claimed his own English improved faster than Ronan's German.

Alexander visited on another drenching day and found Ronan writing.

"He's turning into a Xenophon," Manfred said.

"I am aiding my Reverend Uncle in his history of the Peninsula War. He aspires to be a modern Thucydides," Ronan replied in German.

"He should vait until de var is over," the physician suggested, "Howefer, if he vould like a fiew of it from a medical practitioner, I vould gladly assist. Ve've lost as many men to disease as battle."

"He would tell you the Athenians suffered a plague that killed Pericles. Yes, I'm sure he would appreciate your information," Ronan replied, picking up a fresh piece of paper.

"I bet you haven't written so much since you were at university," Alexander remarked, glancing at a pile of letters Ronan had written. "I see you are still writing to Miss Bodleigh."

"Who is Miss Bodleigh?" Manfred asked.

"The love of his life. The girl he shall marry after the war," Alexander replied, confidently.

"I disbeleife you!" Manfred rejoined.

"You should say 'You are humming me.' more the thing," Alexander advised, teaching Manfred English slang. "Upon my honor, I'm not, am I, Ro?"

Ronan didn't answer, leading his friends to argue the point.

"You see, he doesn't know it, yet," Alexander explained.

"Palderdash!" Manfred scoffed.

~~~

In Boscawden, Berty, Ricky and Sylvan discussed the next painting. To Berty's relief, Sylvan expressed discomfort with posing nude. Ricky suggested drapery. Berty confessed she had not consulted Sarah on the propriety of painting nudes, expecting Ricky would not choose such a painting.

"But father's gone, Berty. I'm twenty-one and can do what I like."

Ricky decided Sylvan would wear breeches and drapery. Berty would request Sarah or Augustus' presence.

Following that discussion, Ricky took Berty aside and asked if she had written to Ronan. She said she had not answered his latest letter.

"He does not precisely approve of my proclivity," Ricky said.

Berty gave him a questioning look.

"Cousin Ronan tolerates much for an army officer. If you mention that I have a good friend in Sylvan, he will surmise the rest," Ricky continued.

Berty still looked puzzled and Ricky realized she didn't comprehend the sexual nature of his relationship with Sylvan.

"Oh, dear, women are so protected," he remarked, "I suppose you've not read much classical history or heard of the Sacred Band."

"No, should I have?"

"Probably not. Suffice it to say the British army does not have a Sacred Band." Ricky refused to elaborate.

When Berty wrote to Ronan, she mentioned this odd conversation.

"Ricky said that you are tolerant for an army officer. I'm glad Ricky has found a friend, although others disapprove. Particularly Mr. Talbert, a frequent visitor of ours. He called Sylvan, chit-faced. Sylvan is only seventeen and very blond. Ricky also mentioned something about a Sacred Band, but didn't explain. I asked Aunt Sarah and Miss Westerly and they didn't know what he meant, either, although Edith says it must have something to do with Ricky and Sylvan being mollies. I do know she means they are gilrlish men. I'm afraid to ask anyone else. Why are women kept in the dark about so many things? I sometimes wish I had a classical education, but Latin and Greek take so long to learn and would serve me no purpose."

In his next letter, Ronan replied, "We enjoy the rain and mud of winter quarters. Regarding the Sacred Band of Thebes, Phillip of Macedon annihilated them. Not only does the British army not have a band of male lovers, but the provost hangs any caught together. I can not comprehend how a man could prefer the company of a chit-faced boy over a charming female such as yourself. Women don't need to know these things. Cedric should not flaunt this friendship and speak of such indecencies to an innocent female."

It astounded Berty that Ronan would write so forthrightly about Ricky, when he was so secretive about his own life.

Chapter 11

Winter 1814, Boscawden

Nasty winter weather kept Liberty indoors more than she wished. When weather permitted, Berty rode Rose. Sometimes she imagined Ronan on a gray horse meeting her in the wood. It had been two years since she had seen him, but she had his letters and thought of him more often than she thought of Gideon Talbert.

Talbert ingratiated himself with Augustus, Sarah and most of Liberty's friends. Since Augustus' illness, her family and friends had become concerned for Berty's future. Even Edith sometimes spoke in Gideon's favor. When Berty felt everyone was against the Ronan, Berty wrote to Miss Penthwaite.

"It seems I will have very little to live on when my relatives die," Berty wrote, bluntly. "I should think I could live off the farm, but they don't agree, although I'm not an expensive person."

She went on to describe how they encouraged her to "kowtow" to Talbert. "Which I refuse to do. He's such a prig. Oh, very considerate to my relatives and all, but so narrow minded. I simply can't bear a person so devoted to propriety. I'm sure if I relented in my coolness to him, he would make an offer. I dread that of all things. I'm afraid Major Trevelyan is not eligible. Everyone agrees he's a libertine and not likely to marry ever. So, I beg of you to let me stay with you for a while. I love Boscawden, but want to escape my friends! And perhaps I can procure some portrait work. Since Uncle Augustus has been ill, I've had little work. "

She could have added, little money, too. Augustus could make it downstairs, on good days, and sit by the fire. He was too weak to leave the house. Liberty took his advice and sold Melody's colts to Mr. Pemberton and Queen's to a farmer. Since the completion of Talbert's house, there had been no work for John. He used Queen and the cart to haul wood, hay or anything else customers wanted hauled. He hauled the new school master and his baggage to the small cottage near the school.

When a fine day arose, Berty hitched Mercury, who needed exercise, to the gig and paced to the Westerly's. Edith was as eager to get out and about as Liberty. She joined Berty in the gig, and they drove nowhere in particular.

"Amy and Tabitha talk of nothing but their babies," Edith complained, "Dead bores."

"They never talked of much before but their silly novels," Berty said, "I've invited myself to stay with Miss Penthwaite. I'm sure she'd welcome you, too. We'd be three old spinsters!"

"We'd sit at tea and solve the world's problems!" Edith remarked with a giggle.

Mercury paced into a narrow, shaded lane that meandered down between hills.

Splat! A gob of mud hit Edith's face. Berty ducked in time to miss a second splat. Cursing in an unladylike fashion, Edith grabbed the buggy whip. They heard wicked laughter in the hedge by the lane. Berty halted Mercury and the two women stepped out to follow the laughter. They saw a flash of red hair as a boy ran away, but could not follow through the briers in their skirts. Berty helped Edith wipe off the mud, ruining both their handkerchiefs.

"That curst Jim Jams! Drat him!" Edith rounded on the retreating red head.

"Who is Jim Jams?" Berty asked.

"What, you've not heard of James Trevelyan's bastard?" Edith asked.

"No, should I have?"

"I would think! Everyone else has. He's the odious brat James got on a maid at the Hall when he was nineteen or so. I reckon Jim Jams is fourteen now. I don't wonder your Uncle Francis hasn't mentioned it. He arranged for the girl to marry one of the tenants, Mr. Jams, a notorious drunkard. He wasn't then, maybe, but he agreed to marry the girl for a measly sum. And now Jim Jams runs wild. Jams rents him out as a plow boy in spring."

Berty asked where the Jams lived and Edith directed her to a muddy track where stood a row of tenant cottages.

"I don't want to drive Mercury in that mire and I'm certainly not going to get out and walk in it," Berty said, staring at the dilapidated cottages in disgust. "Why hasn't Uncle Francis kept these cottages in repair?"

"These are bad tenants," Edith replied.

Loose bricks in chimneys, decayed thatch and broken windows showed neglect and abuse. A swarm of filthy, ragged children ran about with a loose sow. One house showed a slight effort to maintain a front garden. Edith said a widow occupied that cottage. Some of the brats ran up to the gig and stared dumbly.

Edith asked them to fetch Mrs. Jams. After a while, a thin, gray, ragged woman stumbled out of the worse cottage. Although in her early thirties, she had few teeth and her stringy unkept hair was gray either from nature or from lack of washing. She gazed at Berty and Edith from a black eye.

"This is a futile mission, Edith," Berty said.

"I daresay," Edith agreed, but addressed Mrs. Jams regarding her reprobate son.

"He ain't here," Mrs. Jams muttered.

"We know that. He needs to be disciplined for throwing mud at us," Edith said.

"Don't do no good. He's bigger than I am and Mr. Jams don't want to be troubled," Mrs. Jams replied and dragged herself back inside her cottage.

"Then he'll end up decorating a gallows," Edith called after her, then turned to Berty and said, "Mr. Jams is probably to be found in the tavern. We could send someone in for him."

"I don't want to find him. Let's see the new school master. School should be over for the day and I'd like to know why Jim Jams isn't in school," Berty replied and turned Mercury back towards the village.

"I haven't met this new school master. Have you?" Edith asked.

"No, only glimpsed him in a dark corner of the church of a Sunday. If uncle was well, I'm sure Aunt Sarah would have invited him for supper by now. Reverend Wingfield says he has a hideous gash down his face. Major Trevelyan sent him from the war."

"I wish he'd sent a sound one," Edith commented.

"We thought the last one was sound, until Reverend Wingfield found him dead."

They saw Daniel Rollings, still in the school room, checking papers. The notorious sabre wound adorned his face from right forehead to cheek. He wore a patch over that eye. He also limped and his right arm appeared weak. His grim visage usually frightened intransigent boys and if that didn't, he didn't mind acting as provost with a bucket of switches. Berty grimaced when she saw them.

Rollings looked up in surprise. Surely these beauties were not mothers of his students. Ladies did not usually visit gentlemen alone. He rose and bowed when the two women entered. "How have I earned the honor of this visit?" he asked.

Edith began with her description of the encounter with Jim Jams. Then turned to Berty.

"Why isn't he in school?" Berty asked.

"James shows up when he's bored and wants to bullock the other boys, but his father doesn't make him attend. I tried to persuade the lad to enlist, more to get him out of Boscawden than for any benefit he'd be to the army. He's an aristocrat's arrogant bastard, but I say too much."

"Maybe you don't say enough," Berty retorted, "Someday he may get into real trouble."

"Perhaps, perhaps not. He's not a dunce. If he would apply himself, he'd be my best student, but he'd rather fight."

"If that isn't a Trevelyan!" Edith remarked.

"Yes, but they are a rich family and should provide for their love children if they persist in having them," Berty objected, "instead of fobbing them off on a drunkard."

"I quite agree, Miss Bodleigh. I can't condemn them all, though. It was through Major Trevelyan I was offered this position."

"Not an enviable one, I think," Edith said.

"I'm satisfied with it, miss. I am of use. I suppose Major Trevelyan thought a tender hearted soul like myself would make a good school master!" Rollings chuckled at that and his face took on an almost pleasant aspect.

Berty thought he had been good-looking before that terrible injury. "Is that why the major recommended you?"

"He knew I'd graduated Oxford and had tutored. He'd also heard some of my beliefs. Such as that everyone should be taught to read. If they read no other book than the Bible, they will be the better for it. Major Trevelyan hears everything and reveals nothing. I've had my adventures and now wish to live a quiet life. I hope to teach these children to live virtuous lives."

"That's good to hear, sir. I think you would like to meet my aunt and uncle. They take an interest in education. My aunt helped in the school before my uncle took ill. We haven't invited company since his malady. He's better now and a visitor would cheer he and my aunt," Berty said and invited him to tea the following Saturday.

Rollings thanked her and said he would try to persuade James not to throw mud at young ladies. He watched them leave and found it hard to concentrate on his work with such visions of loveliness in his head. The idea of a pair of bluestockings in Boscawden intrigued him.

On the drive back to the Westerly's, Edith commented what a shame such a nice man should be so disfigured.

"Yes, I wish I could paint over it," Berty said, "And you know the same could happen to Alexander and Ronan. Men like Napoleon who invade countries, are truly evil."

"The Corsican monster," Edith agreed. They rode on without incident.

When Berty arrived home, she breathlessly told her aunt and uncle of her adventures, meeting Mr. Rollings and inviting him to tea. They laughed at her excitement.

"Reverend Wingfield said that Mr. Rollings has mostly kept to himself since arriving here. The Reverend sometimes has Mr. Rollings for supper. Rollings shuns society due to his injuries," Sarah said.

"Well that should change. People can just get used to them," Berty declared and then jumped onto another subject on her mind, "Why did Uncle Francis marry poor Mrs. Jams to that awful drunkard?"

"Francis didn't marry them, Berty," Augustus admonished her, "Mr. Jams seemed like a decent, sober tenant at the time and he'd been courting Sally before she took a position as maid at the Hall and encountered James Trevelyan. I won't defend James' abominable conduct, but she never claimed he forced her or promised her anything."

"As it was, Jams was willing to marry her even though she was with child and the family gave him a sum to provide for the child. Francis merely represented the family in the matter. She and Jams both drink when they can get it. I fear she is a slattern and Jams works as little as possible. If it wasn't for the children, Francis would evict them. One can't keep up on repairs when tenants break things."

"They didn't break the roof," Berty remarked, "That thatch wouldn't support houseleeks."

Augustus chuckled. "Francis will have it repaired in due time."

Saturday, Rollings walked from his cottage to the Bodleigh's. He suffered no delusions that Miss Bodleigh had any interest in him as a matrimonial prospect, but thought it kind of her to invite him. Rollings had long found contentment in bachelorhood. He had no interest in the gamble of matrimony even before his disfigurement. He left his stout walking stick by the door and Berty introduced him to Sarah and Augustus.

Rollings immediately recognized the portrait of Major Trevelyan. "Le Diable Bleu est un bel homme!"

Sarah laughed, "My cousin. I knew him as a mischievous boy, but I hope only a devil to the French now."

"Very much so," Rollings replied, but did not elaborate. He admired Berty's paintings and sat down. He and Augustus talked politics and, although Rollings professed no inclination, his opinions tended to agree with Augustus' and he admired the American Constitution. Sarah questioned him about female education. He agreed with her ideas. He kept the sexes separated in his school and stated he preferred separate rooms and instructors, but otherwise thought females should enjoy the same educations as males. "Except in the martial arts, of course. I don't think we need Amazons."

The Bodleighs enjoyed his erudition while he enjoyed Betty's scones. When Liberty escorted him to the door, he confided, "I believe you might be one of Major Trevelyan's secrets."

"What do you mean, sir? I haven't seen the major in two years."

Her embarrassment and the strength of her protest verified Rollings' suspicion. "I didn't mean to offend, Miss Bodleigh. The major could not but notice your beauty, but I collect you are a dedicated and proper spinster with no interest in dashing blades."

He further discomposed Berty with his serious expression.

"I don't apprehend, sir. You seem to be humming me," Berty objected, annoyed at his referring to her as a proper spinster.

"Miss Bodleigh, Major Trevelyan's eyes are like icicles. He has impressed the partisans by being as cut throat as they. Only a few of us know his better side. You have painted our grim warrior with dreamy eyes! Perhaps you are waiting for each other?"

Rollings smiled and departed, confidant he had discovered Ronan's inamorata.

Berty stood stunned for a moment. No wonder Ronan chose such a perceptive man for intelligence work!

Sarah decided there was no reason such a fine gentleman should not enjoy society and determined to ask Mrs. Pendleton to invite him to her next event. "I feel we have neglected this poor man. He shows every refinement of manners and speech," Sarah said.

Berty thought she would like to see Rollings outshining Talbert at their next get together, but she didn't care to hear others state what she thought of herself, a dedicated and proper spinster. An old maid like Miss Penthwaite. Edith Westerly and Berty Bodleigh, the old maids of Boscawden. How irritating of Mr. Rollings to mention her spinsterhood. Not that she was ashamed of it. Better a spinster than married to a Gideon Talbert or worse. Yet, she fumed every time the words crossed her mind, several times a day.

A few days later, Berty rode Rose to Edith's. Taking a shortcut home across a meadow, Rose tripped in a fox hole and fell, throwing Berty over her head. The ground wasn't frozen and Berty tumbled onto soft bracken. Bruised and sore, she mounted Rose and rode home.

Arriving stained and disheveled, Berty made light of the incident rather than upset her family. She awoke stiff and achy the next morning, with a swollen arm and badly bruised hip. Berty had no work to do, but didn't want her relatives to see how stiff she was, so puttered around her atelier and visited the stable, one of her favorite places.

Rose's leg swelled from the injury. Berty rubbed liniment on it and put some on herself. She sat in a pile of hay watching the horses chew and petting Old Tom, the stable's ginger and white cat. Berty had known Tom since he was a kitten and considered him her own cat, but since Tom sprayed, he was not allowed in the house.

Tom displayed injuries common to feline warriors, damaged ears and many scars. He had proved himself a successful lover and many of his ginger offspring roamed Boscawden. Berty thought, first, why had she been unable to imagine a unique name for Tom and second, how fortunate she had been to have escaped serious injury or illness her entire life. She credited most of that to being female. How awful to be male and a warrior!

"Poor Tom," she said out loud, rubbing his scared head. He purred. "I should have named you Ronan! But I think I'll name you Rollings for you do have a scar over your eye."

When Pete came home from school, he watered the horses. He complained how hard it was when the water froze. Berty admonished him for complaining. "No one wants to hear complaining, no matter how justified," she told him, "Look at Old Tom, he never complains, it's unmanly."

"He's not a man, he's a cat," Pete said.

"Uncatly, then. I've decided to name him Rollings," Berty said.

Pete laughed. "You always make me laugh, Miss Berty. Just between me and you, I kind of like Mr. Rollings," he said, "But I don't want to get on his bad side. He's very stern. Officer, you know."

~~~

Mrs. Pendleton invited Mr. Rollings to a Saturday afternoon tea and card party. The Bodlieghs, Westerlies, Palmers, Mr. Talbert and many others attended. It was Augustus' first day out. He, Liberty, Edith and Rollings didn't care to play cards and joined the other non-players in quiet conversation. Sarah loved to play and won several games of whist, beating Gideon Talbert repeatedly.

"Aunt Sarah should bet real money," Berty said, "Perhaps even shillings!"

"Upon my honor, Mr. Talbert seems to be a sour loser," Edith remarked.

He became more sour when he saw Berty and Edith sitting by the impecunious school master. Talbert joined another card table where a game involving chance rather than wits was played.

Augustus committed one of his usual social blunders by asking Rollings how he was injured, as if that was suitable tea party conversation. Berty shook her head at him.

"I mean, where?" Augustus corrected himself.

"Spain," Rollings replied, grimly.

"Oh, how interesting," Augustus began, but before he could ask for details, Berty suggested that Mr. Rollings might want to talk about something else. Perhaps books. Augustus read few books about anything but architecture, agriculture and political philosophy. Edith preferred novels and poetry and Rollings preferred the classics. That subject proved as unpromising as the war, until Mrs. Pendleton joined them and began conversing on a maze of subjects and found that Rollings liked walking in the countryside and riding when anyone would loan him a horse. He also loved music and played several instruments, including violin. Or would when his arm recovered.

"We do love music here and have so few musicians," Penelope informed him, "You must come again when your arm is healed. I'll plan something to use your talents."

Rollings accepted that offer modestly.

After a light supper, the party broke around ten in the evening, for everyone kept country hours in Boscawden. The Westerlies took Rollings home in their carriage.

~~~

Gideon Talbert reasoned he could not possibly be jealous of a hideous cripple, but he didn't like the way Miss Bodleigh and Miss Westerly attended to Rollings at the Pendleton's. Between hunting and an occasional trip to London, Talbert made frequent visits to the Bodleighs. He never found Berty alone, but was too obtuse to realize she avoided that situation.

One chilly afternoon, she was seeing to Rose's leg when she heard Gideon outside. Berty sat in the straw at Rose's feet behind the stable partition, hiding from Gideon as he tied his horse in one of the guest stalls. Gideon whistled tunelessly and marched out without feeding or unsaddling his mount. Berty heard him order Pete to do those chores. When Pete came in, Berty rose from the straw, brushing it off her skirt.

Pete gave her a wry look. "I thought you liked Mr. Talbert. He sure likes you."

"I'm undecided whether I like him or not, if you must know. I own there's nothing exceptional about him and my friends say I SHOULD like him," Berty confessed.

"But you don't, that's clear. I think you like poor, ugly Mr. Rollings better," Pete said. There was nothing obtuse about Pete. "But I don't see why you need to favor any of them. Major Trevelyan's got 'em all beat, you ask me."

"Nobody asked you," Berty feigned indignation.

"Nobody asks me anything."

"Good, because I'm going for a walk and I don't want you telling anybody my direction," Berty said and left the barn by the paddock door.

In the house, Gideon immediately asked for Liberty.

Sarah, alone in the parlor, replied, "I thought she had gone to tend Rose's swollen leg. I'm surprised you didn't see her."

"She must have gone elsewhere," Gideon replied.

"Yes, of course, probably to the milk house to get a cheese for tea. I'm sure she'll be in directly."

Gideon clumsily broached a subject much on his mind. "I've wished to talk with Mr. Bodleigh, but he has been so delicate, I didn't want to bring on a relapse."

"Dear me, what could you wish to discuss that would cause such a thing? Is there a problem with the building?" Sarah spoke with alarm.

"Oh, no, not at all, upon my word, the wing is all I could wish. No, I wished to speak with him about Miss Bodleigh."

Sarah squirmed under her sewing project, which she'd not put away as she should have. "Pray what do you wish to discuss with Augustus that might put him out of health?"

"I dare say, I didn't mean it that way. I should hope he would take it quite positively," Gideon continued awkwardly.

Sarah, more perceptive than Augustus, replied, "If you mean to ask him for her hand, Berty is of age and Augustus would certainly leave any decision up to her."

"Yes, ma'am. That is precisely what I meant to ask him," Gideon smiled with relief at her understanding.

Sarah suspecting it was too soon to ask Berty, carefully replied, "You are quite right to ask me about his condition first. Augustus is still delicate and his fondness for our niece is such that even good news, such as this, might be too much in his weakened state." Sarah felt a brief stab of conscience for telling such a blatant fib, but continued with an even more blatant fib. "And Berty, I don't think she knows her own mind sometimes."

"I quite understand that female failing and Miss Bodleigh being exceedingly maidenly...upon my word, I think she might need your firm persuasion," Gideon stated.

Sarah bridled at the idea of firmly persuading Berty, but admitted, "Yes, she doesn't always see what is best for herself. She is so fond of us, you see, that the idea of setting up her own home, I'm sure she never even considers it."

If Berty had heard that, she would have accused Sarah of telling bouncers.

Meanwhile, fragile and feeble Augustus, having heard Gideon ride up had taken the same idea as Berty of going for a walk. He'd left his office by the back door and, shushing Corky, headed towards Boscawden Park. Augustus entered through the rusted gate that had frozen in place just wide enough for a ridden horse to pass, but not one of the long-horned cows. He'd not gone far under the spreading beeches when he spotted Berty in her garnet riding coat.

"Bit cold for you to be out, uncle," Berty addressed her relative.

"Nonsense, brisk, fresh air is just the thing to revive me and Corky needs the exercise!"

They strode at a good pace to keep warm and soon reached the stream that wove through the park.

"You must have missed Talbert. I heard him ride up," Augustus said.

"Did you? Pray, why didn't you stay to greet him?" Berty asked.

Augustus shrugged. He didn't want to admit he dreaded Talbert addressing him in private as much as Berty dreaded it. "Do you wish to turn back for our visitor?"

"No, do you?"

"Not if you don't. I suppose this is very rude of us."

"Maybe it's rude of him to constantly think we wish to see him," Berty retorted.

Augustus sighed. "This has been a conundrum for me. By all that is obvious, he would make an excellent match for you. And we must consider your future. The pittance I can leave you and Sarah, well it's just that, a pittance, not enough to support you both in the style to which you are accustomed and that you both deserve."

"Oh please, uncle, don't speak of it. We don't have to make trips to London, attend concerts, buy books, buy fine cloth for gowns or any of a hundred such indulgences. And I do hope you live to a hundred!"

Augustus countered, "You don't need those things, but you should have them. And no one in our family has lived past eighty-five."

"Very well, if the choice is to marry Gideon Talbert to have those things or stay a contented spinster and not having them, I prefer to stay a spinster."

"He is that repugnant to you?"

"He's not repugnant and I can't define what it is, but I don"t care to marry him."

"You don't love him. Major Trevelyan has turned your head and you've set your cap on him," Augustus declared.

"Uncle! I have not set my cap on anyone. The major has not turned my head. I'm well aware of his disrepute. I simply don't feel I can ever love Gideon Talbert, fine man that he seems to be."

Augustus thought if Berty had never met Ronan Trevelyan, she'd find Gideon Talbert more attractive, but he admitted, "I do not warm to Mr. Talbert, either. Perhaps in time, when we know him better."

"Well he certainly seems likely to allow us that time," Berty said ironically.

They followed the stream down its many falls to the man made fork. One way followed the stream's natural bed to the large swimming hole and on. The other flowed in a narrow channel to the garden's water steps.

"I'm not up to the path to the swimming hole. Would you mind taking the shorter path to the garden?" Augustus asked.

"Certainly. The pool is too far and probably frozen on the surface. Corky might try to walk across."

They followed the channel to the garden wall, where a narrow gate allowed entrance. Here they took the path over the channel and down along the water steps. In places, the water had frozen on the steps.

"This is so clever. Who thought of it?" Berty asked.

"The same ancestor who brought back the garden statues. Lord Victor's grandfather, I believe," Augustus said.

They walked to the orangery to get warm. There Mr. Gardner picked oranges and tidied the plants. Orange blossoms scented the damp air. Augustus conversed with Gardner about installing an iron furnace and pipes to heat the orangery. Gardner listened attentively, but thought Augustus was a bit light in his head.

"I don't think Lord Alexander has improving the orangery on his mind. Of course, if your brother approves the expense."

"So much for that idea, uncle," Berty said, "but if you could use the heat to start young plants or in some money-making way, Uncle Francis would take to the idea."

That started another lengthy conversation and by the time Berty and Augustus got back to the Bodleigh house, they found the household almost frantic with worry. Gideon was still there and ready to ride through the wood in search of them.

"Oh what a pucker when we are merely late for tea," Augustus objected.

"The two of you should have told someone you intended to walk for hours, which you, Augustus should not have done," Sarah reproved them.

"Oh, but we didn't walk the whole time. We stopped in the Orangery, which was comfortable for uncle. And then uncle would have to go on about a new heating system with Mr. Gardner," Berty explained.

"I daresay, but you can apprehend our concern when Augustus is still weak from his illness," Sarah glared warningly at both and took her husband's hand to give it a hard pinch when he began to object. "A cup of thyme tea, for you, dear, and to bed," she added, firmly, seeing a way to keep Augustus from Gideon's overtures.

After tea and having sent Augustus unwillingly to bed with a pile of architectural publications, Sarah conversed about the Wingfield's latest pledge of their affection, a baby girl. "Cynthia presents the reverend with a healthy babe almost yearly,"

"Yes, she's a good and dutiful wife," Gideon agreed.

"Of course we all would like to have a baby around," Sarah continued, "Unfortunately, Augustus and I were not so blessed."

Berty tried to think of another subject. "Did you know that Mr. Rollings plays the violin?" she asked.

"Yes, Penelope did mention that," Sarah said and returned to babes. "Your friends, Amy and Tabitha, both have children now, Berty. How time flies. It seems just a short time ago, you all played with dolls. You do like children, don't you, Mr. Talbert?"

"Oh, I daresay. Every man wants an heir and a spare."

Sarah disliked that common, crude term, heir and a spare, but did not admonish Talbert.

"What if your wife only presented you with an annual girl?" Liberty asked.

Talbert looked blank, then said, "I suppose eventually a boy would appear."

"After a dozen or so daughters," Berty stated.

"That would be rather unfortunate," Talbert said with sincere sadness, "But I rather think I would produce sons."

"Oh, you are sure?"

"Well, I daresay, I believe some men who are perhaps not men in full, produce girls and others who are more manly, produce boys," he confidently replied.

Sarah and Berty refrained from laughing. "How the reverend must have failed with this last one," Sarah pronounced, "I noticed his sermons were rather tepid last year. Perhaps he isn't eating enough beef."

"Perhaps he'll recover. I thought his last sermon quite powerful," Berty put in with a wry smile. She couldn't wait to share this conversation with Edith.

"Yes, I'm sure these conditions of manfulness come and go, but I shall defer to you, Mr. Talbert, on that," Sarah said, flatteringly.

Gideon appeared at a loss for words and then had the brilliant thought, "I've heard that the female can also be responsible in some way for the sex of the child. Perhaps, as you suggested, diet affects the outcome. I mean, possibly it is not inevitable that a truly manly man always sires males."

"What a scientific mind, you have, sir," Liberty said, "I do think that generally speaking offspring are the inevitable result of marriage and for the sake of good health, it is probably best to postpone the desired bliss of marriage. I consider the marriage of the Duke of Wellington a most correct example of good planning in that line. Don't you agree, aunt?"

"Most decidedly, they waited until they were mature and produced two sons. Far better than the unfortunate marriages of the Earl of Uxbridge. But I should not bring up such immorality in polite company. I assume you know Uxbridge eloped with the Duke's brother's wife?"

Gideon nodded the affirmative. This put him in a brown study. Wellington had waited until his bride was stricken in years. "That is certainly food for thought," he said and thought about such things on his ride home.

As soon as he departed, Augustus came down and demanded to know what all this had been about.

"Really, dear, you looked so worn when you returned from your walk," Sarah said, "And I had just told Mr. Talbert that you were not well enough for an interview he'd wished to have with you."

At the mention of that dreaded interview, Augustus did look unwell. "Why doesn't he just make Berty his offer and get it over with?"

"To be sure, he thinks it improper to speak to the lady first," Sarah replied, "And I hinted she did not know her own mind."

"Aunt Sarah!" Berty objected, but said no more, for there was some truth in that.

The next day, Berty drove to the Westerly's to confide in Edith. After the revelations about Gideon, Edith shared revelations from Tabitha. "She told me this confidentially, of course, and I am not to tell you," Edith began, "Sir Henry doesn't want her to associate with you."

"What? Why not?

"He has many objections. He says you are a bluestocking, a hoyden, an artist, which he considers particularly unsavory, and you have kept company with a reprobate, referring to Major Trevelyan, of course."

Berty fell into a fit of laughter, "I hope he shares these opinions with Gideon Talbert. I collect my character is beyond redemption. That ancient husband of hers is afraid Tabitha will realize her mistake in marrying such an old fool."

"Indeed, I wonder he allows her to speak with me. He's quite stricken in years, what is he, seven and thirty? And Tabitha our ages. And your Mr. Talbert, he's what four and thirty?" Edith speculated.

"He ain't mine and I'm not making Tabitha's mistake. This is why we must go to Miss Penthwaite. If nothing else, she will introduce us to suitable gentlemen, instead of the Gothic old men we have here".

"I've several little landscapes to take to her. She loves our countryside and will, of course, tell all her friends about my great talents. In fact she already does and has written a very warm reply to my letter regarding the dismals I feel here and inviting us to stay as long as we like. As she put it, the country is beautiful, but opportunities are limited."

The young women spent the rest of the day talking of the entertainments they would enjoy come March, when they went to London.

As Liberty drove back, it began to snow. The hot brick the Westerlies provided to keep her feet warm soon cooled, but she loved the beauty of snow on the gray winter landscape. When she got home, she let Pete take care of Mercury while she ran in for her sketch book to make sketches of snow.

On cold days, Berty didn't work in her studio; it took too much wood to heat it, and she had no commissions. Everyone huddled by their fires. Sarah received a new shipment of books, which she and Berty read. Augustus worked on plans for a proposed stable at a neighboring estate.

In February, letters with blue devil seals ceased to arrive. Neither Berty nor Edith received anything for Valentine's Day, although the

Pendletons held a small party and Mr. Rollings played his violin. They especially admired an air written by Major Trevelyan. Talbert did not attend that party. He was in London.

Chapter 12

Le prender en vie!
The Peninsula War and England
Winter, 1814

February, the army marched, driving Soult back. Due to their cruelties to the French, most of the Spanish soldiers had been sent back to Spain. This created better relations between the British army and French civilians. In this prosperous country, the army ate better, too. Napoleon was losing on all fronts.

The British army needed to cross the River Adour. Wellington and several officers, including Major Trevelyan rode along the banks, studying the river, when a French cavalry vedette appeared. The French charged. While Wellington and the others galloped for safety, Major Trevelyan spun Gunpowder around to attack the first Frenchman to reach him, creating a diversion that gave the others time to escape.

The major slashed his sabre across his opponent's neck releasing a gush of blood as the blade hit the artery. At that moment, the major felt a hit in his thigh like a kick from a horse, followed by searing pain. Having dispatched the Frenchman, the major made his own escape, spinning Gunpowder again and galloping hard away.

"Le Diable Bleu! Le prender en vie!" an officer shouted.

The vedette rode after le Diable Bleu, who preferred not to be taken, dead or alive. He directed Gunpowder toward an eight-foot high stone wall, expertly adjusting Gunpowder's gait to reach the optimal distance to leap. With complete confidence in his rider, Gunpowder powerfully thrust himself over the wall.

The vedette came to a complete halt at the foot of the wall with many bitter imprecations from their officer.

Devil landed in a garden bed, laborers scattering from him. One of them opened a wide gate for the rider. Blue Devil galloped on, back to camp, meeting a patrol sent to save him. Hussars formed a protective escort around him. Blood dripped from his leg, but he sat straight in the saddle and drank all the water in his canteen. When they reached headquarters, Devil weakened and his face blanched.

"By Jove, that was a near thing, Trevelyan. You've been hit!" The general exclaimed and ordered his officer taken to a surgeon.

The Hussars rode on to Major Jurgen's hospital in a large house. Ronan dismounted in the courtyard. Pain shot through his leg when his foot hit the ground. He leaned on the saddle until a soldier helped him into the surgery.

"Defil, vat a surprise! You haf managed to get hit between battles. I haf all the time in de vorld to attend you," Jurgens rattled cheerily.

His assistants removed Devil's equipment, baldric and crimson shako before lifting him onto a heavy oak table. Manfred offered him his personal brandy flask and Ronan obliged by taking several deep drafts. While Manfred removed his own coat, rolled up his sleeves and tied on a blood-stained leather apron, an assistant cut off the right leg of Ronan's overalls.

"Let's see vat ve haf here in dis bloody mess. Bone's not broken, artery isn't hit, dough dere's an uncommon lot of blood. You get to keep your leg, vor now."

After announcing that pleasant news, Jurgens took out forceps. Two strong assistants pushed the patient down on the table and held his shoulders and torso, while a third held his leg. With his patient secured, the surgeon dug into the wound, probing for the bullet. In two minutes, he extracted a lead ball with a piece of cloth from the overalls. Since his patient had not screamed or cursed him, Manfred looked over to see if Devil still breathed. Icy eyes stared back at him.

"You alvays a quiet one, Defil!"

Ronan fainted. Jurgens quickly felt his pulse, found that reassuringly strong and ordered his men to clean up and bandage the wound.

"Ingrate doesn't so much as dank me," Manfred expounded, while taking a sip of brandy.

"Such beauty wasted on a man," an assistant commented on Ronan's remarkable face.

"Not a total vaste; he has at least one beautivul daughter," Jurgens informed the man.

"She must be young," he replied.

Another assistant ragged him with, "No beauty would want you anyway."

In the courtyard, Gunpowder refused to move until Sergeant Duncun, the major's horse master and groom, came to lead him away.

Jurgens installed the major in one of his officers' wards, a small, second floor room with three narrow camp beds, two occupied by seriously wounded men. Manfred sent for Jacob to tend his master.

"He didn't like our company," the surgeon joked, "Most soldiers don't."

Jacob started to unbutton the pelisse Ronan wore, but Jurgens stopped him. An orderly placed three blankets over Ronan, instead.

Manfred turned serious, "He must be kept varm. Our Defil's lost a deal of blood. Ven he comes round, get as much brof, vater and vine in him as you can. Anyting you can pour in him. Dis vound needs to heal vrom de inside out. It is quite deep. De ball almost came out de oder side."

The surgeon checked his other patients. One with an intestinal wound seemed surprisingly better. The other, with a lung wound, seemed likely to die. Both had ceased screaming and moaning, but reeked of blood.

Downstairs a messenger waited from Wellington. Jurgens sent back that the patient lived and kept his leg.

Jacob went out to leave a message for Captain Alexander Trevelyan and to find suitable victuals for his master. An hour later, when Ronan woke, Jacob did as the surgeon told him, poured as much into him as he could take.

"What's this, are you drowning my cousin?" Alexander said, walking in with heavy steps. Captain Ramsey followed.

Jacob let Ronan catch his breath after dosing him with beef broth.

"My God, Ro, you're as pale as moonshine. Is there any blood left in you?"

Jurgens walked in then, saying, "I vondered who de loudmouf vas disturbing my patients."

Alexander apologized, glanced at the other two patients and remarked, "I think that one's beyond disturbing."

Manfred agreed. The man with the intestinal wound had died. Ignoring the corpse, the surgeon chatted on, "De var's ofer vor you, Defil. You can go home and marry."

"That's a dreadful thing to tell a soldier," Vivian objected, "Enough to kill a man. Don't listen to him, Ro. You'll be right and tight in no time and back in the saddle living up to your sobriquet."

"No, he von't. He might play de Defil vid London ladies, but not vor avhile," Jurgens retorted and left, passing Captain Langley. Noticing more of Devil's friends outside, Manfred ordered two soldiers to guard the stairs. He allowed no more visitors and specifically warned his guards against a certain "French baggage."

"As soon as you are issued leave, I shall arrange for you to take the next packet for Hampshire," Alexander decided, "You can do as the doctor ordered, go home to Boscawden and marry Miss Bodleigh. That will take a load of responsibilty off me. The more I think on it, the less I like the idea of getting leg shackled. I'm finally a free man. No father, mother or older brothers dictating to me. Why should I saddle myself with a wife? You can get heirs to the barony as well as I."

Ronan poured the rest of his broth down.

"What's this? Devil marrying?" Denton asked, "He don't look in any shape for that. A deuced good chance to get rid of that French baggage, though."

"I'll take care of her. My French is better than yours, Denton. Can't promise the baggage won't murder anyone when she flies in a passion," Vivian said.

Devil shrugged. He'd not seen Clotilde in weeks.

His friends departed. After an hour or so, two men came for the corpse. By then Alexander had left and come back again with a bottle of port.

"Builds the blood," Alexander claimed, "Upon my word, I'm glad that one's gone. Gut wounds smell rather putrid."

Alexander poured himself and Ronan glasses of port and seeing the lung-wounded man was awake and sitting up, offered him a cup as well.

"My God, I've never seen so much blood from one man in my life. How have you survived, sir?" Alexander inquired of the lung man. In reply, the man coughed up another clot into the blood-filled bucket by his bed.

Alexander, accustomed to his cousin's long silences, found nothing unusual in Ronan's not speaking since his arrival. After a glass of port, Ronan spoke, "Arrange for my horses to follow me."

"Ah, I collect you are going to follow the doctor's advice. Do you wish me to arrange the marriage, too?"

"I'll tend to that," Ronan replied with his usual nonchalance.

Jurgens, hearing this interesting interview, joined them for a glass, stating "Ven one can no longer serve Mars, one must serve Fenus."

"Indeed! I rather thought he managed both quite well," Alexander returned. He departed to allow his cousin repose.

~~~

Vivian marched to Madam Soupert's quarters and found her at home arguing with Artemesia. Broken crockery and feathers littered the floor, where Artemesia had defended herself with a pillow. Even so, her arms were cut.

Vivian shooed Alexander's light o' love out of the room and confronted Clotilde, "Madam, I am to inform you that you shall no longer have the pleasure of Major Trevelyan's company."

Clotilde, still panting from her exercise with Artemesia, asked, "What do you mean?"

"Your Frog compatriots wounded our Devil today and he will be removing to England. However, I have offered to take care of you."

Clotilde's response was too rapid for Vivian to comprehend. She slowed enough for him to make out, "Where is he? I must go to him!"

"No, you are not going to him. He has passed you on to me, n'est pas?"

"No, no, no! I want Devil!"

Clotilde pounced on Vivian, snatching at his uniform and scratching his face, while screaming hysterically. He slapped her hard on the face.

Clotilde paused, touching her stinging cheek.

"Devil never hit you, but I will, you ill-natured trollop. Don't try your tantrums with me! Now get that gown off that I may see my new property!"

~~~

Alexander found his cousin much revived the following day. The lung patient remained, but the third bed was empty. Alexander sat on it. He chatted away about Boscawden and Ronan marrying Miss Bodleigh, to keep him safe from hussies like Clotilde.

"Sweet natured girl, Miss Bodleigh. No tantrums, vapors, die-away airs. Not a spendthrift, nor a flirt, either. Time you got hedged, settled down."

"I say, Ro, while you are in Boscawden, you can run for MP. Represent the family and all that. Old Blander's been in for decades, never does a thing."

"You wish me to do nothing as well?" Ronan asked.

Alexander chuckled. "We could count on you to never make a tiresome speech. But what we need is someone to rid us of the horse tax," Alexander said, "A thing ain't really yours if you have to pay a tax on it."

Ronan agreed, "You are growing perspicacious, dear cousin?"

"What ever that jaw-breaker word means, I shall take it as a compliment," Alexander replied, opening a bottle of wine he'd brought and filling the tin cups by the two beds.

More visitors followed, so many that Major Jurgens asked, "Whose hospital is dis?" He posted guards to deter visitors to Major Trevelyan.

~~~

Jacob washed his master with spirits of wine, dressed him in clean clothes and requested crutches. Ronan hobbled downstairs to a chair. Jurgens promptly excoriated him for getting out of bed without his permission. In the middle of this excoriation, Wellington strode in with his ADCs. Ronan struggled up and was told to sit back down by both Jurgens and Wellington. The Duke pronounced felicity at seeing his officer on the path to recovery, wished him well and soon departed. His ADCs claimed Devil had saved the general's life, but Wellington didn't mention that. In fact, he thought Trevelyan had acted somewhat foolhardy. In any case, Major Trevelyan would be unfit for service for weeks to come and the general granted him extended medical leave.

Like many of the major's exploits, a brief description of the action would be printed in the London Gazette. Miss Bodleigh kept a scrap book of these reports.

Alexander engaged a carriage, arranged for Sergeant Bartholomew Duncan's leave to bring along Ronan's horses and took care of the transport of Ronan's baggage. Duncan obtained extended medical leave due to a persistent ague. Ronan wrote to Mrs. Tarkington and Serafina. In three days, Ronan, Jacob, Duncan, the two horses and baggage were at sea on a fast packet to Portsmouth. Jacob spent the voyage reading fashionable novels he'd purchased from another servant. In the cold, rough Atlantic, Ronan needed assistance to walk on deck. He spent considerable time sleeping. During a calm, he wrote letters to Sir Richard, Tristan, Benjamin, the Reverend Brandolyn and his lawyer cousins. He didn't write to Miss Bodleigh.

The ship arrived in Portsmouth towards the end of February. Sergeant Duncun fretted over Moonshine, the gray Arabian, who had injured a leg when struggling in the slings as he was swung onto the dock. The sergeant stayed in a livery stable to watch the horses while Major Trevelyan took a hotel room. Jacob washed him again in spirits of wine and helped him into his dress uniform.

Reeking like a distillery, the major ordered one of his heavy chests loaded in a cab and rode with it to the bank he used. The dazzling, but lame officer presented himself to the bankers. Impressed with Ronan's appearance and address, if not his smell, they offered him a seat at a huge desk and sent men to lug in the chest and set it on the desk. Ronan unlocked the box and lifted the lid. Accustomed to sea captains depositing prize money, the bankers were usually difficult to impress. They gasped. Ronan's chest contained most of the gold and jewels he had plundered at Vitoria. He watched the bankers inventory coins, gold chains, jewelry and loose gems, then lock it in the vault. Ronan requested they copy the inventory and send it to his London lawyers. He intended to write a new will, among other things. Rather than spend this fortune, he might use it for collateral to invest in Brandolyn Arms or other opportunities. He invested his accumulated pay in consoles.

While Ronan passed time at the bank, Jacob bought necessities; soap, white linen civilian neck cloths, shirts and stockings, all of the finest quality, and brandy. He dickered with the liveryman at a posting inn for a post chase and four to take his master to Boscawden.

"That ill-looking carriage will not do. My master's slap up to the echo and desires your finest vehicle, well-sprung, with your best horses," Jacob informed the man. Then he argued the price was too high and threatened to take his business elsewhere. Jacob went so far as to say his master was the famous Blue Devil and any business would be honored to advertise he had used their services.

The liveryman called him a humbug and a young bottlehead.

Jacob bristled, "Very well, you shall see when I bring my master here."

From the bank, Ronan took the cab to a cane maker. The shop owner selected a sword cane of the right length for a tall man. "Quite dashing for an officer like yourself," he claimed, "Gilt lion's head, ebony stick." He showed how to release the sword. Ronan couldn't move as fast with the cane as with crutches and kept both. He offered to make the major a Malacca cane suited to his height. Ronan accepted the offer.

Sergeant Duncan reported back at the hotel that Moonshine was lame on his off front, but it was a superficial wound. He thought the stallion would be fit to travel in a few days.

"No hurry, Bart, bring them when you are in better force and Moonshine is healed."

The major gave Duncan needed funds and ordered the sergeant join him for supper and sleep in the hotel rather than the stable. Duncan still suffered from ague, but would take better care of the horses than himself if the major didn't order otherwise.

Jacob returned, stating he needed the major to impress upon the liveryman that he was indeed a person of the highest quality. Weary as he was, Major Trevelyan used his cane to limp to the posting house, where he made the expected magnificent impression.

"You are quite right, Jacob, this man asks an exorbitant price for such a wretched vehicle. I shall delay my journey until something better is found," he stated with languid hauteur.

The humbled liveryman informed the major he expected the return of his best chaise the following noon and would charge less seeing as how he was dealing with an officer and a gentleman of the highest honor and renown.

That evening, the major shared lobster and oysters with his servants and retired for the night. Jacob spent the morning running errands for his master, including mailing letters, and tending the major's wound. He cleaned the wound with spirits of wine, again, and carefully bandaged it for the journey. That afternoon, Ronan and Jacob boarded the four horse post chaise for the journey to Boscawden over mucky winter roads.

The major took occasional drafts from one of the brandy bottles Jacob had bought in an attempt to deaden pain from the jolting conveyance. A wiser man would not have traveled with such a wound, but Major Trevelyan was not a man to waste time.

~~~

The Halls' skeleton staff sat down to their evening meal. That staff included Francis Bodleigh, who lacking a wife, dined in the hall; Grimsby, butler; Mrs. Goodyer, housekeeper; Mrs. Findley, assistant housekeeper-both these ladies were spinsters, but referred to as Mrs. out of tradition; Stephen Welspent; Henry, head footman; two other footmen; cook; three cook's helpers; four maids; twenty grooms and four assistant gardeners. Forty retainers at dinner when the place stood unoccupied. The head gardener, coachman and stable master, lived with their wives in cottages and dined in their homes. When the house had been occupied by a large family, forty more servants had worked there, including nurse maids and boot boys. The grooms worked in the Hall's massive horse breeding operation.

That evening, after Grimsby said grace, they dug into mutton, ham, potatoes, cabbage, pickles, bread, butter, cheese and fruit pie, all produced on the estate's home farm. With the conviviality of forty people in the servant's hall, no one heard a post chase drive up in the front of the dark house. Ronan sent Jacob around to the servant's entrance.

After considerable banging, Jacob attracted the attention of the diners. Henry opened the door, ran back to the dining hall and announced, "Major Ronan Trevelyan has arrived!"

By then everyone had finished eating. Steward, butler, historian, housekeepers, cook, footmen, maids, gardeners, grooms walked and ran to the entrance hall where the footmen lit candles, and everyone lined up. Henry opened the door and led the other footmen out to lend assistance. Ronan, in full uniform, dark blue caped greatcoat and red shako lowered himself out of the chaise. He slowly limped to the house with his cane and stepped over the threshold into the blazing candlelight. The servants, including the ones familiar with the major, released an audible exhalation. Haggard and exhausted, the major still carried himself with a dominating air. Henry took Ronan's greatcoat, another footman his shako and gloves. Old retainers remembered the tall major's golden wavy hair, broad shoulders and slender waist. They shuddered at his agonizing limp.

Ronan nodded to the familiar faces. Grimsby immediately inquired if the major had dined. He had not. Cook and her help adjourned to the kitchen to heat up the best of the recent supper. An under footman set a place in the vast dining room at the head of the table. Grimsby escorted Ronan into that room, asked if he wanted wine and fetched port. Mrs. Goodyer sent maids scurrying to prepare the major's chamber with a lighted fire and fresh sheets. "Had I known, I would have aired the chamber!" she said.

Footmen unloaded two scarred campaign chests and carried them to that room. Grooms guided the post riders to the stable. Jacob instructed the footmen where to put the chests and told the maids he would need hot water for the major's bath soon after supper. He then walked to the servant's hall for his own meal. The post riders soon joined him.

Francis Bodleigh stood aside watching this bustle with foreboding. He heartily wished, for the sake of his niece, the major had stayed in the Peninsula, dead or alive. He noticed Major Trevelyan was pale as new writing paper and whatever had happened to his leg was recent.

Seventeen-year old Jacob jabbered away in the servants' hall, showing everyone the bullet. He tried to impress everyone, especially the maids, with tales from the war. Sore and tired from the rough journey, Ronan disappointed cook by, in her experienced estimation, barely eating anything. He consumed a pile of mutton, potatoes and cabbage and a quantity of port, before staggering to his feet.

Henry assisted Ronan up the stairs where Jacob undressed him and helped him into a tub of hot water shallow enough to keep the wounded thigh dry. A good wash and Ronan fell asleep in the tub.

"Soldiers can fall asleep anywhere," Jacob observed.

After Jacob and Henry raised Ronan out, dried him off and laid him on the bed, Jacob changed the wound's dressing. Henry took a good look in order to regale the others about the dreadfulness of the wound, not to mention the collection of savage scars ornamenting Ronan's well proportioned body.

Jacob dashed Henry's hopes of impressing the other servants. While his master slept, Jacob told tales of Le Diable Bleu. Intoxicated with his own voice and the mesmerized audience, Jacob described Diable spurring Gunpowder over a twelve-foot wall, of Diable cutting French throats to escape a dungeon, leading partisans in devastating raids, riding hundreds of miles behind enemy lines. Of his master hunting and dining with the great Wellington. Of beautiful French courtesans, captured treasure, Spanish seductresses and other romantic adventures, real or imagined, involving Diable Bleu. Sometimes, Jacob even told the truth.

When he stopped to extricate more stories from his fertile mind, one of the chamber maids spoke. "Sally, at the tavern, says Major Trevelyan has a wife and five children in Lisbon."

"Bag of moonshine," Jacob replied, "The major has never married. If he has a wife, she's not his."

The grooms chuckled. Mrs. Goodyer gave the maid a warning look, but the maid, new to her position, didn't recognize that glare.

"Sally says Lord Alexander told Molly this last time he visited the Cock and Cat," the maid persisted.

"Well it ain't true," Jacob said.

"Sally ain't humming me. She said Lord Alexander said the major had a quiver of brats by a Lisbon lady. Maybe she just thought she was his wife," the maid continued.

"Enough of this!" Grimsby stood up, "We don't have this kind of vulgar, disrespectful talk about the family."

"Indeed," Mrs. Goodyer agreed and turning to the maid said, "Lina, you are new to your position and must learn we do not gossip about the family."

Francis Bodleigh agreed, but wanted to get to the bottom of the persistent rumors about the major. He could well believe Lord Alexander told some draggletail this. Alexander drank and frequented disreputable tavern maids. When Jacob left to return to Ronan's chamber, Francis stopped him in a quiet passage.

"What's the truth about your master?"

"I don't talk about master's mistresses," Jacob replied and continued to the stairs.

Francis caught up, "He has mistresses, then?"

"All officers have mistresses," Jacob exaggerated, "The major don't have no truck with common trulls."

"Then these mistresses have children by him?" Francis persevered.

"I said I don't talk about that. You want to know about that, you have to ask him."

Jacob ran upstairs and into his master's chamber.

"Damned busybody! Why can't these yokels mind their own bread and butter?" Jacob muttered, then turned to his sleeping master. "Burnt to the socket. Not recovering like he should." Jacob returned to the adjoining dressing room, stripped to his shirt, washed and crawled into the trundle bed with a pistol by its side, a habit from the war. Even in a safe country house, he slept near his master rather than in the servant's quarters.

Morning, Ronan slept long after dawn, while the household waited for his awakening. The servants breakfasted. After their breakfast, the post boys left with the rented post chaise.

When Ronan first shifted in the bed, Jacob told Henry, waiting outside the door, to send hot water. By the time the hot water arrived, Ronan sat by the dressing room fire in clean shirt and gray cavalry overalls in need of cleaning. Jacob had not had the opportunity to clean Ronan's uniforms or have laundry done. The major looked refreshed and recuperated from the ordeal of traveling.

Henry presented a glass of milk and egg on a silver tray. Ronan drank it gratefully. "Good of Cook to remember. Give her my deepest regards," he told Henry.

Henry inquired when the major wanted breakfast and left.

"You need a haircut, sir," Jacob told him for the third morning.

"How do you know these things? Is there a law, with which I am unfamiliar, dictating hair length?" Ronan asked.

"I hate it when you wax philosophical, sir. You know that I keep up with fashion for you."

"You know I don't care a straw for fashion," Ronan responded.

"That's why I take care of it for you. Now take these coats left here over two years ago. They are not the latest cut, but I daresay you think them quite the thing." Jacob held up a silver gray cutaway coat, releasing a whiff of lavender.

"Appears to be a fine coat," Ronan said.

"Yes, but out of fashion. However, you have no new ones. Do you wish to wear your uniform or this outmoded coat?"

Ronan chose the coat, passed on the haircut. Out of pure obstinacy, Jacob decided. He shaved his master, trimmed mustache and side whiskers, fluffed the over-grown hair as best he could, dabbed hyacinth scent on Ronan's neck and tied on a white neck cloth. Jacob chose a plain white waistcoat over the embroidered one, which he considered better suited to afternoon and evening.

Ronan struggled downstairs gripping the railing. The pain in his leg had not abated and seemed worse despite the bleeding having stopped. Ronan's mind was preoccupied with other matters, and Jacob was more concerned with turning out his master to perfection, than the condition of the wound. The major addressed Grimsby, "Please tell Barnstable I shall need a vehicle and driver this morning."

Grimsby nodded and passed on the message.

Ronan found the table laid with enough food for a company of Hussars. He thought he acquitted himself well, devouring several eggs and a little bacon, but when the footmen returned most of the food uneaten, Cook declared the major off his feed. At twenty-seven and no longer a growing boy, Ronan could not meet her expectations. He was off his feed.

While Ronan breakfasted, Francis Bodleigh rode to the Cock and Cat to interview Molly. He found the poor drab still abed after an evening serving Boscawden's bachelors with more than ale. After considerable grumbling, she pulled on a dress and came out to speak to Francis in the empty back parlor. Yes, Lord Alexander had confided, when in his cups, that his cousin Ronan had a mistress in Lisbon and a litter of brats by her. When asked how many, she replied, "I don't recollect. Never was good with figures. Seems to me it were five, but could have been two. Lord Alexander spoke like the woman was some great lady, but you can't believe anything he says when he's top heavy. Ain't nothing to us what his cousin does."

Francis rode back to the Hall with the figures five and two tumbling in his head. Then there was the brat Ronan had sent to his godfather. And the rakehell had the nerve to dangle after Francis' niece!

~~~

Augustus sent Liberty to the Hall that morning to deliver a list of good craftsmen that Francis wanted for repairs on some of the tenant cottages. Berty planned to walk about the garden while at the Hall. She would like to have read in the library, but knew none of the fires were lit in the absence of occupants and the day was brisk. She mounted Rose, who had recovered from her injury, and rode through the park to the stables, where she turned Rose out in a paddock.

Berty knocked on her uncle's door, but he wasn't in. She walked back to the stables and talked to Barnstable. Barnstable cued his grooms to keep quiet about the major's arrival. He relished the romantic idea of surprising Berty with the major. He didn't know where Francis was, but suggested she wait in the library. Dreading the frigid library, Berty hung about the stables for a while, watching the stable boys scrubbing Jame's yellow curricle. "What are you doing with the curricle?" she asked Barnstable.

Barnstable confidently expected the major had intended to take it to the Bodleigh's to pay his addresses to Berty. The stableman sent a groom to tell Grimsby she was at the stable. He replied, "We have to keep the horses in training against Lord Alexander's return."

"Lord Alexander drives?"

"He's sure to take it up when he returns. Probably want to drive around those London parks, you know. Otherwise, there's always a good market for a fast team."

Berty accepted this and wandered into the Hall to the library. She was surprised to find the fire lit and burning voraciously. She unpinned her veiled hat. Berty had taken to wearing the veil down due to the appearance of more freckles across her nose, which reminded her of childhood teasing. Liberty considered herself an old maid, but she didn't care to be an ugly one. Having laid the hat aside, Berty took off her cloak and gloves and looked around for an interesting book.

Ronan returned from his chamber, having brushed his teeth, taken a swig of fortifying brandy, pulled his gloves on and taken up his cane. He awaited a footman to hand him his greatcoat and hat. None were forthcoming. Grimsby, Henry and other staff stood idle. The major glanced round them in his usual stolid way, waiting for service that they didn't appear about to give.

"Is my conveyance ready?" he asked.

"Barnstable says you don't need it," Henry volunteered, restraining the urge to smile.

Ronan stared at him, waiting for an explanation. He was accustomed to having his orders obeyed. "Do servants not obey orders anymore?" he quietly inquired. Everyone stood stone-faced without answering. Ronan turned his daunting eyes on Grimsby. A maid giggled nervously. Grimsby slowly smiled, "She's in the library, sir."

Ronan smiled, turned towards the library and hobbled to the door. Henry quickly opened it and Ronan limped in.

Liberty, standing by a table, looked up from a book she held and dropped it on the table. "Ronan!"

He moved to her as fast as he could.

"You're hurt!" she cried, running around the table.

Ronan reached Liberty, picked up her cold hand and kissed it. He stood holding her hand, gazing at her. Berty looked fondly into his eyes, and smiled, a winsome smile that entranced him more than ever. Liberty realized no other man would ever interest her. The major took the shine out of all of them.

Ronan felt he could pick up where he left off two years ago. To him, nothing had changed. He started to put his left arm around her, when the door opened. Reflexively spinning round, Ronan put his weight on his right leg. Pain staggered him. He caught at his cane and the table, managed to stay upright, but accidentally released the sword. Ronan stood holding the bare rapier.

Francis Bodleigh stopped dead. Henry walked up to Ronan, saying, "Sorry, sir. Mr. Bodleigh rushed past me before I could knock. I see your cane's come apart." Henry helped Ronan onto a couch by the fire. Ronan sat down with his legs stretched out and his arms draped across the back in what Francis considered a rag mannered, arrogant fashion. Major Trevelyan behaved as if he owned the world. Francis thought the major took up too much space in it.

"Drat it, Uncle Francis, is that any way to enter a room?" Berty castigated him.

"Is that any way to speak to your uncle?" Francis shot back, "What's wrong with the staff? Letting him in here with you when you lack a chaperon!"

"A chaperon at my age, Uncle Francis? I'm an old maid of one and twenty, not a chit out of the school room! And do you not know the major is injured?"

Ronan listened with amusement, while raising and lowering his sword. Henry, finding the bare sword discomforting, offered to return it to its cane. Ronan allowed that and accepted Henry's offer of an ottoman for his injured leg. Meanwhile, his eyes never left Berty. She was more beautiful than he remembered, even with her hair in a messy braid. Her tight, old-fashioned riding habit displayed her rounded bosom and slender waist. The voluminous skirt and petticoat hid her shapely derrière. Ronan had seen enough nude women to imagined her without the habit. He never thought of her physically when writing to her, but now her nubile figure delighted him. Something about the disconcerting way he was looking at her distracted niece and uncle from their disagreement. They paused, he shrugged, and they resumed their conversation.

"Uncle Augustus, who would never surprise a military man by barging in without knocking, sent me with the list you requested. I collect you intend to replace thatch with tiles on some of the cottages. Uncle Augustus recommends this tile setter." She continued explaining the list and inserting captious comments. "Uncle Augustus says it's about time you made some improvements to those cottages."

"Does he? He should mind his own bread and butter. Now that my lord owns the Kentish estate and is away where he can't spend excessively, I can use Boscawden's income on Boscawden. One can't do that when supporting an expensive family." Francis gave an opprobrious sideways glance at Ronan, although Francis well knew the major had never cost his uncle a cent, unless one included Alexander's gambling debts to his cousin.

"I assume you will be leaving now, dear niece?"

"You assume wrong, dear uncle. I intend to stay. And pray, why didn't you inform Aunt Sarah and I that Major Trevelyan was here?" Berty asked in vexation.

"He arrived last night! And why should I tell you anything? If you are staying, I'll send for Mrs. Goodyer, she has little enough to do these days."

Henry sent another footman to fetch Mrs. Goodyer.

Francis sat down on the opposite end of Berty's sofa. He absolutely was not leaving her alone with this rakehell.

"Miss Westerly and I drove to some of those cottages a few weeks ago," Berty said.

"Why on earth would you do that?" her uncle asked.

"One Jim Jams threw mud at us. Hit Edith in the face! She was quite wroth and we were going after him, but we couldn't pass through a brier thicket," Berty enlightened.

"Are you both hen-witted! What did you expect to do with that strapping bastard?"

"Uncle, such language! And if anyone is strapping, Edith is, a full five feet, nine, and we had the buggy whip."

"A lot of good that would do," Francis sneered.

"Who is Jim Jams?" Ronan asked softly.

"One of your cousin James' by blows. He should be enlisted in the army," Francis declared.

"Lord Alexander says, in our family, second sons and natural children are only fit to be shot at," Ronan commented dryly.

"What an odious thing for Alexander to say, even in jest!" Liberty objected, "Is that what happened to your leg; it was shot?"

"Yes, it's nothing. I'm fortunate."

"I suppose there are worse things, but I wouldn't call it fortunate. What will happen now? Is not the war near an end?" Liberty asked.

"Yes, the Corsican Ogre can't go on much longer. I don't know what the powers will do with him. Napoleon is a better leader and administrator than the Bourbons, but a strong France is not in our interest. He is not to be trusted."

"Certainly not! But I meant what will happen with you and your regiment?"

"My regiment will probably be sent to Ireland. I shall remain here on half pay, until Wellington finds a use for me," Ronan said quietly.

"He seems to have found uses for you a plenty! We read about you in the Gazette." Berty remarked.

Henry ushered in Mrs. Goodyer with her sewing basket. She bowed to the major, who rose on his good leg until Mrs. Goodyer seated herself by a window. Unnecessary for a gentleman to rise for a mere house-keeper, Francis thought.

"I think Mrs. Findley can handle the house while I stay here and catch up on my mending," she said.

"I should think so. That's what she was hired to do!" Francis snapped, "But she can't manage my work; so I must be going. Do not over-stay, Berty. Frankly I think it improper for you to stay at all."

"The major and I have not seen each other in over two years. We have much to talk about," Berty retorted.

Francis considered the major's conversation less than scintillating and departed after a slight bow to the major.

"I thought he would never leave," Liberty said, "I can see why Uncle Augustus and he are always at points. Uncle Francis is so Gothic. If he would remarry, he wouldn't be so spleenish."

Ronan asked, "Do you think marriage would improve his humor?"

"Maybe not, it might only make some woman miserable! Do you think marriage makes men happier?"

"It depends on the woman. Do you think marriage would make an old maid like yourself happier?"

"How dare you call me an old maid!" Berty objected, good naturedly.

"You called yourself one."

"Only out of vexation with my uncle, who would vex anyone! At the moment I couldn't be happier!"

"Nor I. We shouldn't do anything to risk such bliss, should we?" Ronan asked.

"Certainly not. What do you think would do that?" Berty seemed to have forgotten the subject of marriage. Then she recalled his leg. "I should think you would be happier if your leg was healed."

"At the moment, I'm not thinking of it."

Berty noticed that Mrs. Goodyer had fallen to sleep.

"Poor old dear still gets up before dawn to supervise the household," Liberty commented, getting up and joining Ronan on the other sofa. He smiled, picked up her chilly hand and held it to his lips. She felt a light kiss and his moustaches tickled her hand. Ronan put his right arm around Berty and drew her closer. He smelled her damp, woodsy hair, nuzzled her neck and kissed her deeply. He forgot his leg. He forgot everything. Until she drew away and held his hands. Her hands were still cold and Ronan held them in his hot palms.

She'd drawn away from his kiss, Ronan realized. He'd kissed her passionately two years ago and she hadn't minded. In two years, she'd perhaps forgotten and grown unaccustomed to such attentions. The major decided he would need to mind his manners until this inexperienced woman got used to him again. Miss Bodleigh wasn't a soldier's mistress. Although an American peasant, she'd been brought up a lady. She was a blue stocking, not the kind of woman he was accustomed to.

Major Trevelyan dominated women, horses and most men. He expected to be lord and master over a wife when he acquired one. His friends had long encouraged him to find an heiress and take control of her money. Now he considered getting leg shackled to a waif of a woman with no fortune and of a disposition unlikely to be easily ruled. And now this prim female had refused his kiss!

Liberty looked down at his hot hands holding hers. Then up at his eyes and saw a kind of longing. She realized she'd pulled away from his bold kiss. "I tasted spirits," Berty said by way of explanation, "I can't abide the taste of spirits. I suppose you are taking them to ease pain."

Ronan nodded. He'd not realized Berty held the mere taste of alcohol in violent dislike. She could not be more unlike Clotilde! Or any of his mistresses.

Berty, eager to show her affection, drew one hand out of Ronan's grasp to stroke his side whiskers and mustache, a novelty to her. She liked the contrast between smooth shaved skin and whiskers. While playing with his unruly hair, she noticed the livid scar into his scalp. The hair grew white there. Liberty remembered the head injury. There was no point in mentioning it. Ronan would say it was nothing. He gave her the license to do anything she wished. Berty's wishes were mild. She contented herself in touching his face, holding his hand, looking, listening and smelling. His coat was redolent of lavender. His body smelled of soap and medicinal herbs. She caught a whiff of hyacinth near Ronan's neck cloth and a faintly rancid odor emanated from unwashed overalls.

Berty admired his gold seal ring of a dancing devil.

"Your seal should be an angel," he remarked.

"Oh, no, you quite misjudge me. I'm always saying and doing naughty things. I was most trying to Uncle Francis just now. But he is so archaic in his ideas."

"As am I, for I'm in agreement with him," Ronan confessed.

"Say it isn't so! Surely you don't think I need a chaperon at my age," Berty objected.

In reply, Ronan kissed her, again, taking her breath away. When she pushed away from him, Berty asked, "If you thought my staying would do irreparable damage to my pristine reputation, why didn't you say so?"

"That was not in my interest!"

Berty laughed. "Oh, you selfish creature!"

She suddenly felt the library was too hot and asked Ronan if he could walk in the garden. He said he'd like that and called Henry to help him with the many steps. They walked out on the long terrace that gave a view of the gardens. Henry helped Ronan descend the steps to the central walk. The major offered Berty his left arm. She strolled and he limped past the inactive fountain and on to the next set of steps. Berty decided the steps to the grotto would be too challenging for her friend and guided him to the orangery instead. No gardener worked there. Henry opened and closed doors for them and stood aside.

The scent of orange and lemon blossoms filled the warm, damp air. Ronan reached into an orange tree and picked one ripe fruit. They sat on a stone bench. Ronan pulled his sheaved stiletto from somewhere and incised lines up and down the orange, as he'd done two years ago. He lifted off the peel, separated the wedges, bit out the seeds in one and held the wedge to Berty's mouth. She giggled and ate it. They shared the rest of the orange.

Admiring the many marbles that had been brought into the orangery to protect them from frost, Berty mentioned, "Welspent says your great grandfather brought these statues from Italy and this garden is an Italian style garden. I should like to see Italy."

"Yes, it must be beautiful. We should see it together, when Napoleon is gone," Ronan said.

Berty waited for more. Henry, standing at a distance, also expected more. Ronan disappointed them. He merely gazed at Berty in his inscrutable way. She took the initiative.

"How would we see it together?"

"We would pass through the Alps," Ronan replied, innocently.

Berty, puzzled and a little annoyed, asked with surprising boldness, "Would you be offering me carte blanche?"

"Pardon? No, you mistake me. I spoke theoretically," he replied, unperturbed.

"Oh, I discomposed myself," Berty said, feeling herself flush.

"Would you accept such an offer?" he asked.

"Certainly not! Of all things to ask!" Liberty grew heated.

Ronan shrugged at the mutable nature of females.

"I believe you are a flirt!" Berty blurted out.

"Much worse," he admitted.

"Is uncle correct in believing you the worse beast of nature?" Berty asked out of vexation.

"No, I have not murdered babies or raped nuns."

"Well, that's a relief!" Berty retorted and began to giggle, "You are quite shocking, Ronan.! I don't know what to do with you."

"I could suggest something."

Still giggling, Berty adjured him not to. She began to think she had stayed too long. Was it noon? She didn't know. The sundial in the terrace didn't work on such a cloudy day. Yet, she didn't want to leave him after their long separation. "I should go. I'm sure Aunt Sarah wonders why I haven't returned."

"I suspect your uncle has told her," Ronan said.

"Uncle Francis? He said he had work to do. I'm sure she will wonder if I'm not home for dinner."

"Please, stay," Ronan said.

"But Aunt Sarah and Uncle Augustus will worry."

"Send them a note."

~~~

While the two basked in each other's company, Francis Bodleigh rode to his brother's house to announce Major Trevelyan's unwelcome arrival.

"You left Berty with him?" Sarah asked.

"She refused to leave and he's a devil of temptation," Francis declared, "I left Mrs. Goodyer with them."

"Most improper, even with Mrs. Goodyer. I shall drive there," Sarah said.

Augustus listened with concern. "Berty doesn't think of appearances and the possibility of ruining her chances with a decent man."

"He's so much above her and loose in the haft. There can be no good end to this," Francis said.

"You said Sarah was above me, brother, yet we wed," Augustus reminded Francis.

"Not comparable. Berty acts like a hoyden and is just the sort someone like Ronan Trevelyan would take advantage of. I have verified talk I heard in the Hall last night. He has at least one mistress in Lisbon and bastards."

"More children!" Sarah exclaimed.

"Good heavens," Augustus said, "Besides the one in Burlington?"

"Yes, between two and five and this is from Lord Alexander, who confided it to a girl of loose character. And I'm sure he hasn't told Liberty. He tells so little. What can those two do when he has no conversation?"

"I must relieve Mrs. Goodyer and rescue Berty," Sarah decided. "Thank you, Francis. I know it is not pleasant having to deliver bad news. I'm sure if Berty knew more of Ronan's character, she would not have stayed."

Sarah excused herself and walked upstairs to her chamber to change into her best gown for visiting. She and Berty had not had new gowns since Augustus took ill, but Sarah already had many fine gowns and updated them with her expert stitchery. As she slipped on a gown of heavy amber silk, Augustus joined her. "Do you wish me to join you, my dear?"

"I think not. You are still weak from your illness. This is a situation that calls for delicacy, not just with Berty, but in handling that, that person she is with. I never dreamed of such a situation."

Sarah sat down at her dressing table and rearranged her sloppy hair. Augustus wondered why such effort for this confrontation, if such it was. He never quite understood Sarah. Augustus saw that as the cost of marrying a lady of quality. He stepped back downstairs and told Pete to hitch Mercury. Then he told Betty that Sarah and Berty might not be home for dinner, but he and his brother would dine.

Sarah stepped out dressed as fine as any local lady. She tied on her good feathered bonnet and a fur lined pelisse. Augustus noticed she wore her pearls. "You look lovely, my darling!"

She thanked him and Francis murmured something about her going to a soirée.

Sarah arrived as Ronan and Berty sat down for afternoon dinner in the vast dining hall. Ronan rose when Grimsby announced her. He bowed, Sarah curtsied.

"Dear Cousin Sarah, please join us. Did you not get Miss Bodleigh's message?" the major asked.

"I passed the messenger as I drove here. How thoughtless of me to not think of the time. Thank you, I will join you. How kind of you to invite Liberty for dinner," she remarked, thinking it was anything but kind to Berty's reputation. Now Sarah made it right. No one could take exception to a cousinly visit after a long absence. She noticed Ronan's valet had turned him out immaculately, while Berty wore her old shabby, soiled riding habit. Her messy hair and tawdry dress made her look inferior in every way to Major Trevelyan. Berty's careless manners added to the disparity. Could anyone be blamed for expecting him to take her for a mistress rather than a wife?

A footman set another cover on Ronan's left. Cook had concocted a rich repast, but only Liberty, with her healthy appetite, did it justice. Sarah was watching her figure, but wondered at the major's feeble appetite. From his pale, worn look, she realized he was ill. They moved on to the library, where Sarah noticed his painful limp and inquired the nature of his injury.

Gentlemen avoided mentioning details of war to ladies. He repeated it was a mere bullet wound.

"Mere? And Francis never mentioned it!" Sarah said.

So, Berty thought, Uncle Francis had gone rattling to her relatives.

Except for sprawling on the sofa, the major exhibited the example of proper manners. No risqué remarks spiced his speech, nor did he touch Liberty. Yet he exhibited a vivacity they had seldom seen in him. Sarah credited his new-found charm to maturity and being about in the world. Berty suspected it was an act to gain favor with Sarah, who'd never disliked him until gossip mongers had spread word of natural children and duels.

The afternoon passed quickly. After a suitable elapse of time, Sarah announced it was time for her and Berty to depart. Ronan sent a footman to the stables for Mercury and Rose.

"Mercury will have to be put to the gig. I don't like to leave him in harness when I have a long visit," Sarah said, taking her time putting on her pelisse and bonnet.

Berty put on her hat and cloak and Ronan escorted them to the entrance. Grooms brought up the horses and Ronan kissed Sarah's fingers, and not Liberty's, a sure sign he was cognizant of his manners. Henry handed Sarah into her gig and Berty mounted without help. Had he been able, Ronan would have given her a lift up.

When the ladies departed, Ronan started to hobble to the stables. "Your hat and greatcoat, Sir?" Henry asked. Ronan declined them. Henry followed in case he stumbled. The major found Barnstable in the main stable.

"My groom will bring my stallions in a few days. They require rest," Ronan told him.

"Yes, sir. And one of them is Gunpowder, sir?"

"Yes, like me he is temporarily leaving the service of Mars, to pursue Venus."

Barnstable laughed. "He will be in time for breeding season, sir. Glad to have him!"

They progressed past the stalls. Gunpowder's grand sire, Cannonball, lay in one box stall. He struggled up to put his head over the door for Barnstable.

"He's foundered," Ronan observed.

"Yes, poor old thing. Lame on all four. Can no longer service the mares. I shall have the farrier do him in eventually."

"Why wait?"

"I'm afraid I've made a pet of him. I started out as his groom, you know, and he always followed me like a puppy. He's suffering, though. I need to take heart and get the matter settled."

Ronan sent a groom for his pistols. Barnstable saw that Ronan intended to settle the matter. The stable master put a halter on Cannonball and led him out. The old sire slowly stumbled and limped to the closest paddock. Grooms and stable boys followed with shovels. "One's as lame as the other," one commented on seeing the major limp alongside Cannonball.

"Let me say good bye," Barnstable said, giving the stallion a last rub, before stepping aside. Ronan raised the pistol, aimed between the horse's eyes and ears, and fired. Cannonball dropped dead.

"Thank you, sir," Barnstable said as they traveled back, "I hate killing them."

"We killed 400 at Corruna. No worse than killing a man," Ronan remarked.

"So many, what a tragedy! Why?"

"To keep them from the French."

Barnstable shook his head. At the stable, he brought out a promising young bay, one of Cannonball's last get. Ronan studied him appreciatively. When he stood in front of the animal, it stretched its nose to him. The major kissed it. When Barnstable told him the colt hadn't been backed, Ronan said, "He is mine. I shall be first to back him."

"I thought his lordship might want him, sir."

"He is mine. Lord Alexander will give him to me."

"Or you can win him at cards, I suppose," Barnstable remarked.

"Lord Alexander will give him to me out of his love for me," Ronan responded with assurance.

"Yes, sir! How does his lordship get on in the army?"

"Well enough."

"No promotion?"

"Unlikely."

"I see. We rather thought you were the leader of the two of you. A major without buying in and only seven and twenty! You've done us proud, sir."

"Thank you, Barnstable, but never forget, Alexander is a real lord; I'm only a Lord of Misrule."

Barnstable laughed, "Indeed, Blue Devil!"

Blue Devil hung about the stables and paddocks until supper, a light repast, for poor Cook had given up on feeding him like a battalion. Ronan ate his bit of chicken and drank sherry. He asked Grimsby to thank Cook for her delightful meals. She would have preferred a better display of appetite.

"Would you like your port now, sir?" Grimsby asked.

"Brandy, please," Ronan said.

After one glass, he hobbled into the great hall with another. Henry asked if they should light a fire in that frigid room. Ronan commented, "Wouldn't make the least difference would it?"

"No, sir. The Hall's too big to heat," Henry admitted.

Ronan stood drinking his wine and studying the painting of Lord Victor, his grandfather. He drained his glass and threw it at the portrait. Broken glass crashed around it. The footmen looked at each other.

"Henry, remove this picture," Ronan ordered.

"I'll ask Grimsby, sir."

"You'll remove it, now."

From his tone, Henry felt he'd better obey. Grimsby walked in on three footmen carrying the portrait away. "What's this?"

"The major told us to move it."

Grimsby stood thunderstruck. When recovered, he asked, "Where do you want it moved, sir?"

"Any place I won't see it. Bring out that picture Miss Bodleigh did of Lord Alexander."

The footmen took away the offending portrait of Lord Victor and replaced it with Alexander's. Ronan stood admiring it a while before staggering up to bed. The servants, used to the eccentricities of the Quality, found nothing unusual in his wanting the picture replaced. After all, Lord Victor had disowned Ronan's father. They conjectured that the major's wound had affected his appetite and his previous strong head for drink. Jacob verified this theory with, "He ain't been himself."

Chapter 13

Boscawden, 1814

Liberty met Sarah in the parlor after their return. Augustus sat in his chair with Corky at his feet, but appeared uncomfortable.

"Major Trevelyan conducted himself as a complete gentleman of the highest breeding. I find his conversation vastly improved," Sarah began her oration, "I daresay, that doesn't change his opprobrious reputation. Although his conduct may have improved since he earned that repute."

Augustus digested this elevated talk and said, "You mean you no longer believe he is a squire of dames?"

"I don't know what he is, other than well bred. It doesn't change the existence of mistresses and children."

"Mistresses and children?" Berty asked.

"Francis heard the servants talk and looked into it. Lord Alexander told a tavern maid that the major had mistresses in the Peninsula and at least two children, perhaps five," Sarah quietly informed her.

"Five! Besides the one in Burlington?" Berty exclaimed, "Two to six children! That's outside of enough!"

"Precisely," Sarah agreed, sadly, "I wish we had known sooner. Now Ronan conducts himself as if you were in his pocket. I'm afraid, for all his correct manners, he's not to be trusted."

"I'm not in anyone's pocket!" Berty replied indignantly, feeling her face burn. Despair enveloped her.

"I should think not and we must make sure it does not seem so," Sarah said, "Major Trevelyan is an interesting cousin, that is all. Anything else, well, it doesn't bear thinking of."

"Yes," Berty muttered.

She put on an air of quiet contentment through tea and supper, although she didn't feel it. Berty hid her violent emotions from her family, careful not to upset Augustus and cause a relapse of his illness. She excused herself early, washed and went to bed.

There she released her pent-up emotions in tears. When she ran out of tears, Berty wrote her thoughts and feelings in a little notebook. She felt betrayed, as if Ronan had played false with her, but she knew they had made no vows. They had no understanding between them and were free to do as they pleased. A feeling of injustice persisted. He would have nothing to do with her if she had had several base-born children. And why did he not share everything with her like true friends? She accepted that men had their bits of muslin, but to be so secretive and then there were children. That indicated a deeper relationship than a fleeting encounter with a light-skirt.

Liberty also wondered if the major was seducing her. She had no experience of seduction other than Ronan's amorous dalliance. Now she felt ill-used. Ronan promised to visit in the morning. She would express her displeasure. Berty thought and wrote and finally fell asleep.

~~~

Morning at the Hall. Jacob washed his master and wrapped a protective bandage around the wound, although it did not bleed. It was swollen and inflamed. The major flinched when Jacob tied the bandage. Their eyes met. Jacob dared to ask, "Should I send for a surgeon?"

"Not yet.

Jacob dressed his master to Jacob's usual exacting standards, having had the laundry done and coats aired. Again Ronan refused a hair cut.

Again Cook complained that the major picked at his food. At the appointed time, a young apprentice coachman, Joshua, arrived at the entrance in a yellow curricle pulled by two flashy matched chestnut thoroughbreds. The major, dressed in silver-gray coat and gray trousers, pulled himself on board. He didn't need a greatcoat on that balmy morning.

Joshua handed Ronan the reins and started to step off when Ronan grabbed him and pulled him back. "I was going to stand in the back, sir," Joshua explained what a groom was expected to do, forgetting Barnstable's instructions not to speak unless spoken to.

"I've never driven," Ronan informed him.

"Never driven, sir?" Joshua thought all gentlemen drove.

"I've been a cavalryman eight years."

"Sorry, sir, didn't know."

The chestnuts fidgeted. Joshua showed Ronan how to hold the "ribbons" and the whip.

"They have soft mouths and know voice commands. Tell them to walk on and if you want them to move faster, just flick the whip lightly. No need to touch them, they have plenty of spring."

They soon bowled along at a strong trot, that developed into a gallop, that ended in the horses bolting. Ronan, having no desire to control them, let the reins go slack and laughed. His air of levity led Joshua to believe the major mad.

"Sir, we'll overturn!"

A woodcutter approached with a shire horse pulling a cartload of firewood. Seeing the runaway's charging in his direction, the man drove his shire on to the raised verge of the road where his cart tilted and much wood fell out.

Joshua took the reins from Ronan and gradually regained control of the team. Ronan smiled at the lark they had had. "Turn back, I must apologized to that woodcutter."

Joshua did so. When they approached, the woodcutter tugged his forelock.

"Please don't do that," Ronan said and apologized for causing the man trouble. To the man's astonishment, Ronan tossed him a shilling. Joshua drove on, thinking the major a gentleman complete to a shade, although he'd never trust him with the ribbons again.

Liberty pondered indecisively between her old garnet wool and her primrose cotton gowns, finally deciding the primrose yellow was more cheerful. She needed cheering. Peggy helped pin up her hair and claimed Berty was fit to present to the queen. Berty laughed. She and Sarah had mended and remodeled that gown numerous times. The fabric was so worn from washing, it was only suitable for covering the petticoats that kept Berty warm.

Corky gave Augustus an excuse to take a walk at the appointed time. A feeling of foreboding permeated the house. He sought escape from whatever unpleasantness this interview with Sarah's libertine cousin would produce.

Sarah and Berty waited nervously in the parlor. Berty could not resist the urge to go to the door when she heard the curricle. Someone had to go to the door, it might as well be herself.

Ronan struggled down from the rig and limped to the door with his cane. Liberty opened it and as usual, she felt her heart pound when she first saw him, but she didn't smile. He put his hat and gloves on the table, kissed Berty's cold fingers and limped into the parlor. Ronan bowed to Sarah and kissed her fingers before sitting on the sofa next to Berty.

Feeling blithe himself, he found the Bodleighs funereal and waited for them to speak. Sarah mentioned the fine weather for that time of year. An awkward silence ensued.

The things Liberty had thought of saying the previous night, seemed wrong in the light of day. Sarah, too, was tongue-tied. Ronan turned to Berty with his disconcerting gaze.

Finally Berty asked, "Ronan, if I had a child without marrying, would you still address me?"

"That's not in your character," he replied, wondering at the inspiration for such a question.

"Are you sure? Perhaps I believe in free love. Would you care for me in those circumstances?"

He asked himself, had she secretly had a child, but replied, "I don't apprehend," with his usual composure.

Berty sighed. "Do you have a child staying with the Burlingtons?" she asked.

The ardor that had until then illuminated his face, faded, and a coldness descended on him.

"Why do you ask?"

"Why don't you answer?"

"It's impertinent," he replied, insolently.

"I beg to differ," Berty retorted, witheringly, "I'm told you have," she paused; a suitable word escaped her, "concubines and children in the Peninsula."

"Concubines, how Biblical!" he replied with satirical glee.

Berty unintentionally smiled.

"How many concubines am I supposed to have? A dozen? A hundred; pray, make it a hundred!"

"Unsupportable," Sarah interpolated, "Have the goodness to be serious, sir!"

He sat back in sultry silence.

"Oh, this won't answer," Berty said softly, "I'm sure if I had lovers and children, you would have nothing to do with me. I don't understand how you can treat this matter so lightly. Why can't you be forthcoming? Are we not friends?"

"Men and women aren't the same. Even a missish spinster should know that," he replied too harshly.

Missish spinster grated. Tears welled in Berty's eyes. She took a handkerchief out of her sleeve to dab at them, but her emotions got the better of her and tears flowed even stronger.

"Compose yourself," Ronan commanded.

"I'm not yours to be bidden. To hear these things about you from others. That strangers know more of you than I do. Conduct that is an outrage to every feeling. I don't know what you are about. Was I to be another of your conquests?" She spoke between sobs.

"You misapprehend me, but I see there is no reasoning with a maiden of such frail sensibilities."

Liberty rose up and ran out of the room.

Sarah, usually the most good-natured of people, was incensed. Restraining her anger, she said, "I collect you have libertine proclivities and you have revealed a hard heart. Perhaps that was inevitable in the war. I find your conduct towards my niece unpardonable, sir."

Ronan rose and bowed. "Good day, ma'am," he spoke icily.

He limped into the passage where Berty had tried to compose herself. She turned away, hiding her tear-stained face. Ronan threw something on the floor behind her that clinked and rolled. Then he limped out the door.

Joshua had been walking the horses and came to a stop for Ronan to pull himself into the curricle.

"The Hall. Spring them," Ronan ordered and Josiah obeyed.

After the door closed, Berty looked at the floor and saw a ring with a red stone. She picked it up and found it fitted her finger. Sarah walked in then.

"What have I done, Aunt?"

Sarah held Berty while she released a torrent of sobs. "You've done nothing, dear, nothing wrong at all. His kind don't marry to please themselves, but for money. So he flirts. And takes mistresses. And plays with the feelings of decent young ladies. I'm afraid he's a hardened reprobate."

"No, I don't believe it," Berty protested.

"That ring, an ersatz gift to tempt you. You should return it."

"No!" Berty shouted and ran upstairs.

Having seen the curricle leave, Augustus thought it safe to return to his home. He found his spouse angrier than he'd ever seen her and his niece shut in her room.

"I should have stayed," he said.

"I don't think so. I believe you would have been driven to challenge him. I could shoot him myself!" Sarah said.

"Sarah! I've never heard you speak so. Upon my soul this is not like you!"

He placed her in her favorite chair, found her cat and sat the cat in Sarah's lap. He sat in his own chair. "Now, my dear, start at the beginning and tell me what transpired."

Sarah took a breath and began. As she repeated the conversation precisely, she began to calm down. And also see things in a different light. The two sat quietly thinking after.

"We still don't know how many children there are," Augustus observed.

"Arrogant and unkind man," Sarah muttered.

"Who, me?" Augustus asked.

"No, you know who I mean!"Sarah snapped testily.

"Well, yes, he's proud. Touchy." Then Augustus chuckled, "The very thing he accused Berty of, don't you think? Touchy, too sensitive?"

While they reconsidered, Berty lay on her bed, despondently looking at the little ring. A red stone. He knew she liked red. Was it to tempt her or was it something else? Why did he leave it? It must not be of much value, she thought. Maybe he didn't hold her in much esteem.

~~~

The high bred horses caracoled to a stop in the stable yard. Barnstable started to condemn Joshua's reckless driving, but the major waved his hand to stop. Ronan struggled down and limped to the stable, where he leaned against the wall.

"Put horses to a traveling coach," he ordered.

Barnstable stared at him in amazement.

"Now," Ronan commanded in stentorian tones.

The grooms went to work, taking out the family's traveling coach, preparing the team of four Cleveland Bays, wiping down the inside. Barnstable sent for the coachman. Ronan sent a groom to tell Jacob to have his chests packed and brought out. While he waited, Ronan hobbled to the well and dipped a cup of water from the bucket there. He drank several cups.

Jacob did as he was bid, hastily placing every article in the chests and having the footmen carry them out. Then Jacob ran out to see what was going on. When he reached his master, Ronan grabbed him by the front of his coat with his left hand, picked him up and threw him down on the cobbles.

Everyone stopped to stare. Barnstable ordered them back to work and watched the major. Ronan stared coldly ahead.

Jacob lay stunned a moment. Then he got up, rubbing his bruised shoulders. The boy realized something had gone wrong with the visit to Miss Bodleigh and his master blamed him. The gossip, he thought. It had got round to Miss Bodleigh.

"It weren't me, sir. They already knew."

Ronan nodded. He drank another cup of water.

Barnstable studied him. "Where are you going, sir?"

"Hell."

Barnstable restrained a smile and replied, "Coachman needs direction, sir."

"Lisbon."

"You mean Portsmouth?"

"No, Burlington to see my son, then Lisbon, to see Serafina," Ronan said, disdainfully.

Barnstable looked at him searchingly. "You acknowledge them, sir?"

"Of course I acknowledge them. They are nobody's concern but my own."

He took another drink and tossed the cup in the bucket.

Then Barnstable understood what had happened and who was in the wrong and it wasn't Miss Bodleigh. It was the willful, hardened officer in front of him.

"I see," Barnstable said, "not even your future wife's concern?"

Ronan glared at him, saying, "There's no such being," before stumbling to the coach. Henry helped him in.

Jacob spoke angrily to the grooms and servants, "Master ain't himself, you know. He's never lifted a finger to me. It's you infernal clodpoles and your tattle and your Methodists!"

Jacob watched footmen tie the campaign chests on the coach. He took Ronan's great coat from another footman.

"Where's his hat and gloves?" Jacob asked.

Nobody knew. Cook's helper came running with a basket of victuals. Barnstable said the coachman needed guards and Henry volunteered.
He had ridden before carrying a gun. Barnstable ordered two strong
grooms to ride on top. Jacob took the basket and joined his master in the
coach. They rumbled off.

~~~

Berty had no appetite for the noon dinner. She noticed Ronan's hat
and gloves left on the table by the door. After dinner, she changed into her
riding habit, put the hat and gloves into a haversack she used when carrying things on her saddle and walked out to the stable. She didn't mention
where she was going to her relatives, who were trying to seem occupied
with reading. Pete was in school. Berty saddled Rose and rode to the Hall.

Barnstable met her as she rode up to the stables. Berty nervously
told him she'd brought the major's hat and gloves.

"Forgot them, did he? Never known him to forget anything," Barnstable mused, "He's gone."

"Gone? Where? When will he be back?" Berty asked.

Barnstable chuckled. "Said he was going to hell. Going first to
Burlington to see his son. The major's a loose screw."

Berty asked when he left.

"As soon as he got back this morning. You won't catch up with him
on your little pony."

Berty quaked with nervousness. She tried to stay composed, but
blurted out, "I should not have said anything. Now he's wroth with me and
has said the most odious things."

"What shouldn't you have said that brought out his wrath?"

"Oh, Mr. Barnstable, I repeated the idle talk about him."

Barnstable frowned, "What odious things did he say?"

"He called me a missish spinster who should know that men and
women weren't the same."

Barnstable tried not to smile. "Now why would he say a cruel thing
like that, Miss Bodleigh?"

Berty told him and Barnstable assured her she had done nothing
wrong and the major was excessively fractious. "Let him get off his high
horse, see he's wronged you. Missish, indeed, and if he's not a complete
fool, which he isn't, he'll come back and beg your forgiveness."

She brightened a moment, then fell into the doldrums. "I fear he's too proud and bullheaded for that. Lisbon... he'll probably go there where his mistresses live. I'll never see him again."

Berty turned Rose round and rode dejectedly into the wood to the hidden waterfall. She dismounted, sat on a mossy mound and wept without restraint. It began to drizzle. Rose's head drooped as if she were as disheartened as Berty.

Rain descended on the Trevelyan coach as well. Mud splashed on the shiny blue and silver arms. Inside, Ronan leaned against the side, his head and leg aching. Old wounds rebelled with fresh pain at every bump in the road. He found no comfort. Jacob covered him in his great coat, yet he shivered.

They stopped at an inn to change horses. Heavy going had worn them. Ronan entered the inn to take tea and brandy, while the others ate. He asked Jacob for writing materials and wrote one brief line. He melted blue wax and pressed the devil's seal into it. Jacob saw to it the letter would be on the next mail coach to Boscawden. Seemed silly to write to someone you had just seen, but the Quality were like that.

On the road again, Jacob offered his master delights from the food basket. Ronan took an orange. Jacob ate a meat pie and sandwiches. They traveled on in the mist and rain.

In the New Forest, Ronan asked to stop. He told Jacob to bring lint and bandages. Henry and Jacob followed him to a fallen log, where Ronan asked his valet to help him off with his coat and waistcoat. The major lowered his braces and trousers and sat on the log. He took out his stiletto, held it over the swollen and inflamed wound and drove it in. A mass of bloody infection gushed out. Rain washed it away and more oozed out.

Henry thought he'd lose his dinner. "Oh, my God!" he muttered.

Jacob cleaned the wound, wrapped it and helped Ronan pull up the trousers. By then, his shirt was soaked, but he didn't care. Jacob dressed him and Henry helped him back in the coach. The greatcoat and a blanket didn't ease the major's shivering, although Jacob found him hot to touch.

"I knew it was bad," Jacob said.

Hours later, they reached Burlington in a deluge. Ronan stumbled out of the carriage on Henry's arm. He made it up the steps into the entrance hall. Burlington's butler sent a footman to fetch Sir Richard from his office. He arrived as Henry aided Ronan up the main stairs. Ronan collapsed into Henry's arms. Sir Richard's giant footman, George, assisted in carrying the major up the stairs to a vacant chamber. Sir Richard noticed blood soaked through Ronan's trousers and sent for Dr. Waddles in the village and Gervace Markham, usually to be found in the servant's quarters, though a former officer and a gentleman.

While Jacob removed his master's wet clothes and staunched blood, he gave them a running account of all that had happened since leaving Boscawden. When he had covered that, he began afresh with the action in France while George built a fire in the fireplace and Gervace helped cover Ronan with blankets. Jacob did not mention his master's actions in Boscawden.

A dry shirt, blankets and a blazing fire, yet Ronan shivered. Gervase touched the young man's hot forehead and diagnosed wound fever. "Opening the wound should have released the poison. Don't know what Waddles can do, but two heads are better than one."

Sir Richard left to inform Lady Ann, "When the boys come down from the school room, you may tell them Ronan's here, but they must not see him until I've spoken with Waddles."

"This sounds bad, Richard," Ann replied and, with a worried face, followed Richard to Ronan's old chamber.

The patient's pallor and unfocused eyes shocked her. His military whiskers and shaggy mane added to his disturbing aspect. Ann spontaneously felt his fevered forehead and reached for a damp cloth to cool it. Ronan looked vaguely at her when she spoke his name. Ann stayed until time for the boys to come down.

In the drawing room, Ann sat in her favorite arm chair while Tristan, soon to be eight years old, rattled off everything they had done that day. Finally, Ann interrupted, "I have something to tell you."

Tristan grew quiet. Christopher, age four and wearing a skirt, as boys did at that age, sucked his thumb. Sir Richard disliked that habit, but Ann said the poor child had been passed around so much, he should be allowed any comfort.

"Christopher's father is here."

"Capital! We shall have such excitement, Chris," Tristan told his companion. The only damper on Tristan's enthusiasm was his inability to call the major his father. He had figured that out. Despite his loquacity, he had not told anyone.

"Will he take me away?" Chris wondered.

"Certainly not!" Ann assured him, picking him up to place on her lap.

Christopher hardy remembered his mother, but did remember the tall Hussar who had taken him from his grandfather. He liked the Burlingtons very much, but his father was just someone who had passed him from one family to another.

Tristan's buoyant attitude helped assuage Christopher's concerns. "Where is he? When will we see him?" Tristan asked.

"He is not well," Ann said, "After Dr. Waddles has seen him, perhaps you will be permitted to visit a moment."

Tristan's expression fell. He liked doctor Waddles, though, and asked, "Does my godbrother have spots?"

"No, child, why should he have spots?"

"When Chris and I were sick last year, we had spots."

Ann smiled, "You had measles. Major Trevelyan has fever from a wound."

"A wound! I must see it!" Tristan, who took a intense interest in bodily injury, pleaded to be present when Waddles arrived. Ann, as usual, agreed.

Hours passed before Waddles made it to Burlington Hall. Sir Richard allowed Tristan to attend, but not Christopher. Waddles stepped into the warm chamber and stood at the door studying his new patient, Sir Richard's notorious godson, a most perfect specimen of a man. The rumors the doctor had heard were true, this godson was Tristan's father. What were the Burlingtons thinking to choose a blond sire for their son when they were both dark?

Waddles examined his half comatose patient and said, "There's not much I can do since he's already opened the wound with a stiletto. I would have used a probe; the fool could have nicked the artery. However the deed is done and now all we can do is ease the fever and, if need be, remove the leg."

The last comment put Sir Richard and Gervace in a botheration. The doctor ignored them. Tristan observed that the bandages smelled foul. Waddles explained that was from putrid infection. The doctor threw the soiled dressings into the fire and applied a liniment that reeked of thyme and other antiseptic herbs to the wound before Jacob bandaged it.

"Jacob, cut his hair," Sir Richard ordered an old-fashioned treatment in fever cases.

"No, Papa, remember Samson!" Tristan spoke.

"Ronan's no Samson and there's no Jezabel here," Sir Richard replied.

"Delilah, Papa! If you didn't fall asleep in church, you'd know that."

Doctor Waddles grinned, then explained, "Cutting hair won't make a bit of difference to his fever. Bleeding might release some of the poison, but the leg wound is doing that. Try to make him comfortable and assuage his thirst."

Tristan bathed Ronan's face and spoke soothingly as he did to his horse. The patient recognize Tristan and returned his fond gaze. Richard saw Ann's gentle nature in Tristan, something he never discouraged. Waddles left a strong smelling and harsh tasting medicine. Instead of a prognosis, he observed that the patient was young and strong and that was in his favor.

After Waddles left, Gervase remarked, "That was a damned waste. I could have told you that."

He volunteered for the first watch and ordered Jacob to get some rest.

Lady Ann met Waddles in the passage and invited him to tea. "I'm sure you could use it after your rounds."

"Yes, thank you, my lady, I've hardly had time to get a bite to eat today."

He joined Lady Ann and several, more or less, permanent house guests in the drawing room. Sir Richard soon arrived.

Waddles decided to have some fun. "Your godson is remarkably well favored, inspite of his scars. He reminds me of Tristan, same sort of classical face and gold hair.."

"Yes, a coincidence. Of course, most children are blond," Lady Ann serenely replied.

"Tristan is the image of my mother and brother. Both were fair," Sir Richard claimed.

"My mother was fair, too," Lady Ann added, "Tristan has her big blue eyes."

Waddles smirked at this pair of prevaricators. He'd seen the portrait of Sir Richard's brunette mother.

Chapter 14

Boscawden

The Bodleighs worried when Berty didn't arrive home by supper on that cold, rainy afternoon. Towards evening, she wandered in soaked and shivering. Sarah fussed over her, had Peggy run a hot bath and put Berty to bed with a cup of hot chocolate. Tired and miserable, Berty soon fell asleep.

The next morning, a Sunday, Berty was so drained and wistful, her relatives thought it best she stay in bed rather than attend service.

"You've probably caught a chill," Augustus said and passed that news on after the service.

Francis Bodleigh showed up for Sunday tea. Berty decided she was too unwell to join the family. She took her tea alone in her room rather than face Francis. Physically, she felt fine. She heard Francis from her room.

"He's here less than two days and wreaks havoc. If he were here a week, I'd have to give up my position and move in with my oldest son. The Lord of Misrule has disturbed everyone at the Hall. He drove a curricle, which he had never driven before, nearly killed the horses and upset a woodcutter's cart. He shot old Cannonball!"

"Mrs. Goodyer's in a pucker over Lord Victor's portrait. His grandson had it taken to a lumber room and Lord Alexander's portrait hung there instead. The major's got the whole house and village rattling and then there's our Berty, upset and possibly ill from this mischief maker. The Devil only knows his intentions there."

"When I returned from church, there was his groom with his two chargers. A Sergeant Duncan of the fifteenth Hussars, a most detestable and stubborn man. Barnstable told him the major had left, but the sergeant says he had orders to take the horses to Boscawden and he wasn't leaving until he got new orders."

"By all that is dreadful, the man is obnoxious. Barnstable wants Gunpowder for breeding, but we don't need the sergeant. He's as overbearing as the major, eats like a horse and already has the maids throwing their caps at him. The sergeant advertises he will formally introduce his noble charges to everyone tomorrow afternoon in the riding school. Did you ever hear such absurdity?"

The next day, Berty rose and declared herself completely recovered. No one could argue, since she didn't suffer so much as a sniffle and looked as blooming as ever. Edith, having heard Berty was ill, rode over with Claude and found her friend well but wretched.

"Oh, a lover's quarrel," Edith declared, cheerfully, "In novels lovers always make up."

"Ronan doesn't read novels," Berty replied, crossly.

Edith announced that everyone was talking about the display that afternoon.

"How quickly word gets around in Boscawden," Berty remarked.

"Oh yes, upon my soul, Berty, they have it about that you have turned down the major's offer and he left in a pet. Did you really?"

"I told you, Edith, I set his back up before he could make an offer, if he intended to. I think he did not. Perhaps he would have invited me to ride in the curricle. I've never ridden in a curricle," she added, wistfully. "I accused him of keeping concubines."

"Concubines?"

"I couldn't think of any other word at the time. So foolish of me. Of course, he made a joke of it."

They were silent a moment, then Berty said, "I would like to see Gunpowder and this presentation."

Liberty changed into her riding habit and joined Edith and Claude on their mounts. They met many people, adults and children, walking down the Hall's drive, including Daniel Rollings, for he'd closed school early, claiming, "There are so few diversions here."

Sergeant Duncan, a small, slender man with a flourishing dark mustache and side whiskers, had heard the gossip about his major and Miss Bodleigh in the servant's hall. He dismissed it with, "People of his quality don't marry whoever they please. If she don't have money, he didn't offer. Just another of his paramours, I reckon."

This offended the staff familiar with Miss Bodleigh's maidenly virtue and they told him so.

"Balderdash, a virgin at one and twenty? Must be ugly as a mud hut. A man like the major, who has been diverted by the most beautiful courtesans in the Peninsula wouldn't glance at such," Duncan persisted.

"You, sir, should go back to your horses," Grimsby staunchly informed him, "We don't malign decent maidens here and I scorn your vulgar talk."

"Pretty high in the instep for a servant, ain't you?" Duncan said, putting on his foraging cap and marching out.

He returned to the stables where he irritated Barnstable with his exacting orders, including frequent feedings of oats and barley; frequent removal of dung in his horses' boxes and requests for worm treatments that Barnstable had never heard of. Sergeant Duncan required a box stall for his own accommodation between those of the two stallions. It had to be furnished with a rug, a feather bed, chests, a table and chair. Duncan demanded military precision from the lesser grooms, thought Barnstable a know-nothing and said so. When he wasn't haranguing the others, he played one of his several musical instruments, especially a trumpet. He'd worked with Gunpowder when his master was away, in winter quarters or wounded and disliked anyone else near the beast.

That afternoon, Liberty, Edith and Claude sat their horses to see above the heads of the crowd around the riding ring. Sergeant Duncan, in dress Hussar uniform, including tall, crimson, feathered shako, announced his entrance by playing a trilling song on pipes. Gunpowder, wearing no halter or tack of any kind walked proudly alongside him. The tall, gallant animal showed the wear and tear of war. He was thin and scarred. White spots on his back showed where a saddle had been worn too long.

Duncan bowed and Gunpowder also bowed. In a strong voice, Duncan told of the major's exploits and that the French had named him le Diable Bleu. He informed the crowd that le Diable Bleu fought off a French vedette to save Wellington, was shot in the leg and only Gunpowder's leaping a wall saved him. Gunpowder nodded in agreement.

"How high was the wall?" Duncan asked the horse.

Gunpowder stamped his foot eight times.

"Yes, eight feet. Some would have it more, but this noble steed never lies," Duncan said. Gunpowder nodded agreement. The crowd laughed and clapped.

"What did you do after carrying le Diable back to camp?" Duncan asked. Gunpowder dropped to the ground and laid on his side.

"He took a much needed nap."

More laughter. Even Barnstable and the grooms enjoyed this, finding it hard to believe this was the same cantankerous Gunpowder they had known as a colt.

Gunpowder sat up and Duncan mounted. With no visible cues from the sergeant, Gunpowder danced and caracoled around the ring in time to the music Duncan played on his pipe. The sergeant slipped off the horse's back. Gunpowder rose on his hind legs and followed him.

"You wouldn't be showing off behind my back, would you?" the sergeant asked.

Gunpowder dropped down and shook his head no. Duncan led him to Grimsby and asked, "What do you think of that fellow?"

The stallion curled his lip over his nose, bringing on screams of laughter. Duncan smirked.

"Like all soldiers, Gunpowder favors pretty girls," Duncan said. The horse nodded. Duncan asked the men to step back and allow the women to come forward.

"Who is the major's beloved?" Duncan asked the steed.

Gunpowder trotted around the ring looking at the women. Sensing Duncan's unseen cues, Gunpowder stopped in front of Berty and nodded his head.

"What's this, Gunpowder? Do you like the little mare or the hoyden on her back?"

Rose, who didn't like anybody, set her ears back. Gunpowder nickered and trotted back and forth. Berty felt hot with embarrassment and would have ridden away if the crowd had let her.

"Lo que el diable, Gunpowder! No te entiendo!" Duncan spoke in annoyed Spanish, for the horse wasn't obeying his signals. The sergeant walked up to Gunpowder and put his hands on his neck to calm him. Duncan turned to Berty, who he thought singular; her beauty subdued by ill kept hair and obsolete dress. "Who are you, Miss?"

"Liberty Bodleigh."

Duncan stared. "So you're the wench who drove the Blue Devil out of this rural paradise! Ha! He never offered for you, that's sure. Probably left to get away from the tattlers who'd connect his name with yours."

Gunpowder bolted around the ring. Barnstable entered to confront the obnoxious sergeant. "How dare you speak so to Miss Bodleigh, you military rum touch!"

"I'll speak my mind. She ain't good enough to pour his port. You insult Devil! He's got more courage than anyone here and outwits the French every time he rides out! Fine ladies in silk and jewels swoon over him."

Barnstable's patience ran out. "Your Devil is a gazetted fortune hunter, a rake and the worse beast in nature!"

He punched Duncan in the jaw. Duncan punched back and a mill ensued. Gunpowder charged at Barnstable. Three grooms drove him off with sticks. Duncan ordered him away. The stallion wildly charged at grooms who tried to catch him. The crowd picked sides and cheered. Francis and two footmen started forward to stop the fight, but Rollings stepped forward.

"Allow me."

He limped to the combatants, lifted his long walking stick and brought it down between them.

"Cease this foolishness," he ordered in a tone not to be ignored.

The two bloodied men separated, panting. Duncan called to Gunpowder and the horse followed him back in the stable. Duncan cursed in Spanish.

"Such language in front of ladies, sergeant," Rollings chastised him.

Claude cleared a path for Berty and Edith to escape the crowd. They cantered back to the Bodleigh house. Once their mounts were safely in the stable, Berty and Edith ran in the house. Claude had stayed behind to listen to the gossip.

"My goodness, is something wrong?" Sarah asked looking up from her book.

"I must go to London," Berty declared, "I'm disgusted with tattlers and busy bodies. And now insults and violence!"

She and Edith told Sarah of the brawl.

"To have incensed Barnstable! That sergeant must be insufferable. Barnstable has ever been of an easy temperament. One has to be to train horses, I should think," Sarah said, adding, "Hilda expects you next month if you can tolerate Boscawean's gossips a little longer."

A knock on the door interrupted and Peggy let in Mr. Rollings. He seated himself on the sofa with Berty and Edith.

"I hear you had to break up a fight between two overgrown children," Sarah said.

He laughed. "Yes, I've had much practice at that. What's this about my devilish friend arriving and removing in two days?"

Berty and Sarah explained events.

"I don't know what to say. One doesn't discuss a man's mistresses or natural children. Most men don't claim them, indeed most men frequent the most unsavory slatterns rather than involve themselves with one woman. The major is not like that. I don't quite collect the nature of your friendship with him, Miss Bodleigh."

"Neither do I!"

He noticed her ring and stated, " Major Trevelyan gave you that ring."

"After a fashion, how did you know?"

"I recognise that singular ruby. I remember when Ronan bought it from a soldier who had acquired it plundering the French. It had been in a broken necklace, probably plundered from the Spanish by the French. We used to buy such things from soldiers who didn't know their worth and wanted ready money. We sold gold and gems to jewelers for a profit. He had that piece made into a lady's ring, I assumed for a special lady, but he wouldn't say. You will see the jeweler's mark inside. Yes, that's it," Rollings told them when Berty showed him the mark.

"I thought it might have been a garnet or even glass," Berty remarked.

"It's a fine, rare ruby of some value. He's had it three years and the fact he gave it to you bears significance."

Berty hung her head. "Actually, he threw it on the floor."

"Their lovers' quarrel," Edith put in.

"I'm sure he was due for that set down," Rollings said, smiling.

"I completely agree," Sarah said, "However, Berty should not wear the ring. It should be returned to the major, although we are unsure how to do that now."

Augustus returned from walking Corky. Claude arrived and all sat down for tea. After tea, Augustus, always interested in the war, broached the subject with Rollings, specifically asking how Rollings got to know Major Trevelyan.

Rollings grew dour. "A gentleman should not share the grisly business of war with ladies. Although, some ladies, in their ignorance, encourage foolish boys to go to war."

"We are much accustomed to grisly war stories, sir," Sarah informed him, "And as he has disturbed Liberty, we would like to know more about him. He discloses little."

Rollings obliged, "I first met Ronan when he was a captain working behind the lines with the guerilleros. My commander chose me to ride to him and bring back his report. The Quartermaster provided me with the best horses and I rode to a distant mountain town. Captain Trevelyan invited me to dine with him and the partisan chiefs. They displayed a palpable hatred for the French who have tortured the Spanish. The guerilleros extract revenge at every opportunity. I have nightmares of the mutilated corpses I've seen of both French and Spanish. The major has expressed his disapproval to his allies in ways that they understand. He is as deft with a stiletto as with a sabre. Captain Trevelyan provided me with invaluable information, including maps, to take back."

"He is not a man suited to an overnice woman. I suppose he decided you were a woman of delicate sensibilities, Miss Bodleigh, and that is why he left." That's all I shall say on that subject."

Berty looked at him and said, "He is my first love and I don't think I'll ever love another. Please tell me how many natural children has he? Everyone rattles about it, but no one tells me precisely."

Rollings, sympathizing with her, replied, "I don't know. That is for him to tell you. I will not disparage a man who has assisted me. When I was first wounded and underwater from the lateness of pay- I was going to have to sell my uniform to buy food-he brought me everything I needed. When this latest injury occurred, he saw to it I received attention that has ameliorated this gash. It could have been much worse. Men who know him, respect, trust and follow him. He's taken good care of the men under him. As to women, they turn to stare when he passes. I should think it would be hard for him not to have mistresses."

"Well, of course," Edith came to Ronan's defense, "Indeed, the major, Lord Alexander and my brother, Walter, are all quite dashing. I daresay, I wouldn't want to inquire as to my brother's romantic life."

Rollings smiled. "Yes, Miss Westerly, but would these dashing men make good husbands?"

"Upon my honor, they wouldn't bore us to death!"

"That's cruel, Edith!" Berty objected, "Mr. Rollings will think you are referring to him."

"I assure you, as a school master, I'm accustomed to boring people to death," Rollings admitted, with a grin.

The older Bodleighs didn't find Rollings at all boring and invited him to stay for supper. Betty sent out for butcher's meat, an extravagance they had stinted on since Augustus' illness. Sarah and Liberty had not had new gowns or books due to that impairment.

Mr. Rollings studied the varied books they had.

"Many were my parents' books," Sarah told him, "We've not had new ones in a while, but friends loan us theirs and there is the library at the Hall."

"Which has nothing new and half of them are in Latin," Berty came out of her distraction to add.

They talked of books until Rollings commented on Augustus' Argand lamps.

"I have these two and a double one in my office, all of Sheffield plate," Augustus explained with enthusiasm, "Much brighter than candles. Very hard to find now."

"Probably because they are ugly," Berty put in.

"My niece dislikes anything modern except our bath," Augustus said, taking advantage of that opportunity to show Rollings the modern bathroom. That luxury impressed the school master.

~~~

Edith thought Berty needed her company to prevent the dismals over Ronan's behavior. She spent the night.

They rode in Boscawden's park the next morning, Berty showing Edith the secret waterfall. When they returned to the Bodleigh house, they found Sarah and Augustus conversing with Gideon Talbert in the parlor. After the usual social conventions, the women sat on the sofa.

"Gideon's just back from London," Sarah announced.

"How interesting! Berty and I are going next month," Edith said. She inquired if he had attended any concerts, art exhibits or plays.

Gideon said he'd stayed at his club, seen his tailor, attended an opera and some boxing matches.

Sarah asked if he had bought any books. He had not.

Instead of talking about London, Gideon tactlessly mentioned, "I've heard there has been quite an uproar at the Hall over Major Trevelyan. They say he left in a pique at your refusing his offer, Miss. Bodleigh."

"You heard incorrectly. He made no offer," Berty replied frostily, wondering where he heard such tattle so soon after returning from London.

"I see. He sounds like a loose screw."

Sarah diverted the conversation to the improvement in the children since the arrival of Mr. Rollings, a subject Gideon had no interest in. He stayed for tea to Edith and Berty's consternation.

That evening, in Berty's bed, Edith not only told Berty that Gideon was a dead bore, but that he was a ninny. "He has a library, but he doesn't buy books."

"He's an idjit. His library is for show," Berty said, "I do not care for boxing. It sounds so ungentlemanly.

Edith agreed, adding, "Claude thinks it's all the thing. Worse than dogfighting, in my opinion."

"I excessively disapprove of dog and cock fighting," Berty stated, "And boxing, to me, lowers a man," then changing the subject, wondered, "Where do you think he heard that the major left in a pique?"

"Oh, no doubt, the Cock and Cat. I'm sure he frequents the light skirts there, like all the local men do," Edith replied without the slightest blush.

"Edith, how do you know such things?"

"I have brothers, you know. They come home foxed and spill everything to their dear sister! Trust me, Talbert isn't the epitome of moral rectitude your family thinks he is."

Berty smiled at the idea of Francis Bodleigh believing Talbert to be this epitome when he was no better than he should be.

The two friends rode to Edith's home the following morning. Edith invited Berty to stay the night. "We'll have such fun and it will take your mind off, you know."

"I don't know that I want diversion. I need to think," Berty told her.

When she returned home, Liberty put away most of her paints and brushes and packed her drawing materials in preparation for her trip to London.

~~~

Gideon saw Berty's apparent rejection of Major Trevelyan as promising in his own pursuit of her. Francis Bodleigh thought so as well and informed his brother, "Marriage to a respectable man like Talbert would save her reputation."

"What is wrong with her reputation?" Augustus asked.

"She has spent too much time with Major Trevelyan, a known rake."

"Balderdash! He was away two years and in the brief time he was here, Berty was hardly alone with him at all," Augustus said.

"That may be true, but people talk. In any case, it is past time she married and Talbert's the only prospect I see."

"You talk like she was an old maid," Augustus grumbled.

"I daresay, she's nearly on the shelf," Francis retorted.

Liberty was on her way to Augustus' office when she heard them speaking. She stopped, listened and ran back outside. Old maid, on the shelf, missish spinster and, what did that odious man say yesterday, a hoyden! Berty decided to ask Miss Penthwaite for an extended stay. Maybe she would open an atelier in London. She was sure Miss Penthwaite would support her in this endeavor. Berty strode to the stable to visit Rose, one of many things she would miss in London.

The next morning, while Berty was riding in the park, Gideon Talbert drove up in his new phaeton, not a high perch phaeton, a safer more sedate model. When Sarah told him Berty was out riding, he asked to speak to Augustus, but not before saying, "Upon my word, Mrs. Bodleigh, she should not ride alone."

"Perhaps not, but she has done so seven years. She's quite independent, you know," Sarah said.

"I dare say out of necessity," Gideon replied.

He walked into Augustus' office and, after the usual greetings, asked, "Mr. Bodleigh, may I have the honor of obtaining Miss Bodleigh's hand in marriage?"

Augustus sat down and after a tongue-tied moment, replied, "I suppose you may if she is agreeable to the idea. I'm not sure where she is at the moment."

"Mrs. Bodleigh told me she was riding."

"Yes, of course, fine morning for it. She does like to ride on fine mornings. I used to ride with her sometimes, but the press of work, you know. Then, my good gelding died and then my illness," Augustus, feeling ill-at-ease, rambled.

They waited Berty's return, but when she saw Gideon's phaeton in the stable yard, she turned around and rode back into the wood. She considered riding to the Hall, but didn't care to meet that odious groom at the stable. On the other hand, Gideon could stay a long time. "I shan't let a dratted groom keep me from doing as I want," she said to Rose and rode to the Hall.

Liberty met Barnstable as soon as she rode up. His face carried a rare selection of bruises and abrasions, but his main concern was the Trevelyan coach, coachman, grooms and Henry had not returned. "It's as if the major stole it. Which I wouldn't put past him. I suppose he's tooling around Burlington or Portsmouth in it."

Berty laughed at that. "Yes, filled it with paramores and driving them around."

Out stepped Bartholomew Duncan, in his working uniform, playing a flute. He stopped at sight of Berty, approached and bowed. "Miss Bodleigh, I hope you will accept my sincere apology. Had these yahoos told me you were a long-time friend of the major's, and apprised me of the unfortunate occasion of your parting, I would have behaved with the utmost respect and propriety. I fear my behavior was unbecoming a gentleman."

"Not that you are a gentleman," Barnstable interjected.

"Please none of that, Barnstable. I accept your apology, Sergeant Duncan, and must add I admire your way with horses."

"Thank you, miss. I preferr them to people."

Berty dismounted and walked to the gardens, but the gardens reminded her of walking with Ronan and that brought on Melancholy. She didn't know where she stood with Ronan or if she would see him again and that thought increased her sadness.

By the time Berty arrived home, Talbert had left. Over supper, her aunt and uncle praised Gideon and spoke of the advantages of his situation; his fine home, his estate, horses, proximity to Boscawden. Finally, Augustus told her of his offer. "Will you accept?"

"Certainly not! The nerve of him! Why didn't he ask me? Not that I wanted him to, but to ask you when I am a grown woman! And he hasn't shown the least sign of real affection, just his infernal propriety. Drat him!" Berty flounced upstairs.

"I believe that matter is settled," Augustus sighed with relief.

Soon after, Pete came in from town. "The post coach broke down and just got here with the mail."

"So that's why we've gotten no mail in days," Sarah said, sorting through the letters. "Ah one from Hilda. What's this!" She called Berty.

Liberty took the letter addressed to herself and sealed with the blue devil. She quickly broke the seal and read, "Forgive this wretch who loves you. Ronan"

She clasped the page to her heart like a heroine of romance. "He's never told me that," she murmured.

Sarah raised a brow, "Told you what, dear?"

Berty handed her the letter.

"Well, I must say!" but Sarah didn't say. Berty took the letter back and felt like she floated upstairs.

Chapter 15

The mud-splattered Trevelyan traveling coach arrived at the Hall. Henry explained they had waited for news of the major and the news they brought was bad. Major Trevelyan lay prostrated with fever. He'd grown worse and the probability of his arriving back at Boscawden in a coffin increased daily.

Liberty rode up soon after the coach returned and heard the news from Barnstable. She asked how far it was to Burlington and immediately rode on to the Westerly's and told Edith.

"Will you ride with me to Burlington?" Berty asked.

"Now?!"

"No, it's too late in the day. Barnstable says it's twelve leagues. Early tommorow morning. I must see Ronan and we must not let anyone know or they will try to disuade me, even prevent me from going," Berty said.

Romantic adventure appealed to Edith. "I shall go with you, but may I ask Claude to accompany us? He will keep it secret."

Berty agreed that was a good idea. They decided to meet outside Boscawden a little after dawn.

When Berty arrived home, she discovered that Gideon had been there, again, but had not waited. While Gideon was there, Francis had ridden up to deliver the good news (to him) of the major's impending demise. Gideon took this as good news, as well, and returned to his estate confident he would secure Miss Bodleigh's hand.

"She should accept Talbert," Francis insisted to Augustus after Gideon's departure.

Berty took a different view. "Why did you not tell him I do not accept him, Uncle Augustus?"

"You should tell him, yourself, Berty."

"He asked you, not me!" she countered and bounded to her chamber to prepare for the morrow's venture.

Berty filled her purse with coins and rolled her best satin gown, slippers and other necessities into a waterproofed, canvas saddle valise she used for overnight stays. She loaded her pistol, secured it in its holster and wrapped it in canvas. She secured ammunition in a saddlebag. Berty marched to the stable to give Rose extra hay and oats that evening and asked Pete to feed Rose long before dawn. Rose needed time to eat before their ride. Berty returned to the house and told her aunt and uncles, for Francis remained for supper, she would be riding with Edith the next morning and staying the night with Edith. She carefully didn't say where she would be staying the night. They assumed at the Westerly's.

"Berty, Mr. Talbert is sure to return tomorrow and you should be here," Sarah said.

"That, of all things, gives me more reason not to be here!"

"Upon my soul, niece, don't be so violent in your emotions. You may regret refusing this gentleman," Francis admonished her.

"Yes, Berty, I apprehend you are distressed over the major, but pray reflect before refusing Gideon out of hand, " Sarah said in more soothing tones.

" 'Distressed over the major!' I should think you all would be. It's a poor time to be pressing me with Gideon Talbert's ill-considered offer."

Before more arguments ensued, Berty again flounced to her chamber.

"I fear you've set her back up," Augustus pronounced.

"It doesn't take much to do that," Francis replied, "I pity Talbert if he does marry her."

Berty returned for dinner. The family sat down to dinner with anything but good feelings. They barely spoke after Francis said the grace. Berty ate to maintain her strength, but with no appetite. She excused herself, washed well and went to bed.

The next morning, Berty rose before the others, hung her gold chain around her neck, dressed in warm petticoats and her old shabby, patched riding habit. She again ate without appetite, filled her haversack with food and carrying her valise, pistol and small saddlebag, marched to the stable. Rose, who didn't suffer from Berty's lack of appetite, picked up the last wisps of hay. Berty placed a fleece on her back and Pete saddled the mare. He strapped on a sack of oats, Berty's haversack and valise.. When Rose was ready and the pistol hung on the saddle, Berty handed Pete a sealed note.

"Please give this to Uncle Augustus in the afternoon."

"What are you about, Miss Berty?"

"I can't tell you now, Pete, but promise you won't despise me whatever I do."

"I could never do that, Miss Berty!"

She mounted and trotted off in the winter dawn. Frost glittered on brush and branches and decorated tufts of tall grass, crunching under Rose's hooves.

~~~

The previous evening, Claude had staggered into his chamber late, having indulged in too much port and claret with friends. When Edith presented Berty's intentions to him, he grumbled something about damned fool minxes and fell asleep.

Edith could not rouse him the next morning. After consuming an unusually early, hearty breakfast suited to such a full-sized woman, she had the groom saddle her gelding and prepare her brother's pistols, which the groom hung over her saddle. Edith wore a new, stylish blue riding habit, matching cloak and feathered bonnet. She wouldn't have been out of place prancing in a London park.

Berty waited impatiently at their appointed spot. Edith cantered slowly up to her.

"Where's Claude?" Berty asked.

"He came in top heavy last night and I could not rouse him this morning. He quite put me out of humor, but I'm not too late am I?"

"Doesn't signify," Berty replied. They jogged off.

An hour later, Berty halted Rose to look back at Edith. Edith laid her crop on her screw's flank to get more effort out of him. The big gelding fell into a reluctant canter and then back to a slow jog. Lazy at best, Snail had now traveled further from his stall and manger than usual and desired to turn back.

"Do try to make him keep up," Berty pleaded, "As big as he is, he ought to be ahead of little Rose."

"He's a disgrace to his species," Edith said.

They rode on, through the New Forest, making slower time than Berty had anticipated. Toward noon, under a lowering sky, Edith insisted they halt at an inn to bait and water the horses and refresh themselves. Berty objected. She'd brought victuals for both ladies and beasts and intended to picnic briefly by a stream.

"Berty, if nothing else, I need to rest and thaw my extremities," Edith said reasonably. Although Edith claimed to be famished, Berty suffered from a nervous lack of appetite. However, the warmth of a fire appealed. She agreed to stop. Since ladies did not dine in public rooms, Edith, with Berty close beside her, requested a private parlor. The landlord, recognizing the fashionably dressed and dignified Edith as a lady of quality, offered a small parlor for their use. He waited on them personally. Edith ordered a large meal of whatever the inn had available that day, which was roast mutton and potatoes. Berty nibbled bread and cheese she'd brought and drank the proffered hot tea. Edith annoyed her by lingering over her luncheon, ordering more tea and chatting with the innkeeper who thought her a great lady. He couldn't fathom why such a lady would be out riding with her maid.

~~~

Late in the afternoon, when Sarah returned from visiting a friend, she found Gideon hanging about. Sarah explained that Berty was out riding with Edith. A more astute man would have understood that if a woman cared to receive his offer, she would have remained at home, but he assumed Augustus had not informed her. Gideon waited.

Augustus returned from seeing a potential client and led Queen into the stable. Pete deemed it time to give him Berty's note. Augustus read it, frowned, stuffed it in a pocket and went inside to confront Talbert.

Sarah recognized Augustus's unease as soon as she saw his face. He made the required polite greeting to Talbert and announced to Sarah that Berty had ridden with Edith and Claude Westerly to Burlington.

"Burlington!" Sarah and Talbert exclaimed.

"Yes, to see Major Trevelyan on his death bed. Had she only confided in me! If I set out now, it will be nightfall before I reach the first inn."

"This is an outrage!" Talbert exclaimed, "Her reputation is ruined!"

"If only I had attended Liberty, I should have borrowed the Pemberton's coach and traveled with her. He is my cousin, after all. One should not stay wroth with someone who is ill," Sarah commented, ignoring Talbert.

"What will people say of a girl who chases after a rake like that?" Talbert expounded, "He has her in his pocket!"

"Is that all you think of, Talbert?" Augustus asked, "What of her safety? She's never ridden so far. It must be seventeen leagues. Thankfully,

Claude is with them, which proves Edith and he are better friends to her than we have been."

"Now, Augustus, don't blame yourself. This coil is as much the major's fault as anyone's," Sarah responded, "We now must consider what to do. As you said, it is too late to travel, but we can drive to the Westerly's and learn what they are doing. I dare say they did not know their children's intentions."

While she and Augustus talked, Talbert marched out, not to do anything so dashing and romantic as ride after Liberty, but to gallop back to his estate, cursing her.

~~~

"I say, Berty, what will you do if Ronan's existence has come to a period?" Edith asked as Snail plodded along.

Berty quoted the song, Bonny Light Horseman, "I'll kiss his cold dead lips and wander off."

They didn't speak for a while. Then Liberty resolved, "I shall travel to London and stay with Miss Penthwaite. With her help, I shall open a portrait studio and devote myself to my work. I shall never forget Major Trevelyan and never marry."

Edith, deeply touched, dabbed at her eyes with her handkerchief. Then thwacked her lazy screw to keep up with Rose. "For shame that a big lout like you can't keep up with a little pony, a female pony at that!"

"He's a disgrace to his sex and his species," Berty remarked.

The disgrace added to their troubles by developing a limp. Berty dismounted to look at his left forefoot. "The clinches have come loose on one side of the shoe. We will have to stop at the next village and seek a blacksmith. Perhaps you should dismount and walk."

"Walk! In this mud? Upon my soul, Berty, it would spoil my dress even more than it is already."

"Very well, it isn't hurting him. If the mud doesn't pull it looser, it should hold," Berty remounted, They rode at a walk to the next village with a smith and a tavern.

They baited the horses at the tavern and again Edith requested a private parlor and tea. "Oh, Berty, my derriere is numb. How much farther?"

"If you had walked like I suggested, you wouldn't be numb. I don't believe it is above six more leagues."

Edith groaned, poured another cup of tea and buttered her scones. At least, Edith paid for this extravagance from her own purse.

On the rutted road again, Berty observed the ominous sky and prayed the rain or snow held off. She and Edith occupied some time debating whether it would rain or snow and settled on sleet. Edith's gelding resigned himself to a reluctant jog, just keeping even with Rose who continued with her daisy cutting trot as if she were fresh out of the stall. It began to drizzle.

They reached a barren area lacking cottages; only sheep populated the rocky hills. In the misty gloom ahead, they made out four riders coming towards them. The riders wore caped great coats, breeches and top boots like most gentlemen traveling in wintry weather. With walls on each side of the track, Berty decided to move aside and let them pass. Berty took out her pistol and whispered, "pistols," to Edith, who likewise took out her weapons, one in each hand.

"They will think us mad holding pistols like this," Edith objected.

"I don't care a broom straw what they think. They might be highwaymen or rowdy blades looking for sport and I don't want to be their sport!"

The riders reached them and halted, blocking their passage. They looked with amusement on the two women and their pistols. These men, armed with swords and pistols, didn't remove their pistols with three pointing at them. They made no introductions, but their apparent leader, a large man with a martial air and side whiskers, bowed and offered assistance. Speaking in genteel tones, he addressed Edith, "Upon my honor, ma'am, you should not be traveling here with no other companion than your maid. Bridle culls and smugglars about, you know. Put away those barkers and allow us to escort you to your destination."

Edith lowered her pistols, ready to accept the offer.

"Edith!" Berty snapped in a warning tone and replied to the man, "No thank you, sir. We are to meet friends soon and would prefer you rode on. Allow us to pass."

"Friends, eh? Would you, Miss Edith, be eloping with a beau?" he responded with a smirk.

"Certainly..." Edith began.

"Shush, Edith," Berty interrupted, "She may be, but that is none of your concern, sir. Our gentlemen friends will search for us if we don't soon reach our destination. Now please move aside."

"Gentlemen friends, eh? We saw no one on the road. I daresay those barkers are heavy in your dainty hands and you have no intention of using them. Now put them down and allow us to escort you to a convenient place."

"You'll escort us nowhere. Depart at once or I will use this pistol. I'm reckoned a good shot," Liberty declared. She carefully aimed and cocked her weapon. Although terrified, tired and angry, her hands were steady.

The lead gentleman, laughed and moved closer. Berty pulled the trigger. The soft boom startled her and Rose, who braced herself. The smoke obscured Berty's vision a moment, but she heard the man curse. When the smoke cleared, she saw she had hit him. He looked shocked, held his hand over a bleeding shoulder and jerked his horse to a stop. "Damn you, minx !" he shouted.

Edith cocked her pistols and ordered, "Move on!"

Berty quickly reloaded her breech-loaded model. The wounded leader urged his horse away, followed by the others, who studied the women warily. They had never seen a lady use and load a breech-loaded pistol. Berty ordered Edith to pass while she held her pistol on the wounded leader. He looked none too keen on having a ball in his other shoulder. Berty then backed Rose past the men before spinning the mare around and cueing her to gallop.

When the men were out of sight, Berty and Edith holstered their weapons. Berty urged Rose to continue to gallop and Edith's mount, now fearful of being left alone, followed. They pounded down the slippery road in a cold drizzle, verging on snow. After two miles at a pace so furious, the women could not speak, their exhausted horses stumbled into a walk. In the icy rain, they made out Burlington's open gates less than a mile away.

Berty felt renewed vigor at that welcome sight and Rose, sensing it, splashed down the drive at a good clip in the fading light. The blown gelding plodded after.

~~~

When Henry and the coachman had left Burlington Hall, Major Trevelyan lay delirious with fever. Algebraic equations, the French army, guerilleros assaulted his fevered brain. He murmured what X equaled, named numbers of troops, described topography and ordered men forward. He muttered incoherent thoughts in eight languages. He asked for Liberty, which his friends understood to be an ideal, not a person. Except Jacob, and he kept his council. The boy well knew the trouble talk caused.

Sir Richard wrote to the Brandolyns of Ronan's dire fever.

After the Trevelyan servants departed for Boscawden with news of the major's forthcoming finality, the fever broke. Sweat soaked bedclothes and fleeces placed under the patient to prevent sores. Ronan gradually became conscious of his surroundings. He was able to sit up and take court bouillon and Waddles' offensive medicine.

Jacob and Josiah, Sir Richard's old valet, moved him to a chair, changed damp sheets, washed the patient in lavender water and returned him to a clean, dry bed. Sir Richard and his Lady spoke to Ronan, but received little response from a patient overcome with weakness and laconic at any time. He looked up and spoke softly when Tristan and Christopher visited. Lady Ann told the boys to kiss him and then took them away until bedtime, when Miss Brown brought Christopher to keep him company in the night, an old tradition. The boy said his prayers, crawled in next to his father and immediately fell asleep.

The next day, Waddles insisted on rest and no disturbances in the patient's feeble state. The doctor observed healing in the wound and thought the major's spirits should improve in the following days, but they didn't. The major showed no interest in anything but his son and spoke little to him. Overcome with languor, the major barely ate anything and seemed far away. Sir Richard took Jacob aside.

"Why did your master go to Boscawden with such a wound? Then leave again in such haste. The whole thing baffles me."

"I've sworn not to discuss master's amours."

"Amours, what amours?"

"The major suffers from another wound, one of the heart, sir," Jacob practised the romantic flights of language he'd acquired from novels.

"Bosh! Don't be so melodramatic! He doesn't have such a heart; he's a soldier, born and bred," Sir Richard objected.

Jacob walked to one of the major's chests, removed a box and a long, wavy lock of dark, reddish brown hair. He held the lock up to Sir Richard and showed him a stack of letters, which he quickly returned to the box. "Master told me to burn these when we arrived, but I didn't. He was feverish and didn't know what he was doing."

"Who is this troublesome bit of muslin?" Sir Richard asked.

"You will have to ask him, sir. I have already revealed more than I should."

"Had I known, I would have questioned the men from Boscawden," Sir Richard said and went in search of Gervace.

"Lock of hair, eh? Letters?" Gervace replied.

They walked to Ronan's chamber and found him awake. Jacob took that opportunity to take a pile of sweat-soaked shirts to the laundry maid. Gervace sat by the bed and asked, "What's this about a damsel in Boscawden?"

Ronan turned his back to him.

"Fancy woman you have there? Game pullet? Chit out of the school room? None of my bread and butter?" Gervace asked, "Just meant to help. Quite experienced in matters of the fair sex. That's why I never married."

Receiving no response, Gervace said, "Thought you would confide in me of all people. Perhaps when you are at full force again. Ah, here's Jacob with more court bouilon. Has an egg in it. We'll have you back to beef steaks in no time!"

The patient drank his broth with disinterest and lay back in his pillows. When his friends left, Jacob handed him the lock of Berty's hair. Ronan fell asleep gripping it in his fist.

Hours later, Jacob presented him with another bowl of court bouillon. "Has a bit of sole cooked in it this time," Jacob offered, "And if this isn't enough, there's more."

Ronan dutifully ate it and asked for nothing more.

~~~

Liberty and Edith rode up to the door of the great house, glad to see light in the windows. Berty dismounted. She lifted the knocker on the great oak door. A footman answered and looked on the two bedraggled women in surprise. A boot boy scurried out to hold the horses, while the women stepped into the entrance hall, dripping water on the marble floor. The butler took their names and walked upstairs to the drawing room to fetch Sir Richard.

Sir Richard clomped downstairs to see these unknown visitors, took one look and decided the tall woman with the drooping side curls was a lady and the small, veiled creature, her maid. He wondered if the tall woman was his godson's chere-amie. He admired her impressive figure in the wet, but obviously stylish habit.

Sir Richard introduced himself and, addressing Edith, inquired who she was and what she wanted.

"I'm Miss Edith Westerly and I have accompanied my friend, Miss Liberty Bodleigh, who can tell you what she wants, sir."

"Liberty!" Sir Richard ejaculated.

"I must see Major Trevelyan," Berty announced, without a polite sir. She lifted the damp veil over her hat.

"I'm floored," Sir Richard said, looking critically at the slender, wet, shabby girl. He took her for a teenage hoyden and found it hard to believe this was what Ronan meant when he repeated Liberty in his delirium.

"He's not to have visitors. What cause do you have to see him?" Sir Richard stated ominously.

"I must see him," Berty repeated.

"Please, sir, we've ridden all this way. We're bone tired. She must see him!" Edith adjured.

"Why must you see him?"

"To tell him I forgive him," Berty replied.

"Forgive him for what? Are you with child?"

"Certainly not! I forgive him for his secrets. I must see him before he dies!" Berty, in a torment of frustration, started to run past Sir Richard and seek Ronan.

The knight grabbed Berty's arm, bringing her to a stop. "The crisis is over, he lives. Compose yourself, miss. I'll take you to my lady and see if the major wishes to see you."

If he wishes to see me, Berty thought and swallowed to keep from choking. She remembered the letter and composed herself. "Our horses?"

"They'll be taken to the stables."

"Rose must have a box stall and no grain until she's had hay," Berty said.

Sir Richard stared at her. Such concern for her horse touched him.

"My grooms will serve your little jade as they do my blood horses, miss."

While he was giving directions to a footman regarding Rose, Lady Ann, overcome with curiosity, rustled into the hall.

"You poor dears! Soaked to the skin! George, take their hats, gloves and cloaks. Do you have dry clothes? You must get out of those sodden togs," Ann said.

"Our spare gowns are on our saddles," Edith told her, removing her wet bonnet.

They exchanged introductions, Ann exclaiming over Liberty's name.

"I'm American," Berty explained.

"Oh, how interesting, but I was surprised because Ronan repeated Liberty in his fever and we thought he meant freedom!"

"He did?" Berty brightened.

"I collect you are his light o' love," Sir Richard remarked, coldly. Pretty enough, he thought, but not the thing.

Liberty's wing-like brows grew closer. She replied indignantly, "I am no one's light of love, sir! Ronan is my aunt's cousin and we have been friends for years. Platonic friends," she added.

"I can't imagine! Such a hoyden, too," Sir Richard commented.

"Richard!" his wife rebuked him by her tone. She turned back to Berty, "Please, my dear, ignore my lord's rudeness. Worry and wakefullness over his godson has put him quite out of sorts. Until a footman brings in your gowns, warm yourselves by the fire."

"I must see Ronan," Berty insisted.

"Of course," Ann agreed and led them and her husband up the stairs to a long gallery and on to a bed chamber. Sir Richard halted them, saying, "Let me see if he is awake and presentable."

Ronan woke, naked, but for the bed clothes, and unshaven. Sir Richard called for Jacob, but he wasn't about. While Sir Richard looked for a shirt, Berty burst in, ran to Ronan and sprang into his open arms. They embraced each other like anything but platonic friends.

Lady Ann tried to usher Richard out, but he remained and Edith managed to peep in as well. Berty recollected herself and squirmed out of Ronan's arms. She blushed becomingly, her color already healthy in contrast to her faded Adonis.

"Oh, you aren't presentable! I shouldn't have. I ran away when I accidentally saw Uncle Augustus in his braces one day and here I am embracing you like this," Berty blurted out.

Everyone smiled, including Ronan. At that point, Jacob arrived with a stack of clean shirts and hastily covered Ronan's scarred shoulders. Sir Richard ushered everyone out.

By then Berty and Edith's legs felt limp as over-cooked asparagus. They looked as fagged as they felt. Lady Ann ordered maids to prepare chambers and loan them some of her night clothes. The gowns they had brought with them were damp and wrinkled. Berty and Edith felt too tired to eat; a first for Edith. Lady Ann escorted them to their chambers and asked if they would like tea, which they accepted.

After changing into night gowns and robes, they joined each other in Edith's chamber where the maids set a table with tea, delicate sandwiches and biscuits. Following that light repast, they collapsed into warm feather beds and fell asleep.

Chapter 16

A scene of turmoil assailed the Bodleighs when they reached the Westerly's. Mr. and Mrs. Westerly were in high dudgeon with Claude and Edith. Since Edith wasn't there, Claude bore his parents' anger for both of them.

"You muttonhead," his sire accused him, "How dare you permit your sister to ride to Burlington? You should have come to me at once!"

Mr. Walter Westerly, Senior, held his tongue upon seeing the Bodleighs enter. Sarah's dignified approached brought about reason.

"We missapprehended Liberty's attachment to the major and offer our profound apoligies for the disruption she has caused. We must now restore the girls to our families."

Edith's father decided to ride to Burlington with Claude the following morning, followed by the Bodleighs in the family coach. The Bodleighs would return with the young women in the coach the following day.

~~~

Berty rose at dawn and found her riding habit, gown and petticoats clean, ironed and hung in her room. She lit a candle, dressed in the gown, brushed and carelessly pinned her hair.

Carrying the candle, Berty traced the way to Ronan's chamber and knocked lightly.

"Come in, Liberty," he intoned.

She wasn't sure how he sensed it was her, but stepped inside. A fire still glowed in the grate lighting the room enough for Berty to see a small boy sleeping next to Ronan. The major was sitting up. He followed her eyes.

"My son, Christopher. He sleeps through anything."

Of course, they would have the child sleep with him, Berty realized. Adjusting to the fact, she said, "I had to see if you were still well."

Ronan motioned her closer. She set the candle down. He kissed her chilly hands and tried to warm them. Jacob, who had slept in a nearby dressing room, interrupted them.

"Sorry, sir, didn't know you had company," Jacob remarked with a coolness acquired on campaign.

Berty flushed and escaped back to her chamber. She found her cloak and hat and walked out into the cold morning. Berty took the path to the stables, where grooms were busy feeding. Sir Richard startled her when she searched for Rose.

"Up early, Miss Bodleigh!"

Berty felt the gruff knight intimidating and quietly replied she was looking for Rose. Sir Richard had reconsidered his first impression of Berty. Perhaps she wasn't a bit of muslin or one of Ronan's flirtations. Jacob didn't think so, and he would know.

"This way. You'll find her right and tight. A good bit of blood there, but undersized. In better condition than that big jade your friend rode."

"Yes, he held us up with his laziness," Berty agreed.

"Do you ride often, miss,"

"Almost everyday, but not far, nor fast," Berty replied, becoming more comfortable with Sir Richard.

They found Rose munching good hay. She came to the stable door to nuzzle Berty.

"Any further instructions for her, miss."

"She is used to being loose," Berty said.

"Very well, I'll have the grooms turn her into a paddock. Do you drive?"

"I drive old Mercury in a gig," Berty replied.

"Capital! I admire a woman who drives. My lady has no interest in horses, but she sits by me in my phaeton and curricle, which is all I could desire!"

The knight took her through the stables, showing Berty his fine thoroughbreds and Arabians. He observed she not only loved horses, but was a good judge of them.

They returned to the house for breakfast. Berty found the table occupied exclusively by gentlemen, the women sleeping later. "Perhaps I should wait for the other women," she said, timidly.

"Don't be shy, little hoyden! Why should you delay your breakfast because the other women need their beauty sleep?" Sir Richard asked. He introduced her to the others and placed her to his right.

"Miss Bodleigh doesn't need beauty sleep," an officer, with his arm in a sling, flattered her.

Others agreed.

"All quite true," Sir Richard said, "but don't listen to this pack of gazetted fortune hunters and beaus. They'll tell a damsel anything for her favor."

"I'm glad to be included in that discription at my age," Gervace said, "I fancy I'm still a beau, although stricken in years. Wholly at your service, miss. I apprehend you are a friend of the major's."

"Yes," Berty said eager to begin the meal and end the conversation.

She soon satisfied her hearty appetite with an abundance of bacon, sausage, ham, eggs, scones and everything else she could possibly desire. Days of barely eating, followed by a long horseback ride had left her famished. Sir Richard thought the wench had the voracity of a regiment.

Tristan, sitting opposite, watched, but didn't speak as he'd been told not to talk across the table. Berty noticed his striking resemblance to Ronan. The rumors were true.

After the meal, they walked to the morning room to read the latest papers and talk, except Tristan, who had to join his tutor in the school.

"I reckon I can expect more visitors today, your and Miss Westerley's relatives, Miss Bodleigh. My grooms say you carried a pistol and it had been fired. Did you encounter a problem?" Sir Richard asked.

In the excitement of seeing Ronan, that encounter seemed ages ago. Now it hit Berty full force. She feared she may have committed a crime. Unsure how to respond, Berty excused herself and left the room. In her chamber, Berty worried. What if the man died? What did her aunt and uncle think of her for leaving as she had? Would they be arriving that day? Suddenly she was at a stand, not knowing what she would do next. Berty needed to talk to Edith and warn her to keep silent, but Edith, beautifully dressed in the fashionable emerald gown she'd brought, had gone down to breakfast with Lady Ann. Edith spoke of her adventure as they glided down the stairs.

After breakfast, the ladies joined the gentlemen in the morning room. Lady Ann spoke excitedly, "Miss Westerly, do share your adventure with Sir Richard."

Edith, delighted at the attention, described how they had been menaced by highwaymen. "Liberty, I daresay, never one lacking backbone, held her cocked pistol upon the leader and when he approach to offer her an insult, fired and shot him in the shoulder! He'll probably lose his arm!"

At which point, Berty entered the room.

"Here's the gallant Amazon now!" a gentleman exclaimed.

Berty turned to run, but Sir Richard took her arm. "Don't be shy, Miss Bodleigh. We are quite impressed! Describe this dastard."

Instead, Berty asked, "Will they hang me if he dies?"

"For attacking maidens on the road? Of course not! By thunder, if anyone hangs, it shall be this villian," Sir Richard assured her.

She described the man and Sir Richard immediately knew him to be Guy Gayland, a notorious smuggler and suspected thief.

"So he thought to add kidnapping to his accomplishments," Sir Richard surmised, "How dare he threaten women in my domain! The Devil take him! I shall report him to the magistrate."

With her judgement of the man's character justified, Berty relaxed.

Rain and snow prevented outdoor amusement. Sir Richard and the men exercised in a room he used for boxing and fencing, but women, and men not inclined to sport, lingered in the drawing room, where Tristan and Christopher joined them after their lessons.

"Miss Bodleigh and Miss Westerly are friends of your father's from Boscawden," Tristan told Christopher. Tristan asked if they liked music, which they did. Tristan played violin and recorder. Christopher played a whistle. They undertook several simple songs with considerable verve and talent.

When the boys finished to great applause, Lady Ann recalled an art exhibit she'd seen in London. "Miss Bodleigh, are you acquainted with the Mr. Bodleigh who painted a portrait of our major two years ago?"

Liberty looked abashed, but Edith spoke for her. "That's Liberty! She's a painter and I must say, Berty paints famously!"

"A female portrait painter! I must tell Richard! We were much taken with that portrait, but before we could inquire about the painter, friends walked in and we left for the country soon after."

Ann sent a message to Richard, before inviting the girls to her boudoir. "I would like you to use one of my maids. She's quite good with hair. And I'd also like to offer you, Miss Bodleigh, some of my old gowns if you would not mind," Ann said, "I'm afraid I have nothing to fit your statuesque figure, Miss Westerly."

"Oh, that's quite all right. I have plenty of gowns at home, but Berty only has a few homesewn dresses," Edith said, "I daresay my hair does look awful."

"Your side curls look like horse mane," Berty said, adding, "Four dresses are sufficient for my needs."

"Upon my soul, is that all, Miss Bodleigh? That will not do for Burlington. We were going to London this season, but have decided to stay while Ronan is here. This is the first time Christopher has seen his father in two years. When Ronan recovers, I shall invite guests and throw parties. I'd love for you dears to be among my guests. I've always longed for daughters. My sons and their wives live far away and are too old to spoil. I'd love to purchase gowns for a daughter and watch her dance and enjoy herself."

"We'd love to stay, but I reckon our families will be looking for us," Edith said.

"Yes, our relatives are liable to show up anytime and we have provoked them," Berty admitted.

Lady Ann laughed, "Oh famous! I shall mollify them. Since we were preparing to leave for London, I have few guests and plenty of empty rooms."

Few guests, Berty thought. The house seemed full of people. Ann ordered her maids to bring out older gowns that either no longer fitted her forty-six-year old body or were out of style. Lady Ann hated to part with favorites. Her maids and seamstresses pulled lavender scented gowns out of armoires and trunks. They paraded gowns of fine muslin, silk, satin, velvet, a rainbow of colors, elaborate lace and ribbon. The girls gasped at the gorgeous gowns.

"I've never seen such beautiful gowns," Berty confessed, "But they are too fine for me and too large."

Ann giggled, "Of course, you have a dainty girlish figure, but I have an army of seamstresses who can fit them to you. Come choose at least one for now."

"That cerise silk. I've never seen such a wonderful design."

The gown in question was of simple design, with gold ribbon and embroidery on the bodice and sleeves. Diaphanous silk shimmered over a white under dress. Berty took it to her chamber to try on. It almost fitted the way it was, but she had never worn anything so low cut. She returned and Edith and Lady Ann commented on its suitability. Berty asked if the neckline could be raised.

"Why, Berty?" Edith asked, "It doesn't reveal cleavage as it is."

"Quite modest," Lady Ann agreed, "although best worn with stays, like all my gowns. We must show you how to display your gifts to advantage, don't you agree, Miss Westerly?"

Edith, who wore stays to better display her own 'gifts,' laughed. "Berty, you'll stun in that," Edith assured her, "But really, a bit of lift under the bosom would be most flattering."

"I'm not sure I want to stun anybody. I haven't recovered from shooting that horrid man!"

Ann smiled, saying, "I'm proud to know a young woman of such spirit! I wonder if I could have done the same."

Berty relented on the neckline. A seamstress pinned up places to adjust the fit.

Berty picked out a modest red-violet silk gown and a white dress with black ribbon trim. The seamstress said the red-violet gown needed the least adjustments and would be ready that evening.

Edith told Lady Ann that Berty didn't care for a lot of furbelows. Lady Ann replied she admired simple taste and apologized that these gowns were no longer the mode.

"I don't care a fig for the mode," Berty assured her.

Berty and Edith could not help but like amiable Lady Ann. How she came to bear a child by Ronan no longer shocked so much as mystified them.

Edith brought up Christopher, saying, "It is so kind of you and his lordship to take in that child."

"Oh, but he is the quietest, sweetist child. His mother died of typhus, but he barely remembers her and calls me mama."

Lady Ann went on to describe the circumstances of the child's conception gathered from the men who delivered him to her. "Such things happen in war and, of course. Ronan had to find a safe home for the child. And what better home than ours! Tristan longed for a brother and now they are devoted to one another!"

That morning, Ronan ordered and received a proper breakfast of eggs and meat. He also demanded a bath.

"But, sir, you should not bath in your weakened condition," Jacob objected.

Ronan dismissed that notion with his hand and also asked, "Do you intend that my hair grow as long as a woman's?"

Realizing his master felt considerably recovered, Jacob set to work, but after breakfast, a hair cut and bath, his master fell back in the bed to rest until noon, when he enjoyed another proper meal and asked to be dressed in civilian clothes. That and a brief walk with his crutches in the gallery exhausted him. He spent the rest of the afternoon recovering.

Late that afternoon, the Westerlys, Bodleighs and Brandolyns arrived within an hour of each other. This would have daunted any hostess but Lady Ann, who put all at ease. To the provoked families, she spoke with admiration for Liberty and Edith's resolve and perseverance to comfort a friend.

"I don't see why they couldn't have told us," Walter Westerly grumbled.

"You know I would have borrowed a coach and taken you," Sarah said.

"Would you have, Aunt?" Berty asked, doubtfully.

"Had I only known how you felt."

"But what about propriety?" Berty asked, sardonically.

"It would have been proper for me to visit my cousin," Sarah replied, mendaciously.

While Lady Ann mollified the families, Sir Richard took the Brandolyns in hand, apprising them of Ronan's recovery. The reverend, his wife and Benjamin displayed great relief, but they also noticed the two boys watching them. Sir Richard introduced the boys. The Brandolyns kindly acknowledged the children before Richard led them to his office for a private talk.

"I collect my nephew has fathered a child outside of wedlock," the reverend observed.

"Probably more than one," Sir Richard admitted, "But what is done is done, eh?"

The reverend nodded and asked, "Is he well enough to see us?"

"Well enough for a quiet visit, but possibly not well enough for a stern sermon," Sir Richard said.

"He has heard enough of my stern sermons to know right from wrong, sir. I am aware his health is currently fragile," Reverend Brandolyn replied, coldly.

Sir Richard took them to visit Ronan.

Well-groomed, with skin like alabaster, the invalid lay in his bed under an embroidered coverlet. Benjamin greeted him. Aunt Marie held his hand and kissed his forehead and his uncle nodded. Sir Richard left.

Marie sat in the only chair. Benjamin, straight forward, as ever, said, "We saw your son."

"We shall pray God forgives you," the reverend stated, "and ask that you sin no more."

Ronan responded with an indolent nod.

"We can discuss that another time," the reverend said. He took a light publication from a satchel he carried and placed it before his nephew. Ronan reached for his spectacles. He examined the publication, "*Music and Songs for Guitar, Pianoforte and Harp*. Music by a Kings Dragoon. Lyrics by the Reverend Eugene Brandolyn."

"I'll reimburse you for its publication," Ronan quietly responded.

"Not necessary. We have actually made a profit! I have deposited mine in the poor box."

"You may do the same with mine," Ronan said.

"You have a child to support," the reverend, remorselessly.

"I can support him, uncle. My diversions with willing women hardly seem sinfull compared to the the cruelties I've seen in this war. Perhaps driving sabres into men's throats has contributed to my wantoness, but that sounds like an excuse and I make none."

Berty and Edith, waiting outside to pay Ronan a visit, heard this and feeling they were intruding, backed away, but not so far as not to hear.

"You have ever tended to be wild as the Devon moors," his uncle stated. He asked his family to bow and said a silent prayer. "Now we shall let you rest."

Berty and Edith walked quietly and thoughtfully away.

~~~

Lady Ann summoned the two young women to meet with their families and decide the details of their stay. Ann treated the Bodleighs and Westerlies like longtime friends. She flummoxed them by insisting the young women stay with her. "We need youthful jollification here. The house accomodates Sir Richard's military friends, injured soldiers, our poor and elderly relations, but few young women!"

Walter Westerly decided Edith's stay in Burlington would be easier on his purse than her planned trip to London for the season and, although she wasn't likely to meet an eligible husband, readily agreed. Augustus held back. He hesitated to trust the Burlingtons with his niece and Ronan, a proven libertine, who almost certainly was the father of Tristan Burlington. More appalling, Augustus knew Lady Ann was the child's mother.

Sensing his disapproval, Lady Ann invited the Bodleighs.

"I have a business, my lady," Augustus informed her, "And I like to have my family about. Berty intended to visit a London friend, but Sarah would be returning."

"Of course! I beg you to allow Mrs. Bodleigh to stay awhile just to see how dear Liberty gets on. I'm sure having all his friends about will hasten the major's recovery."

"Perhaps for a week, Augustus," Sarah compromised, "You can not begin any projects in this disagreeable weather."

Augustus agreed to stay with Sarah for one week. The Westerly men would depart the following day and Claude return with addition raiment for the guests. "Do send all my best gowns," Edith said.

With that settled, the guests dressed as well as they could for supper. Berty requested that Alice, the maid, turn her back when she changed into a new petticoat suitable to the violet gown. Alice smiled at such modesty. She'd known Lady Ann to appear naked before Sir Richard. Alice showed Berty how to put on light stays and laced it from the back for her.

"I'm not used to wearing these. Can't say I care for them, but I suppose the gown will look better."

The gown fitted perfectly, although Berty felt uncomfortable exposing the top of her bosom. Looking in the mirror, she was surprised how well she looked with proper underpinnings. Not so hoydenish. Alice assured her she was decently covered and had nothing to be ashamed of.

"Gracious, miss, most women with your figure would want to display it!"

"Perhaps if I had a shaw, but I don't," Berty reflected, ignoring Alice's kind comment.

Alice went to work on Berty's thick, wavy hair, suggesting a trim, which Berty would not permit. With remarkable dexterity, Alice pinned the hair into a delightful mass of waves bundled in the back. Liberty almost didn't recognize the beauty who looked back at her from the mirror.

"Alice, my hair has never looked so well. You do have a gift!"

"Thank you, miss."

"Oh, don't 'miss' me! I'm no better-born than you are," Berty objected.

Alice lowered her head, "I'm sure you are, miss. I was left at a church door as a babe."

"Well that wasn't your fault and your papa could have been a great gentleman and your mama a lady for all you know. However, that doesn't signify. My mother's family were what you English call 'Irish bogtrotters,' but in America that doesn't matter a bit! Leastwise, not where I come from."

Alice listened with interest. Miss Bodleigh seemed to come from another world.

"No one will call me a hoyden now!" Berty declared, admiring herself in the mirror.

Berty joined Edith to walk to the drawing room, hoping to see Ronan well enough to join the others, but he dined in his chamber. The company stopped talking at the sight of the two well-groomed beauties. Augustus stared at his niece as if he'd never seen her before.

"Where did she get that gown?" he whispered to his wife.

"I believe Lady Ann has offered Berty some of her out-dated raiment."

Sir Richard turned to his smiling lady, "You've done miracles there, my lady!"

"Nonsense, Richard, they are natural beauties. Miss Bodleigh was like one of your young fillies who has run about the paddock and never had the tangles combed out of her mane."

Sir Richard chuckled, watching the few young gentlemen and some older ones, assail the young women. When the butler announced dinner, the men vied to escort the two into the dining room. Benjamin won Edith's hand upon his arm. Berty, refusing the younger men, honored Gervace.

"I must say, miss, you show refined taste in choosing me," Gervace joked.

Sir Richard sat at the head of his table with the two beauties on either side. Lady Ann reposed at the opposite end. The Reverend Brandolyn said a solemn, but brief, grace and all enjoyed a lavish meal.

After dinner, the men remained to drink and smoke and pass a chamber pot under the table for those who imbibed excessively. The reverend dampened the indulgence of some by sipping a mere glass of sherry and upholding a forbidding persona. A scowl from the reverend daunted many elbow benders. Major Trevelyan's friends recognized that scowl, for they had seen the major exercise it, too, but not to the same purpose.

After an interminable interval, the men, many reeking of alcohol and tobacco, joined the women in the drawing room. Tristan and Christopher roamed the room receiving the admiration of diverse ladies. Tristan seldom indulged in a moment's quiet; Christopher seldom spoke.

The Reverend Brandolyn invited Tristan to join him on a sofa with Mrs. Brandolyn. The reverend and Tristan soon rattled away in Latin. The reverend recited many amusing poems in that language. Christopher stared, until a pause in the conversation, then he repeated every word of one of the reverend's Latin poems.

The reverend smiled.

"He does that all the time. He repeats my lessons to me. Most annoying at times," Tristan said.

"Like his father," the reverend admitted.

At that point, a footman announced Major Ronan Trevelyan. "Speak of the devil," Gervace whispered to Miss Bodleigh and Miss Westerly, seated on a settee, surrounded by admirers.

Ronan entered on a crutch; George the footman following in case he needed assistance. The major wore a pale gray cutaway coat, gray trousers, a white waistcoat and simple white linen neck cloth. He held every eye with his ghostly beauty and took possession of the room with his overwhelming presence.

Ronan's wandering eyes paused on Liberty, his strength improving at the sight of her. He recognized one of Lady Ann's gowns adorned Berty. She was exquisite. His eyes lingered too long for propriety before he limped to Lady Ann. She raised her hand to be kissed and he gracefully did so.

"Always did make a entrance like a damned thespian," Gervace whispered, to the girls' amusement.

Benjamin, seated near Edith, grinned.

The major quietly asked George to place a chair for him in view of Miss Bodleigh. While George went on that errand, several military gentlemen approached the major, shaking his hand and repeating his nom de guerre, "Blue Devil!"

The major escaped his admirers and bowed to Edith and Berty. He took Liberty's hand in his, kissed it, but he failed to smile. Was she still the modest bluestocking he remembered, or had she changed? Ronan wondered if he knew her at all.

Ronan eased himself into the arm chair George had provided and sprawled his long legs in his usual shabmannered fashion. Berty smiled at his indelicacy. Ronan gazed at her without expression.

The soldiers, some of whom had swilled too much port in spite of the reverend's hard looks, replaced the ladies'civil conversation with talk of war. They spoke of the wastage of horses and the decimation of men from disease and battle.

The mention of horses, reminded Sir Richard of Gunpowder."Ronan, how did your Scimitar son stand fire?" Sir Richard asked.

"Like a rock, whether cannon, musket or rocket."

"By Jove, did he? Where is he now?"

"I ordered him taken to Boscawden."

"Is he there now?"

"If Sergeant Duncan breaths, he's there."

Berty interpolated with, "I saw him. The sergeant entertained us with Gunpowder's tricks."

"Tricks, he degraded an officer's charger by teaching him tricks?" Sir Richard protested.

"Winter quarters and wounds lead to boredom," Ronan explained, "How goes Sergeant Duncan in Boscawden?"

"Barnstable drew his cork," Berty answered, grinning.

"Did Duncan do honor to the regiment?" Ronan asked, unsurprised.

"He held his own. A most provoking man!"

Ronan nodded.

The soldiers resumed their martial accounts. Tristan and Christopher listened in rapt attention. Men stamped their feet, tapped the French drum beat and shouted, "Vive le Empereur!"

One bass-voiced gentleman imitated cannon and thus they brought to life a battle in the drawing room. Lady Ann held her ears and complained of the racket, but Sir Richard enjoyed it as much as the boys. When she sighed with relief, believing them finished, they talked of punishing thieves. Was there no end to their impudence? Did they not know how to behave among ladies? Elderly cousins took snuff and kept their smelling salts handy.

"Remember that fellow the provost hung with a mirror round his neck? Muttonheaded thing to steal!" one officer remarked.

"Do they always hang thieves?" a lady inquired.

"No ma'am, we usually flog them, man and woman."

"You flog women!" the shocked lady exclaimed.

"Please, let's not speak of such a sordid subject," Lady Ann begged, to be ignored.

"Well, don't you blue stockings think women equal to men?" the officer asked.

"I daresay, Miss Bodleigh is, riding about, shooting brigands," an admirer put in.

"What's this, Berty?" Augustus asked, in an alarm shared by Sarah and the Westerlies. Even the coldblooded major sat up.

"Some men attempted to prevent our journey," Berty confessed uneasily.

"So she shot the most forward of them," Edith said, proudly, "Before he could offer an insult."

"Is he dead?" Augustus asked.

"I only winged him; so I'm not sure," she replied and turning to Ronan remarked, sarcastically, "A missish thing to do, I'm sure."

With his usual composure, he replied, "Yes, it was, You should have aimed to kill. Now I shall have to hunt him down and give him a taste of the sabre."

"Only a taste?" Berty asked.

"The last thing he will taste, cold steel."

"The majestrate will hang him before you are well enough to do that," Sir Richard remarked, "They are searching for his hiding place. Gone to ground with his wound, no doubt."

Tristan turned to Christopher, "Did I not tell you it would be fun when your papa came here?"

Christopher climbed onto his father's good thigh. Finally Ronan smiled. His son brought him joy, whereas Miss Bodleigh troubled him. He thought she loved him, but did she love him enough? Or did his natural children offend her? He did not smile at her.

Christopher played a short melody on his whistle. Ronan took the whistle, played a short, rapid Irish piece and handed it back. Christopher repeated the piece.

Miss Brown came down from the nursery to fetch the boys for bed. The boys exchanged kisses with Lady Ann and Ronan. Tristan complained that the major's mustache tickled. Ronan bid the company good evening and, with George's assistance, rose and limped out of the room.

~~~

The day dawned bright, good for travelers. Liberty donned her riding habit intending to ride a little way with Augustus and the others. Sir Richard would be escorting the Westerlies a short distance. On the way to the dining room, she met Tristan with Christopher.

Ever loquacious, Tristan told her, "Chris read his favorite book to his papa last night."

Christopher held up a children's book about treating animals kindly. Tristan continued, "Then he slept with him to keep him warm. His papa, I mean, my godbrother, the major, is not well today. His valet, Jacob, says he has the headache. Jacob says the major gets a lot of headaches from an old head wound. It's right here." Tristan halted his oration to point at a place on his head, "The hair grows white there just like the saddle sore on a dark horse. Since the major is blond, I wonder the hair doesn't grow in black like on a gray horse. Why does hair do that?"

Berty didn't know. Tristan continued taking his friend to the nursery.

"That child never stops rattling," a voice came from behind Berty.

Benjamin Brandolyn walked up to her, his imposing height and handsome visage reminding her of the major, but Benjamin's heavier muscles swelled his sleeves, and he spoke with a Devon accent, "I wanted to discuss business with Ronan today, but he isn't up to it. It can wait; I have good managers in Exeter. Where is Miss Westerly, not down with the headache, I hope?"

"Edith never suffers headaches or any other indisposition, but she is inclined to sleep late. If I tell her you were asking for her at breakfast, she might change her habits!" Berty replied with a smile.

Benjamin returned the smile.

All the early risers sat at the table; the Brandolyns, the Bodleighs, the male Westerlies, Sir Richard, Tristan, Gervace and a few officers. After breakfast, the Brandolyns stayed behind with Sarah, while the others rode out. Tristan was permitted to ride a short way with his groom before turning back for his school lessons.

When Berty desired to return, Augustus and Sir Richard rode back with her. Sir Richard astonished them by beginning a long and intimate story about himself and Lady Ann. "As anyone can see, Ann adores children. Allows Tristan to talk excessively. He's like her in that, not like his sire. And I assume you know who that is, everyone else does."

Sir Richard continued telling Augustus and Berty the entire shocking story. In the end, he said, "Ann thinks I did it for an heir, which I did, but I mostly did it because she wanted another child. Deuced fools, both of us. She breached her morals to give me an heir; I breached mine to give her a child. It never occurred to me that Ronan would stamp his get with his fine looks. Yet, I don't regret it. I took advantage of my godson, I admit. He felt he owed me for his education, horses, everything. However, one shouldn't expect a cavalryman to hold the highest morals. Not those reckless Hussar souls!"

"I see you, Miss Bodleigh, are special to him, although not of the docile, submissive nature he would want in a wife. And I understand you are no heiress. Indeed you are as poor as he is. I'd hoped to see him spliced to a at least 10,000 pounds a year."

Berty bridled at these remarks, and Augustus objected,"Sir Richard, how do you know what he wants? He doesn't seem to want to marry at all, even for 10,000 pounds a year!"

Sir Richard shrugged and continued with, "Now what happened in Boscawden?"

Berty returned Sir Richard's forthright words with her own.

"Made a dog's breakfast of it, did he? Told you to compose yourself! Telling a woman to stop crying is like telling the clouds to stop raining! He knows nothing about women and can't stop playing the flirt. Need's a firm hand."

"I thought you said he would want a docile wife!" Berty reminded him.

"What he thinks he wants and what he should have are different things."

Augustus nodded in agreement, adding, "Ronan isn't a stickler for propriety like that gentleman who has been pestering you, Berty. Gideon was more concerned about your reputation than your safety. I feel somehow taken in by him."

"Gideon who?" Sir Richard asked.

"Gideon Talbert."

"Talbert dangling after Miss Bodleigh? Dash it, he belongs to my club. He frequented a London bawdy house until the abbess objected to his mistreatment of her trollops. A man must be rotten to the core when a madam bans him!"

"Is that true?" Augustus asked.

"I heard it from his own lips. Never cared for the hypocrit myself. Or anyone who mistreats a woman, no matter the state of her virtue. Whatever anyone thinks of my godson's morals, he would never harm a woman of any kind. I've heard officers say he risked his life protecting women from battle-maddened soldiers."

"Berty never liked him as we expected," Augustus admitted.

"I didn't feel comfortable about him," she added.

When they arrived back at the stables, Sir Richard asked Berty if she would like to take a drive in a curricle. The fine morning being young, she agreed. The grooms put a pair of well-bred grays to a dark red curricle and Sir Richard handed her up.

The knight demonstrated handling the reins when driving a pair and put the ribbons in her hands.

"Don't be nervous, miss, they can feel it. These are a quiet pair; never known them to bolt."

Thus encouraged, Berty soon got the hang of it, though she couldn't imagine why she would ever need to drive a pair.

"You can take Ronan out for fresh air, with Miss Westerly, of course. She might take up a bit of room, but you don't, so the three of you should fit," Sir Richard said, "Splendid! You took that turn as if you'd been driving a pair all your life. You can spring them on this straight stretch."

"Wouldn't Ronan want to drive himself?" Berty asked.

Sir Richard laughed, "I wouldn't trust him with the ribbons. He's never driven in his life and would drive like a cavalry charge. Dash it, miss, never let him handle the ribbons!"

A group of guests were taking the air along the drive when Berty tooled past at a good clip.

"I say, Miss Bodleigh is a dab with the ribbons," a gentleman remarked.

"Well, of course, she's been driving for years," Edith retorted, knowing driving old Mercury hardly compared with driving a pair of blood horses."

No one but Jacob saw Ronan that day. Jacob knew his master needed warmth, quiet and darkness; no food and no visitors. The following rainy morning, the headache dissipated. Ronan rose, ate a light breakfast in his chamber and allowed Jacob to dress him.

Berty and Edith found him in the long gallery with Benjamin Brandolyn and George, the footman. Ben had prepared a tall staff to replace the crutch. With that, Ronan determined to walk to the end of the gallery and back. He reached the end, turned and slowly limped back before allowing himself to rest in a chair.

"Very good, cousin! You'll be arm wrestling with me in no time!" Benjamin said, "Now, do you feel up to discussing business?"

"May as well," Ronan replied, watching Berty and Edith seating themselves near him.

"Central heating! Piped water! I want to expand the business to building furnaces, pumps, installing systems. What do you say?"

"I find central heating stiffling." As he said that, Ronan shivered.

"Yet you shiver!" Benjamin observed, "But I'll allow you are recovering from fever."

"We shall call a meeting of our investors. If they agree, we will divert profits into this new venture. If not, I will fund it."

Benjamin stared. "You will fund it? How?"

"I can borrow on certain assets. I'm sure our investors will wish to invest in your idea."

"What assets?" Benjamin asked.

Ronan didn't respond. He rose to make another journey to the end of the gallery. He and Benjamin switched to Latin so the ladies wouldn't know their business talk, much of it figures and calculations. Berty and Edith joined them. They stopped to admire one of the many sculptures, a marble copy of Bernini's Apollo and Daphne.

"I think I'd rather be ravished by Apollo than turned into a tree," Berty asserted.

"I agree," Edith said, adding, "But would you want to be ravished by, say, that brigand you shot than turned into a tree?"

"In that case, I'd prefer to be a tree," Berty said, turning to Ronan, she asked, "Would you protect me from wood cutters if I were a tree?"

"Yes, and small boys and birds. First I would challenge Apollo. The brigand is as good as dead when I find him."

Benjamin laughed. "That's the spirit, cousin!"

After another walk down the gallery, Ronan was subdued, shivering and hagged. George took him back to his chamber.

"Got a way to go yet," Benjamin remarked, optimistically. He offered the women his sturdy arms and escorted them to the drawing room.

They found the Reverend Brandolyn discussing the merits of crossing short horn bulls on his red Devon cows. "Produces a fast-growing calf. Of course, I keep a herd of pure Devon reds as well. Marie prefers them for cream and cheese."

"Interesting," Sir Richard admitted, "Perhaps I should try one of your red bulls on my milking short horns."

"You prefer Devon reds for cream?" Sarah Bodleigh asked Marie.

"Oh, indeed. We've always had them."

"I keep a Jersey and two Guernseys," Sarah said.

"Excellent cream producers, but too small," Marie explained, "The calves don't produce much meat. The Devons produce both cream and good sized calves and now with the short horned bull, we get a faster-growing calf as well."

"Mother taught father all he knows about cattle," Benjamin said.

"Benjamin, that's not true," his mother objected, "your Reverend father has studied all the latest publications on scientific farming. I only know what I learned from my father and observed tending my milkers."

As interesting as cattle breeding was, Berty excused herself and walked to her chamber to write to Miss Penthwaite. Lady Ann had given her writing paper franked by their MP. Liberty wrote that she would not be coming to London that March due to the return from the Peninsula and near death of Sarah's cousin, Major Trevelyan. She elaborated on the nature of the wound, the major's known heroism and their closeness to him.

"Uncle Augustus read of the major's latest exploit in the London Gazette. He saved the Duke of Wellington!"

The afternoon passed slowly until the Reverend Brandolyn sat down at the pianoforte. Benjamin fetched his flute and together they played from Ronan's music book. The reverend sang some of his hymns in a resounding baritone. Marie joined in her fine soprano.

Ronan appeared in the drawing room late in the afternoon, past the time the boys should have been out of the school room. He sat by the blazing fire. Edith and Berty moved to the sofa across from him. The spirited boys soon entered. Christopher bounced into his father's arms to be swung over Ronan's head. The boy giggled and begged to be lifted up again and again. When Ronan tossed him up, let go and caught him, Lady Ann admonished them, "Stop that! You'll give me vapours! You are hardly well enough for such frolicks, major!"

"Why were you late, today," Sir Richard asked Tristan.

"We misbehaved, sir," he replied, contritely.

"We? Both of you? What happened?"

"Yes, sir. Chris tossed my ink well and I spoke shockingly to him. Mr. Considine required that I write a 400 word essay in Latin on disiplining my tongue and Chris had to wipe up the ink and sit in the corner while I wrote and we both had to apologise to each other and Mr. Considine."

"What did you say?" Sir Richard persisted.

"Something I should not repeat, sir, and I shall not ever say those things again."

"He called me a verminous army bastard," Christopher cheerfully informed them with perfect diction. He smiled at that accomplishment.

One of Lady Ann's elderly cousins sniffed hartshorn from a dainty bottle.

"I'm sure you don't know what that means, Christopher," Lady Ann stated, believing what she said.

"Yes I do. It means I have lice and papa's a soldier and didn't marry mama. Only it's not true about the lice."

"Yes, Chris, I shouldn't have said any of that, esspecially after the trouble Miss Brown went to to rid you of lice," Tristan said.

One lady swooned, two more took out smelling salts and several gentlemen took snuff to celebrate this conversation. "This is why children shouldn't be allowed in drawing rooms," someone murmured.

"Tristan, we don't discuss such things before company," his mother informed him.

"Did I do wrong, too?" Christopher asked.

Without answering, Ronan picked him up again and lifted him over his head. Two more tosses and both were exhausted.

Benjamin joined Edith on the sofa. The elder Brandolyns sat nearby.

"How go Thomas and Adele?" Ronan asked.

"Adele is increasing again," Benjamin said, "She has presented Thomas with ten tokens of her affection. That gives you how many grandchildren now, papa?"

"Forty-three, is it not, Marie?"

"Forty-four, dear."

"By Jove!" Sir Richard said, "Forty-four grandchildren!"

"That they know of!" Benjamin added, with his mischievous grin.

Reverend Brandolyn bore the trials Ronan and Benjamin presented him with equanimity. He scowled at Benjamin and said, pointedly, "We will have more grandchildren when our remaining bachelor son marries." He then addressed his other prodigal child, Ronan, "You should visit Thomas. He's a don, now, and seldom has time to travel. I'm afraid his oldest still remembers you and has a notion of becoming a cavalry officer."

"Where do children acquire such ideas?" Benjamin asked, ironically. He turned to Ronan and spoke, as usual, ignoring the rules of polite conversation, "There must be some treatment for vermin when men are unable to bath regularly. What do soldiers do?"

"We smoke our uniforms. Added to our usual stench, one would think that enough to discourage lice, but it isn't," Ronan told him, adding, "I'd prefer investing in a remedy for vermin than central heating."

"You, who always sit near the fire! We should set a chemist on the vermin problem, but why are you so set against central heating?"

"If one gets too hot by the fire, one can walk to the other end of the room. With central heating, the entire room is hot."

Lady Ann broke in with, "That's true. When we attended a fete at the Regent's Brighton pavillion, the rooms were unbearably hot, weren't they, Richard?"

"I had to step outside. There must be some way of controlling the heat."

Benjamin, ignoring Edith, thought about governing the temperature in centrally heated buildings and of destroying vermin. "At least vermin don't cause disease," he mused out loud. A decidedly unromantic man, Edith thought. At least Ronan gazed at Liberty.

"Are you sure, Ben? We don't know what causes disease. Vermin may spread disease," Ronan countered.

Tristan walked over to discuss the new month of March, a welcome change in subject. "Mr. Considine told us March is named for the god of war, Mars. He says armies come out to fight in March. They march in March! But you have fought in winter, haven't you, major?"

"Yes. The ancients began their wars in spring. Ours depend on the state of our armies, the weather and roads. Did Considine mention the goddess of peace?"

"Yes, Eirene. Why isn't a month named for her?"

"Peace doesn't interest anyone. Peace is a dead bore," Ronan replied.

Soldiers laughed and ladies sniffed their vinaigrette.

Chapter 17

March began in a warlike fashion with storms, wind, rain and sleet. Augustus returned to Burlington Hall with baggage and Berty's sketching tools. Claude joined his sister. Other guests appeared at Lady Ann's invitation.

Every morning, Liberty found a new dress, hat or a pair of shoes awaiting her, all from Lady Ann's vast supply. Berty wondered if she should accept so much finery, but could not find a polite way of refusing. Meanwhile, she was particularly pleased with a new riding habit modeled after her old one, but of much finer material. She also found walking dresses and morning gowns.

People came and went in drawing room, saloon, morning room, gallery and library. Burlington offered little privacy. The Brandolyns lingered to talk business with Ronan, often before other guests. The reverend told his nephew that the music publisher wished to buy their next compositions and would pay a royalty.

"He would advertise and send our compositions to music shops," the reverend, a good businessman, told Ronan. Together they transcribed Ronan's compositions. Ronan played guitar and harp for brief periods as his strength returned. Ronan also wrote out several pieces for recorders and Irish whistles.

The reverend also collected stories from his nephew on the war and contacts for further information for his history of the Peninsula War.

"I wish to write from the soldiers' point of view. You are correct, though it shocked the ladies, war is more interesting than peace. What would one write about peace? It would be, as you say, a dead bore!"

The reverend found Dr. Jurgen's information regarding soldiers and disease especially interesting. "He states in the papers you brought that as many soldiers die of disease, malnutrition and exposure as die of wounds. I never considered that."

Reverend Brandolyn continued with quill in hand, "You mentioned deserters forming armies of bandits."

"Yes, I organized several guerrillero bands to attack one such band of over a hundred; British, Spanish, Portuguese, even some French deserters. They had robbed and killed civilians. We annihilated them," Ronan declared.

"You led those guerrilleros?"

"With pleasure."

The guests, including Berty and Edith listened intently.

"Did you offered quarter?" the reverend asked.

"No. Guerrilleros never give quarter. We killed every one of those brigands."

While the company listened, the reverend obtained details as to numbers, locations, descriptions of participants and actions; information never published in newspapers.

~~~

Miss Penthwaite replied to Liberty's letter.

"Dearest Berty,

I admire your rumgumption in traveling by horseback to see you dying friend and I'm exceedingly glad he survived. That you shot the villian who threatened you and Edith shows what we women are capable of. I won't swell your head with praise for you courage, for I believe more of us have such capabilities and would benefit from instruction in arms.

I hope Sarah and Augustus had more sence than throw conniptions. You and Edith are always welcome here. Perhaps when your friend is well, you can join me. As it is, I long to meet this dashing officer. I have read and heard of his heroics."

Helen continued with the on dit and news of her political and charity projects.

When Berty and Edith told Lady Ann of Miss Penthwaite, Ann requested the lady's address and sent her an invitation to visit Burlington.

~~~

In a mistaken belief that Ronan would assist him in his desires, Tristan brought up an issue he considered of the highest importance. He did this in the drawing room, an inappropriate place.

"Major, I believe it is time Christopher was breeched. He can not ride our pony properly in a skirt. Mama and Miss Brown refuse to listen to me on this, but they would listen to you."

"I know nothing about these matters. I shan't interfere."

"But Christopher is your son!"

Ronan dampened him with a scowl. Tristan brought up another subject, "Christopher and I want a dog."

Tristan iterated the reasons he and Christopher should have a dog, while Christopher stood nearby giving no indication he cared one way or another. Tristan claimed the only reason he was denied a dog was that Lady Ann abhorred fleas. "We could keep him in the stable," he said.

Unmoved, Ronan told him, "You only want a dog excessively because you can't have one."

Tristan realized that an officer who annihilated brigands didn't hold sentimental feelings about dogs or anything else.

~~~

Sir Richard asked Berty to paint portraits of his family. She sketched them one by one. When she sketched Tristan, he squirmed and talked.

Ronan, who was almost always near Berty, read a letter nearby. He harshly commanded, "Be still."

"And if I don't?" Tristan challenged him.

"I shall have Mr. Considine thrash you."

"Why don't you do it yourself?"

"An officer and a gentleman doesn't thrash boys. He orders some-one else to do it."

"Mr. Considine doesn't thrash."

"I will order him to make an exception," Ronan replied, leaving no doubt he would do so.

"Now the child has an unpleasant frown," Berty complained.

"It will serve him right to be recorded for posterity with that unpleasant aspect," Ronan replied, adjusting his spectacles to finish reading the letter.

Berty dismissed Tristan until he recovered his sunny disposition.

"You are heartless, Ronan," Berty remarked, "and bloodthirsty and cruel and..." She paused, collecting herself and facing Ronan. He'd taken off his spectacles and stared enigmatically at her.

"I'm sorry, I got carried away," she said.

"Yes, women are excessively emotional," he said chillingly.

"And you are excessively cold."

They sat in silence. Neither moved. Ronan, who had long thought Berty the love of his life, didn't feel cold towards her, and he knew he was not cruel, but he would not cater to her missishness with explanations.

Tristan applied to Sir Richard for assistance. Sir Richard would not agree to a dog, but he did suggest to Lady Ann that Christopher should wear breeches or trousers like Tristan. "I never understood why women dress little boys like girls," Sir Richard said.

"There's much that you don't understand, dear. Today you think a four-year old should wear trousers, next you will want him to sit at the table after dinner and drink with the men," Lady Ann said with her irresistible smile.

That evening, Ronan asked Augustus Bodleigh to step into a passage for private speech. Augustus reluctantly did so.

Edith turned to Benjamin, "I bet your cousin is asking for Berty's hand!"

Before Berty objected, Augustus returned, smiling. Ronan limped to his place across from Berty.

Edith giggled and said, "I just told Ben that you were probably asking for Berty's hand."

Ronan didn't respond in any way.

"I wouldn't accept any man who asked my uncle instead of me," Berty snapped, "And you should mind your own bread and butter, Edith." Then she added, "My uncle wouldn't be smiling if Ronan had asked!"

They were more mystified when Sir Richard ordered a post chase prepared for Augustus the following morning. Augustus informed Sarah and Berty he had business to attend to and departed.

~~~

The sun didn't appear to rise on the following cold, wet day. That afternoon, the major took his exercise in the gallery before seating himself by the drawing room fire opposite Gervace Markham. Liberty, Edith and Benjamin joined them on sofas.

"This detestable weather awakens old wounds, does it not, child?" Gervace asked, rubbing his arthritic knees. He still thought of Ronan as a child, even when the child looked haggard and old beyond his years as he did at that moment.

Ronan nodded. He felt every old injury. He'd expected to be walking normally by then, but his leg rebelled at every step. He placed a worn boot on the ottoman George brought.

Liberty noticed and remembered the threadbare, shabby second hand clothes Ronan had worn when she'd first met him after his graduation from Oxford. She realized that the major would probably always be poor. She didn't understand the business he and his cousin had. Guns, central heating, how were they connected? Were such endeavors profitable?

Tristan and Christopher interrupted her thoughts. Released from the school room, they burst into the room. Tristan spoke excitedly about everything that crossed his busy mind. Christopher held a small bowl of liquid soap and a fist full of straws. He walked to his father, sat on his good leg and held out a straw. Ronan accepted it and the two took turns blowing bubbles.

"Trist says he's too old for this," Christopher said, "But you aren't." Ronan smiled and looked younger.

Berty studied the iridescence in the bubbles. Christopher got down and offered her a straw. They all blew bubbles. Benjamin found a clay pipe and dipped it in the soap, but his bubbles didn't float; they bubbled over the pipe, making a mess.

"Ben could invent a way to make bigger bubbles," the major claimed.

Ben rose to the challenge. He stalked out of the room to procure needed materials. Minutes later, he returned with a four-inch wire hoop with a handle and a basin of dissolved soap. He demonstrated his invention, waving his hoop to release large bubbles.

"Bravo, Ben!" Edith exclaimed.

"My cousin will insist I patent it, although my legal brothers will laugh at me," Benjamin claimed. His cousin smiled.

~~~

Ronan joined the others for meals. He sat next to Berty, but seldom spoke. Their friends wondered what went on between them, for they didn't act like lovers and often, Liberty seemed wroth with him for his coldness. They didn't see him reach for her hand under the table and her allowing him to hold it.

When George handed out mail in the morning room, Richard wondered why Ronan always had the biggest stack. What on earth did he do to have so much correspondence? Berty noticed this, too.

March finally, grudgingly provided a fine afternoon for Berty to take her friends for a drive in the curricle.

"Dr. Waddles says you are well enough to take the air," Sir Richard told his godson, "Would you like Miss Bodleigh to drive you?"

"Yes, if it pleases her."

"Would it please you, Miss Bodleigh, to drive Edith and the major?"

"Yes, I'd prefer to drive with companions," she replied with coolness.

"Oh aren't you two cozy!" Sir Richard remarked, taking his godson aside and saying, "Still making a dog's breakfast of things, aren't you?" You can be charming when you want to. Why don't you want to?"

Ronan didn't reply. Unsure of the depth of her vexation with him, he reconnoitered. Gervace uttered something about needing to take him in hand and followed the young people out to the waiting curricle. Berty and Edith wore warm stylish cloaks and feathered hats, the major a caped greatcoat and hat. Gervace helped Liberty up. George helped the major. Benjamin, left out due to lack of space, helped Edith.

"A damsel on each side to keep you warm, my fireburnt cousin!" Benjamin said.

Ronan rudely stretched his arms over the shoulders of both women.

Ignoring him, Berty started the frisky steeds. They trotted briskly down the drive. When Berty took her eyes off the team for a second, she saw Ronan watching her. She deftly handled the ribbons on a turn as they clipped onto the public road into Burlington. They passed working men heading to the tavern at the end of their day. Two crippled men waved to them at the tavern. Ronan asked Berty to stop.

"Major Trevelyan!" greeted Sergeant Lightfoot, "We heard you were back with a wound. Glad to see you out and about and between two prim articles! Lady driver, if that don't beat all! Daresay we shouldn't be surprised what a beau like you would be up to!"

When the sergeant finished his oration, Ronan introduced Miss Westerly and Miss Bodleigh and tossed the two soldiers some shillings.

"Give the grays the office to proceed, Miss Bodleigh," Ronan ordered.

"Well, I never!" from Edith, "Prim articles are we!"

She held her hat as Berty drove the team off at a swift trot. Berty turned them down a coast road Sir Richard had shown her, slowing the team to watch the sea washing against the shingle below.

"I used to swim there," Ronan remarked.

"Do you like swimming?" Berty asked, realizing Ronan's arm had surreptitiously reached round her waist.

"Yes, in summer."

"I wouldn't think you'd like it today, although if you like, we can stop!" Berty commented, "Do you swim, Edith?"

"No, never, have you?"

"No, but I've waded in the Chesapeake Bay on hot days. Grandmama never liked it when I got my skirts wet, though. What do you wear when you swim, Ronan?"

"Nothing."

"I suppose that's why I don't know any women who swim. Do you, Edith?" Berty retorted, not the least discomposed by his answer.

"No, our skirts would prohibit it I think. I say, that would be jolly, wouldn't it, to swim on a hot day? Perhaps we could wear bloomers."

"I wouldn't be caught dead in bloomers!"Berty replied, "What do you think of bloomers, Ronan?"

"I've never heard of them."

"They are something like breeches that some women wear under petticoats. I'm sure there's a way for women to swim while preserving modesty, Edith," Berty continued.

"Why preserve it?" Edith asked, "We should have private places for women to swim nude, if we wanted to. Of course, you wouldn't want to. You won't even undress with me watching. I've heard sea bathing is quite healthy."

"Edith, be careful, you might shock the major!" Berty said, sarcastically, "Next you'll be showing him those cards you had at school!"

Ronan gave Berty a wry glance. "Cards?"

"Picture cards. I've not seen them, but Edith has described them to me, in detail!"

"Berty, please, you discompose me!" Edith protested.

"You've discomposed me numerous times with your risque talk, Edith," Berty said, "I doubt we could discompose the major, not even if you showed him your bawdy picture cards!"

"They have those cards at girls' schools?" Ronan asked.

"We bought them from visitors," Edith explained.

"I shan't send my daughters to school," Ronan decided.

"You'd keep your daughters home with their mama to prevent them seeing a few bawdy cards?" Berty asked.

"I wouldn't want them to become saucy minxes," he replied, pointedly.

"Or brazen hussies like Edith and me! You'd want your daughters to sit and sew until they needed spectacles and receive no education what so ever. And, of course, marry your old army conrades from twenty years before they were born!"

"You misjudge me, miss, but I see you are bent on quizzing me, so have at it."

"Oh that takes all the fun out of it!" Berty turned, shining her sauciest smile upon him. He returned it, for a change.

"You two are as changeable as March weather!" Edith observed.

On their return, the major appeared refreshed rather than wearied by his outing. The women bounced out of the curricle, bright and giggling.

"Brazen hussies," Ronan murmured to Sir Richard as he passed.

"Are they, now? I apologize for subjecting you to such company," Sir Richard remarked.

"Yes, I'm devastated," Ronan replied with a smile.

The good mood continued through dinner. After the women left for the drawing room, the men drank and smoked. The reverend took his single glass of sherry and Benjamin, who preferred ale to wine, also took a glass. Ronan accepted one glass of port and no more.

"Come, major, more port, builds the blood, esspecially this soldier's port you sent us from Porto!" Sir Richard encouraged him.

Benjamin tried it and found it too strong for his taste. Others made up for these cautious drinkers. Including Sir Richard, who reached the point of being half disguised. Which reminded him of his travels in foreign climes. He began with expounding how his older brother had been able to take the Grand Tour and he had not. "Being thought too stupid for a classical education, but broad shouldered and hard headed enough for the army," he said.

Before Sir Richard had gotten far in his discourse, a jug-bitten officer interrupted with a voluble complaint against army surgeons. "The bloody arses, with their butcher's aprons, keep us waiting until our wounds are almost healed, then plunge cold steel in to prod around for a bit of lead. Lucky I still had some ball of fire in my flask."

"That weren't half so bad as the time I caught the clap in the officers' brothel. Why have an officers' brothel if the doxies are no cleaner than common hedge whores?"

"I take my manhood to the surgeon and with out so much as a how do you do, he smacks it with a hammer and..."

At that point, Sir Richard had the footman remove the officer.

"I say, what the deuce is this!" he objected as they carried him to his chamber in the bachelors' wing.

"Cognac anyone?" Sir Richard offered.

Sir Richard's butler brought out bottles smuggled from France. After the officer's diatribe, even the Reverend Brandolyn accepted a glass. They warmed the glasses, inhaled the rich bouquet and drank it slowly.

While the men whiled away the time in drink, smoke and tales, Lady Ann served coffee and tea. Snuff-taking old ladies fussed over Christopher's long golden curls and big, blue eyes. "What a good, quiet boy!"

Sarah and Lady Ann spoke to Tristan about his school work. Sarah spent as much time as she could with the boys. Berty tired of her affectionate praise of them. Berty and Edith grew bored with small talk. "I do wish the men would hurry up," Edith said.

Tristan walked over to praise the sketch Berty had finally been able to finish of him. "Had I known how good it would be, I'd have been prefectly quiet from the first. Some people think I'm incapable of quiet, but it's not true, is it, Miss Bodleigh?"

"No, you sat quite still for our last session. And I'm sure the major's baleful looks had nothing to do with it," she said.

"Well, they did, actually. I'm generally quite fearless, of course, but when my godbrother says he will do something, he will, decidedly. And, you know, he's cut Fenchmen's throats with sabre and dagger. The other soldiers have told me so. One tries not to cross him."

Berty frowned, "He's not really a nice person, is he?"

Tristan thought a second, "No, but he's an out and outter."

Berty looked puzzled.

"He's the most excellent person I know. Papa says if I have half my godbrother's courage and brains, he'll be pleased with me. But, no, he isn't soft. That's a good thing, though. Papa says women are quite incapacitated by their emotions and men hold everything together."

"Gammon!" Berty said.

"I didn't mean to offend, Miss Bodleigh, but that's what papa says. I daresay this isn't a proper subject. It's not what I meant to speak with you about. I meant to ask you if you would do a likeness of my brood mare and her colt."

"Oh, I'd love to. I love mares and foals!"

"Capital! My mare presented me with our second foal last month. Christopher and I waited in the stable all night. We tried to take turns watching, but a groom had to wake us early in the morning. Mares always wait until nobody is looking. Quite shy they are," Tristan went on.

"Yes, I can understand. Our mares always foal in the pasture when alone," Berty said.

The men finally staggered in, disrupting conversation. Sir Richard was obviously too ripe and ready. The Reverend Brandolyn held himself too stiffly. Benjamin was in high ropes. The other officers and gentlemen exhibited various states of inebriation.

"I daresay, Ronan, with a staff to lean on, no one can tell if you be foxed or not," Benjamin said.

"Not," he replied, sitting across from Berty.

"You aren't knocked up from our outing," Edith asked him.

"No, miss. I'm accustomed to activity."

"I was just telling Miss Bodleigh about my mare, Calypso. We watched her drop my new colt, Hermes. She really did drop him, too, but he came in a bag and wasn't hurt," Tristan continued.

"Hermes, god of travel, very good, Tristan," Ronan commented to change the subject.

"Thank you. The grooms call him Herman, though. I was considering Priapus because stallions have such..."

Benjamin interrupted with a guffaw.

"There are ladies present, child," Ronan informed the boy.

Tristan was too naive to blush. He went back to his mare, figuring women wouldn't be disturbed by anything a mare did. "Anyhow, Calypso just plopped Hermes in the straw..."

Lady Ann interrupted this time, taking him aside to whisper that one did not talk of births and genitals in society.

"Plopped Hermes in the straw!" Edith repeated, giggling, "Those Greeks were a vulgar lot, weren't they!"

"Not only shouldn't children be allowed in drawing rooms, they shouldn't be allowed to watch livestock procreate," an old tabby declared.

"Balderdash!" Sir Richard exclaimed.

"A child can't know too much about God's creatures," the reverend said.

"But perhaps children should be seen and not heard?" Lady Ann's cousin quietly remarked.

"What occurs in the stable, stays in the stable, child," Sir Richard said, "Must not talk like a groom around ladies. Noble creatures, horses, but they have no sence of propriety. When a mare's ready for a stallion, she lets him know, no simpering and blushing."

"Richard!" his wife spoke warningly.

"I forget myself," Sir Richard confessed and resumed recounting his travels. "Where was I before that jackanapes interrupted with his whore house woes? Old tabbies may traduce my godson, but let it be said, he never frequented officers' or any other brothels. A cavalier servente, a cisisbeo, but no harm in that, is there? A fine tradition."

"Richard," Lady Ann warned again.

"Oh, yes, Constantinople, the Ottoman Empire, most exciting place after studying the rubble of Athens. I did like those caryatids, though."

"What's a caryatid," Tristan asked.

"A stone woman who holds up a temple. Damnedest thing about those sculptures, the women were clothed and the men naked. Napoleon may have prevented me taking the Grand Tour, but I found Constantinople to my taste. Except for the Turks' abominable unatural lust. For once I was glad to be ugly. And Ronan unhappy in his beauty. He's lost his looks now, but at eighteen, a striking lad."

Some glanced at the subject of this remark. Although Ronan no longer looked eighteen, except for the pallor of illness and the hardness of manhood, the guests failed to see how he'd lost his looks.

"Sir Richard continued, "A pasha offered me a large sum in gold and a fine stallion for him. Tempting, but I passed. He's my best friend's son, one of the greatest satisfactions of my life. No one offered me any-thing for my rodent-faced nephew, who'd I have gladly parted with. He and his brothers have gone to America to make their fortunes, so I don't have to look at them. Where was I?"

"Ottoman Empire," a drunken voice replied.

"Ah, yes. I recieved offers for Ronan all over the Empire. I feared they would try to kidnap him. All sodom..."

"Enough of the Turks, Sir Richard!" Ronan interrupted.

"Yes, Richard, you are getting carried away. There are ladies present," Lady Ann said.

"Ah, so there are and very fine ones, too, diamonds of the first water," he said, glancing at Berty and Edith, "But I'd like to have seen the inside of a seraglio, one with eunuchs guarding them."

"Richard! Do keep a civil tongue in your head!" Ann, again.

Benjamin giggled uncontrollably.

"Poor Mr. Considine," Berty observed, "He'll have to define seraglio, eunuch and many other things to Tristan."

Miss Brown, having no idea what had been discussed, arrived for the boys. Before he left to prepare for bed, Christopher promised Ronan, "I'll read from Aesop's tales to you tonight."

"Yes, anything but the Turks," Ronan replied, excusing himself, to also prepare for bed.

"Not himself," Sir Richard said, gloomily, "Probably never recover. Past time he settled down."

On the way to their chambers, Sarah told Berty, "This is a most outrageous house! I must say, I haven't been bored," Sarah admitted. Thank goodness, Augustus wasn't here tonight."

"Where has Uncle Augustus gone?"

"That is a secret, but I assure you it is a mission that will please you," Sarah said, smiling.

Sarah changed the subject to the charming little boys. "I've not seen two such beautiful, well-behaved boys. Augustus, too, adores them. I daresay, we will miss them most of all when we return home. I wonder if we could invite them to visit this summer, perhaps to pose for their portraits? That is better than painting from sketches, is it not?"

"Yes, but I thought to return here to paint the Burlingtons."

"I shall return with you, then. Christopher has the biggest blue eyes, does he not? Such a charming child!"

"When he's not sucking his thumb," Berty said, disagreeably. How spoiled her aunt's children would have been if she had had them! Then it occurred to Berty, perhaps she was spoiled herself.

~~~

Rain dashed against windows the next morning, discouraging guests from leaving the house. After breakfast, Berty, Edith, Benjamin and Ronan perambulated in the gallery, getting light exercise while admiring pictures and sculptures. Edith and Berty noticed that where ever they went, the two men showed up. George, the footman, reported their activities to Ronan.

Berty thought it suspicious when they went to the library to find books to read, Ronan and Ben showed up soon after. Benjamin browsed books, while Ronan wrote letters. Jacob copied the letters.

"I'm not a secretary, sir," the boy objected.

"You are idle; you will copy these letters rather than read mawkish women's books," Ronan told him.

"What mawkish women's books do you read, Jacob?" Berty asked.

"Books by Miss Burney, Miss Austen, Miss Haywood and Miss Edgeworth. I bought them at auction from a dead officer's effects. They are my favorite possessions, Miss Bodleigh!"

"An officer read mawkish women's books, fancy that, Edith! Aunt Sarah, Edith and I love those mawkish women's books!" Berty exclaimed, "Have you ever read any of them, Ronan?"

Without looking up from his writing, he replied, "One insipid effort by Miss Burney."

"Oh what a grim snob you are!"

"They put foolish romantical notions in Jacob's empty head," Ronan said, scratching away with his quill and wondering why a better writing instrument had not been invented.

"Yes, sir," Jacob replied, "Notions like keeping locks of hair and stacks of letters!"

"Copy this," Ronan said, sternly.

"Do you keep those things, Jacob?" Berty asked.

"No, miss, he does!" Jacob grinned at his revenge, adding, "And they are all from Boscawden!"

"Copy this, also, you impertinent goose!" Ronan replied, putting down his pen and spectacles.

Berty brushed by, smiling. He caught her hand and kissed it.

That afternoon, guests gathered to watch Sir Richard fence with Claude Westerly, Claude had studied under a French master in London and thought himself expert.

"Learned all the Frenchman's tricks, did you?" Sir Richard asked. "By Jove, maybe you can teach them to this old dog, eh?"

Settees, benches and chairs lined the exercise room where Sir Richard practised boxing and fencing. Most of the guests stood or sat around the room.

Ronan, using his cane, limped in and sat on a long settee. Christopher sat on his knee. Berty, Edith and Gervace joined him on the settee. Tristan and Benjamin stood nearby with two young men.

"I remember when Sir Richard told you that gentlemen didn't fight with their fists." Gervace spoke to Ronan, "Now he boxes!"

"He meant to discourage Benjamin and I from fighting," Ronan replied.

"You were the one who always started it, even when I did nothing to vex you," Benjamin retorted, sanctimoniously.

"Humdudgeon, Benjamin, and don't start anything now!" Gervace said.

One young gentleman of the dandy set, a cousin to Lady Ann, Mr. Sitwell, stood nearby. He was rusticating with the Burlingtons to avoid his creditors. An inveterate gambler, he perceived an opportunity to recover some of his London losses. Sitwell commented, "Sir Richard is long in the tooth to be fighting a young buck like Westerly, ain't he?"

The others agreed. "How old is he?" someone asked.

"One and fifty," Gervace replied.

Edith said, "Claude should be ashamed to fight an elderly man like that!"

Liberty studied the well-made knight. He appeared to be solid muscle, not as slender and lithe as Ronan, but not at all thick in the waist. Sir Richard looked younger than fifty-one. His dark hair grew thick and curly. He retained all but one tooth and they were white. By any measure, an imposing man.

Yet, when Sir Richard readied himself for the bout, he moved slowly, stumbled once, dithered in selecting the foils and requested assistance donning the padded vest. Lady Ann cautioned him against taking on young Claude, only twenty, but Berty detected a falseness in her tone, and Ann smiled.

Gentlemen placed bets, mostly on Claude. Gervace bet a pound on Sir Richard. Sitwell turned to Ronan, "What about you, major, care to wager? I know you're loyal to Sir Richard, would you bet on him? Say twenty guineas."

"Forty," Ronan replied.

Benjamin grabbed the settee to support himself. Edith, who had just wagered a pound on Claude, gasped. Berty felt a lump form in her throat. How could he! Was Ronan a profligate wastrel after all?

"By all that is holy, you must be rolling in lard, cousin," Benjamin ejaculated, "Tell me where you acquired this lucre!"

"That sets a bad example for the boys," Berty warned Ronan.

Ronan ignored them. The bout began. As the opponents moved Ronan named most of Sir Richard's positions to his sons. How he longed to be the one fighting! Accustomed to constant activity, he was used to filling empty time with fencing and laying with his mistresses. Now he was crippled and alone.

Claude thrusted and danced with speed and grace. Sir Richard struggled, fell back, stepped slowly, hardly seemed to have a chance. Yet he parried each of Claude's thrusts.

"Sir Richard's been lucky, so far," Sitwell said, "But look at him, he's winded."

Sir Richard panted, drew back, struggled to catch his breath, practically stood still, parrying Claude's advances.

Gervace looked at Ronan and chuckled. Ronan exhibited his usual serenity.

"I don't reckon you'd care to make it sixty guineas?" Sitwell asked, confident he'd won forty.

"Yes, make it sixty," Ronan replied, with a blithe smile.

Everyone in the room gasped. Berty felt a pain in the pit of her stomach. The wretch! She detested gamblers!

Sir Richard appeared ready to collapse, while Claude whisked about energetically. Claude had worked up a sweat and breathed heavily, but no wonder with his exertions. Sir Richard had barely moved. And then he did move, challenging Claude, one thrust after another, driving him back and then one final parry and a thrust to Claude's chest. It was over. Sir Richard won.

Sitwell staggered back as if struck. The room filled with groans. Gervace laughed and hugged Ronan.

"I'll have to give you a vowel until I see my banker," Sitwell told Ronan. In fact, Sitwell had no idea where to get sixty guineas. Even the money-lenders had refused him.

"You have until next Wednesday," Ronan replied icily.

~~~

Ronan remained in his chamber with a headache the next day, a Sunday. In the afternoon, Liberty took Edith and Benjamin for a drive in the curricle. Benjamin claimed Ronan's headache was a clever way to escape an abysmal sermon. "Papa's too polite to condemn another man's preaching, but I will. That was one of the worse I've heard. I've heard better from Methodists. Papa's curate is preaching in Papa's absense and his sermons are above that."

Benjamin amused them with risqué raconteurs collected over pints at taverns in manufacturing cities and London. Benjamin also attended scientific meetings in London, while his conscientious manager and accountant oversaw Brandolyn Arms in Exeter. He engaged the women with enthusiastic talk of his business plans.

"Why do you keep Ronan as a partner? He isn't even here most of the time?" Berty asked.

"He's the brains, I'm the brawn!"

"You do yourself a diservice," Berty said. Edith agreed.

Benjamin laughed. "I can't touch his head for figures, his ability to raise money and his ideas. You notice he constantly writes and receives letters, and they ain't billet deux! He knows people with money and influence and experimenters. He suggested the design for our guns, and very popular they are, too.When he was an ensign, he sacrificed his own money for my experiments. "

"How did he acquire this money, by gambling?" Berty asked pointedly.

"My cousin doesn't gamble, Miss Bodleigh," Benjamin claimed.

Edith snorted.

"It's not precisely gambling when you generally win," Benjamin said, "He played whist, a game that requires intellect."

"Yes, I've heard that," Berty admitted, "I've also heard things about Ronan and wealthy ladies."

Benjamin smiled, "One for the ladies, is our Ronan. A ciscisbeo, approved by husbands who maybe had interests of their own. Meanwhile my cousin escorted their wives to balls and to church."

"So we've heard," Edith said, adding, "I reckon these ladies gave him money for his company."

"Now aren't you a minx to reckon such! Of course, this was before he lost his looks!" Benjamin retorted, good naturedly.

"I find the idea distasteful," Berty said, "Women who take money from men for favors are thought low. Men who do so are no better."

"Now, now, Miss Bodleigh, are you by chance a Methodist?"

"Certainly not, but I do believe in an equality of the sexes."

"Bravo!" Edith agreed.

"That's most interesting," Benjamin exclaimed, "I'm honored to be driven by such a woman. I assure you, I entertain many advanced ideas, myself."

"Do you Mr. Brandolyn?" Berty asked.

"Yes and I often argue with my brothers over their reluctance to enter the modern world. For instance, I see no reason for a man to sire by blows, nor for a wife to be constantly increasing. Six children is an ideal family size, but my brothers refuse to take my advice."

"Yes, six, don't you agree, Berty?" Edith asked.

"We've not had any, so I don't see how we can determine the number, but six sounds reasonable," Berty replied.

"That's true. However the point is, wives shouldn't be slaves to their husband's wants and for many poor families even six would be too many," Edith said.

Liberty nodded in agreement.

"Aye, we agree. And, with the help of Invention, men can enjoy their wives without producing unwanted children," Benjamin went on.

"What Invention do you mean?" Berty asked.

"Oh, pardon, I forgot myself. I shouldn't have entered this subject with maidens. I do get carried away and speak to women as if I were talking to my brothers and workmen," Benjamin replied shamelessly.

"What invention?" Edith repeated Berty's question.

"Inventions and practices. These things are as yet primitive, but someday, I can see people having complete control over their procreation without giving up their God-given pleasures. And when that day comes, there will be no wars, because there will be no superfluous men to fight and die."

"I declare, that is exciting!" Berty said.

"Of course, my cousin Ronan laughs at me and says there will always be wars and doesn't believe there is such a thing as too many children," Benjamin said.

"He would!" Berty said in a tone of disgust.

"So Gothic," Edith agreed.

~~~

The following day arrived with more wind and rain, but the boys ran around joyfully celebrating their birthdays. Since they were born a few days apart and one boy was illegitimate, the Burlingtons chose to have one party for both. No other children were invited and few adults. Those included the Bodleighs and Brandolyns. Augustus had returned the day before from his mysterious mission and could barely retain his glee. Sarah chastised him for secretiveness, but he did not relent.

Cook produced a vanilla cake, sugared almonds, lemonade and other delights. The Burlingtons invited the kitchen and household staff to watch the boys when Cook presented the huge cake.

Most important to the boys was the presence of Christopher's father. The major recovered from his headache sufficiently to join them. He drank lemonade while everyone indulged in cake. After the cake, Miss Brown took Christopher away for several minutes. While everyone awaited his return, Tristan showed them his new violin.

Miss Brown returned with Christopher, dressed like a little gentleman for the first time in buckskin breeches and top boots. Christopher showed off with a cartwheel before standing next to his father.

"Now I shall teach him how to decently ride a horse," Tristan declared.

Augustus slipped out of the drawing room and returned a few minutes later with a red and white spaniel at his heels.

"Corky?" Berty said under her breath.

"Happy, Corky's brother," Augustus announced, "And he is yours, Master Burlington."

Tristan knelt down and hugged Happy. The dog, furiously wagging his tail, slathered him with his tongue. Tristan laughed. Augustus informed him, "Happy is a gift from Major Trevelyan."

"What!" Tristan turned in surprise to Ronan, "You desembled!"

"Did I?" nonchalantly.

Tristan paused, smiling, "Well, you didn't lead me to expect you would give me a dog!" Tristan thanked him profusely.

The Burlingtons laughed. Augustus explained that Ronan had come to him saying he knew nothing about dogs but thought Corky, Augustus' dog, a good sort of dog and asked if Augustus could find one for Tristan. "Happy's owner had died and he was staying with a friend. Happy is trained, which is important for your first dog," Augustus said and demonstrated Happy's obedience at heel and sit. Augustus spent the rest of the day with Happy and the boys.

Liberty sketched Happy for Tristan. She also sketched the four-year-old, miniature gentleman, Christopher, in his new breeches. Unlike Tristan, Christopher stood still. Meanwhile, Ronan played the harp.

After a lavish supper, the gentlemen reposed over wine and cigars. Sir Richard ordered a fresh pipe of port tapped to celebrate the boys' birthdays. He insisted Ronan indulge in a second bumper of the powerful port, a mistake since Ronan no longer enjoyed a strong head. Nor was he the only sufferer. All the military men became top heavy. Benjamin, too, was foxed. Only the Reverend Brandolyn and Augustus Bodleigh declined the proffered beverages. When the military men began singing bawdy songs, they excused themselves and joined the ladies for tea, coffee and chocolate in the drawing room.

The men's loud singing, or bellowing, penetrated the walls and reached the ladies.

"This is outside of enough!" Lady Ann objected, "My lord has allowed too much port to flow, including down his own throat, I fear!"

"Why doesn't she stop them?" Berty whispered to Edith.

"You can't stop men once they start drinking. It's unheard of for a woman to request the men to leave off drinking," Edith replied.

"I would. If it weren't for their stinking smoke, I'd refuse to leave the table. Miss Penthwaite does not allow the men alone at the table after dinner in her house," Berty said aloud.

"I long to see you married to a proper gentleman, Berty. It would be most entertaining!" Edith retorted.

"I long to meet this interesting woman," Lady Ann said, "I fancy we will get along famously. As to the men, my Lord is usually a paragon of sobriety. He rarely allows the men to stay more than two hours at the table after we depart. At most houses, the men sit and drink for hours!"

Other women nodded in agreement.

"Has Miss Penthwaite replied to your invitation?" Berty inquired.

"Not yet, but it is too soon to expect an answer," Lady Ann replied.

At last, the men staggered in, singing The Rambling Soldier, "A-courting all the girls both old and young, with me ramrod in me hand and me flattery tongue, To court them all, but marry none."

Benjamin, singing along, stumbled in, supporting his lame cousin. They collapsed on a sofa opposite Berty and Edith.

"I daresay, this won't do, cousin," Benjamin said, looking at Edith.

They rose and staggered to the opposite sofa. Ronan sat between Berty and Edith and Benjamin squeezed in on the end next to Edith. The men reeked of smoke and alcohol. These pungent odors overpowered the flowery scent Ronan wore. He stretched his arm over Berty. She scooted to the arm of the sofa, saying, "You had best stay away from fire, major. I daresay your breath would catch."

He smiled and looked young again.

When the men settled down, Sarah Bodleigh sat at the piano forte. She played and sang My Bonnie Light Horseman. Edith joined in on the chorus, "Broken hearted I'll wander, broken hearted I'll remain."

"Maudlin," Benjamin voiced.

"It's one of our favorites," Edith said.

"Melancholy, eh, cousin?" Benjamin asked.

"Yes, melancholy. Never liked it."

"Now The Gentleman Soldier, that's not melancholy," Benjamin said.

"No, not fit for ladies, though," Ronan stated.

"Aye, nothing but dreary love songs and hymns fit for ladies," Benjamin opined.

Lady Ann, deciding the gentlemen weren't fit company for little boys, sent for Miss Brown to put them to bed. Miss Brown brought them over to kiss Ronan good night.

"Why do we have to go to bed early on our birthday?" Tristan asked.

"Because we are foxed," Benjamin replied.

Miss Brown took the boys away.

"As if they won't ever dip too deep," Benjamin said with a laugh.

Sir Richard approached and stood opposite them, swaying slightly. He mentioned the likely end of the war with France and speculated on the future of Ronan's regiment.

"Going to be sent to America do you think?"

"No, probably Ireland," Ronan replied.

"I'm so glad you won't be going to America," Berty said.

"I'd like to be ordered there," Ronan replied.

"But it's my country!" Berty said.

"Yes, I'd love to see it."

"But you would fight my countrymen!"

"Of course," Ronan said, adding, "Or I might sell out."

Sir Richard raised his brows. "Sell out! Why?"

"T'is better than a medical discharge."

Sir Richard was not so fuddled he didn't realize Ronan's headaches or his, hopefully temporary, lameness could be considered incapacitating. Yet one-armed officers fought. Sir Richard asked, "And what would you do then?"

"Perhaps purchase an estate near Lisbon. Or continue to partner with Benjamin. Or seek my fortune in America. "

"If my nephew can succeed there, you will surpass him," Sir Richard said, but wondered, "Why did you go to Boscawden?"

"I made a mistake."

Sir Richard looked puzzled. "I thought you might have a chere-amie there," he said, glancing at Berty.

"To court them all and marry none," Ronan sang.

"And what of Miss Bodleigh?" Sir Richard asked.

Ronan didn't reply. Berty did, "I shall not be a slave to any man's lust!"

She rose.

"What of your own?" Ronan intoned.

He caught the ruby ring she threw at him.

"I made a mistake, also," she said, "You are a loose screw, a drunk-ard, a gambler, a squire of dames!"

"A squire of dames? I have not thought of myself as such," Ronan responded lazily.

Liberty marched out of the room. Once out of it, she ran upstairs to her chamber, closed the door and fell on her bed, weeping.

Chapter 18

Alice scratched at the door. Berty got up walked to the window and told the maid to come in.

"Do you wish me to remove your pins, Miss Bodleigh?"

"Do call me Berty! No, thank you. I can remove my own pins."

"Yes, Miss...Berty!"

Berty smiled in spite of her hurt. She watched clouds clearing in the moonlight. The morrow promised to be a good, clear day for traveling.

"Alice, could you arrange for me to have an early breakfast, dawn in fact, in my room and could you procure bread and cheese and could you also have the grooms told to prepare my mare for an early ride?"

Alice noticed Berty's face was teary and thought about her requests. "Yes, Berty, I can do those things. Would you like hot water now?"

Berty would. When Alice returned, she found Berty loading her pistol, something she'd never seen a lady do. Berty washed, put on her night gown, hung up her dress and sat at a little desk. She thought she should tell her aunt and uncle she was leaving, but they would insist on taking a coach and leave with her, or persuade her to stay. Berty disliked such dependence. They enjoyed the little boys so much, they should stay. Berty dipped a quill in ink and wrote to them, explaining her reasoning and begging them to stay and enjoy themselves. She left the note for Alice to give her aunt at breakfast, then got into bed. After much tossing and turning, Liberty fell asleep.

~~~

George reported Alice's requests to Sir Richard. He responded with, "Flighty minx! Tell the grooms they are not to allow Miss Bodleigh to have her mare, the curricle or any other means of transportation. Inform my godson, his cousin and Gervace I will expect them down for an early breakfast." He decided on an hour before dawn.

The three joined Sir Richard at the appointed time. A good night's sleep had restored their sense, but vestiges lingered from their indulgence. With their tender heads and fragile stomachs, they preferred toast and tea to heartier victuals. Jacob had dosed his master with extra tonic, given him a hot bath, dabbed him with violet scent, dressed him in clean clothes and a freshly aired coat. Ronan looked better than he felt.

"I hadn't cast up my accounts in years," Gervace announced, "Usually have an iron stomach. I don't know about you, but I'm not going on the cut again any time soon."

"I underestimated that port," Sir Richard admitted, although little affected by it himself.

"I'm not used to it and don't intend to get used to it," Benjamin said, "Why did you want us down so early?"

"A case of true love not running smoothly," Sir Richard replied, and added, looking at Ronan, "Our beau has made a mull of it again. With the three of us reasoning with Ronan and his damsel, I hope to achieve a reconciliation, at least."

They moved into the morning room where Ronan made to leave. Sir Richard blocked him. They stood facing each other, almost touching, when George burst in with an angry Miss Bodleigh.

"Unhand me, you overgrown brute!" she remonstrated to George, who had taken her pistol and haversack. He'd led her into the morning room from the stables.

"Going somewhere, Miss Bodleigh?" Sir Richard turned and asked. He returned to his glowering godson, "Do sit down!"

A moment's study of Liberty and Ronan eased himself onto a sofa.

Sir Richard stepped over to Liberty. He removed two long pins from her hat. "When you disarm a hoyden, George, don't forget the hat pins. Make yourself comfortable, Miss Bodleigh."

George set aside the pistol and took Berty's cloak, gloves and hat. She wore her new riding habit with its voluminous skirt and heavy petticoats. Ronan gazed at her. Why did that particular apparel arouse him so? It covered her lovely body thoroughly, yet he imagined the body under it. No matter how Liberty dressed, he wanted to stare at her. He wanted her, in every way, physically, practically, spiritually. One always wanted most what one couldn't have, he thought, moodily.

Sir Richard glanced in the haversack. "What's this? Stealing from the larder? You are American, too. Our countries are at war, miss. I declare you a prisoner of war and shall place you in the hands of our gallant major!"

"That is not amusing," Berty replied, "Restore my mare to me and I will be on my way."

Sir Richard laughed. Berty made for the door, but George blocked it. "You are out numbered, Miss Bodleigh, but surrender and we will grant you parole, won't we, major?" Sir Richard joked.

Ronan continued to look at her, but didn't reply. Sir Richard coaxed her to the other end of Ronan's sofa.

"I admit the major is loose in the haft. Damaged goods, too. Gets up on his high horse sometimes, but you are mistaken in thinking him a habitual drunkard. We all were too ripe and ready last night. Nor is he a dissipated gambler."

"You are past seven, my child, of no birth and no wealth and apparently a blue stocking."

Berty carefully raised her skirt to reveal a red stocking above her short boot.

Sir Richard laughed, "My mistake. A red stocking! A pair of rum 'uns, both of you! Petruchio and his shrew!"

"I am not a shrew!" Berty exclaimed, getting up with a flounce and pacing the floor in exasperation.

"Perhaps not, merely provoked. If all Americans are like you, I hope we don't win you back."

"You shan't!" Berty cried, in her peregrination around the room.

Gervace walked up to Berty. "Please, miss, we are all suffering a bit of maliase from last night's excesses. Your pacing makes me queasy, besides, flouncing is most indecorous, you see. Allow me to escort you to a comfortable seat."

Berty accepted his arm. He led her back to the sofa. Gervace pulled up a chair and leaned forward. He pursued his inquiry in a gentler manner than Sir Richard."I collect you and the major have known each other a while."

Berty nodded, "Eight years, off and on."

"That long! Close friends, but not lovers?"

Berty nodded.

"And you are vexed with him for drinking and gambling and, not to wrap it in fine cloth, whoring?"

Berty nodded.

"But you are just friends? No, I don't think so. He travels, too soon after a wound, to see you in Boscawden, out of mere friendship? He doesn't visit us or Benjamin, who I think have been his friends longer than you have. You come riding here to see him out of friendship. Gammon!"

"Are you jealous of his bachelor ware?"

"No. I choose to be a spinster myself; it's not that. I know nothing about his 'bachelor ware.' I've heard he has off spring other than Christopher. He is mysterious, vexing and dangerous. I choose to leave, if you would just allow me to!"

"Missish," Ronan remarked disdainfully.

"She's a miss, what else could she be, boyish!" Gervace remonstrated.

Ronan replied with a quote from a Handel opera, "'Cease to beauty to be suing, Ever whining, love disdaining. Let the brave their aims pursuing, still be conqu'ring, not complaining.'"

"Waxing poetical today, are you?" Sir Richard remarked in an admonishing tone, "But not the kind of poetry ladies wish to hear."

"I'm not whining," Berty objected.

"Of course you aren't Miss Bodleigh," Gervace kindly assured her. "He has no understanding of your sex. I believe our Ronan is dangerous to the French, not to you. They detect a whiff of brimstone about him. Indeed, I often have myself! Mysterious, eh? What do you want to know?"

Berty shook her head. She felt tears building up. She hated that sign of weakness.

"What did you quarrel about in Boscawden?" Gervace persisted, "I apprehend this subject has opened that faucette that so plagues the fair sex." Gervace offered Berty a handkerchief.

She dabbed her eyes. "His secretiveness about mistresses and natural children and his changeable conduct. Everyone knew about these children but me!"

"Changable conduct! Don't you know your own mind anymore, Ronan? Or is it hers you don't know?"

Ronan didn't answer, but continued to watch.

"Dear Miss Bodleigh, I quite understand how disturbing it must be to learn from others of a friend's misconduct. I'm curious myself. How many natural children do you have, Ronan?" Gervace asked.

"You are impertinent," Ronan replied.

"That's what he said to me!" Berty said.

"You should have slapped some sense into him!" Gervace replied and turned back to Ronan. "You should be forthcoming among friends. Or are you going to surprise Sir Richard with a couple more of your bastards? Or, worse, marry this girl and fob them off on her?"

Ronan stared ahead.

"You may add criminal conversations to his sins, miss, for the children I know of have married mothers," from Gervace.

"I have an interest in this," Sir Richard interrupted. "I've told Miss Bodleigh about Ann and our arrangement when you were eighteen, major. You have ever kept that to yourself, like a true gentleman."

"I would never visit calumny on Lady Ann," Ronan responded.

"I knew I could trust you. And you should trust me. If I am to receive additional brats of yours, I'd like to know the number."

"I acknowledge a daughter in Lisbon," Ronan spoke softly.

Benjamin, not yet sober after the previous evening's excess, sat down on the nearest chair before muttering, "One, that you know of. Why don't you pull out and pray?"

"It will perhaps lighten your heart, cousin to learn that my Portuguese mistress will bear no more children."

"Thank God," Benjamin replied.

Berty wondered what pull out and pray meant. She would ask Edith later.

"Who is this Portuguese mistress and why won't she have anymore children?" Gervace asked.

"Senora Antonia Gouveia Serafina Martaus de Sousa," Ronan responded.

"By Jove, I wouldn't be able to remember her name!" Sir Richard interrupted.

"Go on, Ronan, how old is she, tell us more," Gervace encouraged the reluctant one.

"She died at age thirty-nine, from a disease caught nursing orphans. She was a widow with several children. My daughter is in the care of a governess in Lisbon."

"Thirty-nine? You do favor the autumnal beauties, don't you?"

"'No spring nor summer beauty hath such grace as I have seen in one autumnal face,'" Ronan quoted John Donne.

"'Young beauties force our love and that's a rape,'" Gervace completed the quote, adding, "I wonder you can look upon Miss Bodleigh."

Ronan boldly looked upon her, saying, "I look forward to seeing her autumnal face."

"Flummery! Should I add toad eater to your vices, Major Trevelyan!" Berty objected.

Gervace detected a hint of a smile. He gave Sir Richard a turn.

Sir Richard said, "Now Miss Bodleigh. Ill considered of you to elope with out consulting your family."

"I am one and twenty and can do as I please."

"So you think. I shan't allow a woman to leave my house alone and unprotected. Do see reason, Miss Bodleigh."

Berty did see his point and felt she had been too hasty, but stubbornly defended her decision. "I can make better time alone. I'd have reached here long before dusk if Edith hadn't slowed us down. My aunt and uncle enjoy the boys, why put them to a bother over me?"

"Miss Bodleigh, you know your aunt and uncle would be worried," Gervace said, "and may I be so bold as to say someone else would be concerned, although he would never show it. Indeed, I've never seen a couple so incapable of assuring each other of their affection. The two of you are as moody as March weather."

"I am not moody, he is," Berty countered, weeping again. "At least two love children! How can you expect me to show affection for such a rake!"

"I prefered squire of dames, miss," Gervace remarked, "Our major was a cicisbeo or servante gallant when he was a cornet. Too poor to marry; too proud to visit bordellos. Tell, me Miss Bodleigh, how did you come to be aquainted with him?"

Berty sighed and dried her tears. "My first summer in Hampshire after I'd arrived from America, my aunt brought me to the Hall. While she and Lady Catherine talked, I wandered about and witnessed Alexander and Ronan fencing. They followed me to the library."

"I was two weeks from my thirteenth birthday. Ronan was eighteen, quite shabby and still wore his hair long, but very gentlemanly and looked with interest at my drawings. Alexander asked me to sketch both of them. I still have the sketch of Ronan."

"I didn't see him again until he came to Lady Catherine's funeral three years later. That Sunday, he swaggered into church, wearing his regimentals and carrying a sabre. He followed his cousins and outshown them.

Women-everyone stared at him. I think some swooned, he was that striking, but already we'd heard rumors about his amours."

"You didn't stare or swoon, Miss Bodleigh?" Gervase asked.

"Of course not. Handsome is as handsome does. I was not to be
overpowered with beauty! Ronan came to visit Aunt Sarah, later, and he
and I went for a walk."

"And I kissed you," the major interjected.

"Which you shouldn't have done and I wouldn't have mentioned
that! In any case, you rode back to your regiment the next day and at the
end of the year, you were sent to the Peninsula. I didn't see you again for
three years, the end of 1811."

She turned back to Gervase. "He was banged up from his horse
falling and shot in the shoulder. He visited us and we became friends. And
when he was healed, we danced at the Pemberton's ball."

"Almost every dance," Ronan put in.

"Yes, which was quite improper and I should have refused, but
knowing you were leaving and having a soft heart, I, well, I just couldn't. I
don't think my reputation has ever recovered."

"Danced almost every dance even though he was a reputed squire
of dames," Gervace mused.

"I hadn't heeded all those rumors and he'd been in the Peninsula
and he wasn't squiring any dames in Boscawden," Berty proposed a weak
defense, the accusation of missishness informing her speech.

"Except you, I squired you," Ronan added, "You did me the honor
to write to me."

Sir Richard broke into the charming reminisence, "And your
friends had no idea! I thought you had the good sense to hold out for a
bride with several thousand pounds a year, rather than pay your addresses
to a pennyless minx," Sir Richard added.

"Leave us," the major ordered.

"For the sake of respectability, one of us must stay," Sir Richard
said. Gervace volunteered. Sir Richard left for the stables. Benjamin
walked to the library to assemble materials for the presentation he intended
to make to shareholders of Brandolyn Arms.

In the morning room, Gervace sat by the fire nursing his hangover
and aching joints, while Ronan spoke softly to Berty. Gervace soon dozed.

"I was smitten with you when we first met, but you were just a
chit. I thought love was a delusion people chose to believe."

"Perhaps you should have read more mawkish ladies' books and less poetry and phylosophy," Berty suggested.

He ignored that remark and continued, "When I saw you again three years later, I still thought love was a delusion. And I fought it. It was inconvenient, a hindrance to my career.

"Two years ago, when we met again, I surrendered, but you only wanted to be friends, yes?"

"I thought that was what we both wanted," she replied, looking into his big blue eyes. They expressed softness and warmth then, not his usual coldness.

Berty longed for him despite her misgivings and the recurring thought of his children. His beauty still transfixed her. She understood why women desired to have children by him. Berty knew she had wanted more than friendship then and now.

Ronan moved closer, taking her chilly hand and kissing it while still staring deep into her eyes. "Mi belleza."

Berty felt his warmth, as she had that first meeting in the library. Ronan leaned down and kissed her. They embraced.

A log fell in the fireplace, waking Gervace. He noticed his charges had grown quiet and looked around to see Ronan kissing Miss Bodleigh in a more than friendly manner. "None of that! Unless you wish to be leg shackled!" Gervace exclaimed.

"Do you wish to be leg shackled, Miss Bodleigh?" Ronan asked.

"Certainly not!" she replied.

"Damn the wench," Gervace muttered.

"Did you address us, Mr. Markham?" Berty asked.

"No, miss, merely cursing my rheumatism."

"How are we to kiss if we aren't to be leg shackled?" Ronan continued his inquiry.

"You've always managed to find opportunities before," Berty replied with a smile.

He smiled back and she thought him very beautiful.

"No reasonable girl would want to be leg shackled to a half pay officer burdened with children," he admitted, calmly.

Berty thought a moment, before replying, "The Burlingtons have adopted Christopher. I suppose a reasonable girl might marry you, if she didn't believe, as I do, that marriage laws enslave women."

"Another fence to leap," Gervace grumbled, adding, "Miss Bodleigh, I think it reasonable to assume that a man who has practiced criminal conversations might not be too fastidious regarding marriage laws."

"Ah, but men always seek their own advantage," she replied, "and I don't wish to be lorded over."

"I see. I've always avoided the marital state, myself, but I've seen many people happy in it, such as the Burlingtons. Sir Richard certainly does not lord it over Lady Ann," Gervace replied.

"Nor does my uncle lord it over my aunt, but Major Trevelyan is a of a different character than Sir Richard and Uncle Augustus."

Gervace agreed, but added, "Despite the iron in him, Major Trevelyan is gentle with women."

"Enough of this," Ronan said, rising from the sofa and offering Berty his arm. "Do you wish to walk out with me, or do you fear I'll lord it over you?" he asked Berty.

"In my single state, I can always walk away," she replied, accepting his arm.

Chapter 19

On their path to the stables, Ronan and Liberty met Christopher running towards them covered in sand from the riding school. "Please watch me, papa!"

They followed him to the enclosed riding area, where Augustus supervised Tristan and the pony. Happy sat nearby while Sir Richard and the Reverend Brandolyn watched from horse back. Christopher mounted the pony and Tristan, holding a lunge line, cued the pony into an easy canter. Christopher moved with the pony. To show he didn't need to hold on to the mane, he held out his arms. After a couple of rounds, Tristan brought the pony to a halt.

"Chris is proud as a dog with two tails." Augustus said, "Trist has been giving him lessons for weeks."

Sir Richard invited Augustus and Berty to join him and the reverend on a tour of the estate. Tristan longed to join them, but didn't want to neglect his friend. Ronan offered to stay with Christopher, allowing Tristan to ride until his school lessons.

After the others had ridden off, Ronan requested the grooms saddle the quietest horse in the stable. The major carefully pulled himself into the saddle, gritting his teeth as he settled his right leg in position. Despite the pain, it felt good to be in the saddle. He asked for a lead rope for Christopher's mount and they set off at a walk.

Father and son met the other riders on their return and joined them. Berty talked of daffodil meadows she'd seen. "I miss the ones at Boscawden and planting the garden, but we saw foals, calves and lambs, just like at home."

Sir Richard consulted the major on the horse market now that the war was ending.

"You should cull your mares and reduce your breeding stock," Ronan said, "The demand for beef and other farm products will likely diminish, too."

"Yes, I suspect so. The American war doesn't require many horses," Sir Richard agreed.

"I've culled my cattle in anticipation of this," the Reverend stated, "The end of the wars will be hard on farm workers, esspecially with discharged soldiers returning. One can only hope that manufacturing, such as you and Benjamin have devised, will employ them."

"A forlorn hope," Ronan replied.

They watched the major and Miss Bodleigh ride side by side with Christopher. The gentlemen allowed the couple to ride far ahead.

"I'll be happy to see all my children settled," the Reverend spoke, studying their backs.

"Indeed, if that one will settle. He could have married 10,000 pounds a year and didn't. Not your fault if he don't settle, he's only your orphaned nephew," Sir Richard said.

"I did not raise him to be a fortune hunter," the Reverend retorted.

Augustus put in, "My brother, Liberty's father, would have rather she died an old maid than be unhappily married to a libertine with natural children."

"My nephew will settle. If he returns to war, and I pray he does not, he can take a wife with him now he's an officer."

"I don't want my neice following the drum, but she has a mind of her own."

~~~

Sir Richard returned to the house alone and found Gervace, "What are my godson and his minx about, Vacy?"

"The pair of them are mad beyond prayers. Both flee matrimony, yet smell of April and May." He repeated their conversation.

Sir Richard frowned, "Asking a spinster if she wants to get leg shackled is hardly the way to win fair maiden. On the other hand, going down on a knee, if he could, might not improve his chances. She ain't a green girl and he's a downy one. I wager he's playing a deep game, but is it seduction or matrimony?"

Gervace shrugged. "I reckon she's leary of marrying a rake with bastards and he's leary of marrying a blue stocking, but he did ask, after a fashion. I say the problem is the dame."

"Always is, ain't it?"

After noon, Ronan rested in his room, listening to Jacob lecture him. "Too soon to be riding, sir. I'm sure Waddles would object to your doing such a muttonheaded thing. He says there's a lot of damage in that leg, might not ever be right. You was fevered when he said that and maybe don't recollect. And you weren't properly attired for riding."

Ronan fell asleep listening to the soothing lecture.

~~~

Edith and Berty visited the library where Benjamin contemplated the eradication of vermin. Intending to write his speech to investors on expanding the business to furnaces and pipes, Benjamin's mind wandered, distracted with the lice and flea problem. He wondered if lavender would discourage those vermin as it did moths. He remembered his mother wielding a nit comb and insisting her children bath regularly with strong soap. Benjamin found a herbal, but held his own opinions. "Ironing kills them in clothing, but one can not iron a person. The problem is exacerbated in large groups of unwashed humans like armies. Vermin is more a nuisance than anything. It's not as if insects spread diseases like typhus and ague. They are spread by bad air and water. Then there are fleas, which are everywhere."

"Oh, what a distasteful subject, Benjamin," Edith complained.

"Aunt Sarah has an herbal concoction for killing fleas on cats and dogs and in crevices. It consists of fleabane, pennyroyal, bay, tansy and other herbs dried and ground into a powder. Uncle Augustus gave Tristan some for the spaniel. I can't imagine producing enough of it to treat an army. It must be used frequently and sometimes I think it is of questionable effectiveness. Much like her lemon cure for freckles. I must wear a veil or broad bonnet out of doors or become bran-faced."

"A few speckles don't make you bran-faced," Edith assured her, "You have exceedingly fair skin for a brunette. When I get too much sun, I turn as brown as a berry!"

"I think you would look rather attractive brown as a berry," Benjamin opined.

Edith giggled, "Really Mr. Brandolyn, I'd look like a common farm woman!"

"You could never look common, miss," he assured her.

"You should give your cousin lessons in flattery, Mr. Brandolyn," Edith suggested.

"I assure you, Miss Westerly, my cousin needs no lessons regarding the fair sex."

"Really, Mr. Brandolyn?" Berty asked, "It seems you had some advice for him this morning, which I did not quite understand."

Benjamin looked puzzled, trying to recall what she meant.

"Something regarding praying," she added.

Suddenly it came to him and Benjamin blushed for the first time in years. "I do apologize, Miss Bodleigh, I was not fit to be in the company of ladies this morning. Not at all in a state of sobriety. I'm not usually a drinker of port and it quite fuddled me."

"Whatever are you talking about?" Edith asked.

"I wish I knew," Berty said, "Something Mr. Brandolyn asked Major Trevelyan. Something, I collect, would prevent..." Berty blushed now.

She had ignited Edith's curiosity, "Prevent what? Something that would prevent unwanted children? One of the modern inventions you mentioned, Mr. Brandolyn?"

"No, miss, not at all, old as the hills. Mentioned in the Bible, in fact."

"What verse?" she asked.

"Genesis 38:9," he replied, picked up his diagrams of heating systems. He hastily excused himself. Would he ever be able to face these females again?

Edith ran to the huge Bible and looked up the verse about Onan spilling his seed on the ground. "Reverend Wingfield never preaches about this," Edith said, "Nor practices it!"

"Nor does Major Trevelyan," Berty commented, "Two love children, he has, Edith, and others by married women. What am I to do?"

"Read this verse to him!"

"I'm sure he has heard it from his reverend uncle and believes it a sin, but it doesn't mean that does it?"

"Not in other cases, I'm sure," Edith said, "Oh but wasn't that amusing to see Mr. Brandolyn discomposed!"

"I'd like to see 'my major' discomposed for once!"

"Walter says he's the most gallant man in the army and nothing disturbs him," Edith told Berty.

"We'll see about that!" Berty decided.

That afternoon proved fine enough for Major Trevelyan to exercise his leg with a walk in the garden. He sought Miss Bodleigh in the library and asked if she and Edith would walk with him. Both consented. On the way out, they met Benjamin, who agreed to escort Miss Westerly. He'd reconciled himself to the awkwardness created by his loose tongue and hoped the women wouldn't mention it.

The major refused his cousin's assistance and used his cane to carefully climb down the steps onto the gravel walk. He traveled slowly, but no one minded. Particularly not Berty, who took time to study primroses and other early blooming flowers. Although the garden had not leafed out, she recognized many plants.

"I believe this garden has almost as many varieties of roses as Boscawden's, esspecially Gallicas," she said.

"How can you tell what they are when they are dormant," Edith asked.

"Each kind has its peculiar form. Oh, pinks here! Now even you can recognise them with their bluish leaves."

"Oh, yes, I love their smell," Edith agreed.

"Lady Ann tells me her head gardener orders new plants and seeds every year. They would mostly be in the kitchen cutting garden. Mr. Gardner never orders anything new for Boscawden. Uncle Francis would balk at the expense and Alexander, I mean Lord Alexander, doesn't care a fig about the garden," Berty rattled on.

When she thought she'd tranquilized everyone with her talk of gardening, Berty sprung her surprise on Ronan, "At the risk of being accused of impertinance, why did you not do as Onan rather than father children?"

Ronan limped on. She wondered if he was not going to respond. She'd taken him aback. He had to decide whether to reply to such impertinence or not. Ronan knew it infuriated Berty when he ignored her questions. He didn't want to infuriate her. He'd done too much of that. At last, the major quietly replied, "That would have been against nature and the ladies'wishes. These children are none of your concern, Miss Bodleigh," he continued serenely.

"No, certainly not my concern if women wish to have babies by you. Does nothing discompose you, sir?"

The major immediately thought of the Irish soldier who'd died of a flogging, then of Isabella, shot by the French, of the horrors of Badajoz.

However shocking, he had not lost his self-control, but he had challenged an officer over the Irishman, a mistake that almost cost his career.

Berty realized he was considering her taunting question and felt remorse. "I'm sorry. I'm sure you've seen shocking things in the war. You were discomposed when you threw a ring and assaulted your servant in Boscawden," Berty relentlessly reminded him.

"The effects of fever and provocation of an impertinent female," he replied in a lighter tone.

Berty giggled, "Oh you odious man!"

Benjamin spoke, at last, "Then it is settled that my cousin can be provoked, but I already knew that having incited numerous fights in our youth!"

"Ah, Ben, what's this about Onan? Have you been trying to impress damsels with your Biblical knowledge?" his cousin asked.

"More like impressing them with my resounding foolishness and unbridled tongue. Though, in truth, I've always wondered what maidens thought of some of those things in the Bible. Surely father never preached on them to his congregation out of respect for the innocense of young women. I suspect few women read the entire Bible or understand all the terms."

"I certainly haven't," Edith admitted, "Berty's most of it, but not understood all of it."

"Unlike us," Ben responded, "We were taught the meaning of everything in it. Yet we still misbehave! Father would blame our human frailty. Or the Blue Devil!"

He noticed his cousin flagging and Berty felt him shiver. By then, they had reached the orangery and entered it. The sweet odors of orange and lemon blossom greeted them. Ronan seated himself on a wood settee to rest for the journey back and warm himself in the sun streaming through the many tall, arched windows.

While they talked, the head gardener stepped in and immediately apologized for intruding.

"Oh, do stay. Don't let us prevent your work," Ben pronounced.

"No, govner, Sir Richard would not approve of me disturbing his guests."

"Oh, please stay. I wish to discuss the gardens," Liberty begged.

"In that case, miss, what do you wish to know about the gardens?"

"I'm so glad to see an old-fashioned flower garden instead of turf up to the steps. Boscawden, too, escaped that dreadful landscape movement," Berty began.

"Not quite, miss. The old formal gardens had been stripped away and turfed up to the steps, but Lady Ann wanted flowers. Right up to the doors, she said! We kept the terrace and steps: put in the formal walks, walls and hedges that you see today."

Liberty thought a moment, then said, "I'm so glad. I like flowers, too. The landscaped places...I just can't call them gardens, are so boring. Boscawden's formal garden is an Italian garden and so filled with flowers, it hardly seems formal. Lady Ann says you have purchased many new plants."

"We have indeed," the gardener smiled.

"You don't have the special varieties bred by Boscawden's gardeners over the years."

The gardener's smile faded. "What varieties would these be, miss?"

"The Boscawden sweet violet; the Lady Grisella rose, which is a many-petaled lilac; the Boscawden Pippin, which is the absolute best storage apple. The Boscawden pea, the Lord James cabbage, the Trevelyan iris, the Sarah Bodleigh Double Daisy. That was named after my aunt by the current gardener, its breeder. I can't recall all of them."

"I've never heard of them," Sir Richard's gardener admitted.

"No one has except those in the neighborhood. It's a terrible shame and what's more, Mr. Gardner is unable to purchase new stock to experiment with. Which is why I wanted to consult with you. You see, if he could trade Boscawden's plants and seeds for new ones such as yours, both gardens would benefit," Berty spoke intensely before brightening with her delightful smile.

"If Mr. Gardner is willing, I'd be glad to trade."

"Then I shall write to him for a list of what he would like to trade and anything specifically he is interested in that you may have," Berty said, beaming.

The head gardener left for his office to make lists.

"Well, Berty, I knew you had helped inventory every stick of furniture and painting in the Hall, but I didn't know you knew every plant, too," Edith remarked.

"Not every plant, but I know most of the plants, every horse, every servant and, as you said, every stick of furniture and work of art. Uncle

Francis thought I should replace Mrs. Goodyer. Uncle Augustus considered that insulting. He joked I should replace Uncle Francis."

Edith giggled.

"A female steward, why not, eh cousin?" Benjamin asked.

"Miss Bodleigh should be lady of the house," Ronan announced.

Everyone grew silent, until Edith broke it with, "I daresay you don't wish her to marry Lord Alexander any more than she would want to marry him."

"Ne se passe pas," Ronan replied, with an enigmatic look.

They strolled back to the house, where Christopher ran to his father. Tristan soon followed with Happy.

"Major, Chris is afraid of Happy!" he told him, keeping Happy at heel.

"I am not!" Christopher insisted.

They argued into the drawing room, where the major sat on a sofa with his friends. Christopher sat on his lap. Tristan repeated that Christopher was afraid of the dog and Christopher denied it once more. The major said nothing, but glared at each child when they renewed their arguments. He was of the school that children should be seen and not heard.

Tristan described how Christopher avoided Happy and ran away when he licked him.

"Why did you run away?" Benjamin asked.

"I don't like dogs. They eat people."

"You're thinking of wolves," Tristan argued, "Dogs don't eat people."

"They do, too! I've seen them eat people."

Tristan didn't know what to say, not did anyone else, except the major.

"Those were dead people and starving dogs, my child," the major explained, while some of the ladies left the room.

Christopher thought about it while the major told him Happy was not like those Spanish dogs he'd seen on battlefields. Tristan felt terrible and promised he'd never allow Happy to lick him again. Ronan motioned for him to bring the dog closer and stroked his head.

"He lacks decorum, but he won't hurt you," Ronan assured his son. After a while, Christopher stroked Happy's head, too. When Christopher was reconciled to the dog, Ronan told him, "We never speak of the sordid things we've seen on battlefields when ladies are present."

"No, sir. I didn't mean to, papa."

Tristan changed the subject by mentioning it was feeding time for the horses. "The grooms will bring in the mares now. Do come see Calypso and Hermion!"

Once more, the major raised his weary body and hobbled to the stables, followed by his entourage of friends. Calypso chewed hay, while her colt suckled. When Hermion had had his fill, the boys walked in to handle him. Christopher stroked and embraced the colt.

At last, they returned to the house for a supper of lobster and other seafood, followed by music. The Reverend Brandolyn, Mr. Considine and Tristan took up violins, Benjamin took up his flute. They persuaded the major to play the harp. At last, Reverend Brandolyn read from Ecclesiastes 3:1-8 "There is a time for everything, and a season for every activity under the heavens: a time to be born and a time to die, a time to plant and a time to uproot, a time to kill and a time to heal... a time to love and a time to hate, a time for war and a time for peace."

Benjamin sat on a sofa with Edith and Liberty across from Ronan, who sprawled in a chair on the verge of falling asleep. "Cousin," he addressed Ronan, waking him, "Is this another hint from father that we have reached a time to marry?"

Ronan replied, "I've had my time of war and my time to kill and now, my time to heal and my time to love. What of you, Ben?"

Ben laughed, "I don't think my time has come."

The major, by now knocked up, excused himself and limped out of the room. He staggered to his chamber, redolent of a flower garden, and fell across his bed. Jacob, who had been experimenting with scents Lady Ann had given him for the major, undressed and covered the major. When Miss Brown brought Christopher, the boy exclaimed, "Whew, it stinks in here!"

Miss Brown insisted the various flower scents smelled good and Jacob explained the source of the odors. "Strong scents are not the thing for gentlemen these days, but ladies insist on giving my master these scents. He doesn't object when I apply them, lightly, of course. His male friends believe the major would smell like sulfer and brimestone without them. I beleive he smells more like burnt powder and horse. I've just finished mixing Hyacinth, violet, rose and some others. I think I have devised the perfect scent."

He opened a vial for Miss Brown to smell. She approved. "That would definately obsure sulfer and brimestone."

~~~

An hour before dawn. Ronan lay in the quiet before roosters crowed. He planned his strategy to conquer the, hither to, ungovernable Miss Bodleigh. He had dithered enough.

That morning a March wind blew and most of the company stayed indoors. However, Sir Richard walked out to his stables to see Miss Bodleigh. She visited Rose every morning. The major, too, had hobbled into that stable. Sir Richard seeing the two, hung back to see if they spoke. The couple exchanged cool good mornings and walked on. Ronan studied the stallions, while Berty walked on to the mare stalls. She expected him to follow her to steal a kiss away from the grooms, but he did not. She entertained the idea with pleasure, then thought better of it. It could lead to nothing good.

Grooms led mares and foals out to paddocks, leaving Liberty alone with Ronan. She walked back to where he leaned against a stall. He nodded and turned back to watching a stallion. Irritated with his lack of interest, Berty strolled on, looking over the stall doors at the blood horses. Some rushed the bars over their doors with ears back and teeth bared. She wondered what one did with such vicious animals. Most either went on munching hay or came to their doors in a friendly way. She heard a stall door open behind her and turned to see Ronan enter a stall with one of the vicious stallions. Was he mad?

When the stallion rushed at him with bared teeth, Ronan grabbed the steed's tender nose and held it tight. He stroked the big bay, under its jaw, around its ears and down its neck, speaking softly in some of his eight languages. Berty watched, transfixed, until a voice behind her startled her.

"I fancied you'd be seeing to your mare," Sir Richard announced.

"Yes, sir, I was. I don't think the major should be in there with that animal," Berty said.

"Are your frightened for him?" Sir Richard laughed. "Ronan's been gentling unruly horses since he could walk."

"But he's still weak," Berty objected.

"Doesn't take strength to tame a horse. I daresay, Ronan can govern a horse easier than he can govern a woman. That's not a bad horse. A recent purchase, a blood horse that has been mishandled."

Ronan let go the bay's nose and continued stroking it. Then he picked up his cane and hobbled out, while the horse stood placidly. He heard Berty sigh with relief.

"I say, you smell like a horse in a flower garden," Sir Richard declared, to Ronan, "Valet's been dabbling in scents again, has he?"

Not expecting a reply, Sir Richard turned to Berty, "I instructed the grooms to hitch the grays to a phaeton. You should catch on to driving a four wheeled vehical in a flash!"

"A phaeton!" Berty said, with alarm.

"Not a high perch phaeton, a low sensible carriage with two seats so you can tool around with your aunt and uncle, or, more likely, Miss Westerly and Mr. Brandolyn," Sir Richard explained.

"T'is awfully windy today. I fear the horses would startle and damage your phaeton," Berty objected. She didn't like handling unfamiliar horses in a wind; they became nervous.

"Don't trouble yourself about that, child. Are you coming along, Ronan?"

The major followed them out to the stable yard where grooms put the grays to a black phaeton. Liberty presented another objection, "It's too cold and windy for an invalid to be out."

"Indeed it is, but no one's ever pampered the major," Sir Richard said, sending a groom for the major's great coat.

When Major Trevelyan was suitable protected from the weather, Sir Richard helped Berty on to the phaeton. Ronan pulled himself into the back seat. Sir Richard climbed up beside Berty. A groom handed her the ribbons and she cued the team to move out. The brisk breeze gave the grays more than their usual spirit. Their ears flicked back and forth nervously, but Berty kept her hands steady. They settled into a trot down the drive. Wind whipped and tossed branches overhead. One cracked and crashed near the phaeton, sending the horses skittering before Berty checked them.

"Very good! I knew you could handle them," Sir Richard said.

Berty thought him over confident, but made herself calm as they jogged along. Sir Richard rattled on, "I tell my lady that women can drive as well as men. It's not a question of strength, after all. They'll run no matter how hard one pulls on the reins. You have the knack, miss, squeezing the ribbons just so. Now give yourself room for this turn."

Liberty carefully guided the team onto the road.

"Well done! Couldn't have done better myself. What do you think, Ronan?"

"You'll have her boxing next."

Sir Richard guffawed. "I witnessed a woman's boxing match once. Except for some exposed flesh, not very pleasing. No, boxing is not for Miss Bodleigh."

"I'm glad to hear that," she replied.

"You might be glad to hear some news we recieved from an informant regarding Gayland. He has removed himself to France. He'd best stay there."

"I'm greatly relieved," Berty admitted.

Ronan wasn't. He'd looked forward to hunting the rascal down and running a sabre through his throat.

They traveled on without incident and returned to Burlington Hall.

~~~

Major Trevelyan limped into his chamber after the carriage ride to be greeted by his valet.

"May I send to your boot maker for new half boots, sir?"

"There's nothing amiss with my old ones," the major replied.

"I beg to differ, sir. I've had them resoled twice, but they are worn and scuffed, unfit for anything but the stable, yet you wear them in the drawing room."

The major agreed to purchase new boots. Then Jacob suggested new coats.

"I'll soon be on half pay; I must economise," the major replied, to Jacob's dismay.

"But what of your gold?" Jacob persisted.

"What gold?" the major asked sternly.

"Sorry, sir. I know nothing about any gold, I'm sure. I just want to see you dressed to the nines like other gentlemen."

"Wouldn't you rather recieve your pay?"

Without hesitation, Jacob replied, "I'd rather see you turned out bang up to the mark, sir."

Ronan gave him a questioning look.

"You don't understand, sir. We valets take pride in our gentlemen like a groom in a horse. No, I don't quite mean that."

"Why not? It's the second time today I've been compared to a horse," his master retorted.

"It's that old riding coat you're wearing. No matter how much I air it, it smells of horse. Even scent doesn't disguise it. What I mean is, the finer the gentleman, the more respect the valet gets. We ain't anything without our gents."

"Touching," the major commented, but he saw his valet's point.

"And that Mr. Sitwell owes you for that fencing bet."

"I'm unlikely to collect a fraction of that," Ronan replied, "But order the boots and you may send to Suit for a coat."

"I was thinking a summer coat, also, for your honeymoon, sir."

Ronan laughed at the boy's optimism.

Chapter 20

Late in the afternoon, a mud splattered, four horse post chaise arrived at the hall. Miss Penthwaite and her maid alighted with bandboxes and portmanteaus. The butler led Miss Penthwaite to the drawing room and announced her. Lady Ann and Sarah responded with great joy and sent for the young ladies and Sir Richard.

Sir Richard, Gervace and the others saw a slender, averaged sized woman in her fifties, of regular features and great vivacity and spirit. Her raiment consisted of a demure, gray-blue, high necked wool gown, a plain bonnet and good walking shoes. She wore her brown hair in a severe fashion and disdained jewelry. She neither curtsied nor displayed conventional manners.

"If she ain't a blue stocking, I'm a monkey," Gervace whispered.

Hilda Penthwaite shook Sir Richard's and Lady Ann's hands, embraced Sarah and asked for "her" girls. The girls, followed by Benjamin, soon appeared. Hilda embraced the young women and shook hands with Mr. Brandolyn. She thought him brawny and handsome. She then asked, for, "This Major Trevelyan I've heard so much about."

When told he was resting after an active morning, she said, "I collect he's an invalid."

"He is recovering from wound fever," Gervace informed her.

Lady Ann told a maid to show Hilda to her chamber so that she could refresh herself.

"Thank you, but I'm not the least weary and don't need refreshing. She sat down by Sarah and immediately began telling them all the political on dit of London.

Major Trevelyan spent the day in his chamber, writing letters and reading. Jacob thought it a poor way to pursue Miss Bodleigh. Ronan was, practising one of his tactics. His absence would worry her, and she would dwell on him. And she did. Berty wondered if he were ill and looked repeatedly for him in the library or entering a room or at the dinner table, but he dined in his chamber.

After dinner, the major requested a bath. His valet obliged. That afternoon, Jacob trimmed his master's facial hair neatly and combed his golden waves to perfection. Ronan allowed Jacob to dress him in his best civilian clothes, intending to look his finest for Miss Bodleigh, another tactic. Jacob chose white pantaloons and tasseled Hessian boots, plain white linen waistcoat and silver gray coat. He used a light touch with the scent and spent a great deal of time tying a unique, but not ostentatious, neck cloth. He stood back when his master rose. "Splendid! You would outshine anyone in a ton ballroom, let alone this house, sir!"

~~~

As Miss Penthwaite wound up her London report, the butler announced Major Trevelyan.

Hilda gasped, as did many others. Stunning, she thought, an exceptionally beautiful man.

Ronan limped in, kissed Lady Ann's proffered hand and was introduced to Miss Penthwaite. He bowed to her and acknowledged the others, without kissing Liberty's hand. George placed an arm chair in front of the ladies and the major took a seat, sitting upright, the picture of proper manners. He glanced at Liberty, noticing Lady Ann was dressing her again. This time in diaphanous garnet silk over a pearl satin under dress, exposing enough of her softly rounded bosom to cause Ronan to regret allowing Jacob to dress him in tight pantaloons. No woman ever looked more radiant in red. She, too was practising the tactic of enticement, but to what end? It pained Ronan to take his eyes from her, but he steeled himself and did so.

Hilda began, "Major Trevelyan, I must say, I see a resemblance in you to Lord Victor!"

"I didn't have the pleasure of meeting my grandfather, ma'am," Ronan replied in his usual quiet, polar tone.

"It wouldn't have been a pleasure!" Miss Penthwaite replied, with a laugh, "Victor tended to chill people".

"Even when you have provoked me beyond measure, I never compared you to Lord Victor," Sarah told Ronan.

Hilda studied Ronan, now older than the portrait Liberty had painted. No man deserved to be so beautiful. Lord Victor certainly didn't. Ronan had an aristocratic air similar to his grandfather's, and a grimness of his own. Hilda had questioned her friends regarding the major and read the Gazette before deciding to visit the Burlingtons. The war would justify a certain grimness. She noticed the devil watch fob.

"A most interesting fob, major." she commented.

When he didn't respond, Edith explained, "The French have given him the nom de guerre le Diable Bleu."

"Fascinating! I understand you are, what they call, an exploring officer. Or is it spy?" Hilda asked.

"Intelligense officer," Ronan replied.

When he failed to elaborate, Hilda inquired, "I've not met an intelligense officer before. What, precisely, do you do?"

"I ride behind enemy lines to gather information from many sources, including partisans and informants. I watch troops, note terrain, interrogate prisoners and decypher messages."

"Most interesting. Have you had many close calls?"

When he disdained to answer, Hilda said, "Of course, it is considered indecorous for a gentleman to discuss such things among ladies. I quite understand your reticence, major. Perhaps another time."

"I see I have put you off by camparing you to your grandfather, a purely superficial resemblance, I'm sure. I knew Lord Victor. In London, we carried on a long aquaintance. Some even called it a flirtation!"

"You accused of a flirtation with HIM!" Berty expressed surprise.

Sarah smiled, saying, "Hilda quite shocked the Ton with her outrageous behavior!"

"I was young once, you know, and handsome!" Hilda declared, "Lord Victor was quite dashing and enjoyed the company of women. An artist, too, Liberty, who sketched us beauties. And other things, as well, but never painted. Have you not found his sketches at the Hall?"

"No, but we have not gone through several locked map chests, as we are hoping to find missing keys," Berty replied, still astonished that her admired friend had flirted with Lord Victor.

"Yes, that is probably where he kept them and some may be in the London house. I thought he had a sensitive eye and hand. Lord Victor had been devoted to his late wife and once showed me sketches he'd done of her. You, see, I came out the year she died. She was two and thirty and he, five and thirty. They had ten children then. An arranged, but happy marriage. His lordship was deeply affected and never remarried, even after losing four of his sons and falling out with Hector. They were always at points, for Hector was the only one with backbone to stand up to him. James obeyed his father completely."

"After the period of mourning ended, Lord Victor was considered quite a catch, but he wasn't interested in matrimony and by then, neither was I. We became friends, though. Lord Victor was a rum'un; a principal in several affairs of honor, secretive, strong willed, fearless and often very cold."

Hilda stopped and surveyed the surrounding frowning, contemplative faces. She paused at Ronan. He smiled, ruefully.

"Ma'am, your auditors will say my grandfather and I have much in common."

Hilda laughed. "I see I have committed a solecism."

Tristan, Christopher and Happy entered the drawing room. Christopher ran, calling, "Papa," but Tristan grabbed his arm. "No running in the house, Chris!"

The appearance of the two wavy blond heads gave Hilda cause to reflect.

"Papa," Christopher began again when he reached Ronan, only to be subdued by a stern look from that imposing personage. By now the major had impressed upon them that he did not share the Burlington's lenient attitude towards boys.

"We have a guest," the major spoke, again, in his quiet voice. He correctly introduced Master Tristan Burlington and Master Christopher Trevelyan to Miss Penthwaite. Both boys bowed.

"May Chris speak, sir?" Tristan asked.

Ronan nodded and Christopher told him, with as much restraint as he could muster, "I counted to 100 today!"

His parent mustered an approving smile and allowed him up on his good leg while Tristan further described Christopher's accomplishment. "Once he got past twenty, he rattled them off. It was rather tedious but Mr. Considine was quite impressed."

Miss Penthwaite was impressed, too.

Ronan and Benjamin sent for their musical instruments.

Benjamin said Lord Victor's marriage reminded him of the traditional Young but Still Growing. "Should be sung by a female, if any of you ladies know it," Benjamin said, "Otherwise you'll have to suffer with a baritone."

They suffered with Benjamin's baritone.

When they finished, Hilda assured Ronan, "Victor couldn't play a note."

"I prefer that sort of music to your Baroque," Sir Richard said.

Ronan next played a Baroque saraband by Sante, followed by a haunting piece of his own.

"Most unusual. I must transcribe it," the Reverend Brandolyn said, "When did you compose it?"

"After Badajoz."

"Sounds like something for a funeral," Sir Richard decided, "Badajoz was awful, wasn't it?"

The major made no comment. Tristan sent for his recorder and violin, Christopher's whistle and Mr. Considine and his violin. Reverend Eugene Brandolyn joined on the pianoforte. After they had played several pieces, they took a break. Tristan said he'd outgrown his recorder. "Chris may have it. T'is a child's instrument."

The Reverend Brandolyn took it and played a complicated Baroque piece with variations.

"Don't disparage a thing because it is simple and easy," the Reverend warned.

They played until the butler announced supper. Miss Brown fetched Christopher. Tristan was allowed to dine with adults. Berty took Ronan's arm, Edith, Benjamin's, Gervace Markham offered his arm to Miss Penthwaite, who graciously accepted, although murmuring she was quite capable of walking to the dining room unassisted.

Ronan was seated between Miss Penthwaite and Liberty. All enjoyed strong appetites, and talked little. After the last crumb from the last coarse disappeared, Lady Ann rose to lead the ladies back to the drawing room. The gentlemen rose and most of the ladies rose and followed Lady Ann. Miss Penthwaite remained. Liberty remained to support Hilda in her determination. Edith, turned and walked back to join them, too.

The men continued to stand.

"Oh, do be seated, gentlemen. I do like to sit after dinner and talk politics over cognac," Miss Penthwaite announced, before taking a cigaretto from her reticule, lighting it at a candle and sitting back for a smoke. Astounded men sat down and took out their own pipes and cigars.

In the drawing room, Sarah explained Hilda's eccentricities.

"Capital, I'm tempted to peep throught the key hole to see the men's reactions!" Lady Ann said.

"May I go back, Mama?" Tristan asked.

"No, you may not!"

In the dining room, after clearing the table of everything but the sliver candleholders and setting wine cups, the footmen poured from decanters, cognac for some, port for others. Sherry for Augustus, who smiled knowingly at Hilda. The reverend, who retained a dignified countenance under the most trying circumstances, also took sherry.

The footmen neglected to serve Berty and Edith, assuming ladies, except Miss Penthwaite, didn't indulge, but Edith requested sherry.

"Well, Miss Bodleigh, a heavy wet?" Sir Richard asked jokingly.

"May I try just a drop of the port?" she said, curious as to why Ronan was fond of it.

The footman splashed a bit into her stemmed wine cup. Berty sipped, swallowed quickly and felt it burn her throat. She pushed her cup away.

"How can you drink that horrid poison?" she asked Ronan.

"It's an acquired taste."

"Why would anyone want to acquire it?"

"For the effects."

"Such as?"

"To feel happy."

"I daresay, you don't seem to feel happy at the moment," Hilda said, sniffing her cognac.

"Gentlemen are not generally happy to sit between two blue stockings after dinner," Gervace grumbled.

"You are mistaken, Mr. Markham, I am delighted to sit between these diamonds of the first water," Ronan said. He turned to Berty and quoted Ben Jonson, "Drink to me only with thine eyes and I will pledge with mine."

The reverend continued with, "Or leave a kiss within the cup. And I'll not ask for wine."

Ronan continued with, "The thirst that from the soul doth rise doth ask a drink divine; But might I of Jove's nectar sup, I would not change for thine."

Gervace gave Sir Richard a wry look, then turned to Ronan, saying, "Remarkable lot of poetry coming from you today."

"Yes, I'm suddenly remembering it." He finished his port and refused more.

" A most unusual situation here, a blue devil between two blue stockings! Feel free to smoke, major. This blue stocking doesn't mind! " Miss Penthwaite declared.

"I don't smoke, ma'am."

"Then let's talk politics!"

"I have no interest in politics, ma'am."

"A gentleman not interested in politics! You are not of a party?" Hilda feigned shock.

"I'm a Tory and I'm against democracy. Undisiplined soldiers sacking a city is democracy."

"That's anarchy, major!"

"Democracy, anarchy, mobs, all from the same source."

"How disapointing. I thought educated gentlemen-Sir Richard mentioned you had an Oxford degree- were of a more liberal bent."

"I'm not."

"Ronan is quite conservative," Berty said.

"Gothic," Benjamin added.

"A conservative, Gothic? Dear me!" Hilda pronounced, "And I was going to suggest you might run for Parliament."

"Lord Alexander made the same whimsical suggestion to me," Ronan said.

"No! Did he really?" Sir Richard asked, "Surely he joked!"

"He did not joke. He wanted me to represent the family's interest for Boscawden and offered to give me a cottage. Alexander believes I could extinguish the horse tax."

"By Jove, I'd like that!" Sir Richard said.

"He also dislikes speeches and I would spare the public on that score."

Most of those present laughed.

"What of climbing boys?" Hilda asked.

"Do you want them extinguished? With sabre or bullets? Those are the only ways I know of extinguishing them."

"You are roasting me, major!" Hilda replied with asperity.

"As MPs would roast anyone who proposed extingquishing climbing boys."

"You know I meant out law their use. But you are correct; many have jeered at the idea and told me it is none of Parliament's business how sweeps conduct their business. The same with our efforts to end child prostitution."

"Prostituion is already against the law," Captain Algernon Abseaton spoke from down table.

"Prostitution illegal? I had no idea," Ronan replied, blithely, inspiring another round of laughter.

The Reverend Brandolyn interpolated, "Miss Penthwaite, we don't need more laws, we need more Christian morality and charity. Everything doesn't come under the perview of government. Laws can support morality, but they don't make moral men."

"Quite true, Reverend, and these laws would support morality and protect the innnocent," Hilda replied, and continued with, "We also need to expand the franchise and allow women and poor men to vote."

Groans around the table.

"The poor would vote for politicians who promised to take from others and give to them. Women are too emotional too vote. Any good looking fellow who promised to aid women and children would win their votes," the Reverend declared.

Nods around the table.

Hilda looked ready to explode, but realized any display of temper would justify his remark. Collecting herself, she retorted, "Women are equal to men in the eyes of God."

Before the reverend could dispute this, Ronan replied, "But not in the eyes of men," then added to the footman, "Reinforcements, George." George filled his glass.

"Those in power are not going to allow reforms that would weaken their power, but they would take advantage of the ignorant poor and females to strengthen their power," Ronan continued, "The ignorant poor and women voting would destroy the nation, Even in America they don't allow women to vote."

Liberty rose to the occasion, "Spoken like an aristocrat who has no power himself and wishes to keep others beneath him. I suppose you would oppose changing abominable marriage laws that allow a man to beat his wife."

"You must think me the worse beast in nature, miss. I certainly don't condone wife beating and inspite of your low opinion of me, I have never struck a woman," Ronan replied, taking a gulp of his reinforcement.

"By Jove, what would a man do with a recalcitrant wife?" another down table gentleman asked.

"I should think he would make himself more agreeable," Berty snapped.

"And be henpecked?" Captain Abseaton asked.

The men grumbled in agreement.

Miss Penthwaite changed the subject, "A government that can afford wars, can afford to help the poor."

"Ma'am," Ronan began, "The Peninsula war has been fought with inadequate funds from the beginning. We've lost many lives due to lack of siege machines and engineers. The army only recently provided tents."

"Ah, but we've heard you like sleeping under the stars, esspecially when a sergeant's daughter shows up!" A military man said, to a chorus of chuckles.

"Under stars, yes, under rain and snow, not so much." Ronan replied. He then enumerated the many inadequacies of the war's funding, in detailed figures, iterated such things as the questionable quality of provisions and equipment and so on. He spoke for over a quarter of an hour.

"Thank God, you don't make speeches," Sir Richard sardonically observed.

Ronan wasn't finished. "Do you believe England's poor would be better off if the French invaded, Miss Penthwaite?" not waiting for an answer she hesitated to give, he continued, "When the French invaded Spain and Portugal, the army lived off the land, as they say. They took everything the peasants had, tortured them, raped women and killed them. The French army would do the same here. Was it not better to stop them in the Peninsula?"

Not completely daunted, Miss Penthwaite replied, "Yes, of course. I had no idea, but..."

"You had no idea because you believed the rubbish in radical papers," Ronan continued relentlessly.

Hilda broke in, "If the French peasants had not been taxed mercilessly to support an aristocracy, if they had been educated, if they had been allowed a part in their government, then the terror and rise of Bonaparte would not have happened."

"That is mere speculation, ma'am. The Greeks tried democracy. It failed. The French attempt led to mobs, terror and the Corsican ogre."

"Touché!" Sir Richard said, with the desperate hope that this debate was at an end.

Berty sighed. Ronan had beaten her dear Miss Penthwaite, the most intelligent woman she knew, and no doubt he was correct regarding military matters, but she felt he was wrong on other things. Felt! That was the trouble. He didn't trust feelings. He was a man of heartless numbers and cold reason. She must think of reasons for her feelings.

"Isn't the barbarism of child prostitution and the use of climbing boys equal to the barbarism perpetuated by the French?" she asked Ronan.

He looked at her. "It is worse since it is permitted by people claiming to be civilized and at peace, rather than the acts of the worse of men under harsh conditions."

Miss Penthwaite brightened. "You mean you are against these horrors?"

"Of course I am, but that's of no consequence. I'm not running for MP. You forget I'm an army officer, the war is not over and I doubt I shall leave the army as long as Bonaparte can raise an army."

"But the war shall soon end, regardless, major, and we shall enjoy life again," a gentleman remarked.

"We are not meant to enjoy life, but to create it," Reverend Brandolyn pronounced.

"I enjoy every minute of that, uncle," Ronan responded, smiling mischievously at his long-suffering uncle.

"You'll enjoy it more with your own wife, dear nephew. I long for the day when you have a child defy you in that charming way you have always entertained of defying me."

The company burst into laughter, including the major.

Miss Penthwaite laughed with the rest. Liberty feebly waved away some of Hilda's smoke.

"My dear Liberty, I fear you are a milksop," Hilda addressed her protégé, "You can handle neither strong drink nor cigar smoke."

"That's most unkind, Miss Penthwaite. I'm sure the great Queen Elizabeth, after whom my home, Virginia, was named, never smoked. I wouldn't know about her drinking habits, but she sounds like a sober person and I believe she was your kingdom's greatest ruler. Or was it queendom when she ruled?" Berty asked seriously.

Ronan smiled and some chuckled.

"It should have been queendom, of course, but men dominating the language, it was still called a kingdom," Miss Penthwaite explained.

"To the Virgin Queen," Captain Abseaton toasted, "Nay, make that all virgins. Bless their innocence!"

The men and Miss Penthwaite drank. Edith felt Mr. Brandolyn's hand touch her thigh under the table and had the discomforting notion that he did not hold drink well. He'd barely spoken that evening.

The soldiers spoke of women who smoked. "I've seen wives of the KGL smoking pipes with their men," Algernon remarked, "I find a good cigar keeps midges away."

"Interesting," Hilda commented, "And what do you think of women who smoke, major?"

Ronan smiled down at her and remarked, "I'd like too kiss one."

Hilda laughed, "You outrageous flirt!"

"He still has a weak head from fever," Gervace observed, "One cup of port and he talks, two and he flirts, three and he's dangerous. The Devil rarely takes more than two, though."

"How are you dangerous?" Berty asked.

Ronan turned to her, "Vacy exaggerates. I've hung up my sabre for now."

"But is it not sharp and ready to slice French flesh and bone?" Algernon inquired.

"Or perhaps wedding cake?" Sir Richard suggested.

"Would you like your wedding cake sliced with my sabre?" Ronan asked of Liberty.

Startled, she replied, "Oh! How barbaric!"

"You really are a milksop, Berty," Edith teased her.

"Mi dulce amor no es un milksop," Ronan retorted, with his usual sangfroid, "If any gentleman offers Miss Bodleigh such an insult, I shall invite him out to an interview."

"Oh, please, no! I do not want anyone called out on my behalf. If you can not defend me with words, do not defend me at all, sir!" Berty protested.

"I concur, Miss Bodleigh, and very well expressed," the Reverend Brandolyn assured her.

"He's weak headed, shouldn't drink," Gervace insisted.

"Quite so, Vacy. I stand corrected, Miss Bodleigh, Reverend Uncle. This male company is not proper for Miss Bodleigh or any other respectable woman," Ronan stated, rising, "Mr. Bodleigh would you escort Miss Bodleigh?"

Augustus rose and walked round the table to do so. With that, the company rose. The major offered Miss Penthwaite his arm. Rather than laying her hand on it, she hooked hers in his like a gentleman would. Benjamin escorted Edith and the others followed.

Ronan, done with conversation, sat at the harp. Benjamin joined him on flute. Considine and Tristan took up their violins, the Reverend Brandolyn instructed his little orchestra and the music resumed.

"You are fortunate to have such accomplished guests," Hilda told Lady Ann. Lady Ann inquired about their after-dinner conversation.

"We had a most interesting political discussion and I learned a great deal about the war and the dashing major."

Later while the music played, Miss Penthwaite took Berty far aside, where they could not be overheard, "I believe the major has an unrequited tendre for you, Liberty."

"He has spoken so, but he is changeable and of a rakish reputation," Berty replied.

"Indeed, rakish! Does he have other natural children besides Christopher?" Miss Penthwaite asked with dubious ignorance.

"Yes, ma'am, he has a daughter and children by married women, that he can not acknowledge," she replied to gauge Hilda's reaction.

"No wonder you are cool to him inspite of his exquisite beauty," Hilda tried to sound shocked, although she had been inquiring about the major for days. Her friends had refreshed her memory about a notorious Cornet Trevelyan, who had been murmured about before he'd gone off to war.

"Am I? Am I cold to him, do you think?"

"I should say so!"

"I fear his beauty may have deceived me, for I do love him. I believe I have loved him since I was thirteen and I don't want anyone else. But I'm never sure of him. At one time, I thought him very gentle, but the war, perhaps, has brought out the worse in him, or maybe it was always there and I didn't know. I would not want a milksop, but is he not rather wild and bloodthirsty?"

Miss Penthwaite considered. "He is not heated, but of high courage. I do like boldness in a man. I think him capable of gentleness and boldness. He has far more experience of the world than you, Liberty. I daresay, more than I. Does he wish to marry, do you think?"

"Yes, I believe that was his intention. Miss Penthwaite, what of the onerous marriage laws? He says he has never struck a woman and never would, but he is rather dominating, don't you think?"

"My dear, he may be dominating in his way, after all, he is used to commanding men, but he means to please you. Do not fret over marriage laws when your rake has engaged in crim. cons. and apparently kept mistresses. My concern is your painting. I don't think he would prevent you from pursuing your art, do you?"

"I think not. Ronan greatly admires my work. Nor does he mind my driving him in a curricle. Ronan likes to tease me over my hoydenish ways, but he gave me my pistol and taught me to shoot it. He is more broadminded than he would have us believe. Frankly, Ronan's a great humbug!" Berty confessed.

Hilda laughed, "I thought so! Gave you a pistol, gracious! I certainly would not discourage you from a love match. You would have children, of course, but I know many married women who have pursued their interests, after all most have nurse maids and governesses to tend the children."

Berty wondered if a cavalry major could afford nursemaids and governesses, but there would be income from her paintings. One had to leap these obstacles when one came to them.

"There is no better husband than a reformed rake. Major Trevelyan must be reformed!" said the indefatigable reformer, "However, I've heard the on dit, over the years, regarding your major. I didn't connect it with him at first, but having inquired further, I have some of his history of which you may not be aware."

"When he was a nineteen-year old cornet, he met a much older lady who was estranged from her husband. The husband had used her abominably. He threw her down a stairs causing a miscarriage."

"How awful!" from Berty.

"Cornet Trevelyan held crim. cons. with this lady. When her husband learned of it, he called out Trevelyan, although he was only nineteen. He ran the husband through, but the monster survived."

Liberty gasped.

"I collect you were not aware of this?"

"Not the details, no."

"His next mistress was a thirty-year old woman married to an elderly and sickly man. She bore a son, almost certainly one of the major's by blows. When Cornet Trevelyan's regiment moved near London, he had several flirtations until he became cicisbeo to a lady with a tolerant elderly husband. By then he was a lieutenant. Unfortunately, this lady had a jealous former lover, which led to another encounter, involving pistols. I fear Major Trevelyan is a failure as a duelist, for he didn't kill his man this time, either. The ball lodged in the man's shoulder, not far from his heart. After that, Lieutenant Trevelyan sailed to Spain with his regiment."

"Yes," Berty said, "I've heard bits and pieces, but that brings them together. Ronan is, or was, a flirt and an opportunist. Do you really think he can be reformed. "

"He already is, my dear."

Chapter 21

The Brandolyns stayed on longer than expected, Benjamin to consult his partner extensively on business matters and the Reverend Brandolyn to transcribe the major's compositions and add to his notes on the Peninsula War. Besides his nephew, there were other Peninsula officers staying at the Burlington's recovering from wounds and illness. The reverend interviewed them all.

One clear morning, the major and Tristan practised pistol shooting, using Brandolyn Arms' new Blue Devil breech-loading pistol and conventional ones. Some of the other officers and gentlemen joined in. Berty and Edith sent for their pistols. Berty had not fired hers since the incident with the highwaymen.

Guests, including Mr. Sitwell, watched Ronan instruct Tristan, while George set bottles on a bench. A frustrated Christopher watched, also. His father sternly informed him he was not to touch pistols until he was Tristan's age. Trist hit his first dead soldier and reloaded. Ronan shattered another dead soldier. He turned, took a gun Jacob had loaded, spun round and shot a bottle out of George's hand. George continued as if nothing had happened, but Liberty chastised the major.

"Poor George! You could have hit him! That was a terrible example to these children. You needn't show off!" Berty fumed.

"My profound apology, George," the major said.

"Yes, sir, unnecessary. I expect such treats from you, sir," George responded, setting up more bottles for guests. At the major's request, he tossed one in the air. The major blasted it.

George pinned an ace of spades to a tree about twenty paces from the major. Ronan shifted to his left hand, took careful aim and shot the ace of spades.

"Bravo!" shouted some officers. George pinned an ace of hearts on the tree.

Having shown Miss Penthwaite her skill at shooting bottles, Liberty reloaded, took Ronan's place, aimed and hit the ace of hearts. Cheers went up from everyone, especially Miss Penthwaite.

Tristan took a turn at an ace of clubs. He, too, hit the target.

"We need a challenge, George," Ronan told him.

George sent to the kitchen for turnips. He walked further away and offered to toss a turnip. Berty said she would give it a try. George threw up a large turnip, but Berty missed. Before it reached the ground, Ronan hit it. He needed glasses for close work, otherwise, his vision was excellent.

"Drat it, Berty! You let me down," Edith, who hadn't hit anything in four tries, said.

Sitwell watched and wondered how the major aimed with such speed and accuracy. It occurred to the desperate dandy that he could end his misery by provoking the major to challenge him. After others had taken turns shooting, the company returned to the house.

Roger Sitwell requested a private interview with Lady Ann, who knew what he wanted before he asked.

"I will not pay your gambling debts, Roger. I am well aware you came here to avoid your creditors, not to enjoy your cousin's company. Your father has told me you have a generous allowance which you choose to dissipate. I suggest you tell Major Trevelyan you can not pay your debt. He is not that onerous to deal with; after all, you are late in paying and he has said nothing. He may even forgive your debt."

Sitwell approached the major in the drawing room and asked to speak to him in private.

"This is quite private," Ronan replied.

"It's about my vowels," Sitwell whispered, "I'd prefer to speak to you alone."

"I prefer to parley with witnesses," Ronan replied, indolently, carelessly leaning back on the sofa with his arms draped across the back.

"I am unable to raise the full amount," Sitwell whispered, hoping the major's indolence was a good sign.

"Sell your teeth," Ronan replied.

"What?!"

"Sell your teeth," Ronan repeated.

"Good God, I couldn't do that! You are mad!"

"Not as mad as a man who gambles with empty pockets," Ronan replied, nonchalantly, "Your teeth should bring a few guineas. There are

Englishmen wearing teeth from dead Peninsula soldiers. I'll knock them out for you," Ronan continued in the same careless manner.

Two of Lady Ann's genteel cousins reached for their smelling salts. Benjamin and Sir Richard grinned.

"By Jove, your major does cause a stir," Miss Penthwaite whispered to Berty.

Sitwell again attempted to move to another room. "This is a private matter, not something to air before company."

"The bet was placed in public," the major replied.

"Do you mean to shame me in public?"

"You approached me," Ronan retorted.

"I asked for a private conversation. I believe you are trying to disgrace me among friends. I should challenge you. I think I'd rather take my chances fighting you than face my father," Sitwell replied.

The major rolled his eyes. "I'd rather not fight someone with such a want of spirit," he said to Sitwell's chagrin. "Oblige me with an inventory of your possessions and the amount of your allowance."

Sitwell listed a watch, jewelry, raiment, weapons and coins he had with him.

"I will accept them," Ronan replied, graciously.

"I will need something to wear and enough money to pay for coach fair back to London," Sitwell replied.

"A coach? You shall walk."

"But it's over 100 miles!"

"Approximately 125 miles. A soldier could easily cover it in six days."

"And what would I eat and where would I sleep?"

"Half rations and in a bivouac," Ronan finished, turned away and addressed the butler, "Preston, please have George carry Mr. Sitwell's portmanteau to my chamber after he has filled it. I trust George will see that Mr. Sitwell doesn't overlook anything."

George, with frowning dignity, followed Sitwell to his chamber. Sir Richard generously offered to have Cook provide a haversack of six days of army half rations or the equivalent in civilian food.

"By Jove, I'd like to follow the cockscomb to see how he fairs!" Sir Richard added, "I daresay he'll be more carefull wagering in future! He certainly won't bet against aging knights!"

Most of the company agreed, although Miss Penthwaite opined that this was another example of Ronan's resemblance to Lord Victor who was, "Ever severe when collecting his due."

"Do they really take teeth from the dead?" Benjamin asked.

"One heard the hammers all night after battles and in the morning, the dead were picked clean of everything; clothing, rings, teeth," Ronan replied.

"Waste not, want not," Gervace said.

"I must include that in my book," the Reverend Brandolyn, remarked, "One seldom sees such details in most histories."

"That is quite shocking. The dead should have been guarded until properly buried," Miss Penthwaite declared.

Ronan sighed and began a lengthy explanation regarding exhaustion of troops, lack of man power to carry off all the wounded, let alone the dead, use of funeral pyres, scavengers killing wounded, etc.

"I would add that a battlefield stinks worse than Smithfield's shambles on a summer's day," Captain Abseaton remarked, "Dead and wounded horses and men laying in the hot sun, flesh and blood everywhere. Can't half see for smoke and that stinks, too."

"How cheering," Miss Penthwaite acknowledged.guided

~~~

Liberty took up the reins in the phaeton with Major Trevelyan sitting next to her and Aunt Sarah and Miss Penthwaite in the back. She drove at a spanking pace, only slowing to admire a meadow of daffodils or newborn lambs. Ronan annoyed the ladies in back by placing his arm around Berty.

"Your forward and shabby conduct is most unbecoming, major," Sarah remonstrated.

"Yes, Ronan, time to give up your ramshackle ways," Berty teased, "And you shouldn't shock ladies with talk of teeth!"

"Not even to say yours are as lovely as pearls?" he replied.

"Flummery!" she said, revealing those pearls in a smile. Having slowed to admire a flock of Dorset sheep, she gave the grays the office to increase their pace. They drove on to the seaside road, where Berty revived the discussion she had had with Edith regarding women swimming.

"Dr. Waddles told Lady Ann that sea bathing is quite healthful for both sexes, although men do more of it. He said when the weather warms, swimming would be beneficial to Ronan's leg."

"Yes, sea bathing is quite healthful," Hilda agreed, "I've enjoyed it, but modest apparel for such exercise is a difficulty. Petticoats are quite impossible to swim in and shifts are inmodest.Gentlemen don't suffer these handicaps.

"Edith and I had the same discussion. She thinks women should have their own beaches and even swim nude!"

"I volunteer to guard them," Ronan offered.

Berty lightly slapped his arm.

"Really there is no reason the sexes shouldn't be able to enjoy bathing nude together," Hilda decided. Sarah cut Hilda a look.

"I look forward to it," Ronan supported her. Berty slapped him again and admonished Hilda for encouraging him, "You know he lives to provoke Aunt Sarah and me."

"Just as girls and boys should be educated together," Hilda continued, ignoring Berty's remark.

"Oh, no, I disagree!" Berty cried, "That is how my school was in America. I didn't like it and ran home when the master switched the boys."

"In any case, don't you agree, major, that girls should be educated?" Hilda asked.

"Certainly. Girls should be taught to spin; sew; cook; keep house; and obey their fathers and husbands," he answered, to her consternation.

"He's humming you," Berty told her, "He's absolutely the worse humbug, bammer and actor possible! Did I not warn you he lives to provoke?"

"You know me well, mi dulce amigo!"

They drove up to Burlington Hall, where boys played in an open meadow. Upon closer approach, they saw the boys were fighting. "Quite a mill there," Miss Penthwaite remarked, displaying her familiarity with the latest boxing cant.

"Little Christopher is in the thick of it!" Berty exclaimed, driving off the lane into the field, "Do stop them, Ronan!"

He glanced towards the boys and shrugged.

"Are you bereth of human feeling?" Berty snapped.

"No, miss, I simply don't suffer from an excess of it."

"If you aren't going to do anything, I will!" Sarah declared, stepping out of the phaeton.

Ronan sighed in resignation and climbed out of the phaeton. Striding with as much speed and dignity as his limp would allow, he caught up with Sarah.

When the mob saw this imposing, scowling officer approach, most scattered. A few still watched Tristan and another, larger, boy punching each other with admirable determination. Christopher contributed his share by occasionally kicking and hitting the much larger boy assaulting Tristan.

Ronan grimly marched into the fray. He grabbed both older boys with an iron grip on their wrists. The largest boy quit punching with his free hand when he felt the vise on his left. One look at the major's daunting expression, and he squirmed to escape, but the major held him. The boy, feeling his hand grow numb, begged to be released. "Please, sir, don't tell my father. I'm sorry, really I am!"

"If Chris will accept his apology, I will," Tristan said, looking at the major, who glared without speaking, more terrifying than if he had spoken.

Christopher nodded agreement with Tristan. The boy apologized to both. The major released him, and the boy ran off the field of battle. Ronan picked Christopher up, threw him over his shoulder and marched off with Tristan following. Both were dirty and bloodied.

They reached the phaeton with Tristan asking what he had done wrong. The major replied, "Gentlemen do not engage in brawls. Your indecorous behavior has upset these ladies, who don't understand boys."

Berty said, "Christopher's too young to be in a fight with those big boys." She took out a handkerchief and sopped the blood oozing from his nose. Sarah did the same for Tristan.

"I showed them how an army bastard fights!" Christopher proudly stated.

Tristan rattled on in their defense, using boxing cant he'd picked up from Sir Richard, "Jimmy called Chris a bastard and Chris gave him a bit of the home-brewed and then Jimmy drew Christopher's cork and I planted Jimmy a facer and then Jimmy's older brother aimed for my bone box, but I parried and drew his claret and then all eight of us were in a mill. I've never had such a dashed great time! Chris has been fighting since he could walk and he's got bottom to spare. He's going to need it on account of his birth, you know."

"No, I don't know," Berty replied stiffly. Sarah nodded agreement while trying to clean Tristan.

"I won't always be here." Ronan told the boys, "Choose your battles well."

"At least you didn't call us missish," Liberty observed.

"I do hate that term!" Miss Penthwaite interjected, "As if there is something wrong with being a miss. And those young ruffians should be taught not to abuse a child because his parents failed to marry. Boys must be civilized, not allowed to come to blows over anything."

When they alighted from the phaeton, Christopher squirmed to be put down, saying, "I'm too old to be carried, Papa!"

Ronan put him down and limped back to the house with the boys.

~~~

"Gentlemen don't fight with their fists," Sir Richard reprimanded the boys.

"But you do, Papa," Tristan pointed out.

"Don't interrupt! I was about to add, except in sport, such as boxing for exercise."

"This was great sport, Papa, and exercise, too."

"Don't contradict me, child."

"Yes, Papa. What about Christopher?"

Sir Richard addressed Christopher, "You are the son of an officer and a gentleman. We expect you to conduct yourself as such. Gentlemen's sons do not brawl with the sons of servants and tenants."

This admonishment met the approval of Miss Penthwaite and Miss Bodleigh. They did not hear Sir Richard when he later asked the major if the boys displayed to advantage.

~~~

Sir Richard and the Reverend Brandolyn intended to join the last hunt of the season. Officers able to ride also prepared to join. Others would ride in vehicles nearby in the hope of catching glimpses of the hunt.

"I would like to sketch the hunt. There hasn't been one near Boscawden since I arrived ten years ago," Liberty said.

"Boscawden hasn't held a hunt since Lord Victor died," Augustus said, "I used to ride in the hunts, but I'm not up to it now."

"I'm rather glad," Sarah retorted, "I closed my eyes every time he rode towards an obstacle."

Sir Richard chose a groom to drive the phaeton, allowing Liberty to sketch. Ronan, Edith, Benjamin and Chris would ride in the vehicle. Tristan would ride alongside. Augustus Bodleigh volunteered to drive

Sarah, Miss Penthwaite and Mr. Markham in another phaeton. Lady Ann, Mrs. Brandolyn and others chose to keep to the comforts of Burlington Hall.

That night, Berty heard wind whistling in the chimney and rose to find a chilly, ferocious wind gusting without. The men donned their hunting coats, black for the reverend, red for other gentlemen, brown or blue for merchants and farmers.

Upon seeing his elderly father dressed for hunting, Benjamin informed him, "You are too old for this sport, father."

The Reverend Brandolyn raised his head, scowled, and replied, "We shall see about that. I can outride many a younger man, including yourself. I would go so far as to say the only man who can match me is my dear nephew. I pray we shall ride together again."

"I look forward to it, uncle," the major replied, "You will find Sir Richard up to your standards."

Liberty and the others changed their plans. Since it was too windy for sketching, she informed her friends that she would drive. Gervace and Miss Penthwaite decided they would ride with the young people. Augustus decided to drive a gig Sir Richard offered and invited Christopher to ride with him and Sarah, enticing the boy with a chance to hold the ribbons. Tristan agreed to ride alongside.

Berty boarded the phaeton with the major in the center and Miss Penthwaite on his other side. Benjamin, Edith and Mr. Markham sat behind. The men wore caped greatcoats against the wind and jammed their hats down tight. The women wore cloaks; Berty's being garnet. Miss Penthwaite wore a sensible bonnet, securely tied, Edith an elaborate indigo bonnet, also securely tied and Liberty wore a dashing garnet hat, well pinned and veiled. A red feather fluttered in the wind.

Once again Berty noticed Ronan's worn boots under his trousers and that his greatcoat showed much wear. It also reeked of horse and smoke. It smelled like war. These signs assured her that the poor orphan of a younger son was not too good for an American of half Irish ancestry.

The riders struck off and the carriages followed.

Hilda inquired of Benjamin, "You don't care for hunting, Mr. Brandolyn?"

"No, ma'am. I think it an inefficient way to control fox. They should be trapped, not hunted. I only ride from necessity. Poor father, none of his sons is particularly keen on horses, only his nephew. A more neck or nothing rider never existed. The fox is just an excuse for father and Ronan to ride at breakneck speed over every obstacle they encounter. One wouldn't expect a sensible man like father to enjoy such madness. Ronan, on the other hand, one would expect it of him!"

His auditors laughed, except Ronan, who appeared as grim as ever. No one had asked if he wanted to follow the hunt in a phaeton. He did not care to be a mere spectator, but at least expected to admire Miss Bodleigh. Instead, she hid herself under a veil and cloak. He felt no joy as they rode into the heavy wind. He felt particularly irritated when Doctor Waddles rode up.

The doctor, tipped his hat and Ronan coldly introduced him to his companions, then turned away.

"You shouldn't be out today, Major," Waddles admonished him. "Are you following my orders?"

Ronan faced forward, ignoring him.

"The major always follows orders, but he is usually given liberty in their execution," Gervace replied to the doctor.

"I allow no liberties where a thigh bone may be damaged and fragile. He is not riding horses, is he?"

"You don't see him in the field, do you?" Gervace retorted, "No, he is not riding."

"Is he getting top heavy after dinner? Wouldn't want him falling and breaking that leg."

"Certainly not, rarely ever did. As abstemious as a Methodist," Gervace replied.

Benjamin chuckled. Waddles considered that young man an exemplar of good health. He looked like he could lift a horse! His cousin, although broad of shoulder and deep of chest, appeared frail by comparison.

"Is my patient eating better?" Waddles asked.

Gervace hesitated before replying, "You know when a cavalry man rides horses, he eats like one. The major isn't riding."

"Eats like a bird," Benjamin put in, "Mother is quite concerned." Then great tease that he was, Ben added, "Lovesick."

Waddles chortled, "Is that it, major, lovesickness? A disease beyond my perview! Perhaps one of these young ladies next you can cure it!" Waddles laughed again.

Ronan turned and replied, "You have the manners of a battlefield scavenger."

That insult only made the doctor laugh harder. When the doctor had recovered, Gervace addressed Waddles, changing the subject, "Expecting some business today?"

"I do. With 100 riders, I expect someone will break an arm or leg."

"Or worse," Gervace agreed.

"I see they they have found a promising covert," Waddles declared, took his leave and rode on.

After a few minutes of waiting for the fox to appear, some riders dismounted.

"They say hunting is good preparation for cavalrymen, but seems rather tedious to me," Benjamin opined.

"One waits to be called into battle," Ronan explained.

"That would be worse than tedious," Ben said.

Silence followed until Miss Penthwaite inquired of Ben, "Is your family of the Cornish Brandolyns?"

"Yes, ma'am. Father's brother is Sir Aaron Brandolyn, baronet, and father's mother was a daughter of Lord Godolphin. Odd, the Trevelyans are related to the Godolphins, too, hense the corruption of Boscawean. Mother's father was only a country squire, but her mother was daughter of Sir John Tifton."

"Of course our pedigree is nothing like Ronan's. His grandmother was sister to the current Marquess of Leigh, who has only two sickly heirs other than the Trevelyans."

"One, now, a consumptive living in Bath," Gervace corrected him, "If the current Lord Boscawden and his effeminate brother died, Ronan would be his heir. Sir Richard jests of hiring assassins. He refers to Lord Alexander as a cockscomb and the brother as a molly."

Edith giggled in spite of her friendship with Alexander. She now preferred Benjamin to Alexander.

"I consider them both dear friends," Berty declared.

"Alexander is one of my dear friends, as well," Ronan spoke, "I can make my own way in the world."

The horses growing restless in the wind, Liberty gave them the office to move forward. Hunters in the field beyond still waited for the fox.

"Miss Bodleigh," Ronan addressed her, "Please remove that damned veil; you aren't a Mohammedan."

Liberty was stunned. She'd never heard Ronan utter a curse. "Have you acquired the manners of a battlefield scavenger, sir? This veil protects my complexion from wind and sun."

Ronan picked the edge of the veil up and draped it over the hat. Before Berty could object, he ordered, "Turn these beasts about and take us to the sea."

For a moment everyone was speechless.

"I believe one who usually vexes others, is vexed himself," Berty remarked.

"You don't wish to watch the hunt, major?" Miss Penthwaite asked.

"No, does anyone?"

All agreed they were disappointed and bored. Berty dexterously backed the phaeton down a lane and turned the team.

"Well done," Ronan praised her.

They sped off at fast trot. Berty didn't slow the pair until they reached the steep lane to the beach. There she guided them carefully onto flooded shingle. The wind blew so fiercely from the sea, that the men took off their hats and held them, while the women pulled their cloaks tighter. The wind whipped Ronan's and Benjamin's curls . The kind of hair women longed to run their fingers through, Miss Penthwaite thought. Berty gave the tea their heads. They galloped along the beach, water splashing from the wheels and spray damping everyone. Ronan smiled. Liberty knew what he wanted. The exhilarating drive ended when they came to the lane that led off the beach.

By the time they reached the headland, the horses were blown and Berty knew they wouldn't give her any trouble even though the wind spooked cattle in the fields.

"That was quite thrilling," Hilda declared.

"Yes, but this outing is likely to make us brown as plowmen," Edith remarked.

When they arrived back at the hall, Major Trevelyan apologized, "I regret my unconcionable language today. The thought of displaying such want of courtesy before ladies devastates me."

Benjamin snickered, "Yes, you appear truly devastated."

"I'm sure you are frustrated to be left out of the hunting," Hilda said, accepting his apology.

Edith accepted, but Berty commented with sarcastic formality, "Such language desolates me, yet your contriteness evokes my deepest sensibilites. I hope in future you will command your emotions with greater fortitude, but I realize, men are so dreadfully emotional this may not be possible. I could go so far as to say such disgraceful language as you used today is mannish. And mannish is far worse than missish."

Everyone chuckled, even the object of Berty's comments. He was tempted to incur further reproach by stealing a kiss, but exercised command of his emotions, manfully.

"In truth, if you dislike my hat, simply say so, or anything else you wish to say. One never knows what you think," Berty grew serious.

"If you knew, you might say my thoughts were unbecoming a gentleman."

"Try me!"

"I like your rakish hat, but I'd like it better off your head. I'd prefer to see your beautiful hair unpinned and hanging loose. I'd prefer to see you without that cloak," Ronan stated.

Berty giggled, "I dare say, next you will say you'd like to see me without my gown!"

"Yes, I'd like that, too."

Berty turned away, blushing. Her friends giggled.

"Lovesick suckling," Benjamin declared, smirking.

His cousin, standing close, swirled round and punched him in the jaw. Benjamin, attempted to strike back, but Ronan blocked and swung again, hitting Benjamin's cheek before Ben recovered and got a punch in near Ronan's eye. By then, Gervace had sent for four huge footmen, led by George. They grabbed the two by the arms and brought the fray to a stand.

"You always were devilish fast," Benjamin panted.

"And you slow as an ox," Ronan replied.

"And you are both acting like bloody boys," Gervace snapped. "Gentlemen don't fight with their fists,'"he mocked.

The women looked uncomfortable. The footmen released their charges.

"Apologize to these ladies and to each other," Gervace commanded.

"I apologize for this display," Ronan stated quickly.

"As do I," Ben said, "And I will not call you a lovesick suckling again, cousin, since it obviously touches a nerve."

"That was a poor excuse for an apology," Gervace said, "You always were an instigator. I think you are excused from apologizing to him, major."

"Oh, God, I'm sorry, Ronan," Benjamin said with feeling, embracing his cousin, "I've missed you so. I miss the old you. Now you glower like father!"

Ronan embraced his cousin lightly, placing his head against Benjamin's.

"A most affecting scene. By your leave, gentlemen, you are embarassing the ladies," Gervace announced.

The men parted. Benjamin held up his cousin while he picked up Ronan's cane. "The shame of it, unable to knock you down when you have a bad leg."

They locked arms and followed the ladies and Gervace inside.

Sir Richard and the Reverend Brandolyn arrived safely home with the others. They noticed fresh bruises on the Major's and Benjamin's faces. Sir Richard asked, "What's this, did you fall out of the phaeton?"

"A light skirmish," Ronan replied.

"At your ages!" Sir Richard snapped.

Tristan and Christopher looked at each other in wonder at adults.

Inwardly, Ronan cursed himself for straying from the genteel behavior with which he meant to win Liberty. Frustration had overcome his usual calm self, but he hoped Berty was frustrated, too. If she wanted him as he wanted her, she had to be. That evening before supper, Ronan played harp and Benjamin, flute, making a contrast to the ruffians the ladies had seen earlier.

"Men are beyond understanding," Hilda declared. Her friends agreed.

At supper, Ronan sat between Berty and Miss Penthwaite. When he caught Berty looking at his plate, he froze her with one of his frosty looks. He turned and saw Hilda studying his plate. Across the table, Benjamin grinned. The ladies were checking to see if Ronan was too lovesick to eat. He acquitted himself well.

~~~

The Brandolyns and Bodleighs made plans to depart on the following Monday. Berty had decided, with difficulty, to return to Boscawden. She loved spring in the country and felt homesick. Edith said she'd go where Berty went and Miss Penthwaite decided she'd like to sojourn in the country, too. "So refreshing after winter in the city. And it's still early in the season."

Sarah admitted she missed everyone, including Zipporah, her cat. She and Augustus asked the Burlingtons if the boys could visit that summer. The Burlingtons agreed regarding Tristan and the major approved for Christopher. Ronan also announced he would be recuperating in Boscawden until the end of April when he and Benjamin would meet in London on business. Berty's face lit at this news.

~~~

The wars neared an end. The allies expected Napoleon to soon abdicate. By the time the major was in full force, he would likely be on half pay. Meanwhile, he instructed Christopher in horseback riding

"Why can I not hold the reins? Mr. Bodleigh said I did very well driving."

"Head up, heels down. When your seat is secure and correct, we will instruct you in handling reins," Ronan told him. He then mounted a quiet horse to ride with the boys and rode longer than he should have. Dr. Waddles would have declared any ride too long. Ronan refused to be subjugated by doctors or a certain recalcitrant female.

~~~

Friday, April first, the company gathered in the drawing room before supper. Sir Richard entertained with his story of Trafalgar. In the end, he declared, "And that is how Ronan saved my earthly existence."

The subject of that adventure lay abed, recruiting his strength. Jacob informed Ronan it was past time to be dressed for supper.

"Then we must make haste. I shall wear my dress uniform."

Jacob, without questioning this announcement, handed his master a skin-tight pair of pantaloons. The process continued with black neck cloth, tasseled Hessians, barrel sash, laced dolman, medals, sabre, sabretache and pelisse. Neither shako nor fore and aft hat were required for supper.

His silver laced uniform glittering in the candlelight, the major stepped into the drawing room and surveyed the company like a man about to take command. His appearance usually did take command of many ladies' sensibilities. Espying Liberty, he swaggered to her, as well as he could with a cane, and bowed.

Benjamin whispered to Edith, "He's trying to impress Miss Bodleigh."

"He doesn't need to impress her. Berty already loves him," Edith replied.

"She has more sence than marry him, though," Ben reckoned, "He'd want a baby a year! He seems to have managed that without benefit of marriage. He strives to impress her and change her mind."

"Is that why he struck you? I assure you that did nothing to further his cause," Edith said.

Benjamin laughed, "I accept the blame for that. I can't refrain from teasing him, although he never teases me. He's been thwarted in much of late; injuries, missing the last weeks of the war and struggling to win Miss Bodleigh."

"I say those deuced pantaloons reveal the unmentionables. I don't know how such apparel became part of the dress uniform."

Edith tapped him with her fan. "Don't you agree, your cousin displays a fine leg?"

"I assure you, his leg is no finer than mine."

Edith giggled, tapping him with her fan, again.

Liberty glowed in her scintillating ruby gown. Old tabbies agreed Miss Bodleigh and the major made a splendid couple, although she was of no family and he had no money.

Ronan intoned in Liberty's ear, "Would you accuse me of a flattery tongue if I said that you are exceedingly beautiful tonight?"

She smiled, replying, "I respect your honestly too much to accuse you of such, although you might need to use your spectacles."

"Only if I were close enough to kiss you."

"I suspect I'm going to regret my lack of a fan tonight," Berty retorted, "I notice Miss Westerley is wearing the feathers off hers on your cousin."

"I'm sure he deserves worse."

Berty graced the major's arm into supper and sat beside him. At the end of the meal, when sweet meats, cheese and whole fruit were served, Berty chose an orange. Ronan took it from her hand, peeled it with his stiletto and served her the individual wedges, as he'd done before. The company took notice.

After supper, all the ladies departed, including Miss Penthwaite, who felt she'd made her point on the equality of women. The gentlemen partook of their usual wine and cigars. Ronan restricted himself to one small glass of sherry.

Sir Richard glanced at Gervace as if to ask, what is he about? Sir Richard led the men into the drawing room after only an hour of imbibing.

"Prepared to do battle with our blue stockings, major?" Captain Abseaton asked, adding, "I never feel properly dressed out of uniform."

"I feel the same," Ronan returned.

"I don't see how one can feel properly attired in those pantaloons," Benjamin declared.

"I didn't know you had become a prude, Ben. Do you object to the immodest gowns the ladies wear?" Ronan asked.

"What immodest gowns? All the ladies meet the bounds of modesty," Benjamin claimed.

Ronan played one of his lovely compositions for harp before Tristan and Christopher were sent to bed. Then he joined Liberty on a sofa.

Miss Penthwaite rattled on about the rights of women, saying someday England would have a female Prime Minister. "After all, she has had queens. I see no reason why men would not follow a female Prime Minister as well."

"Queens are chosen by God; Prime Ministers by man, ma'am," the Reverend Brandolyn replied.

"And someday, Prime Ministers will also be chosen by women. Plato said women should vote and we shall!" Miss Penthwaite persisted.

"Aristotle thought otherwise, ma'am. He recognised the weakness of the female mind," Ronan commented, mischievously, informing the others that, "Miss Penthwaite and Miss Bodleigh cherish many advanced ideas."

"Yes, Miss Penthwaite has been most vocal in advertising those ideas," the Reverend agreed.

"Do you think America will someday elect a female president?" Ronan asked Berty.

"Eventually, when women are allowed to vote. There are slaves to liberate, too. There may even be a day when the descendant of a slave becomes president. Perhaps the female descendant of a slave," she replied.

"By Jove, that is one of the most radical ideas I've ever heard!" Sir Richard exclaimed.

"Eunuch slaves have attained power in the Ottoman Empire," Ronan observed.

"Yes, but they are barbarians," Sir Richard said, "Are Americans ready to give up their slaves?"

"Some of my father's friends have manumitted their servants-we they don't call them slaves. It was rather difficult as the servants had to be provided with means to live; taught trades or given land. Our friends also had to provide for those too old or crippled to support themselves. Papa was always arguing against slavery. I suppose he is the source of my, so called, radical ideas. I rather think of them as fair and just," Liberty replied.

"Capital!" Miss Penthwaite praised her.

"Entirely reasonable," Ronan stated.

"I'm glad you think so," Berty said, "Of course if former slaves and women are to eventually gain the right to vote, they will need education."

"Of course," Ronan agreed, "Education on the evils of democracy, esspecially."

Some members of the company chuckled.

"Yes, as you know, America does not have a direct democracy, but is a representative republic," Berty replied.

"If they can keep it," Ronan replied, "But let's not refine upon that. Your ideas on marriage particularly intrigue me."

"Do they?" Berty wondered at Ronan's sudden interest and approval on so many of her pet interests.

"Of course they do. Your ideas always interest me."

"How gallant," Miss Penthwaite murmured.

"What specifically about my ideas on marriage interest you that we have not previously discussed?" Berty asked.

Ronan turned further towards her, sitting in his shab-mannered way. "With your ideas of equality, do you think it proper for a lady to offer for a man?"

Berty looked puzzled, as did most of the company. "You mean for a woman to ask a man to marry her?"

"Precisely."

"Yes, I think that should be acceptable," Berty replied cautiously.

"How would a lady offer for a gentleman? What would she say?"

"I suppose she would ask, 'Would you do me the honor to be my husband?'"

"Yes."

"Yes?"

"Yes, I would be your husband. I consider us betrothed," he spoke firmly.

The room fell silent.

"That was an example. I didn't really ask, you know," Berty replied, discomfited.

"You asked and I accepted."

"You're roasting me, you provoking humbug!"

"I'm serious. Are you crying off?"

"How can I cry off when I never agreed to anything?" Berty, annoyed.

"Do you mean when a lady offers for a man it is not acceptable?"

"I didn't say that. I didn't offer. Stop this April foolery!"

"T'is not April foolery, although I might be an April fool. If your offer was nonsense, then you mean only a man's offer signifies? Very well. Miss Bodleigh, would you do me the honor to be my wife?"

Berty stared into his intense blue eyes and realized he meant it. She smiled. "Yes, you fool!"

He kissed her. Then slipped the ruby ring on her finger.

The company broke into laughter and jollification. Sir Richard ordered champagne. The men congratulated the future life tenants and Benjamin feared he would be the next to get riveted. Bodleighs, Brandolyns and Burlingtons sighed with relief at their Blue Devil's and blue stocking's betrothal.

Fini

Made in the USA
Middletown, DE
28 November 2021

53668277R00156